The

QUEEN'S
CAPTIVE

Books by Barbara Kyle

The Queen's Captive
The King's Daughter
The Queen's Lady

The QUEEN'S CAPTIVE

BARBARA KYLE

KENSINGTON BOOKS
www.kensingtonbooks.com

KENSINGTON BOOKS are published by

Kensington Publishing Corp.
119 West 40th Street
New York, NY 10018

All Kensington titles, imprints, and distributed lines are available at special quantity discounts for bulk purchases for sales promotion, premiums, fund-raising, educational, or institutional use.

Special book excerpts or customized printings can also be created to fit specific needs. For details, write or phone the office of the Kensington Special Sales Manager: Kensington Publishing Corp., 119 West 40th Street, New York, NY 10018. Attn. Special Sales Department. Phone: 1-800-221-2647.

Kensington and the K logo Reg. U.S. Pat. & TM Off.

ISBN-13: 978-0-7582-3855-9
ISBN-10: 0-7582-3855-X

First Printing: September 2010
10 9 8 7 6 5 4 3 2 1

Printed in the United States of America

I dedicate this book to
Audrey LaFehr.
My heroes were in exile. She brought them home.

ACKNOWLEDGMENTS

Authors often thank their life partner at the end of their acknowledgments. I will thank my husband, Stephen Best, at the beginning, because that's how important he is to my writing. When I create a new novel I give him a draft of each chapter, and the comments and suggestions he offers are truly invaluable. For this, and for his steadfast support, I thank him with all my heart.

My literary agent, Al Zuckerman, is a near legend in the business, and I am fortunate to have him as a mentor and advocate. He is, in the words my late father used as his highest praise, "a scholar and a gentleman."

I appreciate the creative energy of all the hardworking professionals at Kensington Publishing, New York. My thanks go to unflappable editorial assistant Martin Biro, always helpful and efficient, and to Tory Groshong for her meticulous copyediting. I am especially grateful to John Rosenberg, whose tremendous book business savoir faire has brought my novels such success in Canada.

It gives me the greatest pleasure to dedicate this book to Audrey LaFehr, Editorial Director at Kensington. No author could ask for a more constant champion. Audrey was the first to see the potential of my "Thornleigh" novels—this is the third one—and she breathed new life into these books, shepherding them into the world with passionate commitment. I cannot thank her enough.

HISTORICAL PREFACE

When the corpulent and six-time-married King Henry VIII died in 1547, he left behind three offspring from three wives. Mary was thirty. Elizabeth was fourteen. Edward was nine. Henry could never have imagined the chaos he was bequeathing to England.

As the only son, Edward inherited the throne. He was managed by his powerful and ambitious councilor, the Duke of Northumberland, who took control and hardened the country into a severe Protestant regime. King Edward, always a sickly boy, died before he reached the age of sixteen. It was the summer of 1553.

Edward's legal and declared heir was his half sister, Mary. But Northumberland struck quickly with a coup, proclaiming his daughter-in-law Jane, a great-niece of King Henry, as queen. She was seventeen years old. It was a dangerous time for anyone whom the brutal Northumberland considered a claimant to the throne, and the two princesses, Mary and Elizabeth, lived in fear for their lives. Queen Jane ruled for nine days with the sullen disapproval of the people of England, until Mary rallied dozens of powerful lords to her side, and a fighting force, and took the throne that was indisputably hers. Jane was imprisoned. Northumberland was beheaded. Mary was triumphant.

But not for long. Mary's great cause was religion. She immediately declared her intention to revert the country to Catholicism, and to marry Philip of Spain, "the most Catholic prince in Christendom." Much of England was Protestant by now, and many people, whatever their religion, mistrusted a foreigner becoming the lord and master of their queen. They feared that Mary, controlled by Philip, would turn their small country into a vassal state of the mighty empire of Spain. When Mary gave the church free reign to begin burning heretics, people started to look to her younger sister, Princess Elizabeth, as someone who might give England back to Englishmen.

The people's discontent with their zealous queen festered, and in early 1554 it broke out into open rebellion. The leader was Sir Thomas Wyatt. With the backing of some influential lords he drew an army of several thousand common Englishmen to his base in Kent, where they proclaimed their intention to overthrow the queen. Many among them said they hoped to supplant her with Elizabeth. In February, they marched on London. Wyatt was an experienced soldier, and his men were loyal, but he had waited too long to act. Mary's forces were waiting at London's gates, battle-hardened troops with artillery. Wyatt and his men were cut down and captured. The rebellion was crushed. Once again, Mary was triumphant.

But she did not forgive, or forget. Especially the woman in whose name the rebels had risen against her: Elizabeth.

❧ 1 ❧

The Tower

March 1554

They came for her at dawn.

Through the long, dark hours Elizabeth had stared from the window at the garden made darker by the rain, knowing that if they were coming they would march along the gravel path under the bare, forked fruit trees. For three weeks the Queen's guards had kept her a prisoner in these remote corner rooms of Whitehall Palace. The patch of winter-dead garden had been all she had been able to see of the grounds. Music and laughter from distant banqueting rooms had reached her faintly, like echoes of the life she had lost.

Voices of the guardsmen at her door made her turn sharply from the window. Two lords of the Queen's council marched in past the guards. She had been wrong, they had bypassed the garden. Henry Radcliffe, Earl of Sussex, shook rain off his cap with the air of a man irritated at being burdened with unpleasant business. William Paulet, the sixty-year-old Marquis of Winchester, seemed far more troubled by their mission. Stroking rain from his wiry gray beard, he looked at the floor, and Elizabeth knew the old gentleman well enough to realize he was avoiding her eyes. Both men, with their damp garments and grave faces, brought in a chill that reached her like a cold hand at her throat. She had to swallow hard before she found her voice.

"My sister's reply?"

Sussex clapped his cap back on. Elizabeth felt a jolt of anger. He should be kneeling. They should both be kneeling.

"None, madam."

"But, my letter—"

"Her Majesty did not read it."

It knocked the breath from Elizabeth. One moment—that was all she had entreated of the Queen. One moment, face-to-face, to swear that she was innocent of any involvement in the rebellion. *I pray God that evil persuasions persuade not one sister against the other,* she had written. *I humbly crave only one word of answer from yourself.* But her begging had been for naught. Mary would show no mercy.

Elizabeth stood tall, rallying her courage. She was the daughter of a mighty father, great King Henry the Eighth. She would not let these lords see her terror.

They led her out into the cold March rain. She was twenty years old and on her way to die.

They took her down the Thames toward the Tower. She sat shivering in the barge under a dripping canopy, as pewter-cold waves heaved around her, and pewter-gray clouds poured down their frigid rain. Her fingers, gripping the seat edge, were purple with cold. The turbulent river, reeking now at low tide, churned up smells of dead fish and decaying sea matter, turning her stomach. Above the din of waves beating the hull and rain beating the canopy, church bells clanged throughout London. It was Palm Sunday, the beginning of Holy Week. Elizabeth's pious sister had brought back all the old Catholic rites—there would be creeping to the cross on Good Friday—and she and her council had ordered all the people to go to church this morning. "Keep to the church, and carry your palms!" had been the criers' calls through the muddy streets. An ideal diversion, Elizabeth thought bleakly, for the religious ceremonies would keep Londoners from seeing the barge carry her away. She gazed out at the seemingly deserted capital with its scattered steeples thrusting into the gray sky. All those people crammed into the churches. She thought, *Their palm fronds will have wilted in this downpour. Their stick crosses will be soggy relics for Mary's priests to bless.* She imagined them hurrying to get in out of the rain in their wet clothes—rough, homespun wool on fishwives and apprentices, rich velvets and brocades on the great merchants and their wives, but all of them jostling together, sharing a sense of community that she was now cut off from.

She had been arrested at her country home at Ashridge, and when they had brought her into London she had seen the grisly evidence of her sister's justice. Gallows heavy with decomposing rebel corpses stood at every one of the city's gates and in all the market squares. Body parts of rebels who had been hanged, drawn, and quartered were strung up along the city walls, a nightmare vision of dismembered arms and legs, the stench making the street dogs howl.

London Bridge emerged ahead through the rain. Its three- and four-story houses and shops looked as deserted as the city streets. Its stone arches bristled with spikes stuck with the gaping heads of rebels. Elizabeth thought she could smell the decaying flesh, putrid on the waterlogged air.

The river, squeezed between the viaduct's twenty huge arches, roiled in treacherous rapids, and the bargemen squared their feet wide, preparing to "shoot the bridge." Elizabeth gripped the gunwale to steady herself. The barge rocked and pitched in the angry water as it tumbled through the cavern of the stone arch. The light darkened. The water beat a hollow roar that echoed off the stone. The barge shot out the other side, wallowing in the confused currents, jolting Elizabeth's neck and knocking her knee against the hull.

Her heart thudded as she saw the Tower through the steely curtain of rain. It lay dead ahead on the northern shore. Ancient royal fortress, palace, and prison, its precincts were a labyrinth of stone walls and towers and turrets that rose, massive and forbidding, crushing Elizabeth's nerve.

Again, she plumbed a wellspring of strength from somewhere deep inside her and summoned defiance. "Not in by Traitor's Gate, my lords. I am Her Majesty's true subject and no traitor."

Winchester's voice was sad and kind. "Take heart, madam, the tide is with you." The low water made it impossible to enter by Traitor's Gate, a water gate. Instead the bargemen were rowing for Tower Wharf. Small victory, Elizabeth thought.

Yet Winchester's somber face, showing how little he relished his duty, suddenly gave her heart. She had friends. Many friends. Influential men. Lord Admiral Clinton. The Earl of Bedford. Sir Nicholas Throckmorton and Sir Peter Carew and Thomas Parry and John Harrington, and her favorite, the stolid Sir William Cecil. A mad hope swept her. They would rescue her! Yes, Sir William was hiding there in the windswept rain on the wharf, waiting with a troop of soldiers. They would attack her escort and spirit her away to safety!

But no friends came as the two lords marched her across the drawbridge and into the Tower's western precincts. She splashed through puddles that left her feet and ankles icy. Her sodden cloak, heavy on her shoulders, chilled her to the bone. Loose strands of her red hair plastered her neck, dripping ice water on her skin. The lieutenant of the Tower, Sir John Brydges, met them and led her across the narrow causeway. His soldiers lined the route hemmed in by the high stone walls. Rain drummed their steel helmets. Brydges led the party past the royal menagerie where Elizabeth could hear a lion roar. She did not flinch. She would not show the soldiers her fear.

One of them dropped to his knee and tugged off his helmet as she passed. "God save Your Grace!" he said.

Her heart leapt at this. A few other soldiers pulled off their helmets, too. But the show of loyalty changed nothing for her grim escort, who marched her on. She looked up at the stone walls glinting black with rain. Men were being tortured beyond those walls, she knew, tortured to scream out what they knew of her complicity in Wyatt's rebellion. Wyatt himself was a prisoner here. So was the mighty Duke of Suffolk. Mighty no more.

She passed under the inner tower they called the Bloody Tower and glimpsed, across the courtyard, the scaffold on Tower Green. Terror stabbed her. Just weeks ago her cousin Lady Jane Gray— queen for nine chaotic days—had stumbled up the steps of that scaffold. Trembling, she had groped in confusion for the block on which to lay her head, and the Queen's executioner had brought his axe thundering down. Pitiful, bewildered Jane, just seventeen years old. Yet the rebels had not fought in her name, but Elizabeth's. How much more cause, then, did Mary have to hate Elizabeth?

Her bravado suddenly deserted her, and with it all the strength in her legs. She sank down on a wet stone step, shivering, faint with fear, lost. Her fingers groped the grainy stone, her fingernails grating. The icy wetness seeped through to the skin of her thighs, to her very bones. Mary's hate for her was a well so deep, Wyatt's treason had merely topped it up. Its wellspring had been Elizabeth's mother, Anne Boleyn, despised by Mary for supplanting her own mother, Catherine, as Henry's queen. Mary's years of suffering before coming to the throne all stemmed from Anne. Now, as Queen, she was going to make Anne's daughter pay.

"Madam, you cannot tarry here," Sussex urged.

"Better here than in a worse place!" Elizabeth cried. "For I know not where you are taking me."

The place they took her, through Coldharbour Gate, was both better and worse. Better, for it was no dungeon or filthy cell but a fine room in the ancient royal palace in the inner ward, a room warmed by a brazier of coals and resplendent with a bed plump with satin cushions and fresh, embroidered linens. Worse, though, because this was the very place where her mother, condemned by the King, her husband, had been lodged before he had executed her. This was Mary's cruelest blow! Walking in, Elizabeth smelled coal dust and iron filings, and imagined her mother's terror when she had been brought here, knowing that she would walk out only to her death. Elizabeth had been three years old. Later, she had heard the tales of her mother's reckless courage in those days. Knowing that the axe of an English executioner sometimes hacked two or three times to finish its grisly job, Anne had demanded that an expert French swordsman be imported to make one clean cut.

The guards shot the great iron bolts of the door behind Elizabeth. No one had come to rescue her. Later that very day she heard drums and commotion as they led out the Duke of Suffolk, and then the executioner's axe thundered down again. She tried to muster her mother's courage. She knew she would be the next to die.

❧ 2 ❧

The Bargain

November 1554

The tavern's low ceiling and rough lumber walls had trapped generations of Antwerp's harbor-front smells—fish, stale beer, wet rope and salt-crusted clothes. Boiled turnips, too, Honor Thornleigh thought as she walked quickly through the room. Winter fodder. Staple of the poor. She ate turnips too often these days.

She passed seamen sitting over pots of ale, their desultory talk a stew of many languages—Dutch, Spanish, Portuguese, Italian. One man, dressed in the fine doublet of a ship's master, looked up from his foamy tankard as Honor passed. She lowered her face to hide it behind the edges of her furred hood. She had chosen this sailors' haunt far from her house, but Antwerp's mercantile community was as tight as a gossiping village and she couldn't risk being seen by one of her husband's business associates. Richard had no idea what she was doing behind his back.

She went straight through and out the tavern's back door, and across a cobbled courtyard that stank of gutted fish, where the gusting November wind chased dead, dry leaves. She was relieved to enter the stable with its friendlier smells of hay and horses.

George Mitford was already waiting. He stood at a stall door, scratching the nose of a shaggy bay mare who bowed her head in contentment.

"She seems to love that," Honor said, throwing off her hood.

He smiled when he saw her. "We all love a good scratch."

"Scratch my back, I'll scratch yours?"

"And so the world goes round, my dear."

She gave in to impulse and embraced him. "Thanks to old friends, yes." She paid for her action with a sharp spasm at her rib, cracked by a bullet ten months ago.

"Now, now, don't tease," he said as he pulled back from her embrace. It was his jest, but said with a blush that Honor found endearing, the cheerful fluster of a man who had not forgotten the passionate impulse of youth. She was forty-four and he was ten years older, but he was still fit, still possessed of a thick head of hair, though it was sheened with silver. In the old days, back in England, his hair had been as dark as Honor's was still. Was that really more than two decades ago? He had caught her by the waist under the stairs on Richard's ship as they had sailed into this very harbor, delivering George to safety from the heretic-hunting persecution of the bishop of London, and in that moment he had fervently declared his love to her. She had laughed. George was not the first man she had rescued whose giddy gratitude had flashed into ardor. "And all I had to do," she'd teased, "was save your life."

Now here he was, saving hers.

She noticed the sturdy case at his feet, a strongbox covered with amber leather, secured with studded copper bands and an iron lock. He was never without it. She glanced over her shoulder to make sure she had not been followed. There was no one. Just the soft chomping of horses munching hay, and the keening of wind across the roof's patched holes. She was satisfied that she and George were alone.

She opened her cloak to display the top of her bosom to him, and touched her necklace, an almond-sized emerald pendant on a chain of filigreed gold. The gem was warm against her fingertips, her body's warmth infusing Richard's gift from the summer they were married twenty-one years ago. To her, it held the essence still of that sweet, English summer. She bent her head to undo the clasp, then handed over the necklace. "I couldn't give it to anyone but you, George."

She saw a moment of deep feeling in his eyes before he lowered his gaze to study the goods. His demeanor was suddenly all business. "Milky inclusion in the left quadrant. Old-fashioned cabochon setting. A nick in the clasp."

Honor winced at the criticism. She loved this necklace, a golden filament with its drop of green fire that connected her to happier days. But she stilled her tongue. George knew how much she needed the cash. He had been buying her jewelry, piece by piece, for months. She glanced down at his leather case, aching with curiosity. Were any of her gems still nestled in the black velvet lining, or did they already adorn his pampered clients? Her ruby earrings that Isabel, as a baby at her breast, had reached out to grab. Her rope of pearls bought on a trip with Richard to Venice. The diamond and sapphire ring he had given her seven years ago after a spectacular wool season. Her brooch of opals and topaz, an heirloom from the mother she had never known—Honor had planned to give it to her stepson Adam's intended at their official betrothal. Her bracelets and necklaces of garnets, carnelian, amber, and coral, of lesser value yet cherished all the same. She lifted her eyes from the case, fending off the tug of regret. Her family could not eat rubies and pearls.

As always, George gave her an excellent price. Far better, she knew, than the emerald was worth.

The wind tugged at her skirt as she made her way home along the river Schelde's crowded quay. Tall ships' masts loomed over her, their furled sails stacked in massive tiers that blocked the watery sun. Their taut ropes creaked, straining against the wharf's bollard posts in an age-old sea song. Winter was bearing in from the frosty North Sea and seemed to make the sailors and tradesmen hustle more earnestly in and out of the chandleries and harbor offices and boat sheds. She passed men hefting sacks from the hold of a Portuguese carrack pungent with a cargo of pepper and cinnamon.

She looked to the broad river's western horizon. Was Adam's ship sailing into the estuary right now, she wondered, battered from its battles with Russian ice? Would he make it back for tonight's feast for Isabel? He had written from the port of The Hague to say he intended to be there, and Honor hoped that the wind and tides would indeed bring him. It would be a sadder party without her seafaring stepson.

There were shouts from crewmen on board a magnificent galleon coming alongside the wharf, its bright banners fluttering, and she stopped to make way for a gang of wharf hands jogging forward to secure the ship's hawsers. Venetian, by its flag, and alive with men on the decks readying lines, and boys in the rigging, furling canvas. This controlled chaos of river traffic always impressed Honor. Antwerp was the trading and financial center of Europe, thanks to its fine seaport and crucial wool market, and hundreds of ships passed through here every day, making it an international city, with sailors and merchants and financiers hailing from Spain, Portugal, Venice, France, England, Poland, Sweden, and beyond. Antwerp embraced them all with a tolerance that Honor admired. The sights and sounds of the hectic river commerce reminded her of the busy Thames, and London, and a wave of homesickness rushed over her. How she missed England! But she and Richard were exiles. He was wanted as a traitor. They could never go home.

But what future lay here? The view of the ships dragged her thoughts far out to sea, south to Cadiz, to the storm four months ago that had cost them so much. She saw Richard's two caravels pitch in the storm's black fury. She heard their hulls smash on the rocks, the wood shatter, heard the screams of men hurled overboard. She felt their terror as they drowned, thrashing in the black depths.

She turned abruptly away from the water. Pointless to torture herself with visions of the catastrophe. She left the harbor and headed for home, her purse heavy with George's coins, her heart heavy with regret. And something sharper. For the first time she felt fear. All her jewels were now gone.

John Cheke, a Cambridge don, announced the toast. "To Isabel and Carlos!"

The twenty-three men and women crowding round the Thornleighs' dinner table raised their glasses high. Bright candles warmed the snug town house near the heart of Antwerp's Grote Market. Richard had bought it, a fashionable address, in the heyday of his wool-trading business, to be a second home for his frequent trips from England. Now, Honor hoped their neighbors didn't suspect that they could barely maintain the upkeep. "To the young couple," Cheke cried. "The enemies of New Spain will quake at Carlos's sword!"

"And if that fails," a bookbinder quipped, "he'll unleash a *real* terror—his wife!"

Everyone laughed, the toasted couple loudest of all. Isabel flashed her imitation of a fierce warrior's face at her Spanish soldier husband. It made him throw back his head and roar with laughter.

Even Honor had to laugh—though her daughter's exploits still astonished her. She glanced at Richard down the table and saw him, too, gazing at Isabel in wonderment. Their daughter, just twenty, had proved herself to be not the innocent they thought they had raised, but an audacious rebel who, a year ago, had helped Wyatt's uprising almost bring down England's Queen Mary. It had happened as Honor lay here, barely conscious, sunk in a fever from a gunshot wound, and when she had recovered enough for Richard to tell her the tale, she had found it incredible. Isabel's choice of husband had surprised her almost as much—Carlos Valverde, a mercenary soldier, unschooled, accustomed to very rough ways. But when she heard how he had saved Richard and Isabel, she had embraced him like a son. The wedding three months ago had been a happy interlude in the family's financial troubles.

Adam's wedding would be next. That would be a grand affair, and the rich connection very promising for the family, Honor hoped. It saddened her that the tides had not brought her stepson tonight, after all, but she did not indulge fears of a mishap. If any man knew his way around a ship, it was Adam.

Her eyes met Richard's. He was head and shoulders taller than many of the men here, and with his leather eye patch and sea-weathered face and storm gray hair, he put her in mind of a rugged rock rising above the shallows of other folk. Tonight, though, he looked careworn and all of his age, a craggy fifty-six. As her glance met his, their smiles at the toast gave way to a mutual sadness. This was a farewell party. Isabel and Carlos were leaving for the New World.

All day, organizing the modest feast, Honor had tried not to give in to her sense of bereavement. When would she ever see her daughter again? She watched Richard quickly drain his goblet of wine and then pour himself another. It worried her to see him drinking so much, drowning his own hard regrets. He had wanted to give Isabel and Carlos some of the land he owned in England, determined to keep his family together, but instead, to make a living, Isabel and Carlos were sailing half a world away. Honor knew how it was gnawing at Richard. Queen Mary's officers, in confiscating the moveable goods of all known rebels, had snatched everything at their home in Colchester, from flocks to looms. His fulling ponds and mills sat idle, his tenting yards fell daily into further decay, his warehouses lay stripped bare. And the manor house he and Honor had built—her beloved Speedwell House, named after the wildflower so dear to her heart—was reduced to a hulk. She knew how Richard longed to go home and revive his international wool cloth business, but that could never be. If he set foot in England, he would hang.

"Honor, your tankard is empty. That will never do."

She turned to the affable face of John Cheke, who filled her mug with ale, the twinkle in his eye belying his reputation as a distinguished Cambridge scholar. She shook off her melancholy and quaffed some ale, truly pleased to see these good friends who had come to bid Isabel and Carlos good-bye. All were exiles, many worse off than she and Richard were. With George's coins she had sent her scullery boy to pay off her debts to the butcher, the fishmonger, the grocer, and the vintner, and with her credit good again—for a while, at least—she had set a hearty table of English fare for these fellow refugees from Queen Mary's oppression. The roast beef and beer, eel pie and cider, baked apples and custard, were comforts to a homesick community. A queer little enclave they had created, she thought as she watched John Abel pass the hat. As usual, he was collecting for the Sustainers of the Refugees Fund. There were hundreds of exiles throughout the Low Countries, and for those here in Antwerp her house had become a meeting place, a home away from home for hard-up Protestant gentry and scholars. Erasmus, her late mentor, would have loved the constant chatter about books and the New Learning.

They liked to dance, too. Honor called on the trio of musicians to play, and Isabel and Carlos had just got up to start the first dance when the maid hurried in, wiping her hands on her apron, her eyes shining. "It's Master Adam!"

Honor turned with a happy smile. Her stepson had made it, after all. Adam strode in with a burlap sack slung over his shoulder like Father Christmas, and looking as jovial, if not as old, his beard not long and white but trim and black. Isabel cried out with joy and rushed over to her brother and threw her arms around his neck, crying, "You came!" Carlos clapped a congratulatory hand on Adam's shoulder, saying, "And in one piece." Honor hugged him in delight and welcomed him home. Richard shook his son's hand in heartfelt silence.

The guests hadn't seen Adam since his return from Russia, and as everyone crowded round, welcoming him, Honor looked on with a swell of pride. She knew from his letter the story of the Merchant Adventurers' voyage. They had endured terrible privation, he had written, losing ships and men, and were returning with little profit to show for it. Reading between the lines, though, Honor gathered that Adam had acquitted himself bravely, helping to lead the remnant of the expedition overland to Moscow. At the guests' urging he was telling tales of the extraordinary court of Czar Ivan—of *caviar* and *saunas*, and harbors teeming with whales. She watched him gesture as he talked, thinking how, at twenty-nine, he looked so like his father at that age. Tall and sturdy, with the easy movements of a man comfortable in his own skin, and that watchful gleam in his eye, observing others with alertness but never with fear.

"Where to next, my boy?" old Anthony Cooke asked.

"Back to Moscow, sir, if the company can raise the funds. They're refitting *Spendthrift*. I'll be captain."

Honor caught Richard's dark look as he quietly left the room. Their son's advancement was bittersweet. An expert navigator since he was twelve, Adam had been not just captain but master, too, aboard Richard's ships for years, an equal alongside his father.

But the storm off Cadiz four months ago that had sunk their two caravels with all their cargo—a massive, horrifying loss—had left them stranded on the brink of bankruptcy. Richard's third, much older ship, *Speedwell*, lay moored in the estuary, derelict, for they could not afford to repair her. To bring in money, Adam had signed on with the Company of Merchant Adventurers. It pained Richard to see his son a mere hired seaman. It pained Honor to see their family breaking apart.

She slipped out of the room and found Richard starting up the stairs. To rifle through his account books again, she wondered, searching for phantom profits? Several nights she had gotten up and found him poring over the ledgers in candlelight. The futility of it—his obsession to ferret out some cash—tore at her heart.

"He'll want to talk to you," she said. "Richard, come back."

He turned on the step. "He doesn't need my advice. And words are all I can give him."

"He'll want to tell you everything. Let him give *you* that."

He frowned. "Why don't you wear the things I gave you?"

Instinctively, her hand went to her neck, betraying her.

"That's right, your jewels. You never wear them anymore. Have you suddenly turned Calvinist? No more frippery?"

"There was so much to organize, the food, the wine, I . . . I just forgot."

He looked at her for a long, sad moment. "I hope you got a good price," he said, and went on up the stairs.

She stood still a moment, shaken. Not just at being found out. It was the change in him that unnerved her. She had never before seen Richard despondent. During everything they had lived through, he had always faced the challenges head on, alchemizing dangers and turning them to his advantage, whether outsmarting the bishop of Norwich's henchmen or bedeviling the Church's murderous inquisitors. It almost seemed that he'd thrived on it. But this—being unable to provide for his family—had unmanned him. Honor did not know how to help him.

When she rejoined her guests, Adam was rummaging in his burlap sack and pulled out a sleek, black pelt. The women gasped at its opulence, and Dorothy Hales exclaimed, "A sable!"

Adam draped it around Isabel's throat. "From the forests of Russia, Bel." She beamed as she stroked the silken fur. "And what do you think of this?" he said. He lifted out a carved wooden figure the size of his hand, a Russian peasant woman so plump she was pear shaped, with clothes and a kerchief painted in bright red and yellow and green. He set it in Isabel's hand, then winked at her. "Watch."

He pulled off the top half of the figure. Nested inside was a surprise: another figure, identical but smaller, a baby replica of the original. The guests cried "Ahhh" in delight.

"They call it a *matroshka*," Adam said.

"From the Latin root, *mater*, I should think—mother," John Cheke said helpfully. "What a quaint fertility symbol."

Isabel turned scarlet, tears springing to her eyes even as she kept smiling. She pressed her face against Carlos's broad chest as though to hide her embarrassment. He wrapped a protective arm around her, his face beaming pride. "She was going to tell you later. Isabel is—"

"With child," Honor blurted. She'd guessed it the moment she saw Isabel's happy tears.

Isabel turned back, sniffling and smiling, and nodded to her.

"When?" someone asked.

"Wedding night," Carlos said, grinning.

Isabel playfully swatted his shoulder. "April," she said.

"A little April fool, just like its mother," Adam said, and before she could snap a retort he kissed her cheek.

Honor nudged past the guests and enfolded her daughter in her arms. "Oh, my darling." She held Isabel so tightly it sent a stab of pain through her tender rib.

Isabel saw her flinch and quickly let her go, whispering, "I'm sorry, Mother." She knew how near death that bullet had left Honor. "Are you all right?"

"Yes, yes, fine. And so very happy for you."

The news of the baby sparked new life into the party and the guests threw themselves into eating and drinking with fresh gusto. Some bombarded Adam with questions about how the Russians lived, while others heatedly debated the Spaniards' harsh rule in

Peru, where Carlos was headed to captain the governor's cavalry. And the dancing began. Honor wanted to hurry upstairs and give Richard the sweet news about the baby, but Henry Killigrew tugged her out to join the dance and was bowing to her to the strain of "Greensleeves" when Adam came to her side.

"Can I speak to you?"

His sober look was so at odds with his cheerful mood moments ago. What is wrong? Honor wondered. She excused herself to Henry and followed Adam to a deserted alcove behind the bowl of spiced wine.

"I've been round to the Kortewegs," he said to her quietly. "It's off. No betrothal. No wedding."

Honor was shocked. "But, I thought you and Margriet had an understanding."

"We did."

"What changed her mind?"

"Not her. Her father."

"Why? He found you suitable enough at Michaelmas."

"That was before Cadiz."

Honor felt it as a blow. Margriet Korteweg, daughter of a wealthy Antwerp burgher; Adam Thornleigh, son of a near-bankrupt. "He's refused his consent?"

Adam nodded. He watched the dancing as though he was considering joining in, not for fun but for a diversion. He looked angry, Honor thought. And sounded angry. Not in an ominous way as though he meant to strike back, more like he had absorbed the deep insult and meant to move on, though the anger simmered. Did he love the girl? She was a catch, both pretty and rich, but Honor did not have the feeling that Adam's heart was broken. His pride, yes. And his lively plans.

"Don't tell your father. Not tonight." She knew it would wound Richard almost as much as Adam, and for the same reason. The Thornleighs were suddenly not good enough for the Kortewegs.

"I hoped you might do that task. Better than me." There was a hint of a smile in his eyes, self-deprecating, as though to acknowledge that he lacked her finesse. But she sensed it was to mask the stinging humiliation he felt at his loss. "Money," he said with quiet fierceness. "It's all that really matters, isn't it?" He gave her a determined smile. "Well, from now on, money shall be my guiding star."

There was a flurry of sound through the room, voices abuzz with surprise. Honor realized the dancers had stopped. The music dwindled and died. She followed the gaze of her guests to the door. A lanky man stood there, bundled in a russet cloak against the cold autumn night. A draft of frosty air had rushed in with him, but it was not the cold that held the whole company frozen, including Honor. It was the extraordinary fact of his presence.

Everyone here knew Sir William Cecil, both for his eminence in England as a minister of the late, Protestant boy-king, Edward, and for his tireless support of the exile community. He was thirty-four, and several of the guests were his relations—Anthony Cooke was his father-in-law and John Cheke his first wife's brother. Honor had known Sir William for years. But his home was London, where he carefully balanced a life of partial retirement under the strict, new Catholic reign of Queen Mary. He rarely left England. What had brought him all this way?

"You are welcome, sir," Honor said, going to greet him. "Come in and warm yourself. And sit you down to some supper before these home-hungry souls devour you first."

Cecil did not smile. "Honor, I must speak with you."

"And what of the people? How did they take the Queen's rough handling of her sister?" Honor asked Cecil when they were alone, sitting before the fire in her parlor. She had never met Princess Elizabeth, but hearing now of her plight she recalled how everyone, whenever they talked about the clever and striking young Princess, did so with affection. Elizabeth inspired people. It was a power that Queen Mary could not ignore.

"Widespread dismay," Cecil said with feeling. "Indeed, they showed their love for Elizabeth when the Queen moved her under guard from the Tower and out of London, to Woodstock. That was in May. They traveled by water to attract as little notice as possible, but when the barge passed the Steelyard, the Hanse merchants had their gunners fire a salute to Elizabeth. It brought Londoners running out into the streets to see what the commotion was, and the event that the Queen had wanted to keep quiet turned into a noisy parade." There was a flash of pride in his shrewd gray eyes. Five years ago, when Princess Elizabeth was fifteen, he had been named surveyor of her estates, an honorary post. He had been close to her ever since.

"It was the same when they turned inland," he went on. "The Princess was carried in an open litter surrounded by guardsmen, and the country people rushed from their hayfields and cottages to see her. They thronged her on roadsides and bridges. They showered her with flowers and cakes at every village, even as the guards bristled around her with their pikes. At Aston Rowant some villagers rang the church bells as she passed."

"Which must have put the Queen in a terrible fume?"

"It did. She arrested the bell ringers. But this love the people bear Elizabeth may be what saved her. The Queen faced much hostility after she executed Wyatt and so many scores of rebels. The people grew sickened by the hangings. They would not have tolerated Elizabeth's death."

Honor shuddered. Richard had been about to hang alongside those rebels. "You really think she was planning to execute the Princess?"

"I know it. The chancellor prepared the order, drawn up with instructions to the lieutenant of the Tower. But the Queen did not dare sign it."

"For now," Honor said, thinking it through.

"Exactly. The Princess is far from clear of danger." Cecil edged forward in his chair, tension in his voice. "Honor, the Queen has lost no time wrenching the realm back to Catholicism, just as we expected, since she married Philip of Spain."

The most Catholic prince in Europe, that was how Philip was known. "And the Pope's legate? Has he arrived yet? We heard the Queen had invited him."

"Cardinal Pole will be in London by next month."

"Then the burnings will begin." *All over again,* Honor thought, looking into the fire as it consumed the logs. Once, she had saved men from that fiery death. Once, she had been terrifyingly close to it herself. She thought that such barbarism in England had died with old King Henry. Not so, it seemed. How she pitied the hapless Protestants who crossed this new queen's path.

"I fear so," Cecil said. "An English Inquisition. Which fuels the danger for the Princess. Queen Mary is only waiting for Elizabeth to make an error in religion, to fail to conform. That would give her the excuse she needs to execute her sister."

What a family, Honor thought. Mary had learned from their father when he cut off the heads of two wives.

"It goes even beyond the Queen," Cecil went on. "Ambassador Renard itches to remove Elizabeth. And plots it, I fear. Poison, perhaps. Or an assassin's dagger."

Honor did not doubt the imperial ambassador's agenda to bolster Queen Mary, who was a cousin of mighty Emperor Charles, and now his daughter-in-law as well. Renard would be ruthless, for his master's sake, in removing any obstacle to Mary's reign.

"It is dire," Cecil said. "The Queen keeps Elizabeth as closely guarded in Woodstock as in a prison, allowing no one near her except two women of her chamber, and those straightly chosen for their loyalty to the Queen. And every day she sends her councilors to press Elizabeth to confess her guilt in backing Wyatt's rebellion. Elizabeth has resisted so far. But she is young, and so isolated, and friendless. It has left her adrift, bereft of trustworthy, experienced councilors."

Honor admired his devotion, but could not resist a small tease at his supreme confidence in his own abilities. "Councilors like you, Sir William."

"No, Honor," he said soberly, "like you."

"Me!"

"That's why I've come. To ask you to accept a mission. Come home, I entreat you, and advise the Princess."

She could not hide her astonishment. "Advise her? To do what?"

"Survive."

"You expect much of me!"

"Everyone knows you survived worse."

"Not everyone, I hope, else from a dungeon I'd be advising no one."

"Everyone in our circle. Honor, this is no jest. Your steady strength is needed. The Princess's very life is at stake. She must not fall into the Queen's trap. The hopes of all reasonable Englishmen—the very future of England—lie in Elizabeth."

"Sir William, you flatter me. Truly. And I pity the young Princess. But even if I felt it was in my power to help her, I could not go home. Richard awaits a traitor's death if he ever sets foot in England. You know that. He can never go back. And I will never desert him."

"Honor, hear me out. I—"

"No. I'm sorry, but you've made a long journey for nothing."

He puffed his cheeks and let out an exasperated breath. "How does Richard manage such an obstinate wife?"

She had to smile. "Is Mildred so meek?"

"At least she listens!" He got up and kicked a stray ember back into the fire.

Honor pursed her lips at the rebuke. "Do go on, sir."

He turned, composed again. "I am not such a fool as to come unprepared. I believe I can solve your problem."

"My problem?" Melancholy swept back as she thought how she and Richard were teetering toward bankruptcy. If Sir William could make that problem go away it would be a miracle.

"Richard's, I mean," he said. "I believe I can secure him a pardon."

Her breath caught in her throat. "Good God. How?"

"The lord treasurer, the Marquis of Winchester, owes me a favor. I finessed his purchase of several lucrative manors in Devon formerly belonging to the abbey at Montcross. As one of the Queen's closest councilors, he can draw up this order."

Honor sprang to her feet, daring to hope. "A pardon for treason? Or for killing Anthony Grenville?"

"For everything. A general pardon."

"But . . . the Queen. Why would she sign it?"

"She has signed several other pardons put before her by various councilors. I think it not impossible she would do so again. After all, she does not know Richard personally, his name is just one of many rebels' names, and as I told you she prudently stopped after the first wave of executions, seeing the dark mood of the people. Besides, she is so happy now in the thrall of her marriage, I am told she thinks of little else but entertaining her husband with feasts and jousts and pageants. If Winchester puts the thing in front of her, I believe she will sign it without a second thought."

It *was* a miracle. Honor's heart beat fast with excitement. But her sudden jump up sent the familiar pain flaring through her side, and she reached for the chair and sat again, carefully propping herself on one practiced arm to ease the soreness. Was she mad to consider this undertaking? Was she up to it? Was her body? And what actual outcome did Cecil expect? How long would she be expected to act as "councilor" to this royal personage she had never met?

She put this last question to him, and he seemed about to speak, but stopped and gave a shrug of uncertainty that she sensed troubled him as much as her, for he was a man who loved precision. These were chaotic times, and he was doing the best he could for the Princess, someone he cared deeply about—that was all. Honor saw that the mission was terribly vague, her exact responsibilities unknown. Unknowable. Every inner voice of prudence and experience told her to be wary.

But, to go home! She and Richard could restore his wool trade business. And eventually, when they were back on their feet, they could reunite the family. *Home.* Achingly, she thought of her abandoned garden at Speedwell House. She could be there in time to see the yellow exuberance of spring—scatters of celandines, sprays of forsythia, banks of daffodils.

"We would need more than the pardon," she said, anxious, but needing to know.

"More?"

"We have debts."

Cecil's shrewd eyes registered the satisfaction of a win. "Money can always be found."

Seagulls wheeled, screeching above *Speedwell* as her bow carved the waves, reaching for England.

Honor stood on the foredeck with Richard, hardly needing her winter cloak as the strong midday sun beamed down from a sky of cobalt blue. She had to hold up her hand against the brightness as she looked aloft. Everything was new, from the virgin white sails, to the freshly painted masts, to the taut rope rigging. She glanced back across the ship at Adam, standing high on the sterncastle deck, conferring with the helmsman at the wheel. She took a deep, contented breath of the cold air tangy with salt and freedom. The refitted ship pleased her enormously. But not, she knew, as much as it pleased Richard. It had done her heart a world of good to watch him and Adam these past weeks as they had thrown themselves into overseeing the carpenters, caulkers, riggers and sailmakers.

"The old girl's got the wind in her teeth," Richard said, squinting his one good eye at the new spritsail gleaming in the sun. "It's good to have her back."

"Never count us old girls out, my love."

He laughed. "Never."

She hooked her arm through his with a happy sigh. Her only pang was for her daughter. Isabel and Carlos at this very moment would be sailing into warm, southerly waters, bound for Peru. It was hard to think that, come spring, Isabel would face childbirth in a strange land without her mother at her side. But Isabel could rely on the strong arms of Carlos. He would take care of her. And Honor dared to hope that one day, when she and Richard had reestablished themselves, they would host a homecoming feast for their daughter and son-in-law, and their first grandchild.

She gazed toward the horizon that cradled home. "Will you hire Winthrop back?" she asked. "Is he still in Colchester? And don't forget to ask your sister to recommend a good housekeeper. You'll need someone with her wits about her until I can get home. I don't know low long I'll be with the Princess at Woodstock."

He didn't answer.

"Richard?" She turned to him.

He was looking at her intently, his smile gone. "Honor, it's not too late to change your mind. Princess Elizabeth has other friends to help her. Ones who wouldn't be risking their necks."

"We've been through all this."

"But maybe not enough. We were so relieved at getting the pardon. But now that we're really on our way back, I'm thinking I should never have agreed to Sir William's bargain. In this new Catholic England, it could get you killed."

"I don't accept that. It was so long ago, almost twenty years, it's all been forgotten." Nineteen years, to be exact. She could *never* forget. She had been tried by the church court for heresy, and convicted. Condemned to burn. She had escaped, and later, under the reign of the Protestant young King Edward, she had been safe. She understood Richard's unease now about the zealously Catholic Queen Mary, but Honor wasn't unduly troubled. Her conviction had been so very long ago, and the country had experienced so much upheaval since then, under three different reigns. Her personal history was a mere speck lost in the country-wide dust of all that former chaos. "It's all forgotten," she said again. "A new generation runs things now."

"The past could catch up with you yet. Does Sir William know?"

"About our old missions, yes." Before her arrest for heresy, she and Richard had smuggled persecuted dissenters out of England on his ships. "But about how and why we fled England back then, no. Heavens, Richard, he was fourteen at the time."

"Still, I don't like it."

"It'll be fine. I'll just do what I can to help the Princess, then come home and live as quietly as a mouse."

He cocked a skeptical eyebrow. "Some mouse."

"Other non-Catholics are doing it. Sir William himself is doing it."

Richard's expression turned serious. "There's the Grenvilles. *That* was just ten months ago."

Honor couldn't suppress a shudder, remembering Anthony Grenville's pistol, his deranged face, the searing bullet he had fired into her. She shook off the sickening memory. "Grenville is dead. So is the past." She would not let ghosts frighten her.

"Grenville's dead, but his children are very much alive. And fast friends of the Queen. She's made John Grenville a baron."

"But what can he do to you now? You have your royal pardon. He must accept that."

He said darkly, "Kin do not forget murder."

She was startled by the word. *Murder.* They never used it. They had found it better never to mention how Richard had bludgeoned Anthony Grenville to death.

"Anyway," he said, "it's not me I'm thinking of, it's you." He went on firmly, as though settling the matter, "No, given all the risks, you're safer in Antwerp. When we land, I'll ride home and get the business rolling, you sail back with Adam. Sir William will understand. As soon as I'm on my feet again I'll repay him."

"Go back? Run away *again?*"

"It's not running. We'll just have two homes, Colchester and Antwerp, the way we used to."

"Only I'll be barred from one." She longed for an end to this gypsy existence, never secure, never completely safe. They had established themselves in Antwerp after fleeing all those years ago, but had returned to England in the mild reign of King Edward, and had lived quietly in Colchester for several years and prospered, Richard keeping the Antwerp house for business. But then Edward died and his sister Mary took the throne with a vow to exterminate heresy, and so, with persecution threatening them again, Richard had joined Wyatt's rebellion. When it failed, he and Isabel had barely escaped with their lives. Honor had had enough of it.

"No," she said decisively. "England is our real home. The home of my heart. I won't let these religious zealots run us off again, not the Grenvilles or Cardinal Pole or bloody Queen Mary herself. They can't be allowed to keep attacking their neighbors. Burning people for their beliefs. Making Englishmen quake and dissemble like beaten children. Someone's got to stop them. Until that happens, we'll never be secure, not me or you or Adam or anyone."

He was looking at her now with a frown. "I thought you were going back to advise the Princess."

"I am."

"Are you sure that's all? Because it sounds like you're going back to try to make her queen."

❧ 3 ❧

The Gatehouse

December 1554

Woodstock in Oxfordshire was far from the noisy money-making of London and its hectic royal court. The village lay in a steep, wooded valley with the sluggish River Glyme at its feet. The people lived from harvest to harvest, and when those failed they felt want. The summer had brought the worst rains in years, punishing torrents that had left the fields and gardens an unhealthy bog. By winter, hunger haunted the poor.

Though remote, the village had felt the royal presence for centuries. Woodstock Palace had been a hunting lodge since Norman times, and generations of English kings had come to hunt in the royal forests. Here, four hundred years ago, Henry I had kept a menagerie with leopards and porcupines. Here his grandson, Henry II, had kept his mistress, fair Rosamund Clifford. Yet the palace seemed haunted by death. It was at Woodstock that Henry II first clashed with Thomas à Becket, his friend and archbishop, who was later stabbed to death in his cathedral by Henry's loyal men. Woodstock was a frequent retreat of King John, whose murderous rule, according to legend, kindled the revenge of Robin Hood. Here Henry III survived an assassination attempt. Here, in 1389, the Earl of Pembroke, a Christmas guest, was killed by a jousting foe.

And here, Princess Elizabeth, by order of her sister, Queen

Mary, had been kept under house arrest for eight months. The palace had been in sorry disrepair for decades and was now a palace in name only. Its dilapidated medieval buildings rose from the marshy riverbed, a managerial headache of crumbling stone, leaky roofs, and cracked window casements. The place, never meant as a jail, had few doors with locks, so for security reasons the man appointed as the Princess's custodian, Sir Henry Bedingfield, had lodged her in the gatehouse.

All this, Honor had learned from Thomas Parry, the Princess's steward, as they conferred at Woodstock's inn, the Bull. Each had been alerted about the other by Sir William Cecil, and now they were discussing how they might find a way for Honor to get in to see the Princess. They stood at the upstairs hall window overlooking the main street. The Bull's customers were downstairs at dinner, and the clack of cutlery and whiffs of braised rabbit with leeks drifted up the stairs. Still, Honor and Parry kept their voices low, for they could not risk anyone, guest or servant, wandering by and overhearing. Parry had said he suspected that the village held at least one of the imperial ambassador's spies keeping a vigilant, hostile eye on the Princess.

"Is she allowed out to walk?" Honor asked.

"Once a day, but only in the garden and always accompanied by guards. Usually by Bedingfield as well."

Honor looked out at the muddy street where strips of browned snow lay shredded by the ruts. Across the street the parish church of St. Mary Magdalene with its squat, Norman tower stared sternly back at her. Wind keened through its battlements.

"Do they take her to church? The Queen must insist on that, on her sister attending mass."

"Indeed, but there is a chapel beside her bedchamber. She does not leave the grounds."

"How many rooms in the gatehouse?"

"Four, counting the chapel. The guardsmen occupy one. Elizabeth is left with just two for herself and the women of her chamber."

"Any hope there, among her women? Friends to help us from the inside?"

He shook his head. "Both were strictly chosen for their religion. They are the Queen's women."

"Jailers themselves," Honor said grimly. "And no one's allowed to visit her?"

"No one. Excepting, of course, the Queen's councilors who come regularly to press her to confess her guilt in the rebellion. Or did until this week. I expect we'll see them back again after Twelfth Night."

"May she receive letters?"

"None, unless read and approved by Bedingfield."

"Books?"

"Only approved religious texts, and only after Bedingfield has leafed through every page for contraband."

The challenge seemed insurmountable. How was she to advise the Princess when she could neither see her nor communicate with her? The wind hurled gusts of grainy snow against the window like a tempestuous child hurling handfuls of sand, and Honor hugged herself against the chilly draft. A farmer plodded up the street behind his ox, the beast strapped with a load of firewood on each of its bony sides. Christmas was approaching. Honor had hoped to spend it at home in Colchester. In her absence Richard's sister was overseeing the holiday preparations, and Honor could imagine Joan busily ordering the baking of plum and currant puddings with brandy, while the servants bedecked the great hall with fragrant cedar boughs. But it seemed that she would be stuck in seclusion at the Bull Inn for some time. She felt like a prisoner herself.

At least there was Parry. They had met only this afternoon but already she liked and trusted him. A stout, fleshy, plain-speaking man about her own age, early forties, he had a no-nonsense view of his job and the people around him. He had been Elizabeth's factotum for years, carefully husbanding her estates, for she owned several homes and was the second largest landholder in the realm. Parry had made the Bull his headquarters and from it he continued to manage her tenants, collect her rents, and protect her deer parks, sending his reports to her through Sir Henry Bedingfield and hoping to one day get in to see her. His devotion to the

Princess reminded Honor of Sir William Cecil. So did his pity for her. "My poor young Lady Elizabeth is so lonely, brought so low," Parry had said with a catch in his voice. Honor observed it with some wonder. How this girl could move men.

"Tell me more about her keeper," she asked. She knew that Bedingfield was of an ancient Norfolk family, a stoutly Catholic knight, but little else about him.

Parry rolled his eyes. "A pusillanimous donkey. He fears the Queen's displeasure, fears the council's disapproval, fears even offending Elizabeth herself. Fears his own fart, I shouldn't wonder. His solution is to make not the slightest decision without first asking permission of his betters and getting it in writing. Though the oaf can barely read. But he is blindly loyal to the Queen, conspicuously so during the rebellion, for which she rewarded him with Wyatt's confiscated lands. He'll go far."

They talked for some time about the routines of the household, about who came and went, why and how, Honor trying to spot a gap through which she might slip past Bedingfield's notice. She wondered aloud if she might hide in some delivery cart. "How about deliveries of food?"

"His staff buys here at the village market."

"*No one* goes in?" she asked, adding in exasperation, "Not the butcher, the baker, the candlestick maker?"

He smiled wanly at her jest. "They do, but the guards check every item brought in. Bedingfield's orders. As far as I can tell, the only thing to enter or leave the gatehouse that is not viewed and searched is the Princess's smalls."

Her underclothes? "How so?"

"Bedingfield's orders, again." His voice took on the tone of a pronouncement. "All linen brought to Her Grace clean by the laundress is to be delivered to the Queen's women, and they are to see all fouled linen delivered to the said laundress."

Honor liked this. A plan, at last.

She had slung the burlap bundle over her shoulder. Wrapped in homespun shawls against the cold, her head lowered under a shawl kerchief, she trudged up the road to the palace, the ruts iron hard with frost this morning. Her borrowed dress was brown as a burr and shapeless as a sack, but it was clean, as befitted her pretended occupation. After her years of soft living, the bristly wool grated her skin like sandpaper, and the borrowed leather shoes, coarse as bacon rinds, were already raising blisters on her heels. She was afraid her wincing would give her away. Could she really hope to deceive these people?

No one stopped and stared at her on the road, at least. A drayman rumbled past in his cart piled with ox hides that stank in the strengthening sun. A grimy little girl and boy with sticks prodded a couple of geese that honked their distress, waddling fast as though to escape the death that no doubt awaited them. A priest trudged past Honor munching a chicken leg. She had to stop for a young shepherd driving sheep out of a muddy lane and then across the road to a half-frozen field. He whistled to his dog and it came tearing past her, splashing muck onto her hem. She tried not to flinch like a lady. Dirt was as routine in these people's lives as the gnaw of hunger.

She walked up the gentle slope and reached the palace walls. Four guards were stationed at the gate, all decked in Bedingfield's livery of blue and tawny, complete with his badge of stars over a field of grain. Her heart beat fast as she approached the forward guard.

"Halt there. What's your business?"

"Laundress, sir. Delivering Her Grace's smalls."

He frowned. "The laundress is Meg." He spread his arms to indicate a woman of more than ample girth.

"My sister. Down with a flux, she is. Poor soul can't leave her bed. I'm doing the job till she's better."

He grunted. Was this a negative or affirmative? Unsure, Honor didn't move.

"Let's have a look," he said, beckoning her to set down the bundle.

She did so, very careful to display its sewn-on Bedingfield badge. The guard poked through the clean, folded underclothes— linen smocks and shifts, detachable linings of bodices, stockings both silk and worsted. Honor hoped there wasn't some password the laundress had forgotten to tell her. Parry had paid the woman well, but she had been hesitant in instructing Honor, eager for the coins but nervous about the risk. What if there was something she had missed?

"A bloody flux, it is, something awful," Honor prattled on, hoping to disgust the guard or bore him, anything to nudge him to be done with her. "Bloody mucous running out one end of her, mixed with far worse. And our pease pudding supper chucked up out the other end of her. I can tell you, cleaning up that mess is—"

"Enough of that," he said, making a face. He retied the bundle roughly, apparently satisfied. But then said, "The chamberlain said nothing about Meg."

"It came on her in the night, sir. You can tell his lordship yourself. Unless you'd rather have me go away and leave Her Grace without her underclothes."

"Don't be daft." He waved to his fellow guard to open the gate.

In for a penny, in for a pound, Honor thought as the gate creaked open. "As I don't know the way, sir, could you tell me where I'm to take these to Her Grace?"

He gave her directions, and she walked through, careful not to hurry, to plod on like a working woman who was far from eager to get to her chores.

She had made it in.

The courtyard, surrounded by its jumble of decaying buildings and neglected gardens, was in a sorry state. The palace had been built over springs that left a spongy marsh of melted ice and a stench of swamp grass. Pigs snorted from a pen notched into the crumbling wall. Honor could smell them, along with pungent cow dung. Some soldiers lounged under an archway, talking quietly, a couple of them playing cards at a table while another tweedled a tune on a pipe. Two servant women ambled past Honor, gossiping, carrying baskets of kitchen refuse toward the pig pen. In the center of the courtyard a scullery boy hauled a bucket up from the well, jumping back as he sloshed water on his foot. On the far side, a blacksmith's fire sparked beside a farrier who held a steaming horseshoe in his tongs and bent over the raised hoof of a dappled gelding. Somewhere, a dog was barking.

Honor wasn't interested in the courtyard society. Her focus was the gatehouse. She found the archway the guard had described in a two-story tower, and then the stairs, a rickety affair. She hadn't gone halfway up the stairs when she heard a woman's angry shout in the rooms above her.

"Go! Get out!"

Following the voice, Honor carried on to the top and through a door, and reached a vacant room that was musty smelling but had a stately aspect with an ornate carved ceiling painted blue and gold. A council chamber in the time of King Henry VII, Parry had told her. Her mind flicked back to the gorgeous gilded ceiling of the great banqueting hall at Hampton Court during her days as a lady-in-waiting to Queen Catherine. She was seventeen when she had arrived at Henry VIII's court, wide-eyed at its splendors. It seemed a lifetime ago.

The room was empty but she heard the voice beyond it shout again: "Leave my sight!"

She went on through to the next room, a bedchamber, and saw a middle-aged man on his knees, cringing, and a young woman with a furious red face. She hurled a book at him, yelling, *"Out!"* He ducked the book and clambered to his feet and scurried past Honor, escaping. A servant, she saw from his livery. The young woman wore fine green velvet.

So this was Princess Elizabeth. A red-faced shrew.

Honor kneeled in her presence.

"The man's a toad," Elizabeth snapped, her angry gaze sweeping over Honor as though she were a sack of apples. "I ask for Cicero and get the Epistles of Saint Paul!"

Honor saw they were not alone. The room held two more women, one dark haired and plump, the other sallow and frizzy haired, both well dressed. Ladies. The sallow one bent to pick up the offending book, saying with weary forbearance, "You already have Cicero, my lady."

"I have *De Natura Deorum*," was Elizabeth's withering reply. "It's the *De Officiis* I want."

The dark-haired lady was looking directly at Honor. "Who's this? What's your business, woman?"

Honor repeated her story, still kneeling. They barely listened; none of them seemed to care. The lady who had spoken to her motioned impatiently for her to rise, then took Honor's laundry bundle and dumped it on the bed. The other joined her to see to the linen. Their ages fell somewhere between that of Honor and that of the Princess. Both were smooth of voice and movement, gentlewomen of the court.

Elizabeth flopped down in a chair and stretched out her long legs. "When's dinner?" she groaned, closing her eyes tightly as though to mitigate a headache.

The ladies, sorting the clean underclothes, did not answer. They were serving in duty to their families, friends of the Queen, not the Princess. Their courtesy barely stretched as far as civility.

Honor knew she didn't have long. Time to make her move. Her fist tightened around the folded slip of paper she had brought. She got to her feet and walked directly toward Elizabeth.

"Here! What are you doing?" the sallow lady said.

"The foul linen, if you please, your ladyship." Honor pointed to a wicker basket full of jumbled clothes. Her foot was inches away from Elizabeth's. "Am I not to take it away?"

"Those are rags for the poor, fool. Come here. I'll give you your load."

Turning, Honor dropped the paper on Elizabeth's lap. But Elizabeth did not notice it. Her eyes were still closed.

The sallow lady loaded Honor with the bundle of dirty laundry, then told her to be on her way. She had no choice but to go.

She walked through the council chamber and out the door, her heart thudding. What a botch she'd made of it! Hurrying down the stairs, she expected to hear one of the ladies come after her and shout to a guard to stop her. They would surely see the paper before Elizabeth did and read it. *Call on the laundress to mend your skirt and mend your hope. Written by my hand this 19th day of December. Your servant, William Cecil.* Her mission would be strangled at birth. She could face arrest. Sir William, too. Stupid, stupid move, ill thought-out, she told herself as she hastened through the courtyard toward the closed gate. She should not have been so rash. Should have waited, found a better time—

"Stop!"

She glanced back. The sallow lady was hurrying after her.

"Stop her!" the lady cried.

A guard lowered his pike, barring Honor's way. Her heart banged in her chest.

The lady caught up to her. She was hugging herself against the cold, her face screwed up in irritation. "Her Grace wants you. Can you patch a petticoat?"

They had to wait for the Queen's women to leave. The two were busily airing the Princess's bed, flapping sheets and nattering court gossip, while Honor knelt on the floor, sitting back on her heels, diligently sewing the torn hem of one of the Princess's petticoats. Elizabeth sat in her chair across the room, motionless as a cat waiting to pounce. Her restless eyes were the only clue that betrayed how excruciating the wait was for her. Honor was impressed. This girl could control herself when she wanted.

Glancing up from her sewing, she studied the Princess. She was tall, slim, and upright, with a graceful long neck and long legs like a high-spirited filly. Her most striking feature was her hair, bright as copper, smooth as satin, hanging loose, tamed only by a black velvet headband. Its brightness was made brighter by the whiteness of her skin, which was, in turn, made whiter by the darkness of her eyes. No soft blue or gentle green, the black sparkle of these eyes was the legacy of her dark-haired mother, Anne Boleyn.

Honor felt a chill, recalling Anne's reckless, fiery pride that had fuelled the chaos of those stormy days when Honor had served Queen Catherine. How cruel Anne had been to King Henry's wife of eighteen years, desolate in her failure to give him a son. Anne had demanded the Queen's jewels from her royal lover, and got them. Demanded a noble title, and got it. Demanded marriage, and got it, triumphant in all her pregnant glory as Henry's new queen. She had been crueler still to Catherine's daughter, the sixteen-year-old Mary. She had dismissed all Mary's friendly household, denying Mary her status as a princess in favor of her own daughter, the baby Elizabeth, even forcing Mary, in processions, to carry the baby's train. Anne had installed her own aunt as Mary's governess, giving her complete authority to browbeat Mary, telling her to slap and beat the girl whenever she claimed to be the true princess and to swear at her as a "cursed bastard."

Honor wondered, was Anne's daughter, now a willful twenty-one, driven by the same merciless resolve? Those flashing black eyes spoke of pride, and the spite she had shown to the hapless serving man she'd hurled the book at did not bode well. But bad temper was not brutality. The cruelty now was all on Mary's side. Necessary, Mary would say, to safeguard her kingdom against a likely traitor. But Honor thought the motive was more deeply personal: to punish the daughter of Anne Boleyn.

The sallow lady finished tucking in the last corner of the last blanket and straightened up. "And now, with your leave, my lady, we'll see to your dinner."

"Tell them to warm some cider, too. I have a sore throat. The good cider, from old Bedingfield's stash, not the swill."

"That's in Sir Henry's storeroom," the other lady said in protest. "I'll have to get the chamberlain to unlock it."

"Take your time," Elizabeth said sweetly, then added with a bitter smile, "I'm not going anywhere today."

The moment they were alone Elizabeth dashed to the door and shut it, then whirled around to Honor, who was still on her knees. "Have you a message from Sir William Cecil?"

"No message, my lady. Only myself."

Elizabeth looked startled at the sudden change in Honor's manner and tone, all her subservience gone, authority in its place.

"Stand up. Who are you?" Her questions came fast, tripping over each other. "Why have you come? How did you get in? How do you know Sir William? Who *are* you?"

Honor rose, holding up her hands at the torrent of queries. "Your first and last are easy—my name is Honor Thornleigh. Sir William sent me to you. As for why, he believes you could use some friendly council."

"Council?" Elizabeth said with a skeptical frown, taking in Honor's coarse homespun clothes.

"Philosophum non facit barba," Honor said. The beard does not define the philosopher.

Elizabeth laughed in delight at the Latin. "You quote Plutarch! Ha! Truly, *fallaces sunt rerum species.*" Appearances are deceptive.

Honor glanced at the door. "We may not have much time, my lady. Though I will endeavor to come to you again as soon as I can. First, is there anything I can do for you? Anything you need?"

"Books! Bring me books! That toad Bedingfield allows me nothing but religion. The Queen is bent on making me more Catholic than the pope. I'm choking on those dusty tomes. Bring me books, I beg you. Else I shall die of boredom before my sister gets around to killing me."

Honor was taken aback at the defeatist tone of her last words. "Are you so sure she means to?"

"What else? She hates me. Body and soul."

"Yet keeps you alive."

"Because she has no evidence! She can find no guilt!"

She said it so triumphantly that Honor immediately doubted the girl's former, fatalistic tone. It seemed this Princess enjoyed dramatics. Honor itched to ask her outright if she had indeed conspired with Wyatt in the failed rebellion, but it was not her place to push so hard. Not yet.

"I will try to bring you a book or two on my next visit, my lady. What would interest you most?"

She said eagerly, "Philosophy. Science. Poetry. Ask Sir William. Or have him send you to some learned person—they'll show you what to bring."

"Sonnets by William Dunbar, perhaps? On science, Linacre's *De naturalibus facultatibus*, translating Galen? For philosophy, perhaps *Oration on the Dignity of Man* by Pico della Mirandola. And Thomas Elyot's *Defense of Good Women.*"

Elizabeth looked dumbfounded at the litany. "Elyot . . . one of my favorites."

Of course, Honor thought. Elyot had championed the education of women. "I knew him quite well," she said. "He was a friend of my guardian, Sir Thomas More, and visited us often."

Elizabeth's eyes narrowed. "You grew up in Thomas More's house?"

"I did." She knew this was a double-edged sword. It would cement her credibility for learning, but her guardian had famously gone to his death on the scaffold rather than accept King Henry's marriage to Anne Boleyn.

"You are well read, Mistress Thornleigh," was Elizabeth's cautious reply.

"And you are perhaps the best educated princess in Europe. I heard so from my friend and your tutor, Master Roger Ascham, when he was in Germany."

Elizabeth's cool reserve melted into sudden warmth. "Dear Master Ascham. His name is passport enough. You are very welcome, mistress. Now, these books, will you really bring them? When can you come again?"

"As often as your underclothes need washing. In your daily walk can you manage, perhaps, to fall into a mud puddle?"

Elizabeth laughed. A lovely sound that touched Honor's heart, for it reminded her of her own daughter's laugh.

"The laundress comes every other day, I think," Elizabeth said. "Can you do the same?"

"With pleasure. If the guards remain as compliant as today."

"*Aspirat primo fortuna labori.*" Fortune smiles upon our first effort.

Honor matched Virgil with Virgil. "*Audaces fortuna iuvat.*" Fortune favors the bold.

They smiled together.

They heard voices, the ladies returning. Honor grabbed the bundle of dirty laundry, ready to leave. "One more book," she said. "May I recommend *Il Principe* by Niccolò Machiavelli?"

Elizabeth shook her head. "Never heard of him."

"A Florentine. Brilliant. Not a favorite of the pope."

"Bring it."

"I shall," Honor said. *And with it*, she thought, *I'll teach you how to rule.*

It was two days before she could get back in to see Elizabeth. When she arrived, still pretending to be the laundress, the ladies were not present but Bedingfield was. A weary-looking, jowled man dressed in heavy brown velvet robes, he was on his knees before an angry Elizabeth. Honor hung back, unwilling to have him notice her, but she observed him carefully. The skin below his eyes looked bruised, shadowed with sleeplessness from the stress of dealing with his imperious prisoner, and his chin, though shaven, was shadowed with a black bristle of whiskers.

"I tell you, I must present a petition to the royal council," Elizabeth snapped. "They will not countenance the abuse I endure here, suffering in this miserable, stinking wet and cold. I will ask them to move me to a house nearer London."

"But, my lady, you have been forbidden any pen or paper."

"Good God, man, how you dwell on details."

"No detail, madam. The Queen's order."

Elizabeth almost exploded. "Even a common felon in Newgate jail is allowed to sue for his rights! Am I to be denied even this?"

"I can but follow orders, my lady." He started, laboriously, to get up.

"Kneel, sir, before your betters!"

He sank back down on his knees with a grimace of displeasure. Honor could see how deeply he resented this treatment.

Elizabeth's tight expression showed that she, too, could barely contain her disgust with him. "Since I am not allowed to write," she explained slowly, as if to a dull-witted child, "you must write *for* me. A summary of my petition. You will come here tomorrow and I will dictate. You must bring pen and paper and ink. Can you manage *that?*"

He managed to say that he could, though he looked like he felt it the worst kind of imposition, fraught with danger for himself.

"*Gratia,*" she said with chilly hauteur, "*causarum justia et misericordia.*" Thank you, for the cause of justice and mercy.

When Bedingfield looked perplexed at the Latin, Elizabeth shot a wry glance at Honor, and said, "*Margaritas ante porcos.*" Pearls before swine.

He looked around to see who she was talking to. Honor ducked her head. Bedingfield, she hoped, saw only a laundress.

When he was gone it was Honor's turn to let loose her anger. "You are too familiar with me, my lady. You risk us both."

"What, with that toad? He's as oblivious as a baby. Have you brought books?"

Honor unpacked them, two small volumes, including the Cicero that Elizabeth had requested. "As your keeper he holds the keys to your comfort or pain. And mine. You would do well to show him respect."

"I will not kowtow to an idiot. I am the daughter of a king."

"And as such you have some power. But you use it like a child."

Elizabeth looked shocked. Had no one ever spoken to her like this?

"It is you who are too familiar," Elizabeth said coldly. "Leave the books. Then go. I need no washerwoman's advice."

Honor spent an uncomfortable night at the Bull Inn, unable to sleep, unsure how to proceed. It was going to take time to teach this willful young woman the dangers of the game she was playing.

❧ 4 ❧

Neighbors

December 1554

"**R**ichard Thornleigh? Here?"

It was so shocking, Frances Grenville thought she must have misheard her brother. He had reached her in the outdoor barnyard court where she was overseeing the slaughter of a dozen Christmas geese, and the squawking was hectic as servants restrained the frantic birds and old Mossop's knife hissed at the whetstone.

"Not yet," John said as bitterly as though he'd tasted wormwood. The expression on his bony face was one of grim hostility. It made the scar above his upper lip—a hard, diagonal ridge from the nostril to the lip's edge—go whiter than usual. "Fanshaw galloped across the pasture to say he saw him riding the road toward us."

Frances felt a shudder of terror. The murderer, on his way!

"I want you to stay here," John said. "I've sent Arabella upstairs with the children. God knows what's going to happen." He strode away.

She hurried after him across the court, disobeying his instruction. "Is he coming alone?"

He gave her an irritated glance but walked on. "No, six men ride with him."

"John, you must call out the archers."

"I have." He added with a snort, "A precaution only. He cannot possibly be considering an attack. He's a killer, not a suicide."

That calmed Frances somewhat. Grenville Hall, with its battlements and moat, had stood for almost three centuries against all attacks—not even a madman like Thornleigh would attempt an assault. Especially against the Grenville Archers, so heroic in their defense of London during last year's rebellion against Frances's dear friend, Queen Mary. Keeping pace with John, she asked, "Then what in the name of heaven is he coming for?"

"I have no idea. But he must think he's invincible with his bought pardon."

It made no sense. She knew, of course, that Thornleigh and his wife had come home. Their estate bordered the forest backing that of Grenville Hall, and one heard the servants talking. And she was only too aware that Winchester, the lord treasurer, had wangled a pardon for her father's killer. Bribes had been involved, she did not doubt. Typical, given the corruption rampant in the royal council, a fractious body that poor Mary had inherited upon taking the throne. The blatant duplicity and politicking of so many of the councilors disgusted Frances. But that was London, and the court. Here at home in Colchester, common sense said that the Thornleighs would stay clear of John.

She gripped her brother's arm to stop him. "It's some kind of trick. Don't let him in."

He frowned, exasperated. "How can I know what to do until he gets here?"

"John, the man's a devil. He cannot be trusted."

"Do you think I don't know that?" he shot back. "I hate Thornleigh every bit as much as you do. But I will be the judge of how to handle him. Now stay here, Frances, and let me deal with this."

She watched him go, passing the outbuildings and the stables, heading into the house. She turned and looked across the low stone wall at the snowy, deserted fields that led to the Thornleighs' lands at the Abbey. It would always be that to her—the Abbey. She could never use the name that upstart family had given the house they had thrown up on the Abbey's sacred ground.

Their encampment was a desecration. And the new name itself, Speedwell House, was grotesque for sounding so homey and harmless. She felt again all the horror of her father's death a year ago in that very house, beside their very hearth. His mashed face. His bloodied body. And then, the misery of her mother's melancholic decline, her quick slide into death. Her parents lay in their graves while the one-eyed devil who had put them there was galloping to her door.

She closed her eyes in fury and frustration. Men's work. Must let John handle it. She prayed he had the spine.

But she would not cower in the barnyard, waiting for word. He had interrupted her in the midst of her morning rounds, and she set off now, anxious to keep busy. The bishop was to be their guest tomorrow, and he and his entourage must be entertained in style. John's wife, pregnant again, idled in her bedchamber most days with her female cousins, eating sweetmeats and marzipan and teaching tricks to her spaniels, leaving most of the work to Frances. But she did not mind. Arabella understood little about managing a great house. Frances was very good at it.

Crossing the yard, she had to tread carefully on the slick cobbles filmed with the night's hoarfrost. She looked in at the stone shed where the men were butchering an ox carcass. They were taking their time, some chatting as they stood around the bloodied butcher blocks, others lounging against the walls. She was about to lift the whistle that always hung from her belt, its screech a summons to her steward, Dyer, but the men noticed her and jumped to their business. She would have a word with Dyer about their lazy behavior. Right now, though, she could not keep her mind off the house. Here among the outbuildings she couldn't see anything at the main gate. Had Thornleigh already arrived? She looked toward the kitchen doors, itching to know what was happening in the great hall. When could she go in? What wickedness was the man up to?

Cart wheels squeaked behind her. She glanced around. A cart delivering the sheep carcasses. Good—mutton was the bishop's favorite. She made a mental note to check on the supply of mustard and prunes. Grenville Hall had a reputation for the best festive fare in the county and she was determined to do justice to her late mother's memory. This year's twelve days of feasting would not disappoint.

Moving on to the bake house, she passed through a cloud of clove-scented steam billowing into the cold air. Inside, teams of women, their aprons streaked with cinnamon and golden saffron, were busy turning Frances's orders into Christmas puddings, custard pies, and mince tarts. She looked across at the brew house, where the yeasty aroma from the vats reassured her there would be plenty of ale for the many thirsty guests to come.

She looked up at the house again. John had been firm—stay here—yet her curiosity burned. It was no good. She *must* go in.

She tugged off the buckram apron protecting her gown, balled it, stuffed it under her arm, and set out toward the house. She was passing the stable when the clatter of the sheep cart became suddenly very loud and someone shouted "Look out!" Frances whirled around to see the wheels sliding on the cobbles and the cart careering toward her, the drayman frantically hauling back on his horse's reins. The cart rattled past her, but its rear board struck her wrist with a sharp blow that knocked her back on her heels. The bundled apron under her arm fell and she stumbled, groping the air for balance. Servants rushed to her, calling out, asking if she was hurt.

"I'm fine, I'm fine," she said, mortified at the indignity of almost losing her footing. The drayman had stopped his cart and leaped down. He stood wringing his cap in his hands, fear in his eyes. Careless idiot, Frances thought. "Go on about your business, all of you," she said. They slowly dispersed. The drayman took his seat again and tapped his horse, and the cart squeaked on toward the butchers' shed. Frances stooped to pick up her apron.

That's when she saw blood trickling from her wrist. An exposed nail on the back of the cart? The cut didn't hurt, but the sight of her own blood always made Frances queasy. A wave of dizziness rocked her. Her vision went cloudy. Her legs buckled and her knees hit the cobbles with a sharp pain. She lowered her head, afraid she might be sick.

"That's right, keep your head down," a man's voice called from a distance. "Take slow, deep breaths."

The quiet authority in his tone made her do as he said. She breathed in deeply, grateful for the cold air. It cleared her head enough to look up.

The man was coming toward her, his back to the rising sun as it crested above the outbuildings, leaving his face in shadow and the sun gilding the edges of him. Through her slowly clearing vision Frances saw a tall, sturdy body, broad shoulders, narrow waist. A short, dark beard neatly trimmed, and dark hair whose lazy waves were pushed straight back as though to inconvenience him the least. He wore a black cloak and a tunic of fine blue wool, the blue as dark as the ocean at dusk.

"You're shivering," he said as he reached her, unfastening his cloak. He whirled it off and gently draped it over her shoulders, then crouched down in front of her. "Let's see," he said, taking hold of her hurt wrist. Frances glanced at the dribble of blood. Then looked quickly away.

The man reached up higher, right into her sleeve. She shivered at the shock of his fingers. Then saw the tip of her handkerchief peeking out from the sleeve. That's what he was after—the handkerchief. He tugged it out and pressed it gently against her wound. "You should wash this cut. And can your kitchen maid fetch a good salve?"

"I have a tincture . . . sage boiled in wine."

"Drink the wine, forget the herbs," he said with a smile that crinkled the skin at his eyes. The eyes were dark as molasses. "But, of course, the very best remedy is powdered horn of unicorn, if you have some handy."

A spurt of laughter escaped her.

"Ah, that's good," he said. "A laugh's the best remedy of all."

The sun warmed an auburn cast in his dark hair. Its tumbled waves reached the nape of his neck and glistened with the morning's moisture, making her think of chestnuts pulled from a stream.

Footsteps. Voices. Her servants were back, men and women, surrounding her with questions and concern. The dark-haired gentleman disappeared.

By the time Frances came through the kitchen with her cut bandaged, and reached the great hall, she had composed herself, if not the flutter in her breast. She needed composure, for there stood Richard Thornleigh. Her father's murderer, standing at her blazing hearth.

John stood across the hall, glaring at him. Ranged behind John were five of his liveried men, all with their fighting hands poised on their sword hilts. Behind them stood seven of the Grenville Archers. Their skilled young captain, Giles Sturridge, looked on, calmly alert. Only flickers of their eyes told Frances they were aware of her. In the tense silence, the fire's oak logs sparked, but not a single man flinched.

Thornleigh slowly raised his hands as though he were facing highwaymen. "My lord," he said to John, "I come in peace."

But not alone, Frances saw. A wiry, ginger-bearded man about Thornleigh's age stood beside him, almost certainly a kinsman. And Thornleigh motioned to four other men behind him, who stepped forward, each holding a wooden box almost larger than he could carry. These four were unarmed, mere household servants, harmless. But Frances saw that Thornleigh himself wore a brightly polished and very lethal sword.

"Please, accept my peace offering," he said, motioning his men. They set down their boxes and lifted the lids, revealing trays laden with Christmas delicacies. A whole, cooked suckling piglet, its mouth crammed with a bright red crabapple, its crackled skin studded with cloves. A small bay tree hung all over with dozens of red-ribboned oranges. A baked pheasant, re-plumed in all its glory. A pyramid loaf of pure white sugar a foot high, studded with candied violets.

The sickly sweet smell of the pig's flesh turned Frances's stomach. Did the man think that John's grief and fury, and hers, could be eased with scraps of food? She wanted Captain Sturridge to fire his whole quiver of arrows into Thornleigh, wanted to see arrows pierce him like the stuck pig he had brought into her home.

Thornleigh said cautiously, "Your family has suffered, my lord, and for the loss of your father I am truly sorry. My family has suffered, too—my wife so grievously injured she was brought to the brink of death. And all for what? A pointless feud."

He stopped as though waiting for some response, his expression anxious with anticipation. But John said nothing.

"But those hurts, hard as they were, are behind us now," Thornleigh went on, "and that is where our feud belongs as well. My wife and I have come home, and we long to live in harmony with our neighbors. At this sacred time of year, it is my hope that we can forgive each other, as Our Savior taught us. Come, sir, shake my hand."

He stretched out his arm. John's men stiffened.

John did not move. Frances knew that his hatred ran as deep as hers. Deeper, if possible, for he had been the one to claim their father's broken body from Thornleigh's parlor, bludgeoned by this smiling devil.

Thornleigh turned to Frances. "Mistress Grenville," he said, and bowed. "Will you accept my heartfelt entreaty for peace between our houses? At least, do accept these meager offerings for your Christmas table? It is a start."

If she had been the man of the house she would have spit in Thornleigh's face.

Instead, John astonished her. "Master Thornleigh, you are wise to speak of Our Lord," he said with icy civility. "It is no good thing for a country when neighbors live in discord. Nor for our souls."

"Bravely said, my lord," Thornleigh replied, again extending his arm in friendship.

John stepped forward and clasped Thornleigh's hand.

The armed men relaxed. Thornleigh smiled and guided John over to examine the gifts. They murmured together, looking like old friends, Frances thought. She felt her stomach roil and she thought she might be sick. Her brother had not asked her opinion.

"Frances," John said. "Have the maids take these things to the kitchen, would you?"

She turned on her heel for the kitchen, glad to be going. She heard the far door open.

"And now," Thornleigh said eagerly, "the final gift."

Frances turned. A man walked in from the passage, rubbing his hands from the cold. It was the young, dark-haired man who had stood over her, tended her cut, taken her breath away.

"My lord, I don't believe you've met my son, Adam. He has just delivered a fine, white, Arab stallion from our stable to yours, which I hope you will accept as the seal of our accord."

Frances found herself walking toward the young man.

"Adam," Thornleigh said, "may I present Mistress Frances Grenville."

Adam bowed to her. "I trust that wound does not pain you, madam," he said with a knowing smile. He took her hand and examined her forearm with the mock soberness of a doctor. "Did the horn of unicorn help?"

For the second time he took her breath away. But he was wrong about the pain. The jolt of joy she felt at his touch brought an ache more acute than she had ever known.

Riding home at a trot with his father and his uncle Geoffrey, their horses snorting steam, Adam took a bracing breath of the cold, crisp air. He'd never spent much time in England, had lived most of his adult life either aboard ships or managing his father's shipping interests in Antwerp. But something in these silent, snowy hills and dales touched a heartstring he'd never felt vibrate until they had moved back home for good. For this was truly home. England. Colchester. Their manor house, their fields worked by diligent tenant farmers, their cloth works centered in the old abbey whose lead roofs were just visible now beyond the wooded horizon, all of it managed in their absence by his uncle Geoffrey. The storm of near bankruptcy was behind them, and Adam felt the happy relief that every seaman feels when he sails out of the blow and into the protected waters of his home port. He had a sense that he could make a life here. A life all his own.

He had lost Margriet. He'd been surprised and disappointed by her submissive acceptance of her father's command, and the sting of it was still fresh. But he wasn't bitter. Just sobered. He felt he'd learned a hard lesson about the facts of life.

The most brutal fact, and the most urgent, was that his family needed money. Sir William Cecil's financial aid had got them home—

had refurbished *Speedwell* and discharged their most threatening debts—but that had calmed only the surface of their troubled waters. Their debts went deeper. It would take a year, at the very least from spring sheepshearing to the late autumn cloth fairs of Antwerp, before his father's cloth works showed some profit again. And Adam had launched a project with his father's blessing that would, at first, sink them into even greater insolvency: He was building a new ship. So there was heavy weather to face still, and many trading runs to the Low Countries to pay it all off before they could relax.

Still, Adam felt a ripple of exhilaration. He was keen to get on with it. He'd persuaded his father to let him manage the whole enterprise of the ship—from financing her construction, to over-seeing her eventual trade operations—in return for a fifty percent share in the profits. Such profits, at this point, seemed a mirage that floated in some hazy future, but he felt confident that he could captain the mission to a successful landfall. Life seemed full of promise again.

"God's teeth," Geoffrey exclaimed, looking at their four ser-vants who were riding ahead, one upending a wineskin at his mouth. "Herbert's at it again. Does the man think we're blind?"

"Let him drink," Adam's father said. "It's cold."

"I intend to. Just as soon as he's given me a swig." He rode ahead, leaving Adam and his father exchanging indulgent smiles.

"That went well, mending fences with Lord Grenville," Adam said. "A good day's work, I'd say."

His father grunted. "Don't you believe that charade." He shot a look at Adam, dark with warning. "John Grenville will never for-give."

Adam was startled. "You don't take him at his word?"

"Would *you* give your word to the man who killed your father?"

"You acted in self defense, sir. And the defense of your wife."

"Know thy enemy—that's what the military men say. Think like he thinks. No, Grenville will never forgive. I never expected him to."

"Then why go to his home? Why the"—what was the word he'd used?—"the charade?"

"I found out exactly what I wanted to know. Anthony Grenville's children don't know about Honor's conviction for heresy years ago. If they did, they wouldn't have shown me even the pretense of civility."

Adam looked at him, admiring his shrewdness. Not for the first time. At sea, when he was young, he'd seen his father craftily navigate through many an unanticipated shoal that would have capsized lesser men. Yet, wasn't his wariness now a little extreme? Grenville wasn't a fool—he must realize that the Queen's pardon was an edict, not open to challenge, and therefore the two families had to find some way to live as neighbors. "Well, that's a bonus for us, sir," he said. "He seems willing to let hostilities lapse, at least. That's something."

His father halted his horse abruptly. Adam had to tug the reins of his own horse to stop, too, and turned back to face him.

"It's nothing," his father said, his tone so urgent he sounded angry. "Nothing, you hear? Their hatred feeds on deeper grievances. They hate that we bought the abbey. Hate that we're not acolytes of their religion. Hate that we stood in rebellion against the Queen. They hoard their hatred and let it fester, like rot. Never forget that. Never trust them." He looked over his shoulder, back toward Grenville Hall. "He'd called out his famous archers, did you see? That was his warning shot across our bow." He turned back and added grimly, "Be careful, Adam. Watch your back."

When the frenzy of Christmas and Twelfth Night was over, business on the Hythe, the wharf of Colchester Harbor on the River Colne, resumed its normal bustle. The river traffic was a shifting maze of ships, barges, wherries, and lighters, and on the quay the cranes squeaked and clanged as they hoisted sacks of cargo to and from the waiting wagons and carts. This winter traffic, though, was nowhere near as thick as it was at the end of summer for oyster season. The town of Colchester owned all the local oyster beds by virtue of a grant by King Richard I, and for over three hundred years, each autumn, a small fleet of fishing boats dredged the beds. In October the town staged a great oyster feast in the

Moot Hall and hundreds of people from near and far came to eat Colchester oysters.

But on this gray January day, activity on the Hythe was much more calm. Frances Grenville, on her big-boned bay gelding, followed by her steward, Dyer, on his mare, clopped past a knot of draymen gambling over dice during their dinner break. The men tugged off their caps and bowed to the baron's sister, but she barely noticed their obeisance. She was looking for Adam Thornleigh. He was here, the harbor master had told Dyer. He was working with his shipwright.

Palpitations of the heart beset Frances whenever she thought of Adam. It was a new sensation, one that slightly alarmed her, but greatly excited her, too. She had been near marriage once, last year. It had been a long time coming. As a girl she had made a vow to remain single as long as her dear friend, Princess Mary, was single. But last year Mary had become queen and had wed Prince Philip of Spain, and so Frances had agreed to marry a man her father approved, Edward Sydenham. But God had not approved. Sydenham had betrayed Mary in the dreadful Wyatt rebellion, and was hanged.

Adam Thornleigh was very much alive, and the flutter Frances felt in her breast seemed to set the town's church bells ringing. The fanciful thought pleased her, though of course the bells were only tolling the hour. She was so glad of the return to the old Catholic ways since Mary had brought the country back to the one true Church. Frances knew the sound of all the bells in all the town's churches, most of them very old, built in Norman times. St. Peter's, St. James the Great, St. Runwald's, St. Martin's, All Saints. St. Nicholas, with its spire rising above all the others. Holy Trinity, the oldest, dating back to Saxon times. And the venerable St. Mary at the Walls, so called because it was built against the ancient Roman walls, for Colchester was proudly the oldest town in England. The town's coat of arms depicted its patron saint, St. Helena, the Roman emperor's mother, who had found the true cross of Christ. Frances recalled how her father used to jumble bits of the town's history, telling guests that Helena had been the mother of Old King Cole of nursery rhyme fame. In fact, Frances knew, the rhyme derived from King Cunobelin, Colchester's heathen ruler when the Romans arrived. She felt content with all these ancient ties, for Colchester's past had been intertwined with the life of her family for centuries. Tradition was a venerable thing. The past was a comfortable place.

Then she saw Adam Thornleigh and the present lifted her like a swelling spring tide. He stood on a scaffold of green wood, gesturing orders to his shipbuilders. She had heard the local talk about his family's brash return to business. How they had instantly reopened the former abbey where their cloth works were centered, with their looms and fulling mills and tenting yards. How they had hired scores of men. How Adam had forged ahead building this new ship—so new it was not yet born, a mere backbone with ribs. The smell of its fresh raw lumber cut through the ancient port smells of seaweed and fish. And he himself was new, was young, a man not yet thirty. While she was of an age with her childhood playmate, the Queen, a woman of thirty-nine. Yet he was a ship's master, and something in that image thrilled her. She remembered him standing over her in the courtyard, taking charge of her wound. Imagine such a man taking mastery of *her*. She had to struggle to compose herself as Dyer called up to him to get his attention.

Adam looked down from his scaffold and across the heads of the working men, and when he saw her, puzzlement flitted across his face. But only for a moment. He jumped down to the lower scaffold in one bound, springy as a young lion, then came down the ladder, and in a moment was standing before her, greeting her. He looked up at her on her mount and waited, his fists on his hips as he uttered a quick, formal greeting.

She was so agitated she didn't take in his words, she heard only his tone, a strained politeness, as though he was impatient to get back to work. And worse, as though he was wary of her. She needed to change that.

"What is her name?" Frances asked.

He frowned—a moment more of puzzlement—then quickly understood. "Oh no. No name until she's launched. Bad luck."

"I hope, whatever you do name her, she will not take you too far from home. What is it the fishermen say? There be dragons."

He smiled. "But there be riches, too, in trade. I'll tackle a dragon or two if the return on investment warrants."

He *could* tackle a dragon, she thought. So vigorous, so confident. And even this was new, this self-assurance of the burgeoning new class of gentry with their driving itch for profits. His father was certainly one of them. Not a knight who had done service to his monarch, nor the head of a long-landed family. Just an upstart merchant using every modern tool, procedure, and scheme to rake in cash. An upstart and a murderer.

But she would not let her mind stray into that dark path. She would move beyond that grievance.

"Well, Master Thornleigh, I wish you joy of her in whatever enterprise she may carry you to."

He made a gracious sweep of a bow, lowering his head. She saw a whorl of dark hair at the nape of his neck, just visible above the back of his collar. She imagined stroking it. It brought again the flutter to her breast.

"I, too, have a new enterprise," she said. "Or rather, an old enterprise that wants a fresh start. I wonder if I might interest you in a partnership."

He looked more puzzled than ever. "Me?"

"You are surprised, I see. And no wonder. You and your father"—the word gave her pause, for mentioning the murderer still came hard—"you came to Grenville Hall to offer friendship, and I fear my brother's coldness sent you away dissatisfied. I hope that we might remedy that, you and I. Be friends. Our two families are the most prominent in these parts after the earl, and should be on good terms, for the good of the whole community. Don't you agree?"

"I do, madam. I am of your mind. But what is this joint venture you speak of?"

"A work of charity, sir. To aid the town."

"Ah," he said, his body relaxing, a smile warming his face. "A fine idea." He folded his arms across his chest as though settling in to discuss it. "What is your plan? A fund for the poor? There's many a man hereabouts can't scratch out enough work to feed his family. I can't offer much cash at the moment, but I'll be glad to join you with a helping hand as far as I'm able."

"No, not that." The poor were Father Percy's responsibility. "I want to help the new Grey Friars. Or, I should say, the old Grey Friars." When she was a child these Franciscan monks in their gray habits, as well as monks and nuns of other orders—the Dominicans, Carthusians, Benedictines, Augustinians, Carmelites, Cluniacs—had seemed to be everywhere, in church and market, field and town, as ubiquitous as the birds. Then King Henry snatched all the monasteries and threw these holy men and women out into the world to fend for themselves. An attack on God himself, it had seemed to Frances. Many had gone abroad, while the King sold their vast monastic lands to anyone with the money, whether noble, gentleman, or upstart. But Queen Mary had now encouraged some of the holy men to return, to put on their habits again and live in the church properties that remained in her hands. "It is my intention," Frances said with pride, "to endow a new priory here in Colchester."

"Priory?" He seemed not to understand. She remembered that he had lived mostly in the wicked German lands, molded by his wicked parents. He could not be blamed for their sins.

"Yes, sir. A small monastery. To do the work of God."

His distaste was clear. "I see. Not the work of a carpenter or miller." His meaning was equally clear, that the latter was *honest* work.

It was closer to blasphemy than Frances could allow. "Your family are still new to our good old ways here," she said. "You would do well to show Father Percy and the mayor the faith of your hearts, for the salvation of your souls."

She had not meant it to sound as it did—like a threat—and he seemed to bristle. No, this was not at all what she wanted!

"But more important," she said quickly, "it would be a proof of our families' newfound accord, a thing I am eager to see flourish. I am tired of rancor. It does no one good. I want to open the door of friendship. You came to my home in good faith. Do accept my good faith now."

Again, he seemed to relax. "You say well, madam."

"Then you will join me in this charity?"

He took a moment, his eyes on her as though weighing profit and loss. "I will," he said finally. "For friendship's sake. I ask only one condition."

"And what is that, sir?"

"No hair shirts." He gave her a smile that made his teeth gleam and her breath stop short. "Let us have some merry monks."

Frances allowed herself a smile, too. This young lion could be sweetly tamed.

Grenville Hall was finally quiet after the revelry of Twelfth Night, the Christmas guests gone home. The chattering children of cousins and friends sounded no more throughout the rooms of the venerable old house. It was late in the evening, and Frances and John sat a little distance away from the fire in the parlor, while his wife, Arabella, sat gossiping at the hearth with the last cousin as they plied their embroidery needles, her three spaniels slumbering at her feet. The room was a modern improvement that Arabella had insisted on adding—a parlor was *au courant*—though Frances knew that John preferred, as she did, the old fashion of relaxing in the dignified great hall in the evenings. This room, though lavishly appointed, felt as cramped as a laborer's hut.

"I wonder what his father will think of your partnership," John mused aloud to Frances as he closed the account book of tenants' rents that he had been perusing. She had told him about Adam Thornleigh agreeing to help her build the priory. It would not do for her brother to hear of it through the mean-spirited channels of gossip. By breaking the news herself, she could control his perception.

"I care not what he thinks," said Frances, which was true, though not for any reason John would assume. Adam's good opinion she craved. Adam's father could go hang.

"Don't misunderstand. I approve what you've done," John murmured, absently tugging at the scar above his lip. Frances remembered hearing about how he'd got that scar. He had been fifteen when, late one night, in the kitchen, a pretty scullery maid had rebuffed his advances. He had forced her to the floor, and the girl, struggling to repel him, had groped for a knife and flailed, cutting him. To punish her he had convinced their father to turn her out as a thief. He had told Frances the facts with no more remorse than if he'd ordered a hunting dog put down for biting him. Nine months later the girl gave birth in the woods beside the churchyard, then strangled the baby and hanged herself. "I very much approve," he repeated now.

"I knew you'd like it. I got the idea from your own actions the other day, treating Thornleigh as though you've forgiven him."

"More important, letting him believe so."

"Exactly. And now, through his son, I can keep watch on them. See what they're up to."

"Bide our time."

"Yes."

He fingered the scar, musing.

❧ 5 ❧

The Captive Princess

February 1555

The floor rushes reeked like a London alley. That was Honor's first thought as she carried in Princess Elizabeth's laundry through the gatehouse rooms on a drizzly February morning. The rain that had been pummeling Woodstock for three days had let up only hours ago, reduced to a fainthearted spitting as though weary of the fight. It had come after the freezing cold of January, when the inmates had shivered day and night as wind whistled through the decayed roofs and broken windowpanes. Elizabeth had told Honor on her last visit that her fingers were so cold she could barely turn the pages of her Cicero. Now, her rooms, shuttered tight against the wet, smelled so stale that Honor judged they had not been aired, nor the floor rushes changed, in a week. It was a week that she had used to full advantage, however. She was tingling with the news she had brought the Princess.

But the days of rain seemed to have beaten the fight out of Elizabeth. Honor opened the door to find her slumped in her chair, gazing out the cracked window at the wet, gray courtyard, her legs stretched out, her arms folded, as though she expected nothing to ever happen, nothing to ever change. A black-and-white cat lay in her lap, stretched out as still as death.

Watching her from the doorway, Honor felt a tug of pity. For all of her young life this fastidious princess had been accustomed to moving with her whole household every few weeks from one of her homes to another, so that the rooms could be cleaned and a new carpeting of rushes with sweet-smelling herbs strewn down. She was used to being active, too. A skilled horsewoman, she had delighted in riding her estates, in hunting and hawking. She loved dancing and music and merry company. The squalor and idleness of these eleven months of captivity had been hard on her indeed, Honor thought. How much more would she have to endure? Or—terrifying thought—was captivity just the first stage in her march to the scaffold?

Honor glanced around the room. No ladies. She set down her load of laundry, making the cat on Elizabeth's lap jerk up its head. It jumped to the floor and streaked past Honor and out through the open door.

Elizabeth said, without even making the effort to turn her head away from the window, "You watch the clock well, Mistress Thornleigh. I sent them out, just as you asked."

"How long do we have?"

"Not long. They'll be back soon with wine." Her voice was raspy, a just-out-of-bed voice, as though she could not find the interest to wake it up. "I hope they bring enough wine to fog my head. I long to forget where I am."

The tone of self-pity doused Honor's sympathy. *Rouse yourself,* she wanted to say, *or how can you expect others to rouse themselves for you?* She had thought the girl's former, brazen defiance of Bedingfield a dangerous indulgence, but this sluggishness was worse. She pulled a book the size of her hand out of her bulky shawl. "The della Mirandola volume you wanted," she said, displaying it.

Elizabeth barely glanced at it. *"Oration on the Dignity of Man."* She shrugged and puffed out her cheeks in a weary sigh. "To what end? All my fine learning for naught."

Honor noticed some odd scratches on the windowpane. Three ragged lines etched into the bottom corner. Words, she realized. She bent closer to read them:

Much suspected by me,
Nothing proved can be.
Quoth Elizabeth, prisoner

She looked at the Princess, startled. How had she etched this on the glass?

Elizabeth's smile was sly as she held up her right hand and waggled her index finger to display a diamond ring.

Honor had to admire the girl—she had some fighting spirit. She glanced at the words again—*Nothing proved*—and could not resist asking, "Is there guilt to prove?"

Elizabeth looked her in the eye. "None. I received a letter from Wyatt a few days before he raised his rebellion. He told me I should get as far away from London as I could. In answer I sent word by way of Sir William St. Loe, saying I thanked him but would do as I saw fit. That is all."

"And the French ambassador? They say a letter of yours to the Queen was found in his diplomatic pouch."

"A copy only. As I've told the Queen's councilors a hundred times. And not a word in it about rebellion."

"Yet how could it have got there without your cooperation?"

"Who knows? Some worm of a spy in my household."

"More serious, why would the ambassador have had it unless the French were expecting you to take an active part in Wyatt's revolt?"

Elizabeth sprang to her feet, fury on her face. "Do you worm your way in to spy on me, too?"

It was Honor's turn to be angry. "To strengthen your courage to survive the Queen's questioning. As you well know."

They were standing face-to-face, and Honor saw a change sweep over Elizabeth's. From defiance to fear. "What good is courage?" she cried. "What good is my innocence if my sister means to kill me at all costs?"

"Not at all costs. Which is why we must make the cost too high."

"There is no such thing for a queen!" She flopped down in the chair and buried her face in her hands. Honor could not help thinking of Isabel ten years ago, disconsolate over some slight that could wound only a twelve-year-old girl. It reminded her how young this Princess still was. How untried. How unused to the uses of power.

Elizabeth shook her head as though suddenly too weary of it all. She looked out the window to the courtyard, disconsolate. "I like to let Fool out. Like to see him go about his cat business, whenever and wherever he wants. How I envy him."

Honor followed her gaze. The black-and-white cat was prowling along the top of a high stack of firewood beside the farrier's forge. Through the kitchen's open doors she saw scullery maids scrubbing pots, steam billowing out into the chilly air. One of them stepped outside and hurled a pan of water onto the cobbles, and the cat bolted away.

"Those maids are more free than I am," Elizabeth mused. This time there was no self-pity in her voice. This was a tone Honor had not heard before, though she couldn't have said exactly what the difference was. Longing, perhaps, but honest and direct. "I watch them," Elizabeth went on. "I sit here and I watch. One got her ears boxed last week by the cook. One sneaks out to see her lover, a guard. They have their trysts over there in the farrier's shed. Another one shoves bread crusts into her apron pocket. At first I thought she was hoarding for herself, but then I saw her one evening scattering the crusts for the pigeons. I watch the guards, too. Their quarreling over dice games, and their petty feuds, and then a half hour later their easy camaraderie, everything forgiven. I watch them all, and envy them."

Honor listened, fascinated. And understood something at that moment. The yearning heart in this princess that drew people to her. A phrase of Niccolò Machiavelli came to her mind. *To understand the nature of the people one must be a prince, and to understand the nature of the prince, one must be of the people.*

Elizabeth lifted her eyes to the far wall of the courtyard, as though envisioning the garden that lay beyond it. "You know the legend of Fair Rosamund who lived here? Mistress of King Henry II? He kept her, they say, in an elegant bower inside the garden maze. He hid here there to keep her safe from his jealous wife, Queen Eleanor. He would find his way through the maze to Rosamund by following a silken thread. But the Queen came by one day and outside the maze she spotted the thread. It had caught on the spur of the knight who guarded Rosamund. Eleanor followed it, and it took her to the center of the maze, where she found her rival and forced her to take poison. The bower had hidden Fair Rosamund, but it was a prison that fatally entrapped her."

Honor felt a rush of sympathy for Elizabeth. Felt as protective as a mother for her child. She came close to her and said, "We will not allow this queen to kill you. I promise."

Elizabeth looked up at her, blinking. "How can you be so sure?"

Honor was *not* sure. But she would do her all to make good on this pledge. "I believe there is one cost too high for her to do so."

Elizabeth's eyes widened. "What?"

"The anger of the people. If they know you bear your hardships with dignity, they will love you for it—and resent the Queen. She has no standing army. She cannot risk another uprising in your name, because next time she might lose."

Elizabeth looked skeptical. "All the more reason to kill me."

"Only if she becomes maddened enough, unbalanced enough, to take that risk. That is why we must be cautious and vigilant." Honor looked at the clock on the mantle. It was time. "Listen to me, my lady. The Queen's other gambit is to snare you in her religious trap. I urge you to show more willingness to conform."

"Good God, not you, too! Religion, always religion. I have done nothing to go against her in this. I do not prate like these wild Protestants. But how can she expect me to know each tricky step of the Catholic ways when I never even *heard* her religion until now."

Honor knew this applied to most young people across the country. Attending mass every Sunday was the law, and almost everyone obeyed, but the Queen had forced this change only a year ago, at her coronation. Until then no mass had been celebrated in England for two decades, not since King Henry had wrenched the realm away from Rome to make himself head of the English church. And, after him, his teenage son, Edward, had ruled for six years as a devout Protestant. Queen Mary had now reinstated the old orthodoxy, but Honor believed there was no English subject under thirty who was a true Catholic.

"Bedingfield watches you at mass," she said, nodding toward

the chapel that adjoined Elizabeth's outer chamber. "If he sees your reluctance to participate, you can be sure he is reporting it to the Queen."

"And how am I supposed to convince the toad of my devotion?"

"By show. Ask him for more religious books. Invite him to attend mass with you. Seclude yourself in the chapel every day for private prayer."

Elizabeth looked at her as if Honor had lost her mind. "I'll do no such thing. I have no stomach for groveling and hypocrisy."

"I tell you, you must, for if—"

Laughter interrupted them from the other room. The ladies, returning.

Honor snatched up the bundle of laundry. "Go to the chapel," she whispered. "Now."

Elizabeth smirked. "Or else?"

"Or you'll have no more books, for I shall never visit you again."

Elizabeth's frown showed she was considering the threat. Honor could only hope that the books meant more to the girl than her pride. "Now, tell your ladies you will spend an hour in private prayer. Go."

The ladies came in. Honor kneeled as Elizabeth flounced past her. "I am going to chapel," Elizabeth announced to the room with gloomy theatricality, like a child being punished. "I feel a need to pray." Honor watched her go into the chapel with all the eagerness of a patient going to have a tooth pulled.

It took a few minutes for the ladies to sort the laundry and load Honor with the bundle of dirty underclothes. They were settling down with a deck of cards to play primero as she left them and headed through the outer room. But instead of going out she ducked into the chapel.

Elizabeth sat pouting in a pew. Honor slipped in beside her. Elizabeth looked surprised. "What—?"

"Just wait," Honor whispered. "And it wouldn't hurt you to kneel and say a prayer." In case anyone looked in.

Defiant, Elizabeth sat back, arms folded, to endure the wait.

Not five minutes later they heard a rustling behind the curtain of the confessional. Its rear door adjoined the former priest's room.

The curtain opened and out stepped Thomas Parry. Elizabeth's mouth fell open at the sight of her steward dressed in the homespun smock and leggings of a servant.

He made a low bow to her. "Your Grace."

She jumped up. "Thomas!"

"Shhh!" Honor said.

Elizabeth shot Honor a look of wonder. "How . . . ?"

Honor was pleased with herself despite the dangers that still lurked. "I discovered some interesting byways in this ancient heap." She had found that dressed in her laundress's garb, with lowered head and a plodding gait, she was as good as invisible to Bedingfield's household staff and his guardsmen, both within and without the decrepit palace grounds. On one reconnoiter through the kitchen and down its dank back stairs she had discovered a musty, cobwebbed room, a former root cellar, it seemed. The hinges on its creaking door to the outside were so rusty they half seized as she pushed it open. And it took several hard shoves against the tangle of thorny shrubs outside, grown wild, before she could open it enough to crawl through. She had been astonished to find herself at the base of the courtyard's outside wall. A track led through trees toward the river. An old delivery path, she guessed. The root cellar, so long unused—for generations, perhaps—appeared to have been forgotten. The door was definitely unguarded.

"Master Parry cannot stay long," she told Elizabeth, "but long enough to give you news of your estates and your friends. Even a little news of the world."

Elizabeth laughed and grabbed Parry's hand. "Thomas, you are the answer to a maiden's prayer."

For half an hour the Princess and her steward talked like old friends long apart, eager to catch up. Honor followed as best she could as they discussed Elizabeth's staff and servants at her various homes: her houses at Hatfield and Ashridge, her castle at Donnington, and her other estates. Many of these people had been dismissed by the Queen, and Elizabeth was concerned about them. After hearing all the gossip about an old governess's pregnant granddaughter and a chamberlain's gout, Honor was impa-

tient for substantial news. She wanted reports of Elizabeth's
friends in high places, people the Queen could not slight without
paying a price. She was glad when Elizabeth asked Parry about Sir
William Cecil.

"Have he and Mildred settled into their house at Wimbledon?
How do they find it?"

"Drafty."

They both laughed.

Honor stifled a groan at this chitchat. She asked Parry, "Will Sir
William stand again for Parliament?"

"Yes, his seat for Lincolnshire is all but certain."

Honor's mind ran ahead. Parliament could wield some power if
it wanted to, because of its grip on the country's purse strings, and
Elizabeth could hope for support among its many members dis-
contented with Queen Mary. She said to the Princess, "Parliament
sits in several months, my lady, and if we—"

"Oh Lord, what good can those bumpkins do us?" She turned
to Parry. "What news of the Countess of Sussex, Thomas?" Honor
itched to press her point, but held her tongue. The countess was
Elizabeth's close friend.

"She has fled her husband, my lady," Parry answered. "Been
abroad for months."

"That's the last straw for Radcliffe, I warrant."

"It was. He has washed his hands of her."

"Ah, my dear, good Anne. She suffered enough from that
brute." She added with a shiver, "He positively gloated when he
brought me to the Tower, he and Winchester."

Honor wanted news that *mattered*. She put it firmly to Parry.
"Sir, what doings at court should we know about?"

He thought for a moment, scratching his head. "The brawls get
worse."

"Of course," Elizabeth said with a scoff, "since the Spaniards
rule the roost."

"Aye, my lady. But more of them get their heads knocked every
week they remain."

Honor knew of the enmity between the English courtiers and
the haughty Spaniards of Prince Philip's entourage. When Philip

had arrived to marry the Queen last summer, he had brought with him over a dozen of the greatest nobles in Spain, all strutting their magnificence in everything from their wardrobes to their horses, and all bringing their own enormous retinues. Philip himself was the most magnificent. When his treasure was transported for storage at the Tower, Londoners had watched in resentful awe as twenty carts rumbled through the streets carrying his ninety-seven treasure chests full of gold. Since then, the resentment had erupted in fistfights throughout London between the Spaniards and the English, and there was fighting in the halls of the palace almost every day. Courtiers drew swords at every slight, real or imagined. Three Englishmen and a Spaniard had been hanged after a recent murderous brawl.

Parry said helpfully, "I know of news *outside* the court. Master Gresham has his old place back."

"Oh?" Elizabeth said. "I thought he was not Catholic enough for my sister."

"Seems she cannot do without him."

Honor had heard as much. The government was dependent on the Antwerp money markets for loans to bridge the gap between its revenues and expenditures, and Sir Thomas Gresham, the Crown's agent in Antwerp, had managed this cleverly and resourcefully until Mary came to the throne and sacked him. She had appointed a man whose religion was impeccable but whose inept dealings had forced England to pay ever higher interest rates, up to fourteen percent, leading to a crippling exchange rate. Now, she had been forced to rehire Gresham. One more example, Honor thought, of this Queen's incompetence as a ruler. All that mattered to Mary was religion. Of that issue she was totally in control.

Honor had shuddered at the recent reports. The burnings had begun. One of the first was John Hooper, bishop of Worcester, a tenacious Protestant. He had been in prison for months for preaching that the Catholic tenet of Christ being physically present in the eucharist wafer was absurd. Last week, they had burned him at the stake. With green twigs laid at his feet, and no merciful wind to quicken the flames, he had been roasted alive for three-quarters of an hour.

Parry broke in on Honor's thoughts. "The Queen's physicians say she will be delivered of her child in April," he said. "Cardinal Pole ordered a *Te Deum* sung at St. Paul's in thanks to God."

Old news, Honor thought. She felt disappointed, frustrated. Parry was an able administrator, and fiercely loyal to the Princess, but he was not at court. He could not tell Honor what she needed to know for Elizabeth's sake. The state of the Queen's mind. The state of the Queen's heart.

Elizabeth went on, her tone icy with disdain, "Mayhap, when this blessed royal child arrives, its mother will pull in her claws and molest me no longer."

Honor said sternly, "Do not believe it, my lady. You are in danger as long as the Queen fears you."

"What is there to fear?" she wailed. "I am her prisoner. I can do nothing!"

"You can draw men to you, and she knows it." *As I know it,* Honor thought, *and as Parry knows it, and Sir William.* And how many others? How many men of wealth and influence would rally to this girl's side if needed? But that must wait. Before she could consider such things, she first had to keep Elizabeth alive.

"My lady," she said, "you must ask Bedingfield to write another letter."

Elizabeth rolled her eyes. "Another plea to the council? That dump of deaf old men? It took me weeks just to get the toad to take my dictation, and all for what? They refused my every request."

Honor knew how this had stung Elizabeth. The council had ignored her as though she were a common felon, granting nothing she had asked for. No move closer to London. No more ladies to attend her. No writing materials. No hope.

"I don't mean a letter to the council," Honor clarified. "I mean a letter to the Queen herself."

"Why? She *hates* me."

"You have the power to tame that hate. Quiet her fears. Calm her jealousy."

"Jealousy?" Elizabeth said, incredulous. "I am a captive and she is queen!"

"She is a woman." A plain woman hopelessly in love with her husband, by all accounts, Honor thought. A woman of thirty-nine, nervously facing her first childbirth. "She is human. She once suffered as you do now. She was an outcast, stripped of her titles and rank in the days when her mother was cast aside. You and she have more in common than you think. Write to her, as woman to woman. Be kind. Be gentle. Wish her and her baby well. It may do you a world of good."

Elizabeth was studying her with a quizzical look. "I know not how to judge you, Mistress Thornleigh."

"I think I have proved myself," Honor said with a nod at Parry that said *I brought you him.*

"That you have. Yet you are full of contrary advice. 'Stir the people's anger' one moment. 'Love the Queen' the next. I know not what to make of you."

"Make me right. Follow my advice. Read the book by Machiavelli I brought you, and follow *his* advice." She quoted the Italian: *"Only those means of security are good, are certain, are lasting, that depend on yourself and your own vigor."*

Elizabeth put on her most haughty face, unwilling to be pushed. "I shall consider it."

❧ 6 ❧

The Rosary

March 1555

Honor wiped a trickle of sweat from her brow, her spade idle in her hands as she took in what Adam had just said. "A project?" she asked warily. "What kind of project?"

She was preparing the soil for transplanting some rose bushes to the borders of her herb garden. Dirty knobs of snow clung stubbornly to hollows in the earth, like vagrants claiming squatting rights, and despite the body warmth the work generated, the March wind chilled her nose and fingertips. She had allowed herself a few days at home before returning to Elizabeth at Woodstock, and in this brief time she longed to start things growing. The Princess was proving a frustratingly obstinate pupil, but of *this* endeavor—tending her flowers and her herb garden—Honor was master.

But Adam's news was serious. To steady her spade, Honor jammed it into the garden loam. That shot a pain to her rib that made her wince.

"Here, let me," he said. He took the spade from her, set his boot on the blade's top edge, and sank it effortlessly into the earth. "Why not let the servants do this for you?"

"I like doing it. What kind of project?"

"A monastery."

She stared at him. He couldn't be serious.

"Just a small one," he said. "A priory, she calls it."

"I don't care if it's big or small or covered with honey and feathers. Why involve yourself in such a thing? Especially with Frances Grenville."

"It's hardly involvement." He flung a spadeful of stony dirt toward the raspberry canes trained on a wooden lattice, and frowned as pebbles clattered against the latticework. "What did you plant last year, stones?"

"Roses like stony soil. How much are you donating?"

He rested his hand on the top of the spade handle and gave her an indulgent smile. "Don't worry, it's just a token. It'll be mostly her money."

"Then why involve you at all?"

With a shove of his boot, he dug the spade in again. "She wants someone to help her make decisions."

"There's her brother."

"You're right. The fact is, she has another motive. Her idea is to mend the rift between us, the two families."

Honor took back the spade and hacked the soil with a vigor that took the place of the retort on the tip of her tongue: *a little late for that.* "She could have just invited me to supper," she muttered as she dug.

Adam shrugged. "I think she's a rather lonely old lady."

Honor had to laugh. "She wouldn't appreciate you calling her old. She's of an age with her friend the Queen. Forty, perhaps."

He seemed mystified at the correction. "Exactly."

She laughed again, but more soberly, her suspicion all but confirmed. Adam might be unaware of what a handsome young dog he was, but she doubted that Frances Grenville was unmoved. When would he take a wife? she wondered. They had heard that the Korteweg girl had hastily been married to someone else, a man whose fortune satisfied her father, and it seemed to Honor that Adam had put that misadventure behind him, his heart relatively unscathed. She was glad. She hoped he would settle down with an English girl here at home. But would he want to, given the anxious atmosphere of Queen Mary's regime?

She looked to the house where a pair of swifts darted past the eaves, trading undulations in flight as though they flew as one. The late afternoon sun lit up the windows of her second-story study with a rosy gold light that warmed her in the deepest part of herself. Speedwell House. Home. She heard giggling, and looked down to the water meadow where two maids were strolling up to the house with baskets full of fresh cut rushes. A pair of swans glided on the stream. Behind the house, a horse in the stable whinnied. There was a faint smell of wood smoke. How she loved this place.

But, she thought with a sigh, there was still much to do to get it back to normal. The rooms still felt hollow, echoing. After the rebellion the Queen's agents had confiscated all their moveable goods, and so far Richard had replaced only the most essential furniture—beds, kitchen blocks, dining table for the great hall, desks, not much else. Too much debt. And he was too busy working day and night to reestablish his cloth works, since the Queen's men had taken away everything there, too, looms and all. But they were making progress, step-by-step, and she felt sure Richard would have the business prospering again within a year or so. Speedwell House would soon feel like home again. She cast her gaze across her herb garden. She loved how the hyssop and thyme and winter savory stayed green all through the winter. And soon the speedwells around the sundial would blossom in a carpet of blue. She couldn't wait for warmer days so she could sow parsley seeds and lavender and lemon balm. She took in a deep breath of the chilly spring air, fresh and full of promise.

Then felt a shiver. The Grenvilles had always cast hungry eyes on Richard's property. "Monasteries," she said with a grunt as she dug up a new spadeful of stony earth. "Men forsaking the world and giving themselves to God. What's he supposed to do with them? Such nonsense."

"It's an insurance measure," Adam said.

"What is?"

"My help with the thing. Shows we're conforming. These days, that's important."

She stopped digging. He was looking at her with a serious expression. "And it wouldn't kill us to befriend the Grenvilles," he said. "There's plenty of preferment at court, and access to wealthy investors, and no one's closer to the Queen than Frances Grenville. Good to have her on our side."

"Frances or Queen Mary?"

"Both."

"We don't befriend tyranny, Adam. Seventeen men the Queen has burned this month. Three right here in Colchester. And she's just getting started."

"They were raving radicals. Hot-Gospelers. We're not."

"No," she said tartly, not liking his dismissive tone, as though those innocent victims' suffering had nothing to do with him. "No, we conform."

He nodded, relaxing. "Exactly." He gave her a gentle smile. "It's just a small priory. Ten or twelve monks going about their foolish, monkish business. What's the harm?"

Richard saw it differently. "I don't like it," he said at supper in the great hall, swishing the last of his wine in his goblet. "I told you, Adam, you can't trust a Grenville."

"Can't trust her brother, you said. This involves only the lady."

"Same thing. Same blood. Why's she meddling with us?"

Adam looked about to speak, but then slung one arm over the back of his chair and merely shook his head at his father as though to keep himself from arguing.

Honor spooned up the last of her apple custard, thinking. The three of them were alone. Richard's sister, Joan, and her husband, Geoffrey, visiting from Blackheath, had gone upstairs to the gallery to play cards. The other members of the household who supped with them—Fletcher, the new steward; Dorothy, the housekeeper, and her husband Stephen, the chamberlain; Alford, the clerk—had all gone to finish evening chores. Outside, some children, likely Dorothy's boys, were squealing over a game of football. Honor could hear the thump of the pig's bladder against the courtyard wall.

"Sir," Adam said quietly, "you take this grudge too far."

Richard banged down his goblet. "You didn't see Anthony Grenville fire a lead ball into your stepmother!"

She felt the tremor reach her at the other end of the table. Not just the bang of the goblet but the tremor of memory. Sparks from Grenville's pistol. The searing bullet.

Adam bristled. "I saw what it did to her." He looked at Honor for vindication. "When Isabel sent you across the Channel to my care, I saw."

"And no care could have been more attentive," she assured him. "No one doubts that, Adam." She wanted their argument over. Arriving in Antwerp she'd been delirious, and she recalled nothing of the trauma of her recovery. It was history, and she had other things on her mind. Elizabeth.

"Then how could you so blatantly do something that could bring Honor to the Queen's notice?" Richard challenged his son. "To associate with the Grenvilles is to join the Queen's circle. That's dangerous for Honor and you should know it."

"I believe I know as well as anyone how to protect this family," Adam said with some warmth. "And I believe that the best way to do that is to befriend the people who wield the power in this benighted realm."

His black-and-tan setter had ambled over to his chair and laid her nose on his knee. He stroked the dog's head and scratched behind her ear, gaining control of himself. "Sir," he said more calmly, "I don't dispute the evil or the madness that drove Anthony Grenville to attempt murder. But can we blame his children for that? He is dead and you've been pardoned and they want peace. I say peace is the only way to live sensibly as neighbors."

"They *say* they want peace. What they *want* is retribution, starting with the abbey," Richard said, jerking a thumb toward his cloth works factory across the stream from the house. "Do you think for one moment they'll forget how their old aunt suffered under King Henry?" Honor noted his word *suffered*. The king had sent soldiers to enforce his seizure of all the monasteries and nunneries throughout England, and the story was that the late Eleanor Grenville, the abbess here, had been raped.

"They can't blame you for that. You weren't the only one who bought monastic lands," Adam pointed out reasonably. "The king sold them on the open market. The Grenvilles know that."

"All they care about is that I'm the one who bought the abbey and set up my looms, and they will always see that as blasphemy. I tell you, they will never rest until this property is in their hands and they've sent us packing."

Adam heaved a sigh, not conceding but not willing to fight. "You live too much in the past, sir."

Richard said darkly, "It's them. They won't let the past go."

They sat in silence. From the kitchens came the sound of sloshing water, the scullery maids washing the pots. Someone across the courtyard was hammering.

Honor set down her spoon. It was time to speak her mind. "I think we can make something out of this," she said. "Friends with the Grenvilles, but on our terms. Adam, do you have plans to see Frances anytime soon?"

Both men turned to her. Adam looked intrigued, Richard wary.

"Yes, tomorrow, in Colchester," Adam said. "At the site she's picked for her priory."

"Good. I'll come with you. I want to meet her."

"Really? You seemed so cool to the idea before."

"I'm getting warmer."

Richard's eye narrowed in suspicion. "Honor? What are you scheming?"

She looked at him. "I want Frances Grenville to introduce me to the Queen."

The next morning Honor and Richard's sister, Joan, helped him at the abbey. He was supervising workmen as they hefted in a new loom, setting it in the nave beside five others newly bought on credit, all smelling of fresh wood. Honor and Joan oversaw a team of maids sweeping out the floors of the workrooms and washing windows. Once, these had been the monks' offices and dormitories. Now, they would store bales of wool, as they had before the family fled last year. They would also serve as Richard's headquarters for tenting and fulling the finished broadcloth both here and at the manor at Blackheath managed by Joan's husband, Geoffrey.

Spring wind gusted through the open doors, carrying the scent of wet earth and sending last year's wool fluff dancing through the nave. Birds chittered outside, busily building nests in the belfry and on the sills of the tall clerestory windows. Honor liked how the younger servants, babies when King Henry had dissolved the monasteries, found nothing odd that the clack and *whoosh* of looms, and the paddle thumps of fullers, should echo in the airy space that had once quivered to the chanting of monks. She liked that the clinging odor of incense was being pushed out by the fecund smells of spring.

Yet, as she opened windows and watched the girls sweep, she felt a pinprick of dread. How far did Queen Mary, in her zealous rush to Catholicize the realm, intend to go? "Joan," she said, as her sister-in-law passed by with a pail of water, "have you heard anything in Blackheath about the Queen wanting some of the old monasteries back?"

"Who says that?"

"Oh, there was just some talk in the market square. A couple of lawyers visiting from Cambridge. They thought she might demand it, monastic lands returned to the Church."

"Nonsense," Joan scoffed. "It's been over fifteen years. She wouldn't dare try."

Honor felt the same. It would be political madness, antagonizing hundreds of families who had bought up the old monastic lands. But she had seen religion-inspired madness before. This queen had already provoked a rebellion that had nearly cost her her throne, all because she'd insisted on marrying Philip of Spain. And the burnings continued, many of the victims illiterate villagers confused by twenty years of seesawing official orthodoxy, in which their parish priests had changed doctrines at each new reign. Young people who had grown up being told the pope was the devil were now thrown in prison for disparaging him, and many were going to the stake barely understanding what they had done wrong. It was barbarous. All at the command of this zealot queen.

At noon, she and Richard strolled back to the house arm in arm, Joan beside them, satisfied with their morning's labor, and hungry for the cold roast pork and borage salad the cook had promised.

"Geoffrey's forgotten about dinner," Joan said with a sigh, nodding to the top of the slope where her husband was regaling a group of men outside the brew house and getting their laughter. "I'll go fetch him." She went ahead.

Honor and Richard carried on alone. They didn't talk about her "wild gambit," as Richard had called her plan to see the Queen. They'd been through it all last night and again at breakfast, Richard protesting the danger, Honor determined to go ahead. If she was going to keep Elizabeth alive, she needed to know what the Queen was thinking. She needed to be inside the court. Richard had finally thrown up his hands, unable to budge her. Now, as they crossed the footbridge over the stream and carried on up the sloping lawn to the house, they stuck to safe subjects: the quickest feasible schedule of debt repayment, and how many weavers and fullers they could hire.

Richard went to the stable to check on a newborn foal, and Honor headed for the great hall. When she walked in she found a man standing at the windows, looking out at the distant rooftops of Colchester. He turned, and Honor was surprised to see the ruddy face of George Mitford.

"I know," he said. "Look what the cat dragged in."

"Dragged or not, you're always welcome," she said, going to him and embracing him. She pulled back to look at him. She hadn't seen him since he'd bought the last of her jewels in Antwerp. "But what on earth are you doing back in England?"

"First, are you all right?" he asked with a frown of concern. She knew it had to do with the emptiness around them. The hall did look bleak, given Richard's bachelor-like encampment with Adam since their return to the stripped house while Honor was at Woodstock. There were no sideboards laden with plate. No banquettes plumped with cushions. Not a tapestry or a wall hanging to soften the hall's harsh sounds. She could hardly wait for May, when her flower garden would yield bouquets to waft the scent of roses.

"We're getting back on our feet," she assured him. "It's slow but sure. We'll be fine."

He nodded, apparently satisfied.

"You didn't come all this way to ask me that, did you?"

"No," he said, smiling. "My son's getting married."

"Timothy?"

"Roger."

"Roger! Has his voice even changed?"

"Good Lord, Honor, he's twenty-two."

"And taking a wife—heavens. When?"

"Two weeks from Saturday. Alice Lowry, a lovely girl. Margaret would have been proud."

Honor gave him a sad smile. He had been devoted to his wife, dead for seven years. "Where will the ceremony take place?" she asked.

"London."

"But is it safe? For you?" George was a declared Protestant, devout and outspoken. All very well in cosmopolitan Antwerp, but England these days was a dangerous place for such opinions. It was the very reason he had moved abroad, though his sons had stayed.

"An old codger like me, I won't be bothering anyone. And I'm only staying for the wedding. You and Richard will come, won't you?"

"I'd love to, George, but I can't. I'm sorry. I'll be . . . away."

"Oh? Where?"

"I can't tell you that. Though I'm sure you'd approve."

He gave her a quizzical look. "Not back to your old tricks, are you?"

"I'm no magician. Tricks are for the young."

But it wasn't true—she was in the thick of intrigue, advising Elizabeth, and later today she was going to push things even further, with Frances Grenville. Seeing this face from the old days jangled her nerves a bit. George had been on her side and still was, of course, but might there still be someone out there from the other side? Someone who knew everything and could set the bishop's dogs on her?

"Oh," he said suddenly, remembering. "I'd like your opinion on something." He bent to pick up his leather-covered strongbox with the copper bands. Honor noticed a slight tremor in his right hand. Her old friend was getting on, no mistake. *So are we all.* The thought helped settle her nerves. So many from the old days were dead, and those who remained were out of power, toothless, no threat. Besides, she was accepted now by her community, by the parish priest, and by all Richard's business associates as the properly conforming wife of a proper Colchester clothier. Adam's *modus vivendi:* Don't rock the boat and we'll all get along just fine.

George set the strongbox on the bare dining table, then pulled a brass key from his pocket and used it to open the lock. With the lid lifted, his precious wares winked from their black velvet wells: diamonds, rubies, sapphires. A green leather pouch the size of a melon was tucked in one corner. He took it out, tugged loose the drawstring, and then, giving Honor a sly smile, upended its contents on the table.

Her breath caught in her throat. Her jewels! The ruby earrings, her rope of pearls, the diamond and sapphire ring, her gold bracelets and necklaces of amethysts, lapis lazuli, garnets, and topaz. And, entwined among them, glittering with green fire, her beloved emerald on its golden chain.

She looked up at George, dumbfounded. "You never sold them?"

He smiled, enjoying her confusion, her delight. "I gambled you'd pull through."

She was so moved, she couldn't speak. He could have made a great deal of money. Instead, he had kept her jewels safe for her.

"My banker," she finally managed to say, wanting to make a jest before her feelings spilled over in happy tears. "Though not a very good one, I must say. Bankers *invest* their customers' deposits. You'll never get rich this way."

"Long ago I invested in you, Honor. Invested my life. That's the only reason I'm around today to see my son get married." She nodded, grateful for his gratitude. In the old days, George had been one of the Protestants she had smuggled out of England.

She picked up the emerald necklace and held it to the window's light. How she loved its green beauty—liquid summer kissed by the sun, caught and held forever. "I'll buy them all back," she said impulsively. "Not now, of course." Jewelry was the last thing she and Richard could afford at the moment. "But one day soon, I hope. I'll repay you, George. Every penny."

"Good." He meant it, and it made her laugh. Business was business, after all.

A door slammed. He looked up. Footsteps sounded.

"It's Richard," Honor said.

"Oh dear." George quickly scooped the jewelry on the table back into the pouch.

"It's all right. He knows."

Richard joined them, and she explained what George had done for her, hoping it wouldn't embarrass Richard too much. He listened in silence, then said, with a nod toward her hand, "Can't let that one go?"

She still held the emerald necklace.

"George, we'll take this," Richard said matter-of-factly, lifting the necklace from Honor's hand. "You'll sup with us, I trust?" He undid the clasp. "Wine first, then I'll settle this account."

Face-to-face with Honor, he draped the necklace around her throat and fastened it at the back of her neck. He gave her a long look that warmed her like the strengthening spring sunshine. "Queen of my heart," he murmured, and kissed her.

She smiled up at him. "Thank you," she whispered.

George cleared his throat.

"Wine and food," Honor said brightly. "I'll tell the cook you're staying."

George beamed. "I won't say no to that." He settled the green leather pouch back in his strongbox, preparing to close it. A silver rosary glinted against the black velvet. Honor tapped a finger on it. "Supplying the enemy?" she teased.

He shrugged. "Business, you know."

Richard's words lingered in her mind . . . *Queen* . . . and an idea beckoned. Her hand went to the emerald at her throat, then shot out to George's arm to stop him from closing the lid. "George, wait."

St. Botolph's Church stood squarely in the center of Colchester, just outside the town's ancient Roman wall. It had been part of an Augustinian priory built in the twelfth century by William Rufus, son of William the Conqueror, but the priory had been mostly demolished under Henry VIII's despoiling of England's monasteries, and all that remained was the church. Its Saxon tower overlooked the sprawling ruins.

Honor took a deep breath, composing herself for the meeting as she and Adam followed the parish priest, Father Percy, down the nave. The chancel sparkled with Catholic splendors: a huge silver crucifix on the altar, a brightly painted statue of a doleful Virgin Mary, and gorgeous stained glass windows. The priest led them past the chancel and into his study. It was a cozy, paneled room, warm with a fire laid in the grate against the spring chill. As they entered, Frances Grenville stood waiting, hands clasped at her waist, stiff as a sentry.

Honor had glimpsed her occasionally in the years they had been neighbors, when Frances would pass through the town square on horseback in a procession with her kinfolk, but she had never seen her up close. Her first thought: *a hard woman*. Frances's body was all angles, from jawbone to shoulders, elbows to knuckles. Her light brown hair, flecked with gray, was stiffly pulled back under her jeweled hat. But there was something arresting in her haughtiness, and shrewdness in the pale blue eyes. Frances's glance at Adam kindled a flame in her eyes, which kindled Honor's second thought: *Adam, take care*.

Father Percy, a squat, soft-bellied man with the pallid skin of chronic poor health, made the introductions as the two women stood face-to-face. Adam added some good-natured words about working together for the good of the people of Colchester.

Honor offered her hand in friendship. Frances stood utterly still for a moment, then took Honor's hand brusquely as though she was eager to get this over with.

"Mistress Thornleigh. I am glad we finally meet." Her face showed how little she meant it.

Honor forced a smile. "Mistress Grenville. The pleasure is mine." She suppressed a shiver. This was the daughter of the man who had tried to murder her. She sensed a reciprocal shiver in the woman. Honor was the wife of the man who had killed her father.

Frances's hand was cold. Honor slid her own hand free. They

stood in strained silence for a moment. Then Frances's eyes darted again to Adam, and Honor knew for certain that he was the reason Frances had agreed to this meeting. So, she thought, the lady and I both have a private reason to put the past behind us and make common cause. She was determined to build on that mutual desire. "It is so good of you to see me," she said with some warmth, and more sincerity. "I thank you most kindly."

"Neighbors are meant to be . . . neighborly," Frances said, her frostiness thawing a little as she stole another look at Adam. "Master Adam and I have made a good start, I believe. Father Percy has blessed our joint undertaking." She gestured out the window to the ruined monastic buildings that had once formed a square around a cloister, and though they were now just stone rubble enclosing a square of brown grass, Frances's eyes shone as though she could already see the monks padding in and out of their refectory, kitchens, and infirmary. "Is it not a fine scheme? A brand-new priory?"

Honor nodded. "Rising in glory from the ashes of the old."

"Indeed," Frances said, looking quite taken with the idea. "Like Christ, reborn."

Honor had been referring to the mythological phoenix described by Herodotus, but she didn't press the point. She doubted that Frances had much acquaintance with ancient Greek historians. She had Christian piety instead.

"Adam," Honor said, "this partnership is well done." It was their prearranged signal. She wanted to talk to Frances alone.

Adam took the cue. He turned to the priest. "Father, I'd like to make some calculations of the old priory so we can plan the cost of the stonemasons. Could you show me around the foundations?"

"With pleasure, sir. If you ladies will excuse us?"

When the men had gone, Frances went straight to the window and looked out at the ruins as though Honor were of no significance to her after all. Was she hoping to see Adam striding the grounds, measuring dimensions in paces?

"Mistress Grenville," Honor said to her back, "I asked to see you for a reason."

"Oh?" She did not even turn.

"I know you are a dear friend of Her Majesty the Queen. If you will allow me, I would ask a favor."

Frances looked over her shoulder with a suspicious frown. "Of Her Majesty?"

"Of you. I have something that I believe belongs with her."

That seemed to puzzle Frances. She turned. "I don't understand."

Honor was unfastening a blue velvet pouch that hung from the belt at her waist. She didn't open it, just held it in her hand to keep Frances wondering. "Did you know that I once was a friend of Her Majesty's mother?"

Frances's eyes widened in surprise. "You? Friends with good Queen Catherine?"

Honor nodded. "I served her."

Frances's mouth fell open.

"It was in my youth," Honor said. "I was Sir Thomas More's ward."

"Sir Thomas More." Frances whispered it in a tone of awe. "Who died for Queen Catherine's cause. And God's."

Honor saw that she had struck her mark. Catholics revered Sir Thomas almost as a saint. She tugged loose the drawstring of the velvet pouch and shook out the contents into her palm. A rosary. Pearls and turquoise beads strung on a silver chain, with a pendant cross of silver inlaid with more turquoise, the color evocative of Queen Catherine's Spanish heritage. Though finely crafted, it looked worn, a chip in one bead, patches of tarnish on the chain. "This," she said, dangling the rosary, "was her gift to me. It is my humble wish to present it to Her Grace, Queen Mary."

Frances looked rapt. "It was really hers?"

"Hers. I have cherished it all these years." A lie. She'd bought it just hours ago from George. In her kitchen she had hammered the bead to chip it, and soaked the chain in strong vinegar.

Frances gazed at the rosary, and Honor saw her shrewd eyes calculating its enormous sentimental value to her friend the Queen, and therefore Frances's own increased standing in the Queen's eyes. "It will be my pleasure to give this to Her Majesty," she said, and reached out for it.

But Honor was already lowering it, out of Frances's reach. "I would greatly appreciate the opportunity to bestow it in person."

She poured the chain back into its velvet pouch. Tugged the drawstring tight. She saw that Frances's eyes were locked on it almost hungrily, a treasure now hidden.

❧ 7 ❧

In the Presence of
the Queen

March 1555

Waves slapped the water stairs as the wherry slipped alongside the busy landing stage at Whitehall Palace. The wherryman shipped his oars above the gurgle and chop of the Thames. Honor paid him as her manservant, Ned, hopped out onto the wet stairs, then helped her out.

She instructed him to wait, adding that it might be a while before she would return. She really had no idea what this visit would entail. He ambled over to join a knot of other servingmen lounging on the landing stage, and Honor moved through the wharf's bustle of courtiers, merchants, lawyers, and priests who had come to do business at the palace. She had to quickly step aside for a lord and his retinue of at least fifteen young gallants, all armed with swords, hustling to board boats bobbing at the pier. From one of them she caught an incongruous whiff of perfume. Other men beckoned wherries with impatient shouts of "Oars!" and "Eastward, ho!"

The city of London lived by its water trade, and the river was alive with boats of all kinds, their sails leaning from the March wind as though yearning for speed. There were wherries like cockleshells, graceful caravels, tilt boats with tasseled canopies over the heads of gentlemen and ladies, beat-up scullers, rough barges, smelly fishing smacks, and the heavily laden merchant ships that crowded the city's customs house quays beyond London Bridge. Many smaller boats nudged the city wharves: Blackfriars Stairs, Paul's Stairs, Queenhithe, the Three Cranes Wharf, Old Swan Stairs, and Billingsgate. From where Honor stood on the Thames's north bank, the stately mansions of the nobility spread out eastward along the Strand, each with its own private water stairs forming a series of small quays that stretched all the way to the heart of London.

At this distance from the city Honor could see only one of its three great landmarks, the spire of St. Paul's Cathedral, the tallest in Europe. Farther east, beyond her view, lay the second, London Bridge, the city's only viaduct, crammed with its three- and four-story houses and fine shops. Honor could never think of the bridge without a slight shudder, recalling the desperate flight she and Richard had made all those years ago and her horror at seeing him plunge into the water, bristling with arrows, as her terrified horse had galloped on. It didn't help to envision the city's third great landmark rising just past the bridge—the Tower, icon of the Queen's might with its great cannon, its royal treasury, and its hive of prison cells.

She turned her attention back to the palace, steeling herself for her business here. From flagpoles on the turrets the Queen's pennants snapped in the breeze, signaling that she was in residence. The sprawling complex, which included a bowling green, tennis courts, a pit for cockfights, and a tiltyard for jousting, rang with sounds of horses, carts, wagons, and voices. Honor caught the sound of many horses' hooves clopping on a cobbled courtyard nearby within the honeycomb of buildings, and turned to see a hunting party of courtiers returning from St. James's Park. Across the yard trooped soldiers of the palace guard, a sober manifestation of Queen Mary's power. Honor was well aware of what a formidable power it was, despite the Queen's unpopularity. The might of the Catholic Church was behind her, from the pope with his supreme authority in most of Europe, to her cousin the emperor Charles with his immense armies, to the hundreds of Catholic lords here at home with their entrenched, landed wealth and armed retainers. The Queen could count on all of this support. Wyatt, the rebel leader, had learned that lesson at the cost of his life.

"Mistress Thornleigh?"

Honor turned. A young man stood looking at her expectantly. He wore the livery of the Grenvilles, complete with their green and yellow badge of an arrow flying above three turrets. Frances's servant. "Yes," she answered.

"My mistress bids you welcome. After prayers she will escort you to Her Majesty the Queen."

Honor's heart thudded as she walked beside Frances toward the royal apartments. Conversation between them had gone dry. So had Honor's mouth. Could she really hope to establish a connection with Queen Mary? Was she mad to have come here? Richard was right, this was a wild gambit. But it was too late to turn back. She was committed.

The second-story gallery was lined with windows on one side and exquisite Flemish tapestries on the other, and the spring sunshine glinted off millions of threads of gold and silver, lady-blush rose, royal purple, emerald green, and popinjay blue. Whitehall Palace. Originally called York Place, bought and massively remodeled by the obscenely wealthy Cardinal Wolsey before the late King Henry soured on him, took everything he had, including this palace, and drove him to his death. Memories flooded Honor. King Henry's banquets and masques, and the dancing that he never tired of. His musicians sawing and piping all night and into the small hours until they sweated at their labor. His courtiers, many of them bosom friends since his boyhood, fencing in sport down these very corridors, and dicing and gambling at all hours. The King himself roistering from dawn to dusk, whether on the tiltyard, the tennis court, the banquet hall, or in his mistresses' chambers. He had married Anne Boleyn here at Whitehall. Honor could almost hear her shrill laugh, Anne doubled over at one of the King's jests, often a cruel one aimed at a victim clerk or administrator who stood in red-faced humiliation, fighting tears. What a shabby pair those two had made.

No laughter now. Courtiers, hangers-on, servants, and dogs prowled the corridors as before, but their commotion seemed somehow deadened, all grim business, nothing like the rambunctious revelry that had surrounded King Henry. Two young men strode past Honor, sumptuously dressed in gem-studded doublets of black satin, as shiny as crows. They were agitated, talking in quick Spanish, their voices angry, aggrieved, and one pressed a handkerchief to his cut cheek, blood blooming on the white silk. Another fight, she thought. The hostility between the Queen's English courtiers and the entourage of her Spanish husband of eight months was the talk of London. Inside and outside the palace grudges grew into quarrels, quarrels festered into fights, fights erupted into brawls, and brawls exploded into battles of armed bands. Two days ago a Spaniard had attacked a man in church, badly wounding him, and as punishment he'd been branded on the forehead and lost an ear. Later, at the palace gate, one of Philip's retainers ran an English courtier through with his rapier while two Spaniards held the victim by the arms. The murderer was hanged at Charing Cross, but Mary had pardoned his two accomplices.

Honor finally found her voice. "Is His Majesty at court?" she asked Frances as they walked. She had never seen Prince Philip.

"No, at Westminster. Matters of state keep him there."

Philip was acting like a king, though not officially named one, Honor thought. The royal council had refused to grant him this title he had petitioned hard for. A wise decision, in her opinion. People already so deeply resented Philip of Spain lording it over Englishmen that naming him king would dangerously fuel this fire. But he seemed to be stoking the fire on his own, and no one was rushing to put it out. Legally, he was the Queen's husband and nothing more, a consort, but tradition was stronger than law, and even stronger was the centuries-old teaching of the Church that women were inferior to men in all things, and that a wife must always be subservient to her husband. Before her marriage Queen Mary had been a monarch in her own right, but now the government considered her, by natural law, the lesser partner in the monarchy. The people, too, though deeply mistrustful of Philip, seemed to think of Mary now as merely the King's wife.

The doors to the royal apartments lay ahead, open. Honor heard a commotion inside. Shouting. Many voices, mostly women, in a hubbub of alarm.

A man dashed out and ran past Frances, calling, "Master chamberlain!"

Frances and Honor shared a glance of concern, then walked through the antechamber. The doors to the inner chamber burst open and two ladies-in-waiting scurried out. Frances stopped one. "Amelia, what is it?"

"Her Grace is in a fume," was her answer. Then, in a whisper, "There was a letter—"

"The herbal balm, come!" her fellow lady said, tugging her arm. They hurried away.

Frances and Honor reached the inner chamber and stopped just inside the door. Perhaps a half dozen ladies-in-waiting milled, anxiously murmuring. An elderly lord with a wiry gray beard stood nearest Queen Mary, who was the object of all their attention.

Honor's first sight of the Queen was a surprise. A short, small-boned woman, whose dress, a sumptuous red silk brocade, was so roomy to accommodate her pregnancy that it dwarfed her, like a little girl dressing in her mother's clothes. It made her look childlike and dowdy at the same time.

But there was nothing childlike about her rage. "Infamous strumpet!" she growled. Honor was struck by the surprisingly low timbre of her voice, almost like a man's. Then she groaned through clenched jaws like a dog about to savage a victim, a sound so full of hate it made Honor stare in outright shock.

"What's happened?" Frances quietly asked the lady nearest her, a hawk-nosed matron.

"That," the lady said, nodding to a paper in the Queen's clenched hand. "From her sister."

"Some terrible news of the Princess?"

Dread seized Honor. Was Elizabeth in mortal danger?

The Queen's small eyes flicked to Frances, for she had heard her question. "Terrible indeed, Frances," she said in that oddly low voice, "but not news. I have long known the blackness of her heart." She held the letter at arm's length as though it dripped with an assassin's poison, and cried out like an outraged plaintiff to a judge, "*Innocent,* she says. *Maligned,* she says. Unfair treatment— *at my hands!*"

Honor looked at the letter and her fear for Elizabeth turned to a confused dismay. Had Elizabeth brought this trouble on *herself?* Honor clearly recalled her words of advice to the girl. *Write to her as woman to woman. Be kind. Be gentle. Wish her and her baby well. It may do you a world of good.* Her thinking had been that the Queen, now so content in her marriage and cheerful in her pregnancy, might be magnanimous to Elizabeth and ease the harshness of her captivity. Might even set her free. Instead, it appeared that Elizabeth had written some aggressive indictment of her sister, the exact opposite of Honor's advice. She had written a screed. The fool!

"Winchester!" the Queen commanded. The bearded, elderly lord stepped forward, bowing low. So this was William Paulet, the Marquis of Winchester. Lord treasurer of the realm. Had he brought Elizabeth's letter to the Queen? He was part of the royal council, and Elizabeth would have sent it to them, addressed to the Queen. Mary railed at him, "I will have no more of her letters! Tell Bedingfield. No more of her barbarous insolence! And I want her guard doubled."

"Your Grace, the cost—"

"I don't care if you must pay it from your own pocket, my lord. I will have the strumpet more strictly guarded!" She let out a bitter bark of a laugh, and a flame of hate leapt in those small eyes. "Or maybe I should save the cost altogether. No more strumpet, no expense."

The room went silent. Honor felt fear like ice water seep into her veins. *She is going to order Elizabeth's execution.*

The room seemed to hold its breath. The Queen stood still, as if listening to an echo of her own lethal threat and taking strength from it. "Go!" she ordered Winchester. He hurried out.

"Enemies on all sides!" Mary cried, her voice now rising almost to a shriek. "Renard warned me." Ambassador Renard, Honor thought—the emissary of Emperor Charles, the Queen's cousin

and champion. "At my coronation he said beware of three enemies. The king of France, the heretics, and my sister. Well, I will
abide her no longer, nor her vicious—" Her body suddenly jerked
in a spasm. She gasped and clutched her side in pain. The letter
fluttered from her hand to the floor. She slumped, groping behind
her as though for a chair.

Ladies swarmed her, including Frances, and one of them
shoved a chair toward her. Frances slipped an arm around the
Queen's waist and eased her down into the chair. "Your Grace! Are
you ill?"

The Queen's breaths came quick and shallow. Her face had
gone white. She blinked repeatedly, as if bewildered. "No . . . no,
it is no sickness." She sounded frightened. It drained the rage
from her voice.

"The baby?" asked Frances in alarm.

The Queen's small eyes, tight with fear, locked on Frances, her
friend. "I . . . don't know."

Honor felt an unexpected rush of sympathy. Was the Queen
going into early labor? The predicted date of her delivery was not
for two more months.

Frances said, "Shall I fetch Doctor Ambrose?"

"No, no. Do not bother him. I am quite well, my dear."

She did, indeed, look somewhat better already, Honor thought.
The color was returning to her cheeks. She shifted her position in
the chair, easing her cumbersome body. Honor well remembered
the discomforts of pregnancy, its quirks and frights, how they went
as suddenly as they came. Still, the Queen would soon be giving
birth for the first time at the age of thirty-nine, and the possibility
of death hovered in grim attendance over any woman facing this
ordeal. Honor thought of her own daughter, now in her eighth
month, and felt a pang of regret. Isabel was young and healthy, but
she would still have to face the age-old fear when her time came,
and with no mother there to comfort and guide her.

She shook off that worry and turned her mind to the mission
that had brought her here. Elizabeth.

Mary, looking suddenly very tired, beckoned Frances close.

"My dear, would you please . . . ?" She gave a vague flick of her hand, an indication that she wanted the room cleared.

Frances turned and clapped her hands twice, demanding attention. The ladies, whether used to her authority or simply aware of the Queen's desire, left the room in a quiet flurry. Many looked relieved to be going. Honor stayed.

Frances noticed and said, "Your Majesty, I have brought someone who may cheer you. The neighbor I spoke to you about." She gestured for Honor to approach.

Honor's heart thumped in her chest. She crossed the room and sank into a low curtsy before the Queen.

Frances said, "May I present Mistress Thornleigh?"

Mary's eyes widened with interest. "Ah. The ward of Sir Thomas More, God's martyr."

Honor raised her head. "The same, Your Majesty."

"Is it true that you served my mother?"

"I did, Your Grace. It was my great privilege."

A smile softened Mary's face. "And did you bring it? Her rosary?"

Honor loosened the drawstring of the velvet pouch at her waist and lifted out the rosary. She held it up to the Queen, an offering.

Mary took hold of it as carefully as if it were a sacred relic. In a way it was, for it was common knowledge that the Queen venerated her late, long-suffering mother almost as a saint. Queen Catherine, who, after twenty-three years as the faithful and devoted wife of King Henry, had been cast aside in the most notorious divorce case Europe had ever seen. A divorce that the pope had refused to allow, being then under the heel of the armies of Catherine's nephew, Emperor Charles. A divorce that Catherine had fought for almost a decade with every weapon she had in law and men's fealty to her. A divorce that King Henry finally snatched by severing England's ancient tie to Rome and making himself, shockingly, supreme head of the church in his realm. He had created the Church of England. All for Anne Boleyn. Honor had been there, at Catherine's side, through the whole sordid business.

"I loved your lady mother, Your Majesty," she said sincerely. "It has always grieved me that, at the end, my service to her, though heartily given, was not enough to hearten her. Though I tried to make her life merry, I could never lighten her sadness. She suffered mightily, especially for the lack of seeing you."

Mary looked hungry for more scraps of confirmation of her own past sufferings. King Henry, in spiteful fury at his wife's intransigence, had kept Catherine apart from Mary, the daughter she adored, their only child. He had banished Catherine to a dank house in the swampy fens, until she died in that purgatory at the age of fifty-one, still professing her love for her husband, but still adamant about her God-given estate as queen.

"Were you with her at . . . the end?"

"Sadly, no, Your Grace. I stayed as long as the King allowed me to, but in those final, lonely days she had only her confessor, Dr. de Athequa, by her side." Honor nodded at the rosary in Mary's hand. "She gave me that on the day I was forced to bid her a sorrowful good-bye." Telling the story gave her a tug of shame. Not for embroidering this tale, but for her past sins against Queen Catherine. Her admiration and affection for Catherine had been real enough. A noble lady, and a tragic one. Honor had found it hard, all those years ago, to betray her.

Queen Mary, lost in thought, fingered the rosary's pearls and turquoise beads. She asked Frances to pour some mulled wine at the sideboard for them all, then indicated a nearby stool for Honor, who pulled it close to her and sat. Frances returned, handing them goblets of the warm wine, then sat on a cushion on the floor next to Mary's chair. The wine's spicy aroma enveloped the three of them in an aura of fellowship. Honor could faintly hear, in some distant chamber, someone playing a harp slightly out of tune.

Mary seemed hardly able to hold back. "How long did you attend her? Did she get my letters? What did she say of me?"

"She cherished your letters," Honor said. "She would read them once, twice, three times, then have me read them to her again, often late in the evenings before she retired. Read them in order, over again each night, like a beloved bedtime story."

Mary smiled at that, and nodded for Honor to go on, eager for more.

"She particularly loved your letter about the new pony you had taken hawking, and how it cantered down a slope so fast your gentlemen came galloping after, and Sir Matthew Ponsonby lost his hat and tumbled into the briars."

Mary laughed. "Starlight!" she said, sharing a happy look with Frances. "That little pony was quick as a comet. Remember?"

Frances grinned back at her. "I do, Your Grace."

"My goodness, I was . . . what? Twelve?"

"Thirteen, I believe, Your Grace," Honor said, "for in that very letter you thanked your lady mother for the musical clock she had sent you as a birthday gift."

Mary nodded in delight, but then her smile grew thin. "Not sent by her hand, though. She had to sneak it through a network—from her priest to the Duchess of Norfolk to me. King Henry had eyes throughout my household." The way she said her father's name gave Honor a shudder. So barren of intimacy. So tight with loathing.

Mary and Frances murmured reminiscences together, names and places that meant nothing to Honor. They had been friends since childhood, Frances living in Mary's household as her playmate. As they chattered, Honor looked through the open doors to the adjoining bedchamber and noticed a larger than life-sized portrait on the wall. A blond young man dressed in splendid finery, with an arrogant gaze as flat as a steel blade. Prince Philip, of course. She looked back at Mary with a pinch of wonder at how history had repeated itself. Mary was eleven years older than Philip, just as her mother had been older than her father, by six years. Both women had married younger men they adored. But Catherine had eventually lost her husband's love so completely he had called her "the barren old crone" in public. As for Philip, Honor had heard from Sir William Cecil that the Spaniard was, by all accounts, a courteous husband, but he could speak only a few words of English and made no attempt to learn more—he communicated with his wife in French—and it was common knowledge that he kept a mistress in Spain. According to Cecil, some had heard him refer to Mary in private as his aunt, which was almost the case. They were cousins, Philip a generation younger than Mary.

The Queen noticed Elizabeth's letter still on the floor. She groaned. "That trash should have gone out with Winchester. Frances, would you mind? He can't have gone far."

Frances got to her feet. "Of course, Your Grace." She picked up the letter and left the room.

Mary sighed, shaking her head in sorrowful anger as she fingered the rosary's beads. She said to Honor, "You, brought up in piety by the godly Sir Thomas More—you would be sick to know of the evil I must combat. A constant fight for the souls of my kingdom. How the heretics breed. Priests, even, who desecrate their vows by taking wives—harlots, more like. And now, my sinful sister. Oh, yes, the heretics would love to see her take my place. How can I do God's work with such vipers as *her* at my breast?"

Listening, Honor felt an idea, just hatched, scratch at her mind. "It is truly a mighty battle, Your Grace," she said.

"I have been lenient. I have allowed her to live when other monarchs would have had her head. But she defies me at every turn. Defies me and defiles my trust." She rubbed her forehead as if overcome with weary disgust. "Well, what else can one expect from a bastard, the whelp of a heretic whore?"

Honor flinched at the gross language. Luckily, Mary did not notice, her eyes closed as she kneaded her forehead. Suddenly, she thumped her fist down on the arm of her chair in a flash of anger. "And this viper hopes to inherit my crown. I know she does! It makes me sick. It must sicken God Himself."

Honor took a deep breath. She could not allow the Queen to follow this train of thought. Mary had already shown her brutally vindictive nature when, a year ago, she had beheaded her seventeen-year-old cousin, Lady Jane Grey. She said, "Your Grace, you have good reason to despise the Lady Elizabeth." She added steadily, taking her life in her hands, "So do I."

Mary frowned at her and Honor knew how close to the edge she, a commoner, teetered. In speaking evil of royalty she was virtually speaking treason.

But she also saw that the Queen was interested. "How so?" she asked.

Frances, returning, came through the door, but Mary impatiently gestured to her with an abrupt wave of dismissal. "Not now, my dear. Leave us."

Frances looked surprised. She shot Honor a sharp glance that glittered with jealousy. Then lifted her head high, turned on her heel, and walked out.

Mary pressed Honor again, "You say you hate my sister? Why?"

"Her father crushed the people I loved. I revered my noble guardian as a father, and King Henry executed him because he would not call the King's mistress queen. Why do I hate Elizabeth? Because she is the King's bastard."

Mary looked astonished. And thrilled. "You say true."

Honor went on, "I loved your lady mother, too, the most generous and righteous Queen, and King Henry cast her out and drove her to her death. The King crushed them both in his lust for Anne Boleyn. Why do I hate Elizabeth? Because she is the daughter of that goggle-eyed whore."

Mary was nodding, her eyes glowing with bitter passion. "True. So true!"

"Your Grace, for Sir Thomas More's sake, and for your dear mother's sake, let me serve Elizabeth."

Mary gaped at her. "What? Serve her?"

"Let me serve *you,* by serving her. I will watch her doings, her private words, and make reports to you. And, if I can find a way"— she lowered her voice to convey her dark meaning—"I will serve her in the fashion she deserves."

The light flickered in Mary's eyes, a vicious flame fueled by all the misery of her girlhood, all her youthful love for her mother that her father had despoiled, and it told Honor that the Queen had understood her meaning. Serve. Dispatch. Kill.

Honor pressed the point. "I have good cause, as you can see, and if you will give me—"

"The means?"

"Yes. I promise Your Majesty, I will serve her well."

Mary smiled, as though content for the first time in a long day. "My sister's present ladies have spent long enough in her wearying service. Can you begin at once?"

Frances summoned her steward to her small, private chamber near the Queen's suite.

"I want you to find a discreet man," she told him, "and send the fellow to find out whatever he can about Honor Thornleigh. Especially her life in Antwerp."

"Send him there?"

"Yes. He shall have whatever funds are necessary."

There was something about the Thornleigh woman's claims that Frances found odd. Why would a ward of Sir Thomas More, a lady-in-waiting to Queen Catherine, have spent years living in the Protestant German lands? Her husband's business kept her there, no doubt. Yet something nagged. Something about Honor Thornleigh's sudden and so earnest wish to become a friend of Queen Mary. That was Frances's place. She would not be supplanted by an upstart . . . or worse.

"When did you want this information, my lady? Such an investigation could take some time."

"Then take it. Be thorough. I want to know everything."

✺ 8 ✺

The Queen's Summons

April 1555

Riding homeward to Colchester, munching an apple from the inn's breakfast table, Adam was thinking about ships. A leaner, faster galleon—a new design—that's what he would build and test if he had the means. Say, two hundred tons, with a length-to-beam ratio of three to one. That would create a hull form below the waterline more like the old, small galleasses, but with a deeper draft. He would keep the superstructure low, sweeping upward from waist to stern, and make a more rakish stem to improve handling in rough seas. He'd place the mainmast a little farther forward, too, and rake it forward slightly—that also would make for easier handling. Imagine the efficiency of such a lean, swift ship. Imagine a small fleet of them.

Reality blasted his fantasy. Imagine the cost to build them.

Ships and money. The first was impossible without the second. He had already spent more than he'd planned of the loan he had squeezed from the Antwerp money market thanks to his father's good reputation, all just to maintain top quality on the one hull now taking shape in Colchester's shipyard. He needed investment cash to finish this ship, and soon. Frances Grenville would prove her worth there, he hoped. She had promised to introduce him to some wealthy men at court. He glanced down at his brown breeches and sand-colored doublet of serviceable wool, six or seven years old at least. Christ, he'd have to get some clothes. Couldn't go looking like a bumpkin among the courtiers in their velvets and satins and starched ruffs. A London tailor—that would be more precious cash out the window.

Strange to think of his stepmother moving in that courtier crowd. For two months she had traveled this road back and forth between the royal court and Woodstock, ostensibly as Queen Mary's eyes spying on Princess Elizabeth, though her face-to-face reports to the Queen, she said, were invented, toothless nothings. Adam had escorted her on her return to Woodstock this time, then stayed overnight at the Bull Inn and was on his way home now. He had never seen the Princess and didn't know quite what to make of his stepmother's new position with her. All very clever, of course, but to what end? What did she hope to accomplish? Her double-dealing with the Queen seemed awfully risky. On the road from London yesterday, he had seen how her old wound troubled her, jostling on horseback, so he had kept their pace slow, but it reminded him of the dangers she was facing and prompted him to ask, "How long can you go on like this? I fear the Queen will see through your ruse."

She had shifted in the saddle to ease her discomfort. "You're the one who said we should befriend those who wield power."

"And you said we don't befriend tyranny."

They exchanged wry smiles, acknowledging the odd switch in their positions.

"Trust me, Adam," she had said, and would speak of it no further.

It wasn't a matter of trust. He had been her enthusiastic admirer from the day she had married his father. Adam had been nine, and she had accepted his wedding gift of a model sailboat he had carved for her, thanking him with all the seriousness of a queen accepting a naval commander's tribute. In the years since then, he had watched her resourcefully weather trials that would have left other women weeping on their knees. Now, though, it seemed to him that she had sailed into treacherous waters. But he knew little about royal courts and princesses and politics. She did. He must accept that she knew what she was doing.

Traveling home alone now, he could ride faster and that felt good. He meant to make it back to Colchester in two days, by Thursday. He had arranged to meet Frances on Friday, some saint's day that she felt was auspicious, to discuss her silly priory. Saint Anselm? Whatever, he hoped that at their meeting he could set a date with her for a few important introductions at court. Get some investment cash flowing to his team of carpenters. If it didn't flow soon, he wouldn't be able to launch the ship this summer as he hoped.

He had left Woodstock when the sky had first blushed with dawn, and now, five miles out, the sun was beaming and the morning was warm with a soft breeze as he trotted his horse down the sloping road toward a hamlet of six or seven poor houses. Robins and warblers choired from the hedgerows. Tree buds were unfurling into leaves of a green so fresh you could almost taste it. Spring had burst in all its full-throated glory. Munching his apple, he watched a hawk spiral on a current of warm wind. A kestrel? It banked and dipped as though in jubilation at its freedom, almost as if it were dancing in the air.

He craned his neck, enjoying the hawk's flight, thinking how its soaring had a lot in common with a ship making good way with wind and waves. He longed to launch by August, with luck by July. *Kestrel*—that might be a good name for her. She'd have to swiftly fly the Narrow Seas to the Antwerp cloth markets to start repaying his debts.

The road sloped down to a narrow wooden bridge across a stream that bubbled past banks frilled with watercress. As he neared it Adam took the last bite of apple, thinking he'd toss the core mid-bridge and hear a satisfying splash, when horsemen, at least a dozen, came galloping straight through the hamlet, hell-bent to cross the bridge before him. He felt a tweak of annoyance since he'd reached it first, but he hauled back on the reins to edge his horse to one side and let them have the bridge. There were a lot more of them.

He counted fourteen as they thundered past him. Soldiers of the Queen, one gripping an upright staff with the Queen's banner fluttering from it. They were led by a brawny, blond-bearded captain. Adam turned in the saddle to watch them gallop off. They were heading for Woodstock. A shiver touched his scalp. Did their mission have something to do with his stepmother? Had her double-dealing caught up with her?

He tossed the apple core. It tumbled down the riverbank and was snared by weeds as he kicked his horse's flanks and galloped back the way he'd come.

The entrance to Woodstock Palace swarmed with men on horseback. Thirty or forty altogether, Adam judged as he cautiously trotted up to the gatehouse. Some wore a livery of blue and tawny, likely retainers of Sir Henry Bedingfield, the Queen's man here, custodian of the Princess. Some were soldiers of the guard, in breastplates and helmets. All were armed with swords and rapiers. Horses' hooves clattered and harnesses jangled, and above it all an officer shouted orders to his men. Some people from the village had come out to watch and stood gawking, keeping their distance.

Adam looked up at the gatehouse. That was where his stepmother said she stayed with the Princess. For a moment he took heart, thinking they surely would not make all this commotion about her, a mere merchant's wife. But then he realized that if she had fallen afoul of the Queen, her treason would implicate the Princess in treason, too, a matter of enormous consequences. *Treason.* The very word churned his gut. He had to get inside, find out what was happening. As he approached the gate a soldier halted him. "Name?"

"Adam Thornleigh."

"Your business here?"

"I've come to see my stepmother. She's the Princess Elizabeth's lady."

The guard scowled at him. "Today of all days?"

Dread rose in Adam's throat. *Why not today? What's happened?*

"Dismount."

Adam kicked his feet from the stirrups and jumped to the ground. The guard searched him for weapons, Adam standing with arms outstretched. The guard relieved him of his dagger, searched his horse's saddlebags, then let him pass. "Say good-bye to her, then be on your way."

Good-bye?

Adam led his horse into the courtyard where dozens more men were milling. There were liveried retainers, and more soldiers, and servants running to and fro hefting baggage and leading horses and packing trunks in carts. The blond-bearded captain of the Queen's guard, on horseback, was talking to a stout gentleman on foot who gestured with an air of impatient authority. Bedingfield, Adam guessed.

He spotted a stairway that led up inside the gatehouse. He tethered his horse to a rail, and no one stopped him as he took the stairs two at a time up to the second story. He dodged a couple more servants hustling down the stairs with bundles. At the top he entered a large room with a painted ceiling. He was alone. The room looked barren, as though recently stripped of furniture. The door to an adjoining room was closed. Through it he could hear his stepmother's voice.

"Listen to me, I beg you!" she cried.

Good Lord, was she begging for her life? He lunged for the door and yanked it open. His stepmother turned. She looked pale, anxious. And clearly surprised at seeing him. "Adam!"

"What's happened?"

"Shhh! Come in. Quickly. Close the door!"

"I've no *time* to listen," a woman's voice called from the next room where the door stood open. A bedchamber, Adam saw. "They've only given us twenty minutes," the voice went on breathlessly. "Where's my silver comb? Where's my Cicero?" He glimpsed a figure dash past the bed, then disappear. It had to be Princess Elizabeth.

"Close the door!" his stepmother said again, rushing toward him to close it herself.

"What's going on?" he asked "The Queen's soldiers—"

"The Queen has summoned her. To London."

"To court! At last!" the Princess sang out from the bedchamber.

She sounded happy. Adam saw her flit past the doorway again. It looked almost like she was dancing.

"Why?" he asked.

"For the Queen's lying-in," his stepmother said. "That's the official story." Her anxious look told him how little she believed it. "My lady, *think*," she called as she hurried to the bedchamber. She disappeared inside, but Adam could still hear her saying, "Why should she ask for *you?*"

"The baby," the Princess said. "It has mellowed her. They say that does happen when women come near their time." Adam couldn't see either of them now, but he heard drawers being pulled open, cupboards slammed shut. "It's the coming baby, that's all."

"Or a trap. To lure you there."

The Princess laughed lightly. "No, no, no, you don't understand. It's tradition. An ancient custom. All the noble ladies of the realm are summoned to court to attend a queen's delivery. They'll all be there, you'll see. The duchesses and countesses . . . and me! Oh Lord, to be at court after this mausoleum. I can hardly wait. Music. Dancing. People!" She rushed out through the doorway, then stopped abruptly, seeing Adam. She looked about to laugh as she said, "Here's one now."

The window was behind her and the sun was so bright it seemed to make her glow. But it wasn't just the sun. She was dressed in a dazzle of gold and green. But it wasn't just her clothes, either. He'd never seen anything like her hair, a coppery cascade that shimmered like the sea under a ruddy gold sunset. And her smile had a dazzle all its own. It felt like she was giving off light.

"Stop this," his stepmother said harshly, coming out and stepping between them. "Think what she's doing by getting you back to London."

"Who's this?"

"My stepson. Adam."

He went down on one knee. He was glad that etiquette in the presence of royalty demanded it. His legs didn't feel quite solid.

"Master Thornleigh," the Princess said in an impassioned, conspiratorial voice that sent a shiver of thrill through him, "have you ever felt frightened, but also so excited that you simply had to carry on, no matter what?"

Yes, he wanted to say. Every time a ship under him trembled at the crest of a mountainous wave, about to plunge into its trough. Or right now, as he imagined leaping up and pulling this woman into his arms.

"My lady, please," his stepmother went on urgently. "This summons could just be her ploy."

"To what end?" the Princess said, her eyes still on Adam. He knew he should properly bow his head, but he couldn't make his eyes leave hers. "To dare me to show my face amongst the duchesses? I'll take that dare."

"No. To lure you into the Tower."

Her gaze snapped to his stepmother, and Adam saw a shudder run through the Princess. The mention of the Tower seemed to terrify her, like a dog once viciously beaten who sees its master's stick.

Yet something in her look told him she was facing the fear head-on and carefully calculating the odds. She suddenly shook her head, confident again. "You're wrong. Quite wrong. Master Thornleigh, your mother is my good friend. You know that, don't you? I mean, you know my situation, being persecuted by my sister?"

His head felt like he'd had too much wine. It took him a moment to swallow. "I do, Your Grace."

"Good. Then let me explain, and you be the judge. My sister has persecuted me for one reason only, because until now I was the legal heir to the throne, the last surviving person with our father's royal blood, and she hates that I stood to inherit. But her coming baby changes everything. Don't you agree?"

He blinked. He had no idea what to say.

"Do get up," she said.

He stood. The Princess turned to his stepmother. "Don't you see? The baby will now be her heir, so she can stop plaguing *me*."

"The baby puts you in even *more* danger," his stepmother said. "Until now she did not dare to openly kill the last child of King Henry, for fear of rousing the many lords who support your rights as heir. The baby does indeed change everything, but you have not thought it through. The moment the Queen has an heir of her body, you become expendable."

The Princess went completely still. Adam was horrified by his stepmother's words. For months he had heard her talk of the danger the Princess stood in, but those had been words about a stranger, a distant royal personage. Not this golden, glittering girl. To imagine her death seemed like dying a little himself.

"Forgive my speaking so harshly, my lady, but we have not a moment to lose." She hurried to the window and looked out at the massing soldiers. "Tell them you are ill. Feign some sickness. Stay here, in your bed, and say you are too seriously unwell to be moved. That can give us a few days. Enough time for me to contact Sir William Cecil. He is friends with the lords on the royal council who support you. Once he alerts them, the Queen cannot then act against you without rousing them up. It may be just enough to stop her from—"

"Let me do it," Adam said.

They both looked at him.

"I'll go to Sir William. I can be in London by nightfall."

His stepmother offered a quick, grateful smile. Adam waited. A smile from the Princess, that's what he was waiting for.

All her gaiety had drained away, but also, it seemed, all her fear. Her gaze drifted to the window. The look on her face was open, no art in it, a look of pure yearning. As though her mind had traveled past the window, skipped across the courtyard, and sailed over its walls—as though she were seeing the whole wide world that lay beyond. Trees and rivers and fields. People. London. *Life.* Adam didn't think he had ever seen anyone so hungry for life. He knew then that she had made up her mind and heart. She had been a captive here for a year, and now the Queen's summons had opened her prison door a crack and she ached to bolt through it. She was getting out, and nothing his stepmother could say would stop her. He felt a pang of loss, almost as if something had been stolen from him. She didn't want his help. She wanted freedom.

He would help her anyway. He rode past the dozens of men on horseback outside the palace gate, forcing himself to keep his horse at a trot, not dig in his spurs to gallop as he itched to do. The horsemen had formed themselves into an organized cohort, with the Queen's soldiers in the vanguard, the forward rider carrying the staff with the Queen's banner rippling in the wind. They were followed by Bedingfield's guardsmen and retainers, their ranks stretching back along the road that ran straight to the palace. Outriders from the soldiers' ranks trotted back and forth along the length of the entourage, checking that the whole troop was in order. Scores of villagers had left their cottages and shops and fields and stood crowding both edges of the road.

A cheer went up. Adam halted his mount and looked back. He trotted to one side to watch as the gate opened. The sun was cresting the gatehouse as the Princess emerged on a white horse. She sat tall, as though the world was such a thrilling place she wanted to stretch as high as possible to see it all, hear it all, smell it all. Her horse seemed infused with her excitement, stepping high as it pranced out of the gateway.

"God save Your Grace!" a man shouted from the village throng.

She laughed. Even at this distance, Adam heard her laugh. It seemed to pour into him like cool water on a hot day. She beamed as she trotted forward, taking her place at the center of the entourage, for there were as many horsemen now coming through the gate after her as there were already ranged in front. Adam saw his stepmother, on her stolid brown mare, riding directly behind the Princess.

The whole entourage started moving along the road to London. The villagers moved forward with it, knots of excited men and women and children walking alongside, pointing and chattering. A couple of women tried to get close to the Princess, one calling out, "God bless the Lady Elizabeth!" before the outriders nudged them back. The bearded captain trotted close to the Princess, his royal charge, with his right hand resting on his sword hilt and a stern gleam in his eye. Children skipped after the train like gulls in the wake of a ship.

A skinny little girl carrying a ragged bouquet of wildflowers scampered between the horses, quick as a fish, and darted up to the Princess. "Here, my lady!" She held up the flowers, offering them, as she kept pace beside the white horse.

The Princess looked entranced. Smiling, she reached down for the spindly wildflowers as though they were rare orchids presented by a sultan's daughter.

The captain lunged his horse forward, drawing his sword. He slashed the bouquet, decapitating the blooms from the stems. The little girl screamed and ran. The Princess's face went white. She sat rigid, stunned.

It was all Adam could do to hold back from charging the man and wrestling him to the ground.

Instead, he kicked his spurs into his horse's flanks and bolted down the road ahead of the train. He didn't look back, but he felt her presence—the laugh, the light—as he bent over his horse's neck and galloped toward London to alert Sir William Cecil.

"Perhaps we should begin?" Father Percy ventured.

"Not yet," Frances snapped. She would not start without Adam. The priest folded his hands over his paunch, meekly accepting her command.

They stood outside St. Botolph's church at the edge of the grassy quadrangle, the old monastery cloister rimmed with ruins. Four men—Colchester's master stonemason and his three apprentices—stood at the far corner of the quadrangle, as though they were a team of wrestlers squared off against Frances and the priest. The master mason had rolled up his plans and stood tapping the roll impatiently against his thigh. The bored apprentices murmured amongst themselves. One of them idly kicked at an anthill. The whole party had been waiting for almost an hour.

The sun glared down, unseasonably sweltering for late April. Frances was hot, and she was angry. Where was Adam? It was over a week ago that they had agreed on this Friday meeting, the feast day of blessed Saint Anselm. Adam had promised to be here. He had made her so happy, saying he looked forward to commissioning the masons and approving the first dig, finally launching the project.

Frances squinted in the bright sun, skeptically eyeing her maid, who sat on a large rock amid the ruins, fanning herself with her hand, her eyelids lazily drifting closed. The apprentice kicking the anthill had been stealing regular glances at the girl. It hadn't escaped Frances's notice. Nor had the girl's blowsy appearance, the chemise above her bodice unlaced like a harlot's, showing her plump bosom pink and dewy in the heat. Frances wrestled with the impulse to sack her here and now. She would not tolerate lewdness in her servants. But she hesitated. The maid was quite artful at dressing Frances's hair.

Irritably, she batted away a fly. More flies buzzed thickly over a dead creature by the ruin wall, some large bird. She could smell the thing. An appalling thought struck her. Adam had been hurt. He had fallen off the scaffold at that ship of his and broken his leg. He had been thrown from his horse and snapped his neck. He had been run through the heart by some villainous highwayman, robbed and left to die by the side of the road. He lay gasping in a ditch at this very moment, crawling, trying to get to her. Otherwise, what could possibly keep him from being here?

"Dyer!" she called, turning to the church.

Her steward came hurrying out the door of Father Percy's study. He held the list of tasks that Frances and Adam had written up together, an agenda for this meeting. "My lady?"

"Forget that," she said, waving away the list. "Send people out to search. I fear Master Thornleigh has met some dreadful mishap."

"Have you heard word of this?"

"No."

"Then perhaps—"

"I want him found! Is that understood?"

Dyer shut his mouth. He nodded.

Frances turned to Percy. "Father, dismiss these workmen." She started along the path that led out of the churchyard. Dyer kept by her side. As they reached the maid the girl stood up, ready to fall in behind her mistress. Frances slapped her face. The girl gasped, her eyes big with fear.

"Make yourself decent," Frances ordered. She turned to Dyer. "And I want that shiftless apprentice sacked."

❧ 9 ❧

The Queen's Child

April–May 1555

On a warm Tuesday morning, the last day of April, the news swept London at daybreak. Courtiers told servants, neighbors told neighbors, and soon the whole city was buzzing that just after midnight Queen Mary had given birth to a prince. The boy was fair and without blemish. By midmorning there were bonfires in the streets and bells rang throughout the city. In every church *Te Deums* were sung, the priests jubilantly orchestrating the people's thanks to God for the safe delivery of their queen and the birth of their prince.

By nightfall everyone had learned that the rumor was false. The Queen, in fact, had not yet begun her labor.

Three weeks later, as Honor was climbing the staircase to the Queen's apartments to make another meaningless report to her about Elizabeth, she still didn't know how the birth rumor had started. What mattered was that Elizabeth was safe—for now, at least. Sir William Cecil, alerted by Adam, had spread the word to his influential friends about the Queen removing Elizabeth from Woodstock, and since her arrival in London she had been confined to her rooms in Hampton Court Palace, under guard, but at least she was not in the Tower. Honor did not know if the alarm had stayed the Queen's hand from taking some dire action against her sister, or if Elizabeth's reprieve was somehow connected to the confusion swirling around the imminent delivery of the Queen's baby, including the birth rumor. She reached the top of the staircase and made her way to the Queen's rooms, thinking how everyone was on tenterhooks awaiting the event. Here at Hampton Court, where the Queen had come for her lying-in and the whole court had followed, it was all people talked about. When would the baby come? The Queen was five weeks overdue.

Mary had secluded herself in her private chambers, and the life of the government had practically come to a standstill, while courtiers and the staffs of ambassadors and diplomats met anxiously in chambers, in the corners of galleries, in the courtyards, and on the busy palace wharf, exchanging scraps of information gleaned from the Queen's apartments. Honor was privy to little of their talk, since everyone at court, noting the Queen's shunning of her sister, avoided Elizabeth. They hurried past the cramped set of rooms in the rear of the palace where she had been lodged under guard. Nobody wanted to be seen near Elizabeth. She and her lady were pariahs.

Every day Honor felt the pall of suspense and suspicion grow heavier. It seemed that all of England felt it, for the one program the Queen had pushed ahead with was the burning of heretics, and the bishops had filled the country's prisons with Protestants. A clerk of the French ambassador had told Honor one day, furtively, under a staircase, that he thought the Queen had made up her mind that her child could not be born until every Protestant in prison had been burned alive. The burnings fueled the fury of radical Protestants who met in secret congregations at night in cellars and barns and cemeteries. Their seditious pamphlets were read in taverns, in the streets, in the gambling houses. Honor had seen one of the more distasteful pamphlets with a picture of Queen Mary as a filthy sow, suckling a litter of grubby priests lined up at her teats. As the burnings continued there were riots in Warwickshire and Devon. The Queen's council raised more troops. The soldiers were quartered in the immediate neighborhood of the palace, and they brought artillery with them. Meanwhile it was common knowledge that the Queen's husband was anxious to get to Flanders to see to his father's imperial business and was waiting only until the baby came. His retinue of Spaniards prowled the palace corridors, impatient to get home.

As Honor entered the Queen's apartments she sensed that here, especially, nerves were at a snapping point. The noblewomen of the realm had been brought to court in April to witness the royal birth, and somehow room had been found in the palace for all of them with their maids and lapdogs and trunks of finery, but now it was late May, and Honor heard bickering among the duchesses, countesses, and marchionesses as she walked through the ante-chamber. Eight or nine of them, looking sour and restless, sat idly playing cards, picking at candied apricots at a sideboard, and gossiping by the windows. They had put in weeks of embroidering baby clothes. The sewing was done, the midwives stood ready, the wet nurses had been brought in, the rockers hired. The royal cradle sat in a corner, sumptuously decorated and blatantly empty. Everyone was just waiting.

The gentlewomen kept their distance from Honor, Elizabeth's lady, as she passed among them and knocked gently on the Queen's bedchamber door.

The door opened a crack. Frances Grenville stood like a sentry.

"Her Majesty is expecting me," Honor said.

"She is resting. Come back later." Frances gave off a chill that Honor sensed was jealousy for her, the Queen's new, special confidante.

A groan sounded from deep inside the room. Then the Queen's voice, thin and pinched with pain. "Frances, who's there?"

Honor smelled a cloying odor, like bad meat. The chamber lay in darkness, though it was two in the afternoon. What was going on? Frances started to close the door. Honor slapped her palm against it to stop her. "It's Honor Thornleigh, Your Grace. May I come in?"

She pushed the door open, forcing Frances to step back. It took a moment for her eyes to adjust to the gloom. The windows were shuttered and the heavy velvet curtains were closed—winter curtains, incongruous against the gentleness of May outside. Candle-light flickered at the far end of the room, coming from the alcove with its *prie-dieu*, though Honor could not see it from the doorway.

On a table, a plate sat abandoned with some kind of cooked meat, rabbit perhaps, its gravy congealed. The bed, with its thick carved posts and heavy embroidered hangings, lay shrouded in darkness.

Frances sat down in her chair beside the bed, picking up a baby's silk cap and her embroidery yarn and needle. Honor approached the bed, ready to go down on her knees before the Queen. But the bed, she now saw, was empty. Frances, intently sewing, seemed bent on ignoring Honor.

The Queen was likely at the *prie-dieu*, her private altar, Honor thought. She left the bed and turned the corner to the alcove. The *prie-dieu* stood in lone splendor, its silver crucifix and polished ebony backdrop with inlaid gemstones gleaming in the light of the candles that flared on either side. A red satin cushion lay on the floor in front of it. Honor knew that the Queen knelt here in prayer several times a day. But not now.

She was about to go and ask Frances where the Queen was, when she caught the unmistakable smell of an unwashed body. Sweat.

She heard a groan. She looked past the candles' glare, and her breath snagged in her throat. Queen Mary sat on the floor in a linen shift, barefoot, her hair loose and tangled, her face as white and damp as raw pastry. She looked up at Honor, pain thrashing in her eyes. *She's in labor,* Honor thought.

"Your Grace, is the baby coming? I'll call for your doctor. Try to—"

Mary heaved another groan and her head dropped to her knees. Honor felt a stab of shock—her *knees?* The Queen had pulled her knees up tightly against her chest and wrapped her arms tightly around them. No woman nine months pregnant could possibly sit in such a posture. "Your Majesty . . ." She stopped, not knowing what to say, what to ask.

A horrifying thought struck. The baby had been born, just now. Only . . . where was it? There was no crying. No blood. Had the infant died? Was the Queen in shock?

"Mistress Grenville," she called, hurrying back to her. "What has happened?"

Frances looked up from her sewing, her face as hard as a closed door. "Happened?"

"The baby...haven't you seen?" She stopped. Frances seemed to have no inkling of how impossible the Queen's posture was. Or was she, too, in shock?

"I'll fetch the doctor," Honor said, starting for the door.

"Don't. He was just here, not fifteen minutes ago."

"What? What did he say?"

"That we must be patient. Babies take their time."

Honor could only gape at her. *There is no baby!*

"Her Majesty gets these spells," Frances said, a smug look on her face. "They always pass. God works in wondrous ways." Her tone hardened. "Now, go back to your mistress."

This was madness. Honor pulled open the door and the daylight hit her, making her squint. Some of the ladies looked at her, but most kept on playing cards, strolling, gossiping. She opened her mouth to speak but could find no words. What was she to say? Who would believe her? She scarcely believed what she had witnessed with her own eyes and ears.

She hurried from the Queen's apartments. *No baby*—that was the only clear fact. Should she tell Elizabeth? Honor had left her studying Cicero. But the girl, high-strung at the best of times, had been through so much with her recent feverish hopes of freedom dashed, the last thing she needed was more alarm and uncertainty. And this could not be more bizarre. The Queen, the doctor, the whole palace seemed to be in the throes of a delusion. First, Honor had to sort out what it portended for Elizabeth. She needed to talk to someone with a calm and rational head. Someone in the real world.

Sir William Cecil lived in Wimbledon, a few miles southwest of London. Honor rode, and with the clear, warm weather and dry roads she was there by six, the supper hour. Cecil's house, the Old Rectory, stood on the northern slope of a hill, the view dominated by the spire of mighty St. Paul's across the Thames on the northeast horizon. The house was not luxurious, but Cecil's family lived comfortably: he and his wife and son, along with his sister, his wife's sister, and his ward, plus the two dozen or so servants who saw to the bake house, brew house, kitchen, and stable.

Sir William's wife, the able administrator of this lively household, welcomed Honor and led her to the parlor. "Do stay to supper, Honor," she said. "It's been ages since we've seen you, and Thomas Randall has just come back from Antwerp. He's got plenty of news of our mutual friends there. Do stay."

"I wish I could, Mildred, but it's impossible today."

Sir William rose from a chair beside his desk. "Honor," he said, "what news?"

She took a breath. "I hardly know where to begin."

He looked mildly startled. He glanced at his wife, and she, taking the cue, said, "Yes, yes, I'm going. Honor, do take some of our honey back with you when you leave."

"Thank you, Mildred, I shall."

She left them, closing the door. Honor now saw another man in the room. He was far more elegantly dressed than Sir William, with much jewelry—rings and a chain of gold—and a look of sharp intelligence.

Cecil gestured to him. "May I introduce—"

"Monsieur de Noailles," she said. "*Je vous ai vu au palais.*" I have seen you at court.

The French ambassador bowed, and when Sir William told him Honor's name his face lit up. "The mother of *Isabel* Thornleigh?"

"The same, sir," she said with a swell of pride. Isabel, the rebel. Honor knew that Noailles had been complicit in the Wyatt uprising.

He made another bow, this time as deep and respectful as if she were a duchess. "A young woman of courage. How I relied on her."

"Come, Honor, what's happened?" Sir William said. "Something. I can see it in your face."

She was wondering if she could speak freely in front of Noailles. But Sir William clearly considered him a friend, and Noailles already knew how deeply her family had been involved in Wyatt's failed rebellion. As he had been himself, secretly. His employer, the king of France, was a notorious enemy of Prince Philip's father,

Emperor Charles. The two countries had been warring for decades over pieces of the Italian peninsula. The emperor was lord of half of Europe, and France was his only real adversary, so each was always angling for England's allegiance. Queen Mary's marriage to Philip had incensed the French. Noailles would naturally be a supporter of Elizabeth.

"What would happen to Princess Elizabeth if the Queen delivered no child at all?" she began.

"Pardon?" Sir William asked with a bewildered frown.

She told them the condition in which she had found the Queen. And how no one at the palace seemed to notice. Or at least pretended not to.

"*Mon dieu*, then it's true," Noailles said, his eyes wide. "I didn't believe it when she told me."

"Told you?" Honor asked. "Who?"

"I have a spy among the Queen's women, clever at worming out information. The midwife secretly admitted this very truth to my informant—that there is no baby."

Sir William let out a puff of astonishment. "But what about . . ." He smoothed his hands over his belly as if it were swollen with child.

"Imagined, all imagined," Noailles said. "A fantasy."

"Perhaps a malady," Honor said. She had heard of women suffering bloated lumps in the womb. Sometimes they were fatal. "Poor lady. Not life growing in her, but disease."

"But what about the doctors?" Sir William said with obvious skepticism. "How could they possibly get this wrong?"

Noailles shrugged. "Too ignorant to know the difference."

Honor said, "More likely too afraid to tell the Queen. The same with her women."

Sir William shook his head, unable to accept it. "But, the Queen herself. How can *she* not know?"

Noailles answered with some relish, the satisfaction of an insider. "First, I understand there are more symptoms than just her swollen abdomen. The state of the breasts, for example, tender and somewhat enlarged. And her appetite, diminished and queasy. Second, I am told that she has suffered for years, since her adolescence, with only intermittent monthly bleeding. Still, *this*—I did not actually believe it until now." He summed up with some amazement, "The Queen is either an outright liar or a pathetic fool."

"Or," Honor said with a twinge of pity, "so hopelessly obsessed with proving herself a good wife and queen, she has truly deluded herself." She remembered Mary's mother, Queen Catherine, and her desperate twenty-year quest for a son. The tearful miscarriages, the tragic death of an infant boy, the dismaying approach of menopause. And, through it all, her agonizing sense of failure to her husband. A husband lusting after nubile Anne Boleyn.

"So, no baby," Cecil said, finally accepting it, the bureaucrat getting down to business. "What does that mean for us? For the Princess?"

Noailles threw up his hands. "Back to where we were. Heir apparent, despised by the Queen. I lie awake thinking *how* despised. Ever since Wyatt's uprising, Renard has been urging the Queen to execute the Princess, and it is clear how much she wants to. And then, well, the Queen herself . . ." He seemed now to be thinking aloud, mulling the situation. "If this is a disease, as you suggest, Mistress Thornleigh, perhaps the Queen will die of it."

Honor guessed that his thoughts were bending to the political landscape if both Mary and Elizabeth were dead. Next in line for the throne was Mary Stuart, the late King Henry's thirteen-year-old grandniece. Born in Scotland, and called queen there since her infancy, she had been betrothed to the king of France's son when she was a child of six, and had lived in the splendor of the French court ever since.

"The present Queen is our concern, sir," Honor said firmly. "Though ill, she is very much alive. Frances Grenville told me she gets spells of pain but they always pass. And she has much to live for. A kingdom. And future pregnancies."

"But, good Lord, how will she manage things when the truth is known?" Sir William said. "She cannot keep up this deception for much longer. And when the truth becomes public, just imagine. She'll be an object of ridicule. To her people—to all of Europe."

"Exactly," Honor said. "Monsieur de Noailles thinks things will go back to where they were, but I cannot agree. Nothing will be the same. No woman can go through what the Queen is enduring—and *will* endure, publicly—and remain unchanged. It will devastate her. And a woman in despair, a humiliated and cornered queen—"

"Could be a dangerous creature," said Sir William.

"This queen is already unstable," she added. "Besotted with her husband and fanatical about her mission for God." As these tumultuous thoughts distilled into one, she felt a thump of fear. "It could drive her mad."

Sir William looked as though he was thinking precisely what she was, and dreading it. Who would Mary lash out at in the full fury of her despair? Elizabeth.

She rode as hard as she could, but her mare was old and her gunshot wound plagued her and she did not reach the palace until long after dark. When she hurried into the Princess's bedchamber, panting, Elizabeth was gone. A young maid, no more than fourteen, was weeping in the gloom. Candlelight shadows writhed over her face. Just minutes ago, she said, the soldiers had come for her mistress.

It's happened. "Where are they taking her?"

The girl sobbed. Honor shook her by the shoulders. *"Where?"*

"I know not!" she wailed. "They just . . . barged in and . . . the last thing she said was, 'Pray for me, Margery.' "

Honor dashed to the window. The room overlooked the rear garden and in the moonlight she could see the troop of the Queen's guards, eight of them, marching down the cinder path that bisected the garden, two holding torches to light their way. Elizabeth walked in the middle unsteadily, like someone condemned.

Honor left the sobbing maid and ran out.

She caught up with the troop as they marched, their boots crunching the gravel, their torch flames twisting in the wind. "Wait!" she cried. "I beg you, wait!"

Elizabeth turned, her face as white as the moonlight.

Honor caught up with the captain. "I must attend Her Grace," she said, breathless from running, her wound afire. She showed him her badge. "It is her right!"

The captain stopped the troop. Conceding, though reluctantly, he jerked his head, motioning her to join Elizabeth. Honor flung out her arms to embrace Elizabeth, but the captain thrust his sword between them. "You will not touch her."

They started to march again, the two women side by side. Honor would stay with her as long as she could—all the way to the end. But where were they taking her? Past the end of the garden lay the river, the wharf, boats. Downstream, past the night-dark fields and villages, lay London. In London, the Tower.

"I should have listened to you . . . my letter," Elizabeth whispered, her voice as hollow as Honor's hope. She looked like a terrified child bewildered by an inexplicable punishment. "Will she kill me . . . for a letter?"

They reached the end of the garden and the guards turned. Not to the river then, Honor realized. To a lockup somewhere on the grounds? Or—a far worse horror—a secret palace scaffold? *Summary execution.*

Elizabeth seemed to guess at that horror, too, and gasped. Her footsteps became erratic, her breaths shallow. Her eyelids fluttered as though she might faint. Honor's arm circled her waist to steady her, defying the captain. "Have pity, sir, and stop," she said. "My lady is ill!"

He glared over his shoulder at her and did not stop. But neither did he force her to let go of Elizabeth. They were turning again, taking a path that led back to the palace, to the east wing. Straight ahead lay a flight of stairs. Honor and Elizabeth exchanged a wondering glance. These were the private outer stairs to the royal apartments. The forward guards started up the steps. Honor and Elizabeth followed, the rear guard at their heels.

The antechamber was deserted and lay in gloom, a few low candles guttering. No duchesses now, no ladies-in-waiting, not even a maid to refresh the candles. The room's shadows seemed to shrink in fear as the guards stomped through. They halted before the Queen's bedchamber door. The captain knocked.

"Come." The Queen's voice. Strong and low, in command.

The captain opened the door. He nodded to Elizabeth, telling her to enter. Trembling, she walked in. Honor started to follow. The captain's arm shot out to stop her.

"Let her lady pass," the Queen's voice ordered.

They came into her presence. She sat in a chair, her back straight, her eyes clear, her hair neatly coiffed, though her face was still pale. Honor was astonished at her recovery. Her gown, roomy enough to allow for a baby—and roomy enough to hide the truth— was a sumptuous gold and black brocade. The bedchamber was pleasantly alight with candles, and smelled fragrant with herbs strewn among the fresh rushes that covered the floor. Honor could hardly believe the total transformation from this morning.

Elizabeth moved forward and sank to her knees before her sister. Honor stayed by the door and kneeled, too. The Queen stared at Elizabeth with eyes narrowed in anger, as though trying to decide which accusation to begin with. Honor saw that she held the turquoise and pearl rosary, the one she believed had been her mother's, and there was a restlessness about the way she fingered the beads tightly, jerkily, as though to hold herself back from lashing out. There was a sharp light in her eyes, an impulse to cruelty, restrained.

"What will you say in your defense?" she asked, her tone a cold, quiet dare. "That you have been wrongfully punished?"

Honor saw Elizabeth's shudder. *Defense?* Was there going to be a trial?

Elizabeth's voice quavered as she answered, "I must not say so, if it please Your Majesty, to you."

"Oh yes, so clever. All your answers are so very clever. But what will you say to the world?"

On the scaffold? Elizabeth's terror forced its way out in tears, despite her will to dam them. Honor heard the tears in her voice. "That I am Your Majesty's faithful and loyal servant, and ever will be."

"I would you could swear the same to God. But I will not commit the sacrilege of asking you to, knowing you would to lie to Him as you have done to me."

She sprang up from her chair, eyes ablaze, and hurled the rosary at Elizabeth. It struck her cheek. She gasped. Honor jumped to her feet.

"You plotted with Wyatt!" Mary shouted. "You plotted my death!"

Elizabeth rubbed her cheek, crying quietly, her struggle intensely private, a struggle to stay strong. It tore at Honor's heart to see the girl fighting for her life. "I never did, Your Majesty . . . I swear that I—"

"Enough!" Mary sank back onto her chair as though the explosion of rage had exhausted her. "I will not listen. I care not. I am *done* with you."

Honor felt frozen. Was the Queen sending her sister to her death? Yet that queer gleam in her eye made Honor wonder if she had misjudged what was happening here. Was there something else going on? Something beyond Mary's control?

A scrape sounded across the room. Honor looked past the bed. The sound had come from behind tapestry curtains that divided the room. From inside, a hand pulled the curtain aside. A man stepped out, gorgeously dressed in jeweled black velvet and silver satin.

It was the portrait come to life. The Queen's fair-haired young husband. Philip. Honor dropped to her knees again. The Queen, however, was not surprised by his entrance. She had known all along that he was there.

He sauntered toward his wife, confident, calm. *"Permettez-moi d'accueillir votre soeur, madame."* Allow me to welcome your sister, madam. Honor remembered that he spoke no English, that the Queen had to converse with him in French. He looked down at Elizabeth on her knees. *"Notre soeur,"* he said, as though correcting himself. *Our* sister.

Elizabeth stared up at him in wonder. In fear.

He smiled. *"Très jolie."* Very pretty.

He stepped closer to her and bent and picked up the rosary that Mary had thrown at her. He handed it back to his wife with a look of mild reproach. *"Non plus de cela,"* he told her. No more of that.

Honor's eyes flicked in amazement from him to the Queen. Mary's fury had shriveled, and she herself seemed to have shrunk. She gazed at her husband with spaniel eyes and said, *"Mon seigneur, comme vous voulez."* My lord, as you wish.

Honor could hardly believe it. In one moment this man's presence had transformed the Queen from imperious sovereign into slave.

"My wish?" he said, still speaking in French. "Why, madam, you know it. A son."

Mary's chin trembled as she endured her private humiliation and pain. She raised her hand to grasp his for comfort. He took it and held it. "I pray that God will smile on us with an heir," he said kindly. "If not this time, next time."

He knows, Honor thought in amazement. Knows there is no child. Or at least he suspects it and is going along with the Queen's charade. Does she know that he knows?

"Now," he said, dropping his wife's hand like a pair of gloves, "let us have no more shrill voices. Let our beloved sister henceforth feel your kindness." It was an order, though gently made, and Mary bowed her head, accepting it.

Philip stepped up to Elizabeth and offered her his hand. Mouth agape, she slipped her hand into his. He raised her to her feet. He kissed her softly on one cheek, then on the other. Mary closed her eyes tightly, as though hardly able to bear this further injury.

"The hour is late," Philip said to Elizabeth. "My wife is tired. We will talk another day."

And in that moment Honor knew that the Queen's husband had saved Elizabeth's life.

They sat on the edge of Elizabeth's bed, face-to-face, lost in the wonder of it. The room was still dark but for a single candle. They had no time for candles, or for any other thought beyond the extraordinary thing that had just happened.

"Why would he do it?" Elizabeth was whispering, as though speaking out loud might tempt the gods to snatch away this life-line.

"I think . . ." Honor said, then stopped, still piecing it together. She was whispering, too, but only in case someone might be listening. Noailles had spies, so the imperial ambassador, Renard, almost certainly did as well. "I think he needs you."

Elizabeth frowned, incredulous. "What?"

"Politics. With no baby—"

"A phantom baby," Elizabeth murmured, clearly still overwhelmed by what Honor had explained to her on their hurried way back to her rooms.

"Exactly. With no heir of the Queen's body, you are once again the heir apparent, and he—"

"But I always was. And Philip knew that. So why—"

"Because he's thinking two steps ahead, like the wily Hapsburg prince that he is. He's thinking of his situation if the Queen dies, if not from this malady then perhaps from a childbirth to come. If the Queen kills you and then dies childless, who is next in line for the throne?" She asked it like a good lawyer, knowing the answer.

Elizabeth didn't hesitate. "My cousin, Mary. Queen of the Scots."

"Only it isn't the Scots who worry Philip. Where has your cousin lived since she was a child?"

"In France."

"Betrothed to the French king's son. She has grown up as a beloved part of King Henri's family—"

"Pampered by them like a little pet, I always heard—"

"And soon she'll be his daughter-in-law. No doubt it's the very reason he wanted her for his son, hoping for the day he might see her take the throne of England. With England a vassal state of France, he could control trade. Use England to fight his wars. And confound his enemy, Emperor Charles."

"Philip's father," Elizabeth said, instantly understanding. "So, I'm alive. And, if Philip gets to decide this—"

"Which he obviously does, as we just saw—"

"Then I'll *stay* alive."

For the first time Elizabeth allowed herself to smile. Brave girl, Honor thought. She could have hugged her.

"The question is . . ." Elizabeth paused, thinking, biting at a ragged fingernail.

Honor could practically hear that clever brain at work, weighing, sorting, planning. "The questions is . . . ?"

Elizabeth looked at her, deadly serious. "Am I *free?*"

❧ 10 ❧

News

September–October 1555

Honor was laughing so hard at the actors she couldn't catch her breath. Beside her Adam, too, roared with laughter. They stood in the empty musicians' gallery above the great hall of Hatfield House, looking down at the whole household of Elizabeth's officials and administrators and servants and friends, all of them doubled over, their laughter ringing up to the roof's timbers. Elizabeth sat in the front row, laughing hardest of all.

The trestle tables where everyone ate dinner had been pushed back, and from benches ranged in a semicircle they were watching the foolery on the makeshift stage, where the actors were running around in a fine madness. A buffoon surgeon had tried to pull a patient's tooth with a pair of monstrous tongs while a sly servant tried to rob the suffering patient, and now the surgeon chased the patient and the patient chased the servant and the servant chased a pretty boy-actor playing a maid, and the hall rocked with laughter at their antics.

"Look out!" Elizabeth shrieked as the servant's partner in crime tossed an orange peel underfoot in the path of the patient. The patient slipped on it and tumbled, the tooth popped out, the surgeon dove and caught it, the maid whirled around, the lusting servant plowed into her, knocking her down on her back, and fell on top of her.

The audience howled. Adam threw back his head and laughed. Honor laughed so hard she had to pull out her handkerchief to wipe her eyes. After the months of shared captivity with Elizabeth it felt so good to laugh. The Princess was free. She was back at her beloved Hatfield House where she had spent most of her childhood, and all of her loyal staff were with her.

Another five minutes and the play was over. Elizabeth, clapping, jumped up and skipped to the edge of the stage to talk to the actors, who grinned and wiped sweat from their brows. Several of Elizabeth's household people followed her, handing goblets of wine up to the actors.

Honor sighed, dabbing at the last of her mirthful tears. Adam continued to gaze down at Elizabeth as she chatted with people left and right, making them smile.

"They love her," he said.

Honor heard the warmth in his voice. Amazing, she thought, the effect Elizabeth had on people. The more lowly their station, the more passionate their admiration, from fishwife to butcher to carpenter's apprentice. Honor believed it was because they sensed her genuine interest in them. "Ah, you should have seen it when we left London," she told Adam. "The people went mad for her. Cheering, and rushing to give her cakes and flowers. She would stop and banter with them, which just brought more people running. It happened at every village. Took us days to get here."

Honor was quite sure no European monarch or prince showed such affection for their common people. In fact, they would be shocked by Elizabeth's easy familiarity. A fine quality in her, in Honor's estimation, and one Elizabeth had earned the hard way— the terrors she had endured had given her an understanding of the insecurities most people lived with. Though a princess, she knew what it was to be friendless, fearful of the future, and at the mercy of rulers. People saw that in her, and it touched their hearts. Just as she has touched mine, Honor thought. The girl now felt as dear to her as her own daughter.

Well, almost. What joy she had felt when she'd read Isabel's letter back in July, with the news that she had been delivered of a fine, healthy son. Nicolas, they had named him, in honor of

Richard's late father, Nicholas, but with the Spanish spelling. He would be four months old now. It had taken Isabel's letter over two months to reach England from Peru. Nicolas had been born on May Day.

"Who's that?" Adam asked.

"Who?"

"That oaf with his hand on her shoulder."

Honor followed his gaze down to Elizabeth. "Oh, that's Doctor Dee. Mathematician and philosopher. Her friend."

"And that fellow? The one speaking in her ear?"

"Roger Ascham. Her former tutor. Another good friend."

"What about the one at her back? Black beard."

"A new friend, Senor Castiglione. He's teaching her Italian."

"An awful lot of them."

"What?"

"Friends."

"Well, naturally." Honor was settling herself down on the bench, tucking her handkerchief back in her sleeve. "She's been alone for so long."

He looked over his shoulder at her. "She's had you."

"Hardly the same. It's young people she needs." She patted the spot beside her on the bench. "Come, Adam, I want all the news." He had arrived just as the play was starting and she had whisked him up to the empty gallery to watch, but also to get him alone for a few minutes. She was hungry for news of home. "How is your father? How is everyone? Tell me all."

"I can do better than that." He was pulling letters out of his pocket. "One from Isabel. One from Father." He handed them to her.

She tore open Isabel's and read it quickly, gobbling the words. Carlos had been promoted in the viceroy's horse guard. Baby Nicolas could now hold a rattle. Isabel had made friends with a captain's wife and had become so fluent in Spanish she was writing poetry in it. Honor sat back, sated by wolfing down what she needed to know—that they were alive and thriving. She would read the letter again later, slowly and indulgently, to savor all its tastes.

She opened Richard's letter.

> *My dear Honor,*
>   *You will be glad to know that the Flemish weavers we
> hired are settling in well and are fine craftsmen all. I be-
> lieve that paying for their passage and settlement will
> prove to be a good investment. I may hire more if Walton
> can get to Antwerp before Michaelmas to arrange it.*

He went on to tell about a delay in delivery of the wall paneling
she had ordered, and the death of his niece Cecily's grandfather,
and a sick hunting dog, and the wedding of one of their maids to a
Colchester tanner, leaving the housekeeper on the lookout for a
replacement.

> *Here's the real news, my love. Lord Powys and Sir
> Nicholas Graves stopped in yesterday and stayed to sup
> and they told me Henry Jernigan is dead. Seems he caught
> a flux in Ireland and was gone the next day. That leaves
> his seat in Parliament vacant just as an urgent bill is
> coming up that touches all our rights, as Powys and
> Graves put it. The upshot of their talk was that Powys has
> asked me to stand in Jernigan's place. Powys thinks it a
> fine idea, and Graves seconded it, and they asked for my
> answer, yay or nay, and when they told me the dangers of
> the Queen's bill I was ready then and there to tell them yay.
> That made three men saying the same thing, which is a
> foolish way to weigh an issue. I wish you had been here to
> argue the point. I told Lord Powys I would think on it
> and send him my answer. If I do say yay, the Grenvilles
> are sure to howl, but they have no claim to the seat now
> that John Grenville has moved up to sit with the Lords.
> His brother lives too far away, in Northumberland.*
>   *The Queen's bill is called the Exiles Bill, so you will
> have some idea of where her interest lies. If passed, it
> would allow the Crown to confiscate the property of any
> Englishman who has fled abroad. Protestants, of course,*

are her intended quarry, particularly the hundreds of families in the Low Countries. Powys left me reams of paper on the issue, which I will study before I decide. In the meantime keep this knowledge unto yourself alone. I have not told Adam. But write to let me know your mind and send your letter home with him.

Trusting that you are in good health and steadfast in your service to Her Grace the Princess, I commend me unto her.
Your loving husband,
Richard

"Good heavens," she murmured, excited.

"Hmmm?"

She looked up from the letter. Adam stood with his back to her, arms resting on the railing, still gazing down at Elizabeth.

"Nothing. A delay in getting my wall paneling." It was not like Richard to keep such important news from Adam, but she thought she understood why. Ever since Frances Grenville had roped him into her project of rebuilding the priory in Colchester, she often called him to the site to discuss it whenever she was home from court. It would not do if Adam inadvertently let this news slip to Frances before Richard was ready. *The Grenvilles are sure to howl.*

Let them, Honor thought. The Commons seat was virtually Lord Powys's to bestow. He was the largest landholder in the county—much of that land being former monastic holdings he had bought from King Henry—and the mayor of Colchester and all the leading citizens followed his lead. Except, of course, the Grenvilles.

Richard must accept, she thought, her excitement building as she folded the letters and put them in her pocket. In the House of Commons he would be a part of the very sinews of government. More important, and definitely more urgent, this Exiles Bill sounded threatening. A blatant money grab by the Queen. One that would immediately impoverish all their Protestant friends abroad. And it might be just a first step. If she was targeting the wealth of Protestant exiles now, how long until she targeted suspected Protestant sympathizers right here in England? Honor shuddered, thinking how with a pen stroke of Parliament she and Richard could lose everything they were working so hard to rebuild. The Queen had to be stopped. Parliament had been called for October. It would convene in five weeks.

She looked up at Adam, who was still at the railing watching the milling household. He had come for a quick visit after meeting with a merchant in nearby Hereford about investing in Adam's shipbuilding venture. An unsuccessful meeting, he had told her when he'd arrived—seems the man had recently suffered some financial loss and was no longer interested. Tomorrow Adam planned to ride home. But Honor was thinking it might be wise to keep him away from Frances Grenville for a while.

"There are some people here you should meet," she said, joining him at the railing to watch the hubbub below. Servants had brought out platters of fruit and cheese and more wine, and Thomas Parry had started playing his lute, and the hall rang with chatter and laughter and music. "Powerful people."

"Oh?" Adam said. She could see he was barely listening to her. He had eyes only for Elizabeth.

"You might consider staying for a few days. Get to know some of these men. There's always a group out hunting or hawking. You could sound out a few of them about investing."

He looked at her as if she had said something remarkable. As if he wished he'd thought of it himself. "I could, couldn't I?"

"The more the merrier with the Princess. She's making up for lost time."

He was all attention. "She rides with them?"

"Almost every day the sun shines."

"I'll stay."

"Good. I'll introduce you to a few people before I leave."

"Leave? Where are you going?"

She smiled and kissed his cheek. "Home."

Frances was torn between anxiety about Adam and anxiety for the Queen. "Urgent business in London"—that was what had kept Adam from their meeting at the priory in the spring, so his note back in May had said, and in the months since then he had cancelled two more meetings, one just two days ago. It grieved her so much, she had sent her steward to investigate. What "urgent business" could now be keeping him from her?

But the Queen. Poor, dear Mary. Her claim on Frances was greater at the moment. She was weeping over the letter from her husband. Frances did not know how to comfort her.

"The abdication arrangements could take months," Mary said, lowering the letter and lowering her head in misery. "Oh, when will he return to me?"

Frances reached across the table and took her friend's hand in solidarity. Emperor Charles, the most powerful monarch on earth, ruler of Spain and the Netherlands and the limitless New World, was stepping down and passing on his lands to his heirs, giving Philip the choicest of these, the Kingdom of the Netherlands. But divesting himself of half the world was taking time. The official ceremonies were dragging on and on.

"The King will surely be back soon after Michaelmas," Frances said to bolster Mary's hope. It still felt strange to call him king, but Mary insisted on it since it was Philip's wish. He was her lord and husband. "He will want to join you for the opening of Parliament."

Mary looked across the room at the life-sized portrait of him. Her face darkened and an angry growl came from her throat. She jumped up from her chair and ran at the portrait, arms raised, and pounded her fist against the canvas. Philip's image continued to gaze out over her head, oblivious. "Dorothy!" she shouted.

The young lady-in-waiting appeared at the door, looking nervous at the Queen's harsh tone. "Yes, Your Majesty?"

"Take this picture away! I will look at it no longer!"

Dorothy glanced at Frances, bewildered. In answer, Frances shook her head to the girl: *Wait.* "Your Grace," Frances suggested, "it will take some time to bring in the workmen at this late hour. Perhaps we should leave the portrait for now."

Mary lowered her arm and her head drooped again. "Yes. Yes, leave it. I would not have it moved." Frances shooed Dorothy away. Mary came back to her chair and sank into it. "I would have him near me." Her face crumpled as she tried to hold back tears.

Frances again reached out and took her hand. "Courage, my dear," she said, and Mary nodded bleakly, suffering in silence.

The Queen *had* shown courage, Frances thought. All through the hellish summer. Back in April, still happily awaiting the baby's birth, she'd had her secretaries write letters announcing her safe delivery, ready to send to the pope, the emperor, the kings of France and Hungary and Bohemia. The date of the birth had been left blank, as was the sex of the child. Mary had signed the letters herself. Then came May, and the awful anxiety of waiting, and Frances suspected Mary's horrible mistake. By June people were sniggering that the Queen was apparently eleven months pregnant. Their insolence appalled Frances, but she knew by then that her friend was tragically deluded. All through July they had waited for a miracle. But no miracle came.

Finally, at the end of July, the household received orders that the Queen was moving so that Hampton Court could be cleaned. It was an unstated acknowledgment that her confinement was over. The bored, impatient inhabitants of the palace heaved a sigh of relief. Philip's attendants had already been leaving for weeks. The noblewomen who had been shut up with Mary and Frances for three months swiftly ordered their servants to pack their trunks and left for their own summer houses. On the third day of August the Queen and King quietly moved to Oatlands, a modest manor house outside London. The ordeal was over.

But Mary's agony was not. After that soul-wrenching humiliation, she then had to watch her husband leave England. Frances saw her trying to be cheerful and dignified, saying good-bye to him in front of scores of courtiers as he and his retinue boarded ship at Gravesend. But as soon as she was alone with Frances, her tears flowed. The King had promised that his stay in Flanders would be brief, and indeed he had left behind most of his vast personal household, including his Spanish soldiers, his Burgundian cavalry, his physicians and chapel clergy, most of his horses and grooms, and even the pages of his chamber. But as the weeks passed, all these members of his entourage left, one after another. Ships carrying Philip's personal effects sailed out of English ports every day.

Mary took some comfort in the presence and support of Cardinal Pole, who moved his lodgings into the palace. He was her cousin, and Mary loved him. He was the symbol of her proudest accomplishment, England's reunion with Rome. This alone had kept her strong—her duty to God, her avowed battle against heresy and wickedness. Frances was in awe of her dear friend's determination. But she feared that the King had little intention of returning to England this year, or even the next, if at all. The King had abandoned his wife.

There was a soft knock on the door. Dorothy poked her head in. "Mistress Grenville? Your steward is come to see you."

She practically ran down the corridor away from the Queen's apartments. Dyer was waiting for her in her private chamber. Hurrying in, she shut the door behind her. He turned from the fire that crackled in the grate, still rubbing his hands to warm them. His face was pale.

Dread clutched Frances's heart. "Dead?"

"No, madam, he is alive."

Relief overwhelmed her. *Thank God.*

But the next moment anger pinched. "Then where is he?" Yet again, Adam had not come after saying he would—a court banquet two days ago in honor of the visiting king of Poland. He had seemed keen when she'd extended the invitation, offering to introduce him to many gentlemen of high rank at the affair. He had promised to come. But she had ended up sitting alone. "Where?" she demanded again.

Dyer heaved a tight sigh. "You will not be pleased, madam."

Not a good beginning. "Go on."

"He is in Hertfordshire."

"What's in Hertfordshire?"

"Hatfield. Princess Elizabeth."

"Ah," she said, relaxing. "He is visiting his stepmother." The Thornleigh woman had persuaded the Queen to let her attend Elizabeth—or, as Frances always thought of her, the whore's daughter—though she did not think Honor Thornleigh's reports had been much use to the Queen. It was merely her low way of worming into Mary's good graces.

"Yes and no," Dyer said carefully.

Frances was tiring of this cat and mouse game. She went to the sideboard where her maid had left mulled wine. "Get to the point, man," she said, pouring herself a goblet full.

"My informant in the house told me that Mistress Thornleigh left Hatfield six days ago. Master Adam stayed."

Frances drank some wine, eyeing him with growing alarm. His tone told her there was much to be alarmed about. "And what's he been doing all this time?"

"Hunting. Hawking."

"There's more. I can tell."

"Madam, I am your faithful servant. Please remember that. What I have to tell you, I do so out of the greatest sense of duty to—"

"Yes, yes, man. Out with it."

"He rides out hunting with the company of ladies and gentlemen who follow the Princess, but it is not the deer he has his eye on. It is the Princess."

"Hoping for her notice? For some preferment?"

He shook his head solemnly. "For love, madam. For sheer love."

Frances shivered in London's morning fog the next day as she rode with Dyer under the arch of Moorgate, heading for Finsbury Fields. She barely glanced up at the heads of rebels impaled on pikes atop the arch. Twenty months after Wyatt's rebellion the shriveled heads remained as a warning to any would-be traitor. Frances had not slept, had thrashed in anguish all night, and now she felt almost dizzy from fatigue and the unrelenting heartache.

Adam and the heretic Princess. The whore's daughter. Lewd, blasphemous, and almost certainly a traitor. Frances had wanted to tear her hair. The only thing that kept her from it was Dyer's assurance that Adam had not become intimate with the object of his desire. "My informant in the house tells me that Master Adam loves, but loves from afar," he had said. Of course, Frances thought. The whore's daughter kept so many men around her that every new one had to join the queue. That was something. Adam had not touched the trollop. Not yet.

Not ever, she vowed as she left the Moorgate arch behind her. The fields outside the city walls were busy. In Moorfields, to the right, laundresses spread shirts and smocks and household linens on the grass, waiting for the autumn sun to burn off the last of the fog. Past them, closer to Bishopsgate, were tenting grounds where apprentices stretched wool cloth, tapping hammers at the tenter-hooks. Ahead, past grazing cattle, rose the windmills of Finsbury Fields, where the shouts of men drifted from the archery butts. Through the trees and the last shreds of fog Frances could see them, a troop of twenty or so. Their shouting was exuberant and good-natured, young men taking pleasure in their prowess.

Just the kind of man Frances was looking for. These belonged to her brother's troop, the famed Grenville Archers. John had commanded them at the battle of Ludgate, and for playing this crucial role in saving London from Wyatt, the grateful Queen had made him a baron.

Frances halted her horse and looked among the archers for their young captain, Giles Sturridge. She spotted him letting an arrow fly. It pierced the straw target with a satisfying *whomp,* dead center. A tall, lusty fellow of twenty or so, he grinned as he accepted the praise and backslaps of his mates. He knew he was the best of the best. Frances had heard John say as much, but had wanted to see for herself. Even better, she had heard from Dyer that Sturridge had once been arrested for molesting a girl and had spent time in jail for it.

Exactly the man she wanted.

She turned to Dyer. "Tell him eight o'clock."

Church bells were tolling the nightly curfew all over London when Frances left her supper plate of roasted partridge with olives and followed the maid to the parlor. Except for the servants, Frances was alone at the Grenvilles' London house on Lombard Street, and it was quiet except for one of her brother's hounds snoring in the hallway. John and Arabella were visiting the Duchess of Norfolk at her house on the Strand. Their children, with the governesses, were asleep upstairs.

Giles Sturridge, waiting in the parlor, stood twisting his cap in his hands. He bowed when Frances came in, a little uneasy at being summoned, she saw. No doubt he felt out of his depth in the elegant surroundings. But there was also a look of interest in his clear eyes. He knew he would not be called here for a trifle. She admired that, his sharp mind.

"I understand you have no wife, Master Sturridge."

He blinked. "No, my lady. I mean yes—no wife."

"With no family, you could embrace the adventure of starting a new life in some other land."

He frowned, not understanding. "My lady?"

"I am going to pay you a great deal of money." She slipped a ruby ring, a very costly jewel, off her finger and held it out to him. "This is a mere token of what is to come. Please take it."

He stared at the ring in astonishment, then at her, obviously lost.

"If you carry out the commission I have for you," she said, "I will give you enough money to live comfortably in France for the rest of your life without ever working another day."

Wonderment filled his eyes. And a flicker of excitement. *Good,* she thought. "If you refuse the commission, however," she said calmly, "I will tell my brother that you molested me, and he will have you hanged."

11

The Princess's Defender

October 1555

"You underestimate your fellow sea captains," Elizabeth said to Adam. "Some have traveled far. Look at Hawkins of Plymouth—he sailed to Brazil. The Countess of Sussex has a popinjay he brought back. He's sailed to the Guinea coast of Africa, too, and brought back ivory. And there's Thomas Wyndham—what about his Barbary trade?"

"It's all just coastal roving—limited," Adam said. He tugged the reins to pull his horse back a little, keeping side by side with the Princess on her mare. They were riding in through the gates of Hatfield after a day of hawking—a hot, sultry day, though late in autumn. The whole company of Elizabeth's guests, almost twenty tired gentlemen and ladies, trotted in behind them, crossing a drift of spongy, fallen leaves that muffled the horses' hooves. "Spain and Portugal have monopolized the luxury trade for too long and taken the lion's share," he said, warming to his subject. "We have to become lions, too."

"How? Where?"

"Persia, for starters. I believe we can get there overland through the northeast route via Russia. Cut out the middlemen, the Venetians and the Arabs, and establish our own trade thoroughfares to Persia."

"If that's for starters, then what, pray tell, is left?"

"The New World."

Her eyes widened in delight. "But, it's off-limits."

"Only on paper." The artificial demarcation had always seemed absurd to Adam. Decades ago Spain and Portugal had signed a treaty, sanctioned by the pope, that carved up trading and colonizing rights between them, excluding all other nations. The fiat was both tyrannical and ludicrous. Who knew what lands lay out there?

"That's what I feel," Elizabeth said in a conspiratorial whisper. "What care we for a mere pope's injunction?"

It thrilled him. How bold she was. "My lady, can you imagine an English fleet plying the Atlantic? It would take some foresight from our government, and a little encouragement to merchant adventurers in the form of prize money. But with that, I believe our little nation could send trading expeditions to all corners of the world. We could become master of the seas. I've been dreaming of a new type of galleon, faster and leaner and more—"

"Yes, yes," she said, suddenly sharp. "Your ship. Its construction. I know." Then, less sharply but with a new coldness, "We will talk later, sir." They had reached the stables and she turned her horse's head and briskly moved away. Three grooms ran to meet her.

Adam watched her go, not sure what had happened between them—the sudden chill that cut short their friendly discussion—but sensing it was his fault. The rest of the company trotted in around them, making the stable courtyard ring with the clack of hooves and the jangle of harnesses and the shouts of grooms. A groom dashed up to Elizabeth with a stool for her to step down from the saddle. Adam watched her hand over the reins, and noticed how everyone's eyes always darted to her. Gentlemen, ladies, servants, no matter what anyone in this crowd was doing—dismounting, unsaddling, strolling away, chattering—all attention continually returned to the Princess to check what *she* was doing.

They all want something from her, he thought. Positions, posts, preferment, either for themselves or their kin. People were constantly wangling, all very charmingly, for posts as stewards of her estates or chamberlains in her houses, or for other jobs on her administrative staff. Some wanted her influence to sway a judge in a court case. Others wanted introductions. Others, cold cash. He had known it, of course—had heard all these requests and more in his eight days here—but he'd never felt it so clearly as at this moment. Because he realized that the sudden chill in her *was* his fault. He had asked her earlier, on the ride out, if she would like to invest in his ship, his request as blatant as the appeals of all these other questing fellows.

But for him it had just been a way to talk to her, be close to her. He would find the cash to pay the debts on his ship somehow, even without a farthing from her. Her interest in what he was doing— that's what he wanted. Her warm, intense awareness. He hated to think she considered him the same as these hungry hangers-on.

He had to let her know the truth.

He swung out of the saddle, tossed the reins to a servant boy, and pushed through the people, heading straight for Elizabeth. Dismounting, too, she set her foot on the step the groom had set in place, then hopped to the ground. A dew of perspiration damp- ened the coppery hair at her temples, and with one gloved hand she absently pushed at the edge of her chemise collar, open to her breastbone, to cool her neck.

Adam was a few strides away from her when he caught a motion from the corner of his eye. Something so swift . . .

"My lady!" he yelled.

She turned.

Adam didn't think. He lunged for her, face-to-face, gripped her shoulders and pushed her back against her horse, shielding her with his body. He felt her startled breath warm on his throat.

The wallop to his back was like a cudgel. It slammed him hard against Elizabeth. He heard a dull crack of bone, felt it splinter in- side him. Fire erupted in his chest. She gasped, looking up into his eyes.

Men were shouting, running. Adam staggered back a step. He looked down at the hand's breadth of space between him and Elizabeth. Three beads of blood glistened on the white skin at her breastbone—a scrape the size of a fingernail paring. An arrow tip jutted from the top of Adam's rib cage, the metal barb glisten- ing red.

He held his breath, because to breathe was agony. His vision went as dark as the sky in a squall at sea. His legs gave way.

He felt her tremble as she struggled to hold him up. He wanted to stay with her but his leg muscles felt severed. He felt a moment of fury at the thing invading his body and taking him from her, and then he slid down, sinking into darkness.

The choir of St. Botolph's intoned its plaintive chant. The faithful of Colchester stood listening with bowed heads. Father Percy shuffled up the steps to the pulpit to begin his sermon. The congregation raised their heads.

Roses, that's what Honor was thinking about. She had deadheaded the drooping blooms of autumn as soon as she had arrived home, and now she was pondering a further expansion of the rose arbor next spring. Maybe transplant the foxgloves and irises to nearer the pond, and that way she could extend the rose trellis all the way to the house. Roses climbing right under her library window, that would be lovely. Imagine the scent on a sultry summer evening when the daylight to read stretched almost into night.

The choir finished and Father Percy began to drone. A prayer for the Queen's health, then St. Paul's Epistle to the Galatians. Honor stifled a groan. How Christians loved to promote Paul as the Jew who converted to Christ.

She glanced at Richard beside her, his head bowed over his prayer book. She smiled when she saw why. He had slipped a paper in between the pages, a letter from his Antwerp agent, and was reading it. They both found Sundays a trial. Necessary, though. They attended regularly, as was the law, always partaking of mass. Honor had even contributed a costly pair of silver candlesticks for the altar. She trusted it was enough.

They were near the rear of the congregation, and she glanced diagonally across the heads toward the front rank where Baron John Grenville and his wife, Lady Arabella, listened intently to Father Percy's words. Frances, beside them, looked quite engrossed, too. Despite Frances's partnership with Adam—a situation that Honor still found odd—the baron hadn't deigned to speak to Honor since she'd been home, beyond a barely civil

"Good day" at church, which was fine with her. There were friendlier faces in the community. Like Lord and Lady Powys, situated
closer to the pulpit, both listening with inscrutable expressions
honed to hide their Protestant inclinations. What a fine country of
hypocrites we've become, Honor thought. The Queen's brutal religious policy demanded the deception. Forced to choose between
death at the stake and the pretense of piety, what rational person
would not choose hypocrisy?

She cleared her head of such galling thoughts and let her mind
drift back to her garden, and planning for spring. Time to prune
back the purple mulberry bushes bordering the swath of daffodils
down to the water meadows. She had already had Baird, her gardener, plant ten dozen more daffodil bulbs. She loved April's riot
of yellow. One could never have too many daffodils.

The church door banged open. Honor turned her head to look.
Ned, her young footman, hurried in. A few other people in the
congregation glanced around, but latecomers were a regular interruption almost every Sunday and in a moment all eyes turned back
to Father Percy.

Except Honor's. Ned was heading straight for her and Richard.
His normally cheerful face looked so disturbed, she knew at once
this could not be good news.

He reached her side. His whisper was a rasp. "There's been a . . .
it's Master Adam . . . he's . . ."

"He's what, Ned? Has something happened?"

"Something terrible . . . Master Adam . . . he's—"

Dead. As he said the word the priest's voice thundered in his sermon, and all Honor could think was *I heard it wrong.* This stone
vault we're in twists the sound.

Richard leaned in, looking curious. "What?" He hadn't heard
the word. "What's happened?" Heads turned all around them, he
had spoken so loudly.

Honor gripped his arm. *Don't. If Ned doesn't say the word, it didn't
happen.*

But he said it again. *Dead.*

The motions of Honor's mind halted, as still as a frozen stream.
She could not recall why she was standing in this stone vault. She

looked at Richard. Saw the fearsome word drill into him. *No. No. This is not happening.*

"Where? How?" Richard said, his voice a croak.

Hatfield, Ned told them. An assassin on the dovecote roof. Crossbow. Tried to kill the Princess. Master Adam jumped in the way. The arrow went right through him. And he fell. *Dead.*

It punched the breath from Honor. *My fault! I told him to stay there!*

She felt Richard's hand grope hers. She turned to him, and the anguish on his face buried her in a panic so crushing that she had to look away, toward the altar. The crucifix gleamed, the man impaled there twisting in agony. Hot bile rose in her throat. She felt she would be sick.

Voices hummed like hungry insects buzzing the news across the congregation. More people turned, and the voices grew to a drone of horrified excitement that rushed all the way up to the pulpit. The priest stopped his sermon. He looked in consternation across the backs of heads.

Honor and Richard shared a glance of agonized agreement. *We must go to him.* Still clutching each other's hands they started to push through the bodies. They had almost reached the door when they heard a woman shriek, "No!"

Honor staggered on the spot and glanced back. Frances Grenville was running toward them.

"Stop!" she screamed.

They shared another look—what did the woman mean by this affront?—and then again, in tortured agreement, they turned and made for the door.

Frances caught Honor by the arm and jerked her to a halt. "Tell me it's not true!"

Honor stared at her in shock, the woman's hand painfully squeezing her arm. Richard said, his voice hoarse, "Madam, our son is . . . please, let my wife go." He pried Frances's hand off Honor and again they turned to leave.

But she lurched around them and cut them off, a wild look in her eyes as she spread her arms wide to corral them. "Let me come with you! I must see him . . . alive or dead . . . I must—"

"Take pity, madam," Honor said, her mind thrashing in confusion at the woman's behavior, her heart bleeding. "Leave us be to—"

"I beg you!" Frances cried. She fell to her knees. Honor and Richard stepped back, recoiling. Frances clutched Honor's skirt and cried, "Take me with you! We'll use our horses, they are fresh. I *must* be with him!"

They stared, dumbfounded. The woman was mad.

"Frances!" John Grenville pushed through to his sister. "What are you doing? Get up. Let these people go." He looked at Richard. "They are grieving."

Honor saw the gleam in Grenville's eyes, a sadistic glint of satisfaction at Richard's suffering and hers. "My condolences, sir. My sister and I know what it is to grieve for a loved one." He was enjoying their pain.

Richard groped for Honor's hand and pulled her away from the Grenvilles. As they stumbled out the door she could hear Frances wailing.

Soldiers in half-armor were posted in the torch-lit darkness around Hatfield House. Sir William St. Loe, captain of the Princess's guard, waited on horseback to meet Honor and Richard as their horses plodded through the gate at three in the morning. St. Loe was a hardened soldier who had done distinguished service in Ireland under young King Edward, but as he escorted them in silence to the house he looked grim-faced with shame at the tragedy that had occurred on his watch. Honor looked up at the red brick walls that loomed dark in the moonless night, the windows black voids except for a few where candles flickered. Something dying screamed from the forest. Then a howl from the victor. A wolf?

"My deepest sympathy, sir, madam," St. Loe said, his ramrod posture at odds with the quiver of emotion in his voice. "I honor Master Adam Thornleigh."

Neither of them could muster the voice to thank him for this touch of kindness.

A soldier with a torch lighted their way up the stone steps. Had the forbidding stone portico always been at this entrance? Honor could not recall. The exhausting, bone-jarring ride had left her mind too numb to think clearly. But the merciless memories were all too clear. Adam at nine, sailing his first little boat, a skiff he had slapped together from leftover lumber at Richard's fulling ponds, the sail a linen sheet he'd cajoled from the housekeeper. Adam at thirteen, buying a gingerbread doll for baby Isabel at the fairground in Brussels. Adam, just last year, striding into their Antwerp house with a grin, thinner and with a new beard, back from his voyage to Russia.

They reached the top step. She hesitated. She was not sure she could find the strength to go in and see his body. She glanced at Richard. His face, gaunt in the torchlight, broke her heart.

Preparing to face the ordeal, they again clasped hands. His hand was so cold!

The soldier knocked. The door opened and candlelight flooded them. Two guards inside stepped back to make way as Elizabeth hurried to greet Honor. "Mistress Thornleigh," she said, her voice low with feeling.

Honor felt dread cram up in her throat. She could not swallow. "My lady—" She licked her dry lips. "This is my husband, Richard."

He bowed, stiff with his own dread. "Your Grace."

Elizabeth reached out both hands, offering one to each of them, a gesture of such sweet sympathy that Honor had to fight not to weep. She and Richard stood rock still, too numb to respond.

"I am so, so sorry," Elizabeth murmured. "How the villain got past my guards, I know not. He climbed to the dovecote roof. Your son was the only one who saw him."

They listened, eager for scraps about Adam even as the details savaged them.

"He saved my life, of that I have no doubt," Elizabeth said. "I am in your debt, and ever will be."

Richard managed to ask, "May we see him?"

Elizabeth frowned. "Are you sure? Now?"

Oh God, Honor thought, *is he so mutilated?*

"Now," Richard said, a croak. "Please."

"Yes, of course. Come. I'll take you myself."

She led them. A staircase. A long gallery gloomy with flickering rushlights in wall sconces. A harsh smell of lye soap. At the end of the gallery, a closed door. Elizabeth opened it and stepped inside. The room was stuffy, and dark but for a candle on the windowsill, its lonely flame standing as still as death. Richard stopped in the doorway. Honor saw a bed. On the bed, a body. She heard a breath dragged from Richard, a sound shuddering with pain. His face was white. She slid her arm around his waist for support. "My love," she whispered.

They shuffled forward in the unwilling steps of a funeral march. They reached the bed. Adam lay stretched out, eyes closed, lips blanched. A blanket covered him from his toes to his neck.

Richard shocked Honor—he reached for the cover and flung it off his son. She understood, though. He needed to see. Adam lay shirtless in his breeches, a linen bandage wound around his chest. A massive bruise spread out from under the bandage. A small, bright spot of blood had wept through the cloth. Honor stared at the blood. It looked still wet. Fresh. How . . . ?

Richard suddenly turned to her as though unable to bear the sight. "Honor," he whispered, "I think I'm going mad. I can see him . . . breathe."

Elizabeth said, apologizing, "I assure you, this dressing will be changed. I allowed the doctor to go and get some sleep, but he'll be back at dawn."

They both stared at her. *Doctor?*

"He's alive!" Richard blurted.

Honor gasped so hard it pinched her throat.

Elizabeth said, perplexed, "You didn't know?"

"We were told—" Honor felt Richard grab her hand with such fierceness it was pain. They looked at each other, and her tears broke forth, a dam bursting. She leaned against him and wept in sheer joy. He threw his arm around her shoulders and squeezed so tightly she knew it was to keep himself from weeping, too.

Elizabeth regarded them with a sad smile. She said gently, as though to prepare them, "Yes, good people, he is alive. But for how long, we know not."

Honor's wild joy died. But cautious hope took its place. Richard was already studying Adam's face for hopeful signs. Honor sat on the bed's edge and touched the back of her hand to Adam's forehead. He was burning up.

Elizabeth, looking on, said, "The doctors fear his fever has lasted too long."

"He's young. He's strong," said Richard.

"I've had three doctors examine him, sir. They all agree. They also warn of the danger of infection."

They spoke in hushed tones, as though to keep Adam from hearing. If only he could, Honor thought. *Don't leave us, Adam. Please.* "We are so grateful, my lady," she said, "for the care you have given him, calling in your doctors."

She reached for the basin of water on the nightstand, dipped a fresh linen cloth into the water and squeezed it, then gently set the cool cloth on Adam's brow. Richard took a stopper the doctor had left beside a pitcher of water and filled it, then came to the other side of the bed, sat on the edge and dripped water drops onto Adam's parched lips.

Elizabeth said, her voice tinged with wondering admiration, "I doubt not that kind parents will do him more good than ever doctors could."

Honor glanced up at her. Elizabeth's remarkable parents had stamped her life, but she had never really known them. Her mother had been executed when Elizabeth was three. She had rarely seen her father, the King.

"Doctor Rufus comes back at dawn. Until then I will leave your son in your care," Elizabeth said. "I have had the room beside him prepared for you." It showed a subtlety of understanding that Honor blessed her for. "Do not hesitate to call on the servants for anything you need." She looked down at Adam and her voice, still low, rang with feeling. "God keep Master Adam with us."

They sat up all that night. Adam never moved.

The next day the doctors came, one after another, shook their heads, then left. Elizabeth looked in every hour. Honor and Richard did not leave the room all day. They stoked the fire in the grate, opened the window a crack, closed the window, called for fresh water, fresh linen cloths, fresh pillows. The maids brought them meals. They took a few bites, then sat again at the bedside, dabbing Adam's brow, coaxing him in low tones, holding his hand, reading to him from Elizabeth's books. Aesop's fables. Marcus Aurelius.

All day, he never moved.

When dusk came they took turns at naps in the chair by the fire, the chair turned to face the bed so they could see Adam.

All evening, he never moved.

A hand jostled Honor. She jerked awake. Bleary, blinking at the cold light of dawn, she saw Richard standing over her. His face was haggard. Tears glinted in his eye.

She dragged her voice from the pit of her despair. "He's gone."

He shook his head. And smiled. "No, my love. He's awake."

❧ 12 ❧

Allies and Enemies

October 1555

Hatfield, the house in which Elizabeth had grown up and which she now, once again, called home, was not just a fine country estate, it was also a working farm. Cattle and sheep grazed its pastures, yielding beef and mutton for the communal tables of Hatfield's great hall and also for market. The life of the manor house and its scores of workers moved in rhythm with the seasons. Spring was for plowing, seeding, shearing, and felling timber. Summer, for cutting hay, harvesting the gardens and orchards, collecting honey. Autumn, which had settled on the woods around Hatfield like a tapestry of gold and orange and red, was the busiest season. In preparation for winter, the yeomen chopped logs for firewood and the kitchen staff laid up victuals, while the gardeners covered the strawberry beds and the sweeps scoured the chimneys.

Despite their dawn-to-dusk tasks, the servants had been instructed to move quietly and keep their voices low as they cleaned the bedchambers, for the Princess wanted no one disturbing the man lying in the chamber next to hers, the hero who had saved her life. During the first days, when everyone was sure he would die, the maids had whispered in tones of grief as they worked. Then, when his fever broke, the chamberlain announced it to the household at dinner in the great hall and the news brought a cheer. After more days of rest, with the chambermaids cosseting him and the doctors bleeding him daily, he was proclaimed out of danger.

Adam could have done without the bleeding. But he was very glad to be alive.

"Sit, do sit, sir," Doctor Rufus said, indicating a stool before the fire. "That's enough exertion for this morning. You're still weak as a newborn pup." A portly, balding man, he was laying out his wares on a table beside the stool—scissors, a basin of warm water, a sponge, a jar of herbal ointment, fresh linen bandage strips.

Adam eased himself down on the seat. "Feels good to be up, though," he said. Awaiting the doctor's ministrations, he looked across the room at the window. Though he sat bare-chested, the fire was warm, but outside cold-looking drizzle slid down the leaded windowpanes, and the sky was the color of a bruise.

He had gotten quite familiar with his own huge bruise that spread out from under the bandage binding his chest. He looked down at it, a nasty greenish black with striations of angry red. The one on his back was even worse, the doctor had told him. He'd also gotten used to the dull pain that constantly grumbled in his chest, but it was definitely lessening with each passing day. He counted himself very lucky.

He heard footsteps in the hallway, and women's voices. Elizabeth? She was early. Usually she came after the household's noonday dinner, and again last thing before she went to bed, but at this hour the hall could barely have finished breakfast. Then he realized: no hunting or hawking in this wet weather. He blessed the rain gods.

The door opened and in she came, followed by two maids. Adam quickly got to his feet to grab his shirt and greet her properly, but Elizabeth, her eyes darting over his bare chest, flicked her hand, a command to sit. He did, for the doctor was right, he was still weak. Jumping up like that left him a little light-headed. The maids bustled around them, collecting his empty breakfast dishes.

"Today, Master Thornleigh, I shall be your nurse," Elizabeth declared, all business. She shooed out the maids, then told Doctor Rufus he need not stay, either. He left, still issuing instructions as she closed the door after him. "It does not require a genius to change a bandage," she said as she turned back to Adam. "Now, sir. Let us begin."

"Hold on," he said sternly. "Where's my news?"

Her businesslike expression melted and they shared a smile. It had become their daily routine: news, first thing.

"I humbly crave your pardon, my lord," she said in mock submission, making a deep curtsy.

It sent a thrill of arousal through him. He almost had to laugh at himself. On death's door just days ago, and the pain still so harsh it *hurt* to laugh, but all she had to do was let her eyes meet his—those sparkling black eyes—and desire throbbed through him like he was fresh and strong.

"Allow me to inform you of the doings of the great and the good," she said, rising. "Item, the lord chancellor, Bishop Gardiner, lies very ill, like to die, they say. I say Gardiner's a toad and his passing would be no loss to the realm." Surveying the doctor's paraphernalia, she dropped the sponge into the basin of warm water. "Item, my good friend Lady Cavendish comes to visit me on Thursday and brings my little godson Harry, who is not my favorite of her children, and baby Charles, who is." She pulled the stopper from the jar of herbal ointment and sniffed, wrinkled her nose, and shoved the stopper back in. "Item, Parliament opens in six days. Your father has been telling me about the Queen's proposed bills. He has been studying them diligently, readying to join the opposition."

"He's green at it, but eager for the fight," Adam said. He'd been surprised to see his parents sitting at his bedside when he surfaced from the fever. It was the first time he had ever seen his father shed tears. They were still here, Elizabeth's guests.

"What tigers you Thornleighs are," she said. "Your father girding himself to combat the Queen. Your mother conniving to keep me from harm at her hands. And you . . . well, *you . . .*" She stopped, looking suddenly very serious. Her voice became soft. "To risk your life . . ." Emotion pinked her cheeks, but she did not look down in maidenly embarrassment. She looked straight into his eyes, her own eyes shining with wonder.

Adam wanted to sweep her into his arms. Instead, he cleared his throat. "Any idea yet who was behind it?"

She shook her head. They had already discussed this, and suspected an agent of Simon Renard, the imperial ambassador, a fierce friend of the Queen. Or even someone sent by the Queen herself.

"Has St. Loe posted more guards?"

"My purse, sir, only goes so far."

She said it lightly, but Adam sensed it was a mask to hide how deeply the assassination attempt had shaken her. Someone was bent on killing her.

"Now, sir," she said, holding up the doctor's scissors, "may I begin?"

He hesitated. It didn't seem right for a princess to be doing this task. On the other hand, how could he refuse a princess? He nodded, and she bent to begin removing the bandage. She gently snipped the fabric at his breastbone, the scissor tips cold on his skin. Her head was lowered and he watched the firelight dance on her flame-colored hair. He took in the smell of her, some faint perfume, a scent of sandalwood.

Her eyes flicked up to his. "This will not do for purchase," she murmured, and went down on her knees between his legs. It made him catch a breath.

She snipped through the remaining cloth. "Raise your arms."

He did, sending a jagged pain through his chest, but it was worth it just to feel her fingers' light touch as she unwound the bandage. It fell to the floor. Her fingertip brushed his nipple. He swallowed hard.

She went still, staring at the puckered wound in the center of the massive bruise. She raised her eyes to his and whispered in awe, "How you have suffered for my sake."

He could barely find his voice. "This is not suffering, my lady."

"Then, sir, you must be more than human."

"Not so. Believe me." His body betrayed how very human.

The faintest smile curved her lips. "Flesh and blood, then?" She lifted the sponge from the silver basin and squeezed water from it, the drops pinging into the basin. "Can you turn? I'll start on your back."

Again, he hesitated. A king's daughter, washing him? But he craved her touch, and the determined look in her eyes was all the persuasion he needed. He pivoted on the stool so that he was facing away from her. She gently laid the sponge against his wound. He sucked in a breath at it. The warm water. Her tender pressure.

"All right?" she asked.

He nodded. *More than all right.*

Gently, she smoothed the sponge over the wound, washing away the dried blood. She patted his skin dry with a fresh cloth, then reached for the jar of ointment. He couldn't see her face as she smoothed the balm on his back in slow, radiating circles, and he was glad she could not see his, his eyes closed, savoring her touch. The pleasure was almost excruciating. It made his heart pound so hard he was sure she could hear it. He couldn't help his breathing getting ragged.

"Turn back to me," she said.

He did, hoping and longing for her fingers to continue, though it was hellishly hard to keep still, not reach for her. He could not refuse a princess . . . but neither could he touch a princess.

Still on her knees between his legs, she reached again for the ointment to apply to the wound on his chest, but then stopped. Her eyes met his. She raised her hand to her own white skin just above the swell of her breasts, and touched the thin scar on her breastbone, faint as a fingernail paring, carved by the arrow's tip.

She reached for his hand and lifted it to the spot, and when his fingers touched her skin he thought his heart might stop. He understood what she was silently telling him—that her scar was their bond.

"When will he *leave* that cursed place?" Frances practically shouted it, making Dyer wince.

"I understand he is recovering, my lady," he said. "I imagine it will take some time."

She was pacing, feeling as trapped as the caged lion in the Tower's royal menagerie. She had hurried from Colchester to her brother's London house. It was that much closer to Hatfield, a day's ride closer to news about Adam. But still not close enough. It was *him* she wanted to be close to. Every time she thought of that arrow piercing him, it felt like an arrow ripping through *her*. He was recovering, yes, and thanks be to God for that, but she was trapped here, waiting for every crumb of information that Dyer could glean from his spy in the Hatfield household. While the whore's daughter was near Adam day and night, pampering him, petting him. It made Frances wild with frustration.

"Does she touch him? Nursing him, you said. Do they say she touches him?"

"I believe she changes his bandage, madam, so I presume she must. But as to any further—"

"Stop. I don't want to hear." It was so unfair! She had not seen Adam's face for months. First his ship had kept him away, the building of it taking forever, and then his quest for financial backing took him all the way to Hatfield, and now he was held hostage there by that red-haired shrew. How much longer until she could lay eyes on him? While the whore's daughter laid hands on him.

She went to the window and rested her forehead on the cool glass, trying to settle her fevered thoughts. She had suffered fitful sleep for days, had barely eaten. The news in church that he was dead had almost killed her. She had been so sick with grief, John had brought in Doctor Markham to examine her. Then, when word came that Adam had survived, her joy was so intense she had swooned and John brought back the doctor. But Frances had dismissed the fool, for nothing mattered except being with Adam. If only he could get free of that harlot's clutches and come to her. She kept this small, third-floor parlor for herself, removed from the household noise below, and she could make him so comfortable here. John was away on business all day, and Arabella was always out visiting friends. Adam could rest on a bed she would make up for him here by the fire. She would tenderly bathe his poor, hurt body and he would love her for it . . .

Dyer cleared his throat. Frances set her dreams of Adam to the back of her mind. Business first. She turned. "Bring him in," she said.

When she heard Dyer's footsteps clomping down the staircase, she turned back to the window and looked down at darkened Lombard Street, crowded with houses and shops. It was a chilly night, with only a scatter of people hurrying home before curfew, the shops mostly closed. A linkboy held his torch high to guide a pair of gentlemen on their way, and they passed a beggar standing on the steps of the church across the street, a scabby man wearing a filthy cloak. He scratched the back of his hand at the brand that was his license to beg. After the linkboy's torch passed, the beggar was a mere shadow in the moonlight. A cat streaked into the alley beside the church and was swallowed up by the darkness. Frances went to her desk and opened a drawer and took out a purse of coins.

Giles Sturridge, captain of the Grenville Archers, walked in and bowed low. When he had reported to her last week, caked with dusty sweat after his frantic ride from Hatfield, he had looked terrified of her fury at his failure, but Frances had told him to return to his troop and breathe not a word of what had happened and no one would be the wiser. She might still need his services, she'd said. He had been mightily relieved.

Now, she handed him the purse of coins and made it clear that this time he must succeed. He was effusive in his thanks, bowing deeply again and assuring her that he would not fail her.

She dismissed him. When his footsteps died on the stairs she went back to the window and looked out at the church steps. The beggar had stopped scratching. He was looking at Frances's front door as it opened, flooding the patch of street with light.

Sturridge walked out, swaggering now as he pocketed Frances's purse. The door slammed shut, cutting off the light, leaving Sturridge alone in the moonlight. He smoothed back his hair with both hands and looked up and down the street with an expectant look, but unhurried, as though pondering which alehouse to visit.

The beggar on the church steps threw back the side of his cloak, revealing a dagger in his hand. Another man stepped out of the dark alley, and another moved forward from behind Sturridge. The three came slowly toward him, stalking. He tensed, taking in the two brutish faces before him, and their knives. He twisted around, saw the one coming behind him with an even longer knife. He shot a look up at Frances's window, horror leaping into his eyes.

The beggar's blade rammed into Sturridge's back. He arched in agony. The others' knives stabbed his neck, his chest. He dropped to his knees. The three men bent over him and hacked.

When Sturridge lay still and bleeding, the beggar dug into his pocket and yanked out Frances's purse. The other two carried the body to the church alley and heaved it, facedown, into the darkness. The three men dispersed into the night.

Frances looked up for a moment at the moon. Was Adam looking up at it, too, and thinking of her? She pulled the curtain, blew out the candles, and went downstairs. He could sleep now, safe. She would always take care of him. No one could hurt him and live.

The horses were saddled. Richard was booted and spurred. Honor had tipped the servants and said her thank-yous. Adam was bidding Elizabeth good-bye. They were leaving for London, Richard to take his seat in the upcoming Parliament in Westminster, Adam to launch his ship in Colchester, Honor to report on Elizabeth to the Queen.

Another toothless report to lull Mary's fears, Honor thought as she made her way down the stairs of Hatfield House to join the others outside. How much longer could she keep up this subterfuge with the Queen? The chilly autumn wind whipped her skirts as she crossed the gravel path to where Elizabeth stood talking with Richard and Adam beside the waiting horses and grooms, and she wondered if now was the time to warn the Princess. There was no crisis yet, and indeed Mary had grudgingly accepted her regular assessments that Elizabeth, well frightened by her imprisonment in the Tower and her year under house arrest, had been sobered by the reality of Mary's reign and was now properly conforming in religion and eschewing any contact with a single soul who grumbled against the Queen. But almost weekly, festering rumors of rebellion burst like boils in Mary's court, panicking her councilors and enraging Mary herself, and each rumor invariably peaked with the whisper that, naturally, any rebel leader's aim would be to put Elizabeth on the throne. It maddened Mary. Which made Honor's task of lulling her more difficult with every passing week.

"Careful, careful," Elizabeth said, sounding as anxious as a mother as Adam swung himself up into the saddle.

He laughed. "I can sit a horse, my lady. The wound's not in my backside."

The grooms chuckled, and so did Richard as he mounted his horse beside Adam. It was good to see the healthy color back in their son's face, Honor thought. Good to see him on his feet at last. He was still a little weak, and she feared his chest still ached, but the moment word had come from his shipwright that the work was finished, Adam had started packing. Honor had urged him to stay another week to get all his strength back, but she knew it was pointless. Nothing short of multiple amputations would keep him from captaining his new ship.

Elizabeth saw her coming and held out her hand, in both greeting and farewell. Honor clasped it, wondering how to begin. A groom stood holding Honor's horse for her, but she wasn't ready yet to mount.

"I wish you and your good husband could stay," Elizabeth said with feeling. "You return to the great world to do battle, while I can but watch and wait. You have my deep thanks, both of you."

"These gifts are thanks aplenty, my lady," Richard said, patting the horse's neck. Elizabeth had given them three of her finest mounts and a couple of her servants to ease their journey.

"It is small recompense, sir, if you can forestall the Queen."

A sober look passed between them all. Last night over supper they had discussed the bills that Queen Mary was going to introduce in Parliament to seize the estate revenues of all English exiles abroad, denouncing them as heretics. The Thornleighs had scores of exiled friends in Antwerp alone, and there were hundreds more throughout the German lands and in France. Some of the most prominent were Elizabeth's friends, too. Honor feared that this cash grab of the Queen's would be just the beginning. Not content with burning every self-declared Protestant in England, her apparent aim now was to ruin the exiles. And then, how long would it be before she moved against Protestant sympathizers here at home, even those she merely suspected? If her bills passed, as royal bills almost invariably did, it would put the Thornleighs and all their friends in peril.

"We're not alone, and we're ready," Richard said. "The Queen will get a fight."

Elizabeth smiled her thanks, but Honor knew this girl so well now she could read the tension in the smile. Though showing a courageous face, the Princess was still afraid of her sister.

Elizabeth took a deep breath as though to shake off the fear, then brightened her smile. "I have another gift, sir. For your son." Adam looked at her, clearly surprised, but she continued to speak to Richard. "Words cannot express my gratitude for his brave act to save my life. But perhaps my purse can." There was a twinkle in her eye as she turned to Adam. "Master Thornleigh, will you allow me to invest in your new ship? Say, three hundred pounds?"

Honor and Richard exchanged a look of astonishment. A huge sum. It would almost completely discharge Adam's debt.

Adam grinned in delight. "It would be my great honor, my lady."

"Partners, then?"

Honor caught the warm look that passed between them. How Elizabeth's eyes held his. This, it was clear, was no everyday business transaction.

"Give me a gold coin right now," said Adam. "An angel."

Elizabeth looked shocked. "You doubt my word?"

"Good God, no. It's to set under the mainmast."

When she frowned in puzzlement, Richard explained, "It's a custom with shipbuilders, Your Grace. For luck."

Elizabeth smiled her delight. "Really? How charming." She dug into the velvet purse that hung at her waist and handed an angel coin up to Adam.

"My lady," Adam said, his voice low with feeling as their fingers touched, "the ship is yet unnamed. Will you allow me to call her the *Elizabeth*?"

She practically glowed. "An excellent name. You have my consent. May she bring you joy, sir, and riches. As I do not doubt she will if you always abide by one rule."

"What's that?"

"That you master the *Elizabeth* tenderly."

Honor's eyes flicked to Richard and he cocked an eyebrow as if to tell her that even *he* could see the spark between these two. Well, Honor thought, it's natural. A handsome young hero and a lovely, grateful princess. How could they not appreciate one another? But in her mind a warning fluttered its flag. Appreciate from afar, Adam. This is a princess of the blood.

Elizabeth broke the spell. "Now, sir, what surety can you offer me for a return on my investment?"

Adam looked crestfallen. "There's the cargo, of course . . . and—"

"I'll have something for my angel right now, if you please. Your whistle."

He blinked in confusion. "Pardon?"

"In your pocket. You're always toying with it. I've never seen you without it."

He pulled it out. His captain's whistle carved from stag horn. A gift from Richard several years ago. He handed it to Elizabeth, and as she took it her expression became very sober. "I will treasure it always, to remember what you risked for my sake."

The sentiment was so genuine, so unadorned, it moved Honor. Both these young people were dear to her. And both had been in mortal danger at the assassin's hand. It jolted her back. She had to speak up now. She took the reins from the groom holding her horse and waited until he ambled away. Then she said, "My family is proud to serve you, my lady, however we can. My husband in the House of Commons to protect your interests, our son whenever you may need him, and I at court to forestall the Queen, if I can. But you must acknowledge the danger you are in." She glanced around to make sure the servants were out of hearing. "Someone sent that assassin. We agree that it was almost certainly the Queen. She will not hesitate to try again. I fear the time has passed when you can simply watch and wait. You may have to do more."

Elizabeth's face went pale. "No one is more aware than I am of the threats I face. But I have taken every precaution, and so has Sir William St. Loe, increasing my guard. What more would you have me do?"

Honor was about to speak, but Richard stopped her with a hand on her shoulder, gentle but firm. His look warned, *This is not the time or place.*

But someone had to say it. With so many lives at stake, Elizabeth had to prepare to use her power. "It may come to a fight beyond words hurled in Parliament. Your many friends here and abroad would serve you faithfully to unseat this queen. But you alone can lead them."

Elizabeth looked aghast. Honor could almost see the teeth of terror bite in her mind: *Wyatt fought Mary. She cut off his head. And cast me in the Tower.* When she spoke her voice was harsh with anger. "I will not be her prisoner again. Unless you want to send me to the block, madam, forswear such talk. Forswear the very *thought.* I command you."

Frances was nearly nauseated by the smell. The priest's house squatted in a lane around the corner from meat shops where carcasses hung in the windows, and the air held a putrid odor of decaying flesh. She almost wished she hadn't come, but her steward, Dyer, had said it was important. Months before, she had charged him to investigate Honor Thornleigh's claim of friendship, long ago, with Queen Catherine and what had subsequently taken her to the Low Countries, and Dyer's search, following up on his German agent's report, had led him back to London and this shabby house in the filth of Southwark across the river. "You'll want to meet this priest and hear his tale, my lady. And soon, for he is dying."

Perhaps that accounted for the smell, Frances thought as Dyer ushered her into the cramped bedchamber. The priest lay in a narrow bed on sweat-stained sheets, his eyes closed. She felt a little ashamed at her uncharitable response, since he was a man of God, but she had always felt disgusted by the fetid odors of the sick and the old, and this priest was both. She was also a little unnerved by his deformity.

Father Jerome Bastwick wasn't ugly so much as startling. His hair, standing in dry white bristles, grew on just one side of his head. On the other side, perfectly bald, the ear was as shriveled as a bacon rind, and the skin was an angry red, and stretched so tightly over his skull it was shiny. Frances knew from Dyer's report that Bastwick had once been a royal chaplain to King Henry VIII, personally raising the host to the old King's lips, but the old King's son and heir, the Protestant King Edward, had made life hard for the faithful, and it was clear how far the priest had sunk since those glory days. From the look of the place—the grimed wooden walls, his soiled clothing scattered on chairs, a bowl of congealed porridge abandoned on a stool—he had not even a housekeeper.

Bastwick's eyes sprang open. He fixed them on Frances with surprising clarity. "God sent you," he said, his voice a rasp.

She was taken aback at his fervor. "I hope I walk in God's path always, Father," she said. She glanced at the door for Dyer, but he had gone outside to wait. She wanted to leave. "I am very sorry to bother you when you are ill, Father, and perhaps I should come back another—"

"I will be dead. Your man told me why you've come. I am glad you did. It was ordained."

"Do you, in fact, have information about Honor Thornleigh?"

"What is she to you?"

"My neighbor."

He looked appalled. "She has returned?"

"She and her husband and their—" She stopped before mentioning Adam. She wanted to keep his name untainted. "Yes, she recently came home."

"Home, bah. Her home is hell." He was groping with one hand under the bed. He dragged out a metal box the size of a large book and, with a grunt of effort to lift it, landed it beside him on the mattress. He lay back, exhausted from the exertion. "Open it."

Eager to conclude this bizarre interview, Frances raised the box lid. Mottled papers lay inside.

"Take them." When she hesitated, he commanded "Take them!" in a voice so urgent and so full of authority, she obeyed. She lifted out a sheaf of dog-eared papers.

"She is a devil," Bastwick said. "I knew her first as Honor Larke, and she did me a wrong once, long ago. But that is nothing compared to the foul deeds she committed while serving Her Majesty Queen Catherine. The Thornleigh woman is a viper in the breast of Christendom." He held up a bony finger and shook it, pointing at the papers. "It's all there. How she befriended heretics who plotted against the Church. How she carried these vermin to safety across the Narrow Seas to laugh at God's priests. How she wrote filthy books to bewilder and inflame the gullible. And how, in the end, she came before my court, the bishop's court, at St. Paul's. We examined her and found her foul with heresy. She abjured, as so many of Satan's minions do to save their skins. But I brought her back, and proved her rankness with her own writings. She was condemned to burn. We had her chained to the stake and the fire lit under her, and she was about to breathe the last of her contagion. Read, madam, read. It's all there. The Church's record, faithfully transcribed. I have kept it for a day of reckoning."

Frances was stunned. "She was . . . about to burn?"

Bastwick was groping inside the box. He took out a key. Holding it up, he said, "Take this." He pointed to a high wooden chest across the room. "Open it."

Afire with curiosity now, Frances took the key and slid it into the lock and opened the chest's twin doors. Dozens of glass vials stood in tidy rows, the kind apothecaries used for herbs and ointments.

"Imagine the execution ground of Smithfield," Bastwick said, "and the crowd around the stake. Imagine St. Bartholomew's church hard by. Imagine a devil, leaping on the church roof, howling its fiendish cries, setting the people to run in terror. Imagine the fiend hurling boiling pitch down on them." He turned to her, a wild gleam in his eyes as though he was reliving the chaos and horror. "Flaming tar that struck some poor souls, who screamed in pain." His hand groped at the bald side of his head with its red, shiny skin. Burned, Frances realized—burned beyond recovery. "Imagine vile wretches planted in that crowd who raced to the stake and freed her, Honor Thornleigh, Satan's own."

He stretched out his thin arm to proudly indicate his collection of vials. Listening in awe to his story, Frances had not looked closely at what was in the vials. She looked now. Not herbs. Not medicines. Each vial held a small bone. Some as thin as pencils, some charred black, some white as chalk. She realized with a shock that they were finger bones. Human fingers.

"Each one from a heretic burned in England since I took holy orders," he said. "Gathered from the cinders, or bought, or bartered for. For twenty-one years I have been waiting to add Honor Thornleigh's."

Frances could not get away fast enough. She rode onto London Bridge with Dyer riding behind her, and kicked her horse to move as quickly as possible through the traffic of wagons and riders and people on foot, all plodding their way in and out of the city. The truth about Honor Thornleigh appalled her. A heretic! Condemned! And another realization was creeping over her—that her father had known it all. That had to be the reason why he went to Speedwell House that night, that terrible night over a year ago when he shot the woman, wounding her, and her husband killed Frances's father.

What was she to do with this dumbfounding news? Tell her brother? John would be maddened beyond imagining. Maddened enough to attack the Thornleighs. Attack Adam!

No! John must never know. She must tell no one. She was shocked at her own decision. It was terribly wrong to withhold knowledge about a convicted heretic. But how could she not, when it would endanger Adam, so dear to her heart?

In her saddlebag were Bastwick's papers. They would stay in her possession. The old priest would soon die, and then she would be the only one who knew. Dyer had heard, of course, but Dyer she could trust. Honor Thornleigh's secret would stay with her.

❧ 13 ❧

Smithfield

November 1555

"A silver rattle?" Honor suggested. "How about a silver cup?"

"Richard, the child's still suckling."

"Not for long."

"You'd send him a beer tankard if you could."

"Good idea. Why wait?"

She laughed. "A silver rattle," she said, ending the debate. She would order it this very morning and hope it would reach their baby grandson before Christmas. George Mitford would have just the thing.

Stepping out of London's Crane Inn they started to make their way along busy Thames Street, and as Honor hooked her arm in Richard's she felt buoyed by life's fullness. Nicholas was a thriving babe of six months. Adam would soon launch the *Elizabeth* on her maiden voyage to Antwerp with a cargo of finished wool cloth, the fruits of Richard's hard work. And she and Richard were now on their way to deliver a gift for another of life's passages, a wedding present for George Mitford's son Roger, whose marriage would take place next week. Honor had enjoyed searching out the gift at Chastelain's, one of the finest shops on Goldsmiths Row—a set of Venetian crystal goblets tinted blue like a spring sky at dusk, and etched with a delicate pattern of stars.

Arm in arm, they navigated through the stream of apprentices hustling to work, and maids heading to market, and school boys with satchels slipping through the crowd like fish darting through shallows. Carts and wagons rumbled past. The bells of several churches clanged in oblivious discord, and from the river with its hundreds of boats and wherries came the screech of seagulls and a shout of "Oars!" and between the buildings Honor glimpsed the thicket of masts of merchant ships bobbing at anchor beyond London Bridge. The crisp air carried the smells of fresh lumber, fish, and burning charcoal. A boy jostled Honor's elbow as he dashed by her and then bumped a woman ahead carrying a basket of bread loaves. A loaf tumbled out and the boy caught it and tossed it back into the basket and ran on without breaking his stride. Honor laughed.

"You're in a good mood," Richard said as they sidestepped a mound of horse dung steaming in the November chill.

"I'm just glad we'll see George before he sets sail for home."

He nodded. "And I'm glad I can finally repay him."

She felt the same. Weeks ago George's courier from Amsterdam had returned the last of her jewelry, and today, as soon as they saw George himself, they would discharge the loan he had so generously extended when they had so desperately needed it. A great deal more debt still hung over their heads, but Honor was adamant that George be repaid first. Friendship. Another of life's blessings to be thankful for.

"Will you sup with Sir William again tonight?" she asked, thinking of loyal friends. Richard had been in the House of Commons for three days, and as a novice in its arcane procedures he was relying on Sir William Cecil's guidance.

"Into the small hours again, I imagine. Along with Peckham and Kingston and the rest. Plenty of organizing to be done for the vote."

She didn't like the sound of that. The House had begun debate on several of Queen Mary's bills, and the first—a proposal to return the Crown's ecclesiastical revenues to the Church—was a seemingly mild request from the Queen, since it involved only her personal income. If the House couldn't muster the opposition to defeat even that, what chance did they have of defeating the far more significant Exiles Bill, scheduled next? "I thought you had all the support you need."

"We will. Members of the House will be furious as soon as they realize they'll have to make up the revenue shortfall through taxation, from their own pockets. We just have to explain that to enough of them."

"But the vote will be called soon, won't it? Will you have time?"

"That's why I'll be at Cecil's most of the night." When she frowned in concern he assured her, "Don't worry. We'll win this one." But then he added darkly, "We have to. If we let the Queen give these revenues back to the Church it could embolden her to try giving them back *land*."

Unthinkable, it seemed to Honor. Almost every man in the House of Commons, or his father before him, had bought up the rich, rent-producing manors and estates that had flooded the market when King Henry had dissolved the monasteries and pocketed the cash for himself. They would never relinquish such property on their own. But this ecclesiastical bill had originated in the House of Lords, whose members had a very different view. The nobility abhorred the rise of the merchants and gentry they called "upstarts." Baron John Grenville, who sat with the lords, hated Richard for buying the abbey where his aunt had been the abbess, and also—and far more deeply—for his father's death. Honor could not forget Grenville's leer of pleasure in church when they had all thought Adam was dead.

She was about ask what strategy Sir William Cecil had planned for defeating the bill, but her question would have to wait, for they had arrived at the Mitfords' house on Bucklersbury Street. It was the home of George's elder son, Timothy, and its imposing facade proclaimed his success. Timothy had established himself as a goldsmith and jeweler just as successful as his father. As Richard knocked at the door, Honor admired the orchard and garden just visible through a high lattice fence.

The door opened a crack. The first thing Honor heard was weeping.

A maid's face appeared, drained of color. She opened the door and without a word, as dull-eyed as a sleepwalker, she beckoned them to come after her. Honor and Richard shared a puzzled glance, then followed her into the great hall where they found the family apparently in the throes of a hasty departure. Open trunks, satchels, caskets, and scattered clothing lay helter-skelter like the belongings of a decamping troop of soldiers. The communal dining table was littered with the half-eaten debris of a roast pork supper. Servants bustled in grim silence, packing.

Timothy Mitford, a lean young version of his father, sat slumped on a chair at the cold hearth, his head down, like a broken puppet. His grandmother sat on a stool, clutching a child's straw doll to her breast and quietly weeping. Timothy's wife, Alice, helped a maid hurriedly pack armloads of children's clothes while holding back tears herself. Timothy's brother, Roger, who was to be married in four days, was tossing gold candlesticks to a footman to pack into a trunk when he noticed Honor and Richard. He gaped at them, his normally cheerful face haggard and bleary-eyed.

"Roger, what's happened?" Honor asked anxiously. Her gaze swept up the staircase where three little children huddled together on a stair, their eyes huge with uncomprehending fear. In another room, a baby wailed.

Richard set the gift box on the table and said soberly to Roger, "What's amiss, my boy?"

"Master Thornleigh. Mistress . . . dear God, you have not heard."

They exchanged a glance of dismay. Roger plowed a hand through his disheveled hair and said, as though suddenly remembering, "Account books," and turned to quickly look into a trunk, searching, then dashed to another trunk, then another.

The old lady fumbled the doll, dropping it, and Honor went to retrieve it for her. Richard stopped Roger in his tracks and gently sat him down at the table and asked again what had happened. Roger blinked, as hollow-eyed as if he had not slept for days. "They took him . . . we were at supper . . ."

"Took who?"

"Father."

Timothy, at the hearth, groaned in misery.

"Who did?" Richard asked. "Why?"

Roger told it all. He and his brother, though passionate about their Protestant faith, had always been careful to hide it, unwilling to follow their father into exile. But a month ago a zealous friend of Timothy's had ordered some religious pamphlets printed, but then could not come up with the cash for the printer, so Timothy paid. He did it in secret, but a disaffected neighbor got wind of it and told the parish priest that the Mitfords were spreading heretic filth. Timothy, fearing arrest, prepared to flee to Antwerp. George, here for Roger's wedding, had been set to sail with Timothy today. Then, last night, the subdued family had just sat down to supper when the bishop's men banged on the door.

The old lady sobbed in a new spasm that made Roger flinch.

"They came for Timothy?" Richard said, to prod him back.

Roger nodded. "They started to drag him away. Father stopped them, asked where they were taking his son. To the bishop's cells, they said, and after that he'll burn. They had him almost out the door when Father stopped them again. He told them that Timothy did not do the deed."

There was a strangled moan from Timothy. "He told them *he* had done it."

Richard and Honor looked at each other in shock. George had taken the blame for his son's action. And been arrested. And now, it seemed, the rest of the family was preparing to flee. No wonder. It would be just a matter of time before officers of the bishop's court arrested both the brothers for questioning, and Alice too—likely even the old lady. And if their answers deviated from orthodoxy, any one of them could stand trial for heresy. Then, if they did not abjure their beliefs at trial, they would suffer death by fire.

"Have you the means to sail immediately?" Richard asked, taking charge. "I can have my agent arrange passage for all of you on the next tide."

"And we can give you money," Honor added quickly, though she was so shaken by George's arrest she could hardly keep her voice steady.

Roger said, "I thank you, sir. Madam. But we are well provided.

Our father saw to that." His mouth trembled. He hunched over and buried his face in his hands. A little boy on the stair burst into sobs. His older sister, white-faced, threw her arm around the child to comfort him.

It was too much for Timothy. He jumped up from the hearth, his face a map of guilt and pain. He bolted for the door. But Richard stood in his way and caught him by the arm. "Where are you going?"

"To tell them the truth. Let me go, sir!"

"Don't be mad, boy. If you confess, they'll kill you."

Timothy tried to wrench free. "They're going to kill *him!*"

Richard held him fast. "Your father knew what he was doing. Look around you. Look at your children. Your family needs you."

The trail was sickeningly familiar to Honor. Richard was with her as they made their way to the one place she had hoped never to see again. Northward they walked in frozen silence, holding hands so tightly her fingers were almost numb. Westward they turned along crowded Newgate Street, all the way to the city wall pierced by the massive arch of the gate. Wagons lumbered through it, and people streamed, coming and going about their business. Newgate Prison rose in three stories above the arch, and felons peeked out in misery from its barred windows. A mad-eyed girl with an ear cut off. A wildly bearded man branded on the forehead.

Outside the city wall they turned north onto Pie Corner, where the road broadened into the wide expanse of Smithfield fairground. Cattle and sheep were sold here all year round, the farmers walking the livestock in from Essex, Suffolk, and Kent. Horse markets were held regularly, too, and every kind of mount was bought and sold, from priests' mules, plow horses, and ladies' palfreys, to finely bred Arab hunters and Barbary coursers. In August, Smithfield was home to Bartholomew Fair, when throngs tramped in from all over the country. Jugglers, balladeers, fire-eaters, and clowns milled with pickpockets, lovers, families, and whores. There were contests in wrestling and archery. Bakers hawked meat pies, gingerbread babies, and saffron buns. Country women sold asparagus, scallions, radishes, cherries, and ripe, fragrant plums.

But now, in the thin, cold November light, the merriment of August was only a memory. The empty cattle pens were a bog of soupy mud, the grass a blight of brown, and hoarfrost iced the Elms, the name given in grim jest by Londoners to the trio of gallows ever since, years ago, these gibbets had replaced a stand of elm trees. There was no scent of fruit pies and cinnamon buns to overcome the stench from the slaughterhouses and tanneries crammed, by law, outside the city walls, where the waste of entrails was slopped daily into the Fleet Ditch. Yet the place was almost as crowded as on any fair day, for Smithfield was also the city's execution ground. People had come to see a burning.

The crowd, perhaps a hundred men and women and children, formed a wide semicircle around a roped-off square of sand that the night's frost had turned to rutted muck. At the center of the square a wooden stake ten feet high was impaled in the ground. A narrow ledge was nailed to it two feet from the bottom, assuring that when the victim stood on it they could be seen by the whole crowd. There was no victim yet. At the foot of the stake lay faggots—bundles of sticks and twigs—and straw was heaped knee-high on top of them. This was the pit. A lone guard stood sentry. A platform for dignitaries, with three tiers of wooden benches, rose at one side, deserted.

Amongst the waiting crowd, many had come for the sport, snatching an hour off work for the thrill of watching the primal drama of death, and they chattered and fidgeted in eager anticipation. A man yawned as he swung a little boy up onto his shoulders. A skinny woman suckled her baby and gossiped with a blowsy friend who was picking her teeth. Three youths wearing the blue smocks of apprentices had brought a small hogshead of beer that was perched on the broad shoulder of one, and they clinked brimming tankards to toast the event. But many more of the onlookers stood in the mute stillness of mourners. Honor knew by their long-suffering expressions, pinched with anger and dread, that they were secret Protestants.

"There," Richard said, pointing.

She turned. Twenty or so people had broken away from the crowd and flocked alongside a procession on horseback, plodding up from Pie Corner to deliver the victim. The grim parade passed Honor and Richard close enough that they heard the people's jeers.

"Stinking heretic!"

"Burn, you God-cursed Lutheran!"

Leading the procession were a dozen guards armed with spears and swords. They were followed by a member of the Queen's council dressed in a fur-trimmed brown velvet robe. By law, one councilor was designated in rotation to attend each burning. Following him came four stolid officials representing the mayor. Then three black-garbed priests representing the bishop of London. At the rear, a mule dragged a wooden hurdle and on it, strapped down by lashings of leather, his wrists bound in front with twine, lay George Mitford. His face was as bleached as boiled linen, and his red-rimmed eyes stared out of sockets so dark they looked bruised. He was barefoot, in a filth-stained shirt and breeches, his hair matted with mud and sweat. Ragged children tagged after him, daring one another to toss handfuls of muck. One pitched a clump of dung that splatted his shoulder.

It sent such a shock through Honor she opened her mouth to cry out to George, but Richard jerked her hand in warning. "Don't," he said quietly, sternly. "Not even a word."

She closed her eyes in agony, knowing he was right. The Queen's new proclamation. Anyone showing sympathy for a victim being burned would be arrested and flogged.

"We're here to bear witness," Richard said. "That's all."

She nodded, knowing he was as horrified as she was about their friend's fate. But they could do nothing to save him now.

The procession stopped and dismounted. The lone guard at the pit lowered a rear section of the rope barrier, raising a gleeful shout from the people who had come for the show. The whole crowd, gawkers and mourners alike, shuffled closer to the front barrier to watch, and Honor and Richard moved nearer, too, until they were separated from the pit by just two jostling rows of people. Being this close to the stake made Honor's mouth go dry as dirt. For twenty years she had kept the memories chained in the cellar of her mind, but they sprang back now, snarling. *Stepping barefoot onto the stake's ledge. The splinter gouging skin between her toes. The stench of moldy straw at her feet.*

Six of the guards fanned out, taking up positions along the semicircle and facing the crowd. The city officials and two of the priests took their seats on the viewing platform while two guards stood sentry at its steps. The third priest, an austere man whose gold chain of office proclaimed him as Bishop Bonner's chancellor, went into the pit and stood beside the wooden stake, where he waited with the impatient air of a man with a busy schedule. Ignoring the crowd, he shook out a handkerchief from his pocket and blew his nose.

A guard went to the mule-drawn hurdle and pulled his dagger and sliced the leather straps, freeing George. He tried to stand, but with hands still bound he could not get his balance and he stumbled and fell to his knees. Honor flinched at the sight . . . and the memories. *Twine scraping her wrists raw. Summer-hot sand of the pit scorching the soles of her feet.*

The guard cut the twine binding George's wrists, and he and another guard grabbed him under the armpits and dragged him facedown to the stake, his toes carving channels in the muck. The bishop's chancellor stepped back to let the guards do their job. They prodded George to stand up on the ledge nailed to the stake. It raised him enough above the piled faggots and straw so that everyone could see him. They jammed his back against the stake, and another guard came carrying a chain that he wrapped around George's waist so it pinned his arms to his sides, then hooked the chain to a nail at the back and passed it around him again at his hips. George watched the guard snug up the chain, like a grotesque parody of a man watching his tailor measure him for a new doublet. *The chain they wrapped around her chest . . . its links black with soot . . .*

Another guard brought two head-sized sacks of gunpowder tied together with a short length of rope, and slung them around George's neck so that they hung at his sides.

"Thank God," Richard murmured. The gunpowder would speed up the burning.

But this measure of mercy in the brutal ritual brought a low hum of disappointment from several in the crowd. Gunpowder was not used at every burning, and they were not pleased that it was going to cut short their enjoyment today.

The bishop's chancellor, this drill dully familiar to him, stepped up to George's side. Raising his voice so the crowd could be both taught and warned, he intoned the charges to the victim. "At sundry times you have alleged that the sacrament of the altar is only bread, not the true body of Christ. You have alleged that no priest can absolve a man of sin. You have alleged that the blessings and pardons of bishops have no value . . ." While the chancellor droned these crimes of thought, George closed his eyes tightly, as though struggling to summon every shred of courage to endure. It was all Honor could do to not scream.

When the bishop's chancellor was done he turned and walked away, blowing his nose again, and nodded his signal up to the platform of dignitaries. Although the Church condemned a heretic, it handed over the victim to the state to carry out the sentence, saving the Church from committing murder. At the chancellor's cue, the mayor's representative on the platform stood. He raised his arms above his head and declared, *"Fiat justitia."* He sat, and the crowd hushed.

The ritual was done. The burning could begin.

A guard stepped forward with a flaming torch. Honor groped for Richard's hand. She held her breath as fiercely as if by saving it she could save George's life.

The guard plunged the torch into the piled faggots and straw. There was a *whomp* of the straw bursting into flame. Voices in the crowd sighed a loud "Ah!" of approval. Hearing it, Honor could not breathe. In sympathy, Richard's hand almost crushed hers.

Flames leapt from the straw and licked George's feet. His body stiffened. His red-rimmed eyes bulged white with terror. Smoke boiled up around him in the windless air. Honor's parched lungs forced her to suck a breath, and the smell of the smoke sent an acid shock to her stomach that brought sickness boiling up her throat. She forced down the bile. *Please, let the gunpowder catch.*

The flames died a little, the straw consumed. But the fire took hold in the faggots piled around the stake, and these flames, more determined, leapt up, making George's breeches smoke. He kicked in an involuntary spasm, but he was above the fuel and there was nothing to kick but the scorched air. Honor saw the sole of his foot charred black like meat on a spit, and she gagged. His abdomen pumped under the searing hot chain. His head rolled against the stake, his eyes wild with pain. At his agonized moans Honor thought she would go mad. In the crowd, a few men and women were openly weeping.

Soon George's breeches were smoking black shreds. Flames ate at his charred legs. His eyeballs bulged as he writhed against the chain. His shirt hem curled and smoked, then caught fire in an orange burst of flame. Sparks jumped to his hair, setting it smoking. He screamed. Someone in the crowd laughed. The flames leapt higher.

A slosh of liquid from the crowd hit one of the canvas gunpowder sacks, and then the other, wetting them. It was the apprentices flinging beer from their tankards, wanting to prolong the show. The sacks hissed steam, an almost comical sound that brought more laughter. The watching guards did not budge.

"No!" a man in the crowd shouted, hoarse with grief.

His cry unstopped the anguished fury of others like him. Two young men charged the pit, one banging Honor's shoulder as he barreled past her. He jumped the rope. The next man trampled it. That set loose a half dozen others who stampeded after them.

Guards sprang into action, chasing them. The dignitaries on the platform jumped up, shouting, pointing.

But the enraged sympathizers, nine of them now, were racing toward George. A woman cried out to him, "Hold on, friend!" One of the on-rushers, a man huge like a wrestler, with long, fast strides reached the stake and pulled off his heavy gray cloak and hurled it at the burning faggots to smother the fire.

Hope flashed through Honor. Without thinking she bolted forward, driven by a pure, primal need, mad to join the rescuers. She was over the trampled rope and at the heels of the young man running ahead. George, writhing in his agony, loomed so near! She heard Richard shouting her name behind her. Then his voice was smothered in the shouting all around.

She was almost at the stake. Flames had quickly eaten through the man's flung cloak and now raged up around George. Guards reached the sympathizers who had run forward first, and they set on them with fists and clubs. A man toppled at Honor's side, blood gushing from his nose. A youth stumbled and fell, then instantly jumped to his feet and swung his fist at a guard. Another young man broke free from a guard and lunged at the bishop's chancellor. His knuckles smashed the priest's face. The priest collapsed and fell facedown in the muck.

As Honor reached George, the heat of the flames hit her like a fist. She smelled his charred skin. He looked down at her from the ledge, his dried eyes stuck open, and recognition leapt there—a spark of joy at her presence—even as he continued to writhe. Wildness overtook her. She could not stop herself. She dropped to her knees and pawed at the burning faggots. She batted away scorching chunks of straw, scattering blazing sticks, feeling nothing but a surging desperation to kill the fire.

"Here!" a man yelled at her. Liquid splashed over her hands. She gasped at the cold relief, suddenly aware of the stabbing pain, and looked up. The wrestler had grabbed the hogshead of beer from the apprentices and was sloshing it all over the straw and burning sticks. The flames died. The faggots hissed steam and billowed smoked. Honor looked up at George in a daze of elation. The fire was out!

A cheer went up.

Then, a scream. Honor staggered to her feet. The apprentices were leading a vicious counterattack on the sympathizers. Men and women were fighting all around her. Punching, kicking, gouging. With hands throbbing, she looked around for Richard. Through the mass of bodies she spotted his face, smeared with blood. He was fighting two guards. For every blow he landed they returned doubly brutal punches. His ear was ripped, streaming blood. A fist to his stomach made him double over. One of his attackers pulled a dagger.

Something ferocious shot through Honor. She grabbed the closest stick, as thick as her arm and sharp at the tip, still smoking from the fire, and pushed through the flailing bodies, frantic to get to Richard. He chopped at the dagger hand of his attacker, knocking the man's blade to the ground, but the other guard landed a punch to his jaw that sent him reeling. A third guard had fallen to his knees behind Richard, and he snatched the dropped dagger. Gripping it with savage determination, he aimed the tip upward for an underhand thrust at Richard's back.

Honor reached the man and stabbed with the stick, its tip spearing his throat. Flashing her a look of shock, he gasped and dropped the dagger. Blood spurted from his throat. He groped at his neck, smeared black from the charred wood and red with blood. He gasped for air with a gurgling sound, and fell. Richard punched one of his two other attackers, who staggered in place, and before the second one could swing, Richard grabbed Honor's hand and pulled her away. Hacking with his free arm, he cut a path through the crowd.

They reached the edge of the melee and she realized he meant to pull her all the way clear of Smithfield. She dug in her heels. "No! We can't go! We can save him!"

"We can't. Look." He jerked her around by the shoulders to show her.

A troop of the Queen's guard was galloping up from Pie Corner. At least thirty soldiers in half-armor. With swords held high, they thundered toward the rioting crowd with all the terrifying power of cavalry. Some in the crowd saw them coming and started to run. The soldiers expertly broke into a three-pronged formation and galloped after the escapees. Women screamed. Swords slashed. Blood gushed. Men toppled. Some soldiers swung down off their mounts and joined the guards in beating the troublemakers to their knees. Victims curled up beneath the merciless blows. Within minutes the Queen's soldiers were dragging their quarry away, bloodied and broken.

Honor felt Richard snatch her hand and yank her, like the sharp tug of a rope. They ran.

They were almost at the Elms when a woman shrieked. Honor looked back at the pit. Fresh flames had burst around George, leaping as high as his waist.

When they reached Newgate they melded into the oblivious, plodding crowd of farmers, maids, draymen atop wagons, lords on horseback—all passing in and out through the great arch. Panting, dazed, Honor and Richard leaned against the stone arch wall, out of the stream of traffic, hiding in its shadows. Standing behind her, he wrapped his arms around her and pulled her backward to him. Her head thumped back against his chest, her burned hands pulsing pain, her spirit beaten. She felt his chest heave in a torment all his own. She slumped in his arms, her throat scalded by sobs she could not control.

In the busy city, the bells of St. Paul's clanged.

❧ 14 ❧

Commons and Lords

December 1555

The River Thames was sluggish under thickly falling snow as the wherry's bow nudged the Whitehall Palace wharf. Honor ducked her head as she moved out from under the boat's canopy, and found the wharf as busy as ever with people who had come to do business at court, though they bustled with cheerless determination in the damp December chill. Cheerless, indeed, was her own state of mind. There were just three weeks until Christmas, but she felt no connection to the lighthearted joys of the season. Stepping onto the water stairs, she tugged her fur-lined cloak tighter using just her fingertips, but even that motion made her blistered palms sting under the linen dressings. Yet how paltry her pain was, she thought, compared to what George had suffered.

Her heart was so heavy she could not have said which weight was the more punishing—her grief at George's death, or her revulsion at the woman whose policy had condemned him. The same woman, she was sure, who had sent an assassin last month to kill Elizabeth—or at least connived the attack with the imperial ambassador—and almost killed Adam instead. The very woman she was on her way to see. Queen Mary. Honor wondered if she could bear to make yet another empty report to her about Elizabeth. How could she manage to hold back her fury? Yet she had to, for Elizabeth's sake. Had to find out from the Queen herself the truth behind whispers of a new dark design she had against her sister. Honor had been warned of it by a trusted source, the French ambassador. Parliament was to be the Queen's instrument.

"I have heard," Noailles said as they had dined alone at his house in the city, "that she has asked the Duke of Norfolk to draw up a bill in the Lords to declare Princess Elizabeth illegitimate. That would instantly bar her from the succession."

Honor had been appalled. "And leave open the door for the Queen's husband to seize the crown."

Noailles nodded in grim agreement. "Philip of Spain on the throne of England." It was the French king's nightmare.

An English nightmare was what it portended to Honor—for Elizabeth and the whole country. Philip taking power would so enrage Englishmen it could unleash civil war. But that did not seem to concern this criminally irresponsible queen. Far more important was saving her subjects' immortal souls from the pollution of the sister she considered a bastard and a heretic. But, though the House of Lords might ram through such a bill, would the House of Commons agree to pass it? Honor fervently hoped not. But hope was no defense. It was up to Richard and their friends in the House to actually fight the Queen. He was in Westminster at this very moment, fighting her other bills.

She made her way through the courtyard where courtiers and servants trod gingerly over cobbles slick with ice. A troop of the Palace Guard marched past, the battle-axes atop their halberds glinting through the falling snow, and Honor's mind flashed back to the guard she had stabbed in the throat at Smithfield. That charred stick. His shock and horror. His spurting blood. Had he survived, or had she committed murder? The possibility sent a shiver through her. But she realized, with a calmness that shocked her even more, that the guilt she felt was a mere surface discomfort. The man would have killed Richard. The Queen's tyrannical rule, she thought, has made savages of us all.

She continued past the clock tower and around to the rear of the palace and through the snow-deadened gardens, then climbed the private outdoor stairway to the royal apartments. She entered the warmth of the antechamber and was still batting snow off the hem of her skirt with the back of her swollen hand when a young lady-in-waiting came and told her that Her Majesty was ready to see her. Honor took a deep breath to stifle her revulsion. *Play the part. Be her friend. Get the information.*

The moment she was ushered into the Queen's private chamber she felt a flutter of alarm. Queen Mary sat at dinner before a blazing fire, but not alone. To her right sat Frances Grenville. To her left, John Grenville. When had *he* become so close to the Queen?

"Mistress Thornleigh," the Queen said in that mannish voice that always unnerved Honor. She thumped her goblet down as though declaring a challenge. "You and yours have been mightily busy since we saw you last."

Honor made her curtsy, her skin prickling. "It has been some time, indeed, since I have had the pleasure of seeing Your Majesty." The Queen looked ten years older, she thought. Pining for her husband? Philip, it was said, had been living with his mistress in Brussels these last four months. Honor nodded civilly to Frances Grenville and the baron. "And it is always a pleasure to see my neighbors."

"Do not be so sure. Lord Grenville has brought me very grave news. I will have the truth from you."

News? Truth? Honor had the queasy sense that she had fallen into a trap. The scene before her—the ladies-in-waiting quietly bustling with dishes of food at the sideboard, the musician across the room plucking a sweet tune on his lute, the cheery fire—it was all at odds with the dread creeping into her breast. The three of them at the table sat watching her like judges. Why?

"But first I want to speak of your son. Of his action that saved my sister from an assassin's attack. I am informed that he intentionally risked his life to save hers. How can you account for his behavior? Does your son not share your view of this pernicious woman?"

It was hard for Honor to find her voice, choked by her certainty that the Queen had ordered the attack herself, and horrified that

Adam was under suspicion. "I can vouchsafe for him, Your Majesty. He is a young man trained in dealing with danger on the seas. His action was a kind of reflex, an unthinking response."

"*You* can vouchsafe? And why should I believe a word you say? I trusted you, madam, gave you my friendship, and look how you repay me." She pushed away from the table so abruptly it made the chair legs shriek. Both the Grenvilles immediately rose, too. John watched the Queen with a barely concealed excitement that made Honor feel suddenly cold.

The Queen stumped to the sideboard, to a silver basin of water, and thrust her hands in to cleanse them, splashing them about like panicked birds. A lady-in-waiting bowed as she handed her an embroidered hand towel. Mary wiped her hands roughly, glaring at Honor the whole time. "What happened to your hands?" she demanded.

"A foolish accident, Your Majesty. A brazier of hot coals came loose from its bracket. Unthinking, I reached out to steady it."

"Unthinking? Like your son?" Mary's eyes narrowed on her. "You were indeed unwise. Burned flesh is a serious business."

Honor thought of George writhing in the flames, and had to bite her tongue.

Mary flung the towel onto the sideboard. "Enemies on all sides," she said darkly. "My bastard sister. This wretched Parliament. Your family."

All Honor could think of was saving Adam from the Queen's wrath. "We are no enemies, Your Majesty. My son has proven his good heart in his devotion to your pious concerns. He is helping Mistress Grenville reestablish the priory in Colchester." She looked to Frances, desperately hoping for support.

A strange light shone in Frances's eyes, as though she relished Honor's fall. But Honor believed that the woman's keen interest was also fed by her infatuation with Adam. Her hysterical behavior in church was hard to forget. Disturbing as that was, Honor now needed Frances on her side. Looking right at her, she said, "He takes such delight in doing this work with Mistress Grenville."

Frances blurted eagerly, "He has told you so?"

"Often."

The Queen bellowed, "We speak not of monks but of treason!"
The lute tune died. The ladies-in-waiting ducked their heads. Honor felt frozen with dread.

John Grenville cleared his throat, trying to hide his pleasure at the Queen's outburst but not succeeding. "Your Majesty, if I may question her?"

"Do. I have no patience with the woman."

He turned to Honor with the coiled aggression of a prosecutor. "Misguided your son may have been, madam. We shall see. At the moment, though, another member of your family more nearly endangers Her Majesty's peace. In Westminster, in Parliament, an unruly faction at this very moment is stirring up unrest in the Commons to thwart her Majesty's bills, and among the rabble-rousers is your husband. How do you account for *his* behavior?"

Honor had barely recovered from the attack on Adam. This was worse. The vicious gleam in Grenville's eyes spoke of his hatred for Richard, a hate that had festered since his father's death at Richard's hand. "My lord, my husband's actions—"

"His duplicity!" the Queen burst in. "And this is not the first time. I have just been told that he joined the heinous uprising against us led by the traitor Wyatt. My councilors advised me at the time that many men were duped by that villain's lies and deceits, men who otherwise were loyal subjects, and on that advice I pardoned many in an act of mercy, including, apparently, your miserable husband. But now he rails against me in Parliament. Is this how you and yours value my benevolence? My friendship?"

Honor swallowed. "My husband is green in the ways of Parliament, Your Majesty. I trust that a sovereign as wise as you can forgive a novice's mere bluster."

Mary's lip curled. "When I pardoned him I, too, was green— new to my calling as God's chosen servant. I know better now. I rule for His glory."

She came forward until they stood just inches apart, her eyes boring into Honor's with all the hurt pride of a woman abandoned by her own husband. Mary was shorter, and Honor, sensing that her taller stature was a further indignity to the Queen, dropped to her knees and bowed her head.

The Queen gave a snort, then turned and walked back toward the table. "My lord, I am done. Have the sergeant of the guard take her elsewhere."

Honor could hardly breathe as she raised her head to John Grenville. He looked as if he could not believe his good fortune. "And what is your will, Your Majesty?" he asked. "Further interrogation?"

She fluttered her hand impatiently over her shoulder. "Do with her what you will."

Frances's eyes flicked between the three of them—her brother, Honor, and the Queen—as though a battle of indecision was raging inside her. Suddenly, she moved toward the Queen. "Your Majesty, may I have a word?"

They met at Arundel's Tavern that evening to strategize. It was well away from Westminster, deep in the old city, a few hundred yards west of London Bridge on Poultney Lane. Richard poured ale from a pitcher for the nine of them around the table. They were all tired, hungry, and thirsty after the intense Commons debate over the Queen's ecclesiastical revenues bill. It had started at eight in the morning and gone on all day, and when the vote was called they had lost. Richard had been shocked—he'd thought they had the support they needed. But he was quickly learning about Parliament. He wouldn't again underestimate the Queen's allies in the House.

Robert Young growled, "I hear Cardinal Pole called it a great victory."

"A disaster," said Sir Henry Peckham.

They sat in silence, chewing on their grievance and the challenge that lay ahead. Next up for debate in the coming days was the Exiles Bill. They could not afford to lose that one.

A cockfight was noisily underway in the next room. The battling birds flapped and squawked in their frantic fight to the death while the gamblers yelled encouragement. The bloodlust sickened Richard as he thought of George Mitford and that rabble who had come to watch him burn. And poor George was just one of so many—well over two hundred had been sent to the stake. This Queen had much to answer for.

He took in the bitter faces around him. To his left was Honor's friend, the indefatigable Sir William Cecil, Richard's astute leader in this fight. There were no official parties, but Cecil had been the driving force behind organizing a loose alliance of those opposed to the Queen's bills. He was a skilled politician, and as Richard worked alongside him he had admired how the man kept at it day and night, coaxing MPs at suppers at his town house on Canon Row, calling informal conferences in local taverns, making common cause with men from all parts of the country, honing their discontent. And, perhaps most important, organizing the other leading men of the opposition, the others around this table. Peckham, Young, William Courtenay, Sir Anthony Kingston, Christopher Chamborne, Sir John Perrot, Alfred Roper. They were more than disappointed by today's loss—they felt cheated, humiliated, outraged. And ready to fight back, Richard hoped. Roper's pockmarked face was still red with fury. How many others felt the same? A hundred and nineteen had voted with them today—astonishing, he now realized, since it was rare for any bill promoted by the monarch to incite such opposition. But still it wasn't enough. They needed a hundred and fifty-five. Defeating the Exiles Bill would be an uphill struggle, and Richard wasn't sure it could be done, but a plan was starting to form in his mind. These men, he thought, are hungry to settle the score, and revenge is a powerful spur.

Cecil said quietly, "If we lose the Exiles Bill the danger goes beyond the threat to our property. It could embolden the Queen to move against Princess Elizabeth."

"How?" Courtenay asked.

Richard said, "With a bill to declare her illegitimate and bar her from the succession." Cecil had told him this morning.

"Good God," Chamborne said, "I'd heard the rumors, but—"

"All true," said Cecil.

There was a hush of dismay. "Would she dare?" Kingston said. "The Lady Elizabeth is a princess of the blood."

"Northumberland did it," Cecil answered darkly.

Richard well remembered those dangerous days not two years ago. At the death of the boy-king, Edward, the succession fell to his sister Mary, but the Duke of Northumberland made a grab for power and set his daughter-in-law, Lady Jane Grey, on the throne. The hapless seventeen-year-old was queen for nine days, until Mary rallied men and troops from all over the country, took back what was hers, and beheaded her cousin Jane.

"Northumberland's scheme failed," Cecil said, "but the Queen's may not. I fear she dreams of passing on her throne to her husband."

Peckham let out a low whistle of alarm. "Englishmen will never abide a Spanish king. Has she no sense?"

"Damn her eyes!" Roper growled.

"She has made no such motion yet, gentlemen," Perrot said brusquely, "so let us stick to the issue at hand. The Exiles Bill. We must do our all to keep this malicious attack from becoming the law of the land."

There was no argument. Every man here, and most other MPs in the Commons, too, had friends and relatives among the refugees who had fled the Queen's policy of persecution. In Antwerp, Richard and Honor had hosted suppers for some of them, including Cecil's brother-in-law, John Cheke, and his father-in-law, Anthony Cooke. Many were men of means, including the Earl of Bedford and Princess Elizabeth's friends Sir Francis Knollys and his wife Catherine, Elizabeth's cousin. The departure of these Protestants had begun as a trickle when the Queen had come to power, but became a flood as she'd stepped up her program of burnings. Richard downed his ale, trying not to worry about Honor's long-ago conviction by the heresy court, and the threat that lurked for her because of it.

The immediate threat was to the exiles, for the bill would allow the Queen to confiscate their estates' revenues, but Richard and the others were convinced that if she won this, she would set her sights on the property of suspected Protestants at home, and that threatened every man here and a good portion of their Commons colleagues, too. The trouble was, those colleagues were cowed by the Queen's enormous power to punish and reward. She could make anyone who opposed her suffer, by stifling their advancement, while those who backed her got gifts of rent-rich lands or posts that brought windfalls of cash benefits.

"Our task is twofold," Cecil said, getting down to business. "First, to keep on our side the hundred and nineteen who voted with us today. Some may be wavering, so we must be resourceful and vigilant in holding them to our cause. Second—and much more difficult—to win over the thirty-six we need for victory."

"The great thing is we have Pollard," said Chamborne. On the first day the Commons met, they had elected the Speaker of the House, who ran the proceedings. Sir John Pollard was a known Protestant sympathizer.

"We've got more than him," Richard said, indicating Cecil. "Sir William, you've done miracles."

Cecil looked far from convinced. "I'm afraid that's what it's going to take."

Richard felt a pang of doubt. Cecil was the expert in this arena.

"A miracle . . . or else an uprising." The quiet comment was from Sir Anthony Kingston, and it sent a subdued thrill through Richard's colleagues around the table. He saw that they were all watching Kingston, waiting, as though wanting more.

"Anthony, have you had further talk with our friend?" Alfred Roper asked. His words were cautious but his tone rang with a fiery eagerness.

Kingston nodded. "Last night."

Richard leaned in to Cecil. "Friend?" he whispered.

Cecil answered quietly, "Sir Henry Dudley."

Richard knew the name. Dudley was a lifelong soldier, and had served as captain of the guard at Boulogne. During the Queen Jane debacle, the Duke of Northumberland had sent him to France to try to win backing for Jane.

"And does he still stand ready to command for us?" asked Roper. They all kept their voices low.

"Ready and willing," Kingston said.

"As long as we will fund him," Young put in. It wasn't bitterness that steeled his voice, just realism.

"And pledge our retainers as his troops," Perrot agreed.

"Still, as a last resort . . ." said Courtenay.

Richard wasn't sure what to think. It was bracing to know that an experienced military commander was at hand should they need to resort to a real fight. And he did not doubt the commitment of these men. But he had marched with Wyatt, a brave commander, and seen Wyatt's support evaporate overnight. Where Wyatt had failed, could this man Dudley succeed?

"War is always a last resort," Cecil said grimly.

"But often the only way, sir," said Roper. His pocked face had reddened again with zeal, and his eyes were alight like a Crusader's. "And think, if we take Whitehall Palace, we can carry out the work of Christ. Destroy this devil-spawned queen and wash the streets clean with her papist blood."

"No, sir, we will not," Cecil said firmly. "If revolt is necessary, our goal will be to exile the Queen, not to kill her."

The zealot, Roper, disgusted Richard. The last thing the country needed was to replace one tyrannically religious regime with another. Twenty years ago he had seen abominable cruelty in Münster, the work of fanatic Protestants. It was not love of Christ that drove them, but hatred of Catholics. Cecil obviously had faith in the war-eager Roper, so he must be reliable, but all Richard saw was a dangerous weak link of extremism. Zealots love to preach, he thought, and one unguarded word about planning an insurrection could lead them all to the gallows. But he was no strategist, so he held his tongue.

"Let us endeavor to win the battle without shedding blood or treasure," Cecil told Roper. "Let us look to Parliament and rally our troops there." It was a clear order to cut short the talk of rebellion. "Now, here is what we must achieve tonight."

He talked on while the fight in the next room climaxed with a cock's crow of victory and the winners' jubilant hoots. By the time the nine of them adjourned, each had a roster of names of fellow MPs whom they had pledged to persuade or cajole into seeing where their best interests lay. They had to accomplish it by tomorrow's vote.

As they were leaving the tavern, Richard said to Cecil, "Do you know the sergeant-at-arms?"

"Of the House? Martin Rowland. Why?"

"We just might need him on our side."

They all bade each other good luck for the evening's work ahead, and Richard walked up Fish Street under dark clouds pregnant with snow. He was heading back to the Crane Inn, where he and Honor always stayed when they were in London. After the taste he'd had of the tavern's pork and pease, more like gristle and lard, he was hungry for a trencher of something decent before setting out to visit his list of MPs. The wind was still sharp, and as he turned the corner onto Thames Street the first snowflakes scuttled down past the rooftops. He passed Fishmonger's Hall, and through the snow he saw the Crane Inn's bright red and blue sign depicting the river's three famous loading cranes. The inn felt like a second home. He had known its owner, Leonard Legge, since the day twenty years ago when he'd fished Richard, pierced with three arrows, out of the Thames. Legge hadn't been able to save his eye, but he had saved his life. A fine friend. Richard remembered how Isabel, at age seven or eight, used to love coming along on his trips to London's Blackwell Hall cloth market, just to stay at the Crane and play with Legge's boisterous young brood. Those children were parents themselves now, and it was Legge's little grandchildren who served the guests their meals and fetched their beer.

How the years fly, he thought as he opened the door to the warmth of the inn's common room. Isabel was now a mother herself. He knew Honor longed to see their first grandchild, and so did he. But if and when Isabel and Carlos came home to England with their baby son, what would they find? John Grenville had always cast greedy eyes on Richard's property, especially the abbey. It spurred his resolve to rope in those fence-sitting MPs. He would not let Grenville strip his children of their patrimony.

He climbed the stairs and opened the door to their room and stopped cold. Honor was on her hands and knees, scrabbling to reach something on the floor. She turned to him, white-faced. Dread thumped his chest. He had never seen her look so frightened.

❧ 15 ❧

Discord

December 1555

Honor gasped when the door swung open. Richard walked in. She sank back on her heels, weak with relief.

She had been so shaken when she left the palace, her legs felt so limp she hardly knew how she managed to hire a wherry for the downriver trip to the Queenhithe Wharf and then walk the two blocks to the inn. She could still see the Queen's furious face . . . Grenville's wolfish smile . . . the steel battle-axe atop the sergeant's halberd. She had started to pack almost in a panic, and fumbled a money casket that crashed to the floor, spilling coins. She dropped to her knees and pawed at it with her bandaged hands to see if it was broken, but she was trembling and had to steady herself against the rim of the trunk she was packing.

"What are you doing?" Richard said, frowning at the jumble of clothes she had thrown in the trunk, more clothes heaped on the bed, another open trunk across the room.

"Leaving." She abandoned the broken casket and began scooping up coins in handfuls despite her cumbersome bandages, and dumping the money straight into the trunk. "We have to leave."

"Leave? What's wrong? Has something happened at home?"

"Can't go home, either. They'll come for us." Coins had rolled under the bed and she crouched lower, reaching out blindly to grope for them. She and Richard would need every ounce of gold now.

She heard his boots come closer, heard the worry in his voice as he asked, "Honor, what's happened?"

"You cannot go back to Parliament."

"What? Of course I'm going back. The Exiles Bill comes up for debate first thing in the morning." She was still grubbing under the bed, desperate to reach the coins. "Forget those and look at me, would you?" he said. "You know what's at stake. If we don't defeat this bill we could lose everything we own."

She turned on him. "If we stay we'll lose our lives!"

She struggled to her feet and started toward the other trunk, but he grabbed her arm to stop her. "What in God's name has happened?"

She looked up at his face and felt a shot of strength from his firm grip. Enough strength to pull herself together and tell him everything. How the Queen had turned against her in a rage, had cast doubt on Adam's loyalty for saving Elizabeth, had questioned Richard's loyalty for inciting the Commons, livid that she had ever pardoned him. She told him how John Grenville had been about to march her away with the palace guard. "And if she had agreed, I would not be here to tell you."

"Good God." He took her in his arms and held her close. "What hell for you."

She closed her eyes, her cheek against his chest, and took comfort in the smell of him, that familiar mix of laundered linen, sweat, and horse.

"How did you stop her?" he asked.

"I didn't. Frances Grenville did."

He said baffled, "What?"

She pulled away to look at him, still not quite believing it herself. One moment Grenville had been about to march her off to some cell for questioning, and the next moment Frances was whispering to the Queen, and then the Queen told Grenville to let her go. "I think, maybe, it's because of Adam."

That seemed to stun him even more. "Is she so besotted with him?"

"Enough to want to save his good name, I think. And the Queen has such affection for her she relented." It was the only explanation that made sense. There was a bang out on the street and she flinched. Just a wagon, she told herself, but it shook her back to the crisis. "Richard, the Queen's last words were 'Rein in your husband.' She means it. You cannot go back to the Commons."

He was looking across the room, his mind moving on. He said grimly, "This changes the battlefield."

"Exactly. We have to get away as soon as possible. Back to Antwerp. For good. Come, help me pack."

She started to turn, but again he took her arm to stop her. He looked at her for a long moment.

"Let me go. There's so much to arrange before—"

"Honor, stop. We're not going back. Now that we're under suspicion, there's no way to go but forward. We have to stay and fight."

"Stay and . . . ?" She did not want to say *fight*. The word felt sharp in her mouth, like a nettle. From the corner of her eye she saw snow fall past the window, jerking in the gusts as though in pain. Downstairs, someone was laughing. "Don't you understand? We have to save ourselves."

"I've given my word. There are good men counting on me. We need every single vote to defeat this bill, you know we do, because—"

"Damn the bill. Let *them* defeat it. It's *you* the Queen is watching."

"Because if we don't," he said pointedly, "if we let her have her way, we'll be handing her a weapon to ruin us. I won't let her steal everything we've built. We have to take a stand."

She didn't want to hear this. She turned to the bed and snatched things—a linen shirt of his, a silk shift of hers—and balled them up and threw them in the trunk.

"You know it's true," he said. "You knew it when you warned the Princess back at Hatfield. You told her she may have to fight."

"I was wrong!" She grabbed an armful of clothes and dumped the things into the trunk. "I was wrong about everything. I told Adam to stay with Elizabeth and it almost got him killed. I told you to take the seat in Parliament and it could get *you* killed."

"What's happened is not your fault."

She slammed down the trunk lid. "No, the fault is all the Queen's. And the *power* is all hers, too." She went to the trunk across the room and picked up books stacked on the floor and threw them in.

He came to her. "People are counting on me, Honor. I have a job to do here." He added gently, "And so do you. The Princess needs you. Cecil knew that when he asked you to advise her. Elizabeth is in as much danger as we are. More. You cannot desert her now."

She looked at him, trying not to tremble, not show how deeply his words cut her. She shook her head, hardly able to find words. "I've had enough of danger, Richard. Enough of terror. George was . . ." She fought the quaver in her voice. "I cannot fight them anymore. I cannot bear another day of this."

He seemed to take her weak tone as a surrender, and started to pull her into his arms. "I'll do the fighting."

"I don't need pity!" she cried, pushing him away. "I need you to see sense and come away with me!"

He said very soberly, "I can't do that. I will not slink back to Antwerp and forfeit everything we own. Honor, we have a good chance of winning this fight in Parliament if we—"

"*That's* what you want. The thrill of Parliament. And for that you would bring down the Queen's wrath on us."

"Thrill? I'm scared to death."

"Then come away!"

"No. I will not let her run us off again. We ran last year, left everything behind and ran like dogs. And it was the worst year of my life. Looking bankruptcy in the face. Watching Adam work as a common seaman because I couldn't employ him. Watching Isabel sail off to God knows what hardship in the New World because I had nothing to give her and Carlos. Watching you sell your jewels—"

"I don't need jewels. And we have *some* money. We have the house in Antwerp, too."

"And how long before we'd have to sell it to feed ourselves? I am not a young man. I don't have the luxury of time to start earning a living from scratch."

"Richard, I would take in washing before I'll stay another day here."

"You're talking nonsense. And you're not listening to me. Nothing will make me run away again."

"Nothing can make me stay. I'm going to get away from this madhouse country, and on the very next ship that sails. I hope that ship will be the *Elizabeth* with Adam captaining her, because I need to get him to safety, too. And if you have any sense you'll come with us."

His face darkened. "Don't rope Adam into running. Don't force him to take you there."

"Once he hears what's happened he'll *want* to go. He has more sense than you."

"Don't do that to him. He needs to build a life here."

"You can't stop him."

"I think I can."

"You would order him?"

"If you make him choose, yes. Don't, Honor."

They stared at each other, she breathing hard, he rock still. Suddenly, he turned and strode to the door.

"Where are you going?"

"To work. *Someone's* got to keep their word."

"If you go out that door, consider it locked."

He walked out, slamming it behind him.

❧ 16 ❧

The Jaws of Victory

December 1555

The temperature had plunged overnight. As the House of Commons convened to debate the Exiles Bill, wind blew in icy gusts that blasted the precincts of Westminster along its waterfront expanse. Going up the steps into Westminster Hall, Richard rubbed his hands to warm them after the frigid boat trip from the city.

He had spent a sleepless night at the house of his London agent. The awful quarrel with Honor had unnerved him. It wasn't like her to buckle under pressure. He understood her fears, of course. Watching George's terrible death. Facing down the Queen's wrath. And she must be in pain with those burned hands. But she knew that she had bound herself to Princess Elizabeth's cause. And the damned thing was, she was right about that cause. As long as Queen Mary ruled, they would be forever hiding, dissembling, forever fearful of her power to ruin them, to even take their lives. And John Grenville, now so close to the Queen—he would do his all to hasten that destruction, Richard was sure. Now, as never before, they had to take a stand. Honor had to see that, he felt. Now that she had slept on it, she would see it.

In any case, he couldn't stew about it now. He had to stay focused on today's fight. So as he walked into Westminster Hall he welcomed the din of legal business that engulfed him. The sheer

size of the place always awed him. It was one of the largest medieval halls in Europe, and from the honeycomb of shop stalls that
lined its length, hundreds of haggling voices echoed up to its massive hammer-beam roof. The place teemed with members of Parliament, lawyers and their clients, judges, priests, clerks, scriveners,
pages, footmen, food vendors, ale sellers, and soldier-guards of the
sergeant-at-arms. Richard made his way past stalls that spiced the
air with the smell of their wares, the tang of meat pies and saffron
buns alongside the mustiness of books, paper, and parchments.
Outside, faint cries of "Oars! Eastward ho!" came from the busy
wharf where gentlemen, lords, and servants shouted for wherries
to take them back to the city.

Richard bought the paper and ink he needed, jammed them in
his satchel, and left the Hall to make his way toward the House of
Commons, squeezing past a rookery of black-robed lawyers bickering outside the Court of King's Bench, while inside a lawyer
thundered his case in Latin. To the east and south of the Hall lay
a warren of offices, library, chapel, kitchens. These had once been
the domestic apartments of the monarch's household, for the
centuries-old Palace of Westminster had been a royal residence
for generations of kings until Henry VIII moved his main residence to Whitehall Palace, leaving Westminster solely as the hub
of government. All this Richard had learned from his mentor here,
Sir William Cecil. The place now housed the Court of King's Bench
and the Court of Common Pleas, the Treasury, and the Chancery,
the administrative branch of the Crown, as well as Parliament
when in session, both the House of Lords and House of Commons. Westminster was such a crowded place that for over two
centuries the Commons had met in whatever room was available.
But five years before Queen Mary took the throne, they had been
granted a home in the chapel originally used by the monarch's
family. St. Stephen's Chapel became the permanent House of
Commons.

Richard pushed through the throng of hangers-on outside the
House, showed his badge to the guards at the door, and walked in.
St. Stephen's Chapel was not large—Adam's new ship was bigger—
but it was magnificent. Its slender stone piers and vaulted ceiling

seemed to float above the splendid stained glass windows. But Richard imagined that the ghosts of past kings would be shocked by what the place had become. Built as a spiritual oasis of peace, it was now as packed as a bawling market square and as raucous as a boys' dormitory. Three hundred and nineteen MPs milled among the sloping choir stalls on either side, and on the stone floor between them. The word Parliament came from the French word *parler*, to talk, but right now there was a great deal of shouting. Everyone was on edge after the seemingly endless days of debate.

Richard especially. He felt on tenterhooks as he strode across the chapel floor. So much depended on this vote. He spotted Cecil and climbed the steps to the choir benches, elbowing past MPs standing in ragged groups. Cecil, who stood listening to the member from Buxton rant at him, had cocked his head in irritation, his customary calm civility obviously pushed to the brink. He saw Richard coming and made his way toward him. They met in the aisle.

"I count it at a hundred and forty-three for us," Richard said, raising his voice above the ruckus. "We're so close."

Cecil nodded, cautious hope apparent on his weary face. "They'll have to call the vote today."

Richard looked around. "Or face a mutiny."

Cecil jutted his chin toward the elderly MP from Coventry, shuffling to his seat in the lower choir stalls. "Did you talk to old Perkins? How did that go?"

"Sweet-talked him for an hour last night," Richard said. "Even promised him ten ells of Florentine silk for his daughter's wedding. No good. He won't budge."

"Old fool."

"But a dozen others are leaning our way." Richard and Cecil and their seven friends from the tavern had been at it all night—and the three days and nights before that—visiting undecided colleagues at their homes, stopping them on the street, in shops, in taverns, laying out the horrors that awaited their mutual friends among the exiles if the bill passed, and outlining the potential dangers to them personally, namely the confiscation of their estates and impoverishment of their families. Richard had been heartened by the response—the bill incensed most of them—and he felt that a small majority were ready to kill it. But he was nervous after losing the ecclesiastical bill. These fair-weather friends could waver if they had much time to think about the Queen's persuasions. Hard for principles to compete with a post that brought bags of money. What was essential now was the timing.

He scanned the faces for Kingston, Peckham, and the rest. "Are all the others here?"

Cecil pointed them out around the room, the seven men of their faction. Each was engaged in earnest talk with some MP.

"And the Speaker?"

Cecil nodded. "Pollard will support us." He looked at Richard. "Ready, then?"

"Ready."

They moved down to the floor and spent the next hour milling among the three hundred and seventeen other MPs, shoring up votes, urging others to join them. Just before ten o'clock Richard and Cecil and their seven friends stood near the closed chapel doors, set to enact their plan. Richard was nervous, but eager to make this happen.

Speaker Pollard caught his eye and Richard nudged Cecil to get his attention. Cecil turned and nodded to Pollard, and the Speaker nodded back. Richard felt a thud of hope. This was it.

"Order!" the Speaker called out. "This House will come to order! Order!"

It took a few minutes for all the MPs to hear him and calm down, but soon they began heading for their seats. Cecil, Peckham, Courtenay and Perrot did, too, as planned, while Richard stuck by the closed doors with Kingston, Chamborne, Young, and Roper. They all had their roles. The first four fanned out to steel the nerve of the suspected waverers, while the other five would stop anyone from slipping out the doors to avoid voting. Richard would call loudly for the vote the moment Cecil gave him the nod, and Kingston would second it.

The debate began. The Queen's spokesman, Sir Matthew Aylesworth, got to his feet and delivered a diatribe against the exiles. Warming to his subject, he denounced them as "These wretches, these heretics, these traitorous, execrable villains!"

Richard looked around at the brooding faces in the choir stalls. Aylesworth either didn't know or didn't care how his invective was infuriating many of these men. Though every one of them outwardly conformed to the state religion, just as Richard and his family did, many sympathized with the Protestant cause. *Aylesworth is pushing them into our arms,* he thought. But he also sensed that others, even among those he had visited who had earnestly agreed that the bill was wrong, might now, at this penultimate moment, be too timid to ally themselves with the exiles.

Two members from the west shires rose from their seats in the far stalls and made their way as inconspicuously as possible toward the doors. *Cowards,* Richard thought. Just this morning on the wharf both had assured him they were with him. He stood with his back to the doors, ready to halt them if they got this far. But Peckham and Young stopped them first, engaging them in low, urgent talk. *Good,* he thought. *Keep them here. Make them vote.*

Cecil was on his feet now, speaking to the House. ". . . which touches the rights of every Englishman, born into Her Majesty's protection as well as her service. The rights of property are enshrined in the laws of this realm, both common law and statute."

There was a scraping sound at the door. It opened, forcing Richard to move back. The sergeant-at-arms, Martin Rowland, stepped in and came to his side.

"What is it, Martin?" he asked quietly. He had befriended the man, promising his son a job as secretary to his trading agent in Antwerp. It never hurt to have muscle on your side.

"Some lords on their way, sir."

Richard glanced back at Cecil, who was still speaking with energy as the members of the House listened. Richard stepped outside into the corridor, past the two guards who stood on either side of the doorway looking bored. Three men were striding down the corridor. The Duke of Suffolk, Cardinal Pole, and Baron John Grenville. The Queen's men.

Richard ducked back into the chapel, his pulse thumping. The

bastards were coming to stir things up. The cardinal could inter-
vene in the proceedings with impunity, could request a postpone-
ment. His immense power could easily intimidate most of the
MPs, and all of them would fall into their customary deference to
the authority of a duke, even a baron. And then? Richard did not
doubt that the lords would use bribes, threats, whatever it took to
enact the Queen's will.

He turned to the sergeant. "Lock the doors."

Rowland looked surprised, and not exactly willing.

"Your orders are to guard the Commons, are they not?"

"Aye, sir."

"And it is our right to debate in private. Those men have no
business here."

Rowland considered this, still hesitant.

"Speaker Pollard expects it, Martin," Richard warned. The
sergeant held his job at the pleasure of the Speaker.

That was enough to convince him. He lifted the ring of keys
that hung at his belt, fitted one in the lock, and twisted. The doors
were locked.

Richard turned back. Aylesworth was holding forth again, sug-
gesting that a nay vote could be considered disloyal, even treaso-
nous. Cecil jumped up, furiously ready to rebut, for they could not
let Aylesworth frighten even one of their hard-won allies.

A fist banged on the door. A few faces turned at the sound. The
sergeant ignored it, standing wooden-faced with his arms firmly
crossed.

Richard saw Aylesworth take a breath to continue his screed. *No
time for this*, he thought. *If we don't call the vote now, we're lost.*

"Gentlemen!" Richard called out. Hundreds of startled faces
turned to him, for this was outside the rules of procedure. He
should be in his seat. And he should let Aylesworth finish.

No time for that, either. He stepped forward, just paces from the
doors, and declared, "Three days ago members of this House
pushed through a bill in defiance of many consciences. They must
not do so again. The provisions of this bill are clean contrary to our
rights and the rights of our good fellow countrymen who travel in
foreign parts."

The pounding on the doors got louder and many MPs looked anxious and began murmuring, questioning one another as to what was happening.

"I am a merchant trader," Richard called out. "I own a home in Antwerp where much of my business lies. Would this House, by passing this bill, call me an exile, too, and seize my English property? Many of you likewise do business in the Low Countries, in France, and in the German lands. Would this House call *you* exiles and seize your English property?"

Behind the doors came a muffled shout of "Sergeant, open the doors!" amid more banging.

"This bill must not pass!" Richard cried. He looked to Cecil for help. Cecil looked perplexed, unsure what was happening. This was not the plan.

But two of their friends, Peckham and Courtenay, were closer and immediately left their seats and joined Richard at the doors. It gave Richard a jolt of hope. He threw his arms around their shoulders and declared, "These gentlemen stand with those of us who stand for the rights of Englishmen. Stand with us now, all of you," he challenged the House. "Any man who loves his country, stand with us to fight this bill!"

Kingston, Chamborne and Young stood and cried, "Hear, hear!" and "Down with the bill!" and started for the doors, beckoning others to join them.

There was a hum of confusion. The pounding at the door became a furious hammering. A few more men left their seats, grinning like emboldened schoolboys, and hurried to the doors. Several others stood, looking uncertain but excited. Throughout the chapel, faces that moments ago had been brooding broke into bright looks of anticipation.

Richard shouted, "Mister Speaker, call the vote!"

Cecil finally took the cue. "Mister Speaker, I second the motion. Call the vote!"

Pollard seemed only too ready to do so. Despite the din from three hundred and nineteen excited MPs, he called on them one by one, and each quickly called back "Yay" or "Nay." It went so fast, and Richard was so worked up, he found it hard to keep count.

Finally, amid the raucous babble of the members, and the lords' loud banging at the doors, the Speaker called for silence. He was ready to declare the vote tally.

"Just the one trunk, mistress?" The carter kept his eye on his two adolescent apprentices who were hefting Honor's belongings into his cart.

"Yes," she said, rooting in her pouch for money. She was so distracted by worry she could barely count out the coins. Where was Adam? And Richard—was he at this very moment doing reckless battle in the House of Commons? No word from either of them.

An old man brushed past her, making for the door of the Crane Inn behind her. "Here," she said, handing the carter the money. "Deliver it to the *Bona Esperanza* at Billingsgate Wharf." She added another coin, a large tip. "Get it aboard ship before the bells of St. Paul's ring compline and you'll have another shilling."

He happily pocketed the coins. "Consider it done, my lady."

She felt a small, sharp coldness at her heart. Fleeing England. Again. The Spanish ship was bound for Bruges with the evening tide, the soonest passage she could get. From Bruges she could make her way to Antwerp. But alone, it seemed. Richard had not come back last night and their argument festered inside her like a canker. It made her feel almost ill to be leaving him like this, but her mind was made up. It was madness for them to stay here courting danger. He *must* realize that and follow her to Antwerp. She had written a note to him saying as much, and left it with the landlord.

The apprentices hopped onto the rear of the cart, their legs dangling over the back. The carter settled himself on the bench and flicked his horse's reins, and the vehicle clattered off into the noonday traffic of Thames Street, a skinny dog running after it, barking. Honor watched it go, then pulled her cloak tighter against the damp chill and turned into the arched alley that led to the Crane's stable. A beggar was hunkered beside the arch wearing the coat of a soldier, but tattered and torn. She dropped three pence into his grimy palm.

Ned had her mare saddled in the stable courtyard. She asked him, "Did you get a bite to eat?"

"Aye, my lady. Master Legge had some cold game pie left from breakfast. I thank you."

He looked as though he'd gotten as little sleep as she had, and she felt bad for having made him travel back and forth to Colchester overnight in this bone-chilling weather. She had sent him home with a message for Adam, explaining that they needed to get away from England immediately. She had included another message for Geoffrey and Joan, warning them to be on their guard if the Queen's agents came sniffing. But Ned had returned this morning to report that Adam was not home. "They said he's come to London town, my lady."

What was he doing here? Could she find him before the *Bona Esperanza* set sail?

Mounted, she and Ned left the stable at a walk, their horses clopping along the alley's cobbles under the arch. They paused to let a well-dressed lady march past, her maid hustling at her heels with satchels of market shopping, then they set out along Thames Street, Honor trying to quash her fears about her family. Adam was used to facing danger, she told herself. During the most perilous voyages he had always managed to keep a clear head, for himself and others, and make it through. She would go to the Merchant Adventurers' hall to look for him. If he was not there on business, perhaps someone might know where he was. But if there was no sign of him by five, she would sail alone on the *Bona Esperanza*.

Alone. It made her feel cold to her marrow. But she was doing the right thing and there was no use crying about it.

The traffic, both mounted and on foot, was thick and noisy, making her progress slow. She and Ned hadn't gotten three blocks from the Crane when she had to nudge her horse to one side and wait for a farmer driving seven shaggy cattle in the opposite direction toward the Fleet Street slaughterhouses. The plodding beasts seemed to sense their destination, for they bawled and bellowed.

"My lady . . ." Ned was saying something, but Honor could not hear him above the cattle.

He turned in his saddle and pointed behind them.

She looked back over her shoulder. A man was hurrying down the street toward them, shouting something. Her name? She suddenly realized who it was.

"Sir William!" she called. She turned her horse to face him.

He caught up to her, panting. "Honor—" He took hold of her horse's harness to steady himself as he tried to catch his breath.

"Sir William, what news?" It could only be about Parliament.

He looked up at her, his face pale as ash. "Richard—" He could not speak between tortured breaths.

Something has happened, she thought. *Something terrible has happened.*

The light was dazzling. That was Adam's first thought as Thomas Parry, Princess Elizabeth's steward, led him into the great hall at Somerset House. Not so much a house as a palace, Adam thought, and the construction so new he could smell fresh lumber and paint and marble dust. Everyone in London knew the story. The late Duke of Somerset had ordered it built as his grand new home on the Strand, to lord over the city alongside other riverfront mansions of the nobility. But three years ago, as building neared completion, the duke had fallen afoul of councilors of the boy-king, Edward. He went to the block, and his palatial house was confiscated by the young king, who gave it to his sister, Elizabeth, as her London residence. The final labors of the teams of carpenters, plasterers, and painters had taken until a few months ago.

Adam's boot heels clicked over the marble floor laid out in bold diamonds of white and dolphin blue. Shiny, linenfold paneling the soft color of sand rose forty feet or more to a ceiling spangled with silver stars against a painted background of cerulean blue, breezy as a summer sky. But it was the light from the soaring lead-paned windows that defined the place. Even on this dreary winter afternoon it shone into the hall with the sparkle of spring. Suits her perfectly, he thought.

"Did she get the plans?" he asked Parry. He had sent her his shipwright's designs of the finished *Elizabeth*, feeling sure she would enjoy looking them over. She liked feeling part of his enterprise, and that fired him with a warmth like fine brandy. Arriving here, he had told Parry that he wanted to report to the Princess on her investment in the ship, and indeed he would happily rattle off numbers if she wanted, but in his heart it was a lie. He had come just to see her.

"She did, sir," Parry answered. "Though I cannot vouchsafe that she has yet looked at them."

That disappointed Adam. Deeply. And so did the small crowd chattering around her. She hadn't even noticed him yet. She sat lounging in a chair at the far end of the long table, laughing with three men who stood with tankards of ale. Halfway down the table two ladies played backgammon. Two more sat trading secrets on the blue velvet banquette that lined the wall, while a knot of gallants chatted under a gleaming wall display of swords and crested shields. There were the ever present musicians plucking and bowing a lively tune on their lutes and viols, and some children giggled over a basket of kittens near the massive hearth. He told himself he should be used to it. It had been the same at Hatfield, all these friends of hers, no one much over thirty, everyone taking their ease in her company in games and gossip, dicing and dancing, hunting and hawking. He recognized a few. Among the gentlemen were the captain of her private guard, Sir William St. Loe, and scholars John Dee and Roger Ascham. Among the ladies, her close friends Kat Ashley, Mary St. Loe, Lady Cavendish, Blanche Parry. Adam had enjoyed the company of these people. He just wished they weren't here now.

As if she had heard his thoughts, Elizabeth looked right at him. A spark shot through his chest at the way her eyes met his, so direct, so forthright. He was struck again by the wonder of her—that hair like beaten copper, the blazing red silk dress, the ruby necklace dipping to her breasts, that skin as white as cream. But in an instant her features tightened as though in suspicion or anger, or both. She flicked her gaze away in a gesture so heartless he almost lurched in place.

He hadn't imagined it. Parry said, as though to soften the slight,

"She's tired, sir. We've been mightily busy, moving the whole household in for Christmas."

Adam appreciated the man's subtle kindness. He had come to like Parry when he'd stayed at Hatfield. "I'm sure you've got the place running as smoothly as a Spanish admiral's muster."

"Thank you, sir, but if we're in ship shape I hope it's purely English fashion."

Adam smiled. And as he watched Elizabeth resume chattering with her friends, it was hard to dwell on that odd moment of rebuff. All this light and music and laughter—he couldn't imagine her any other way. How had she been able to bear those two terrible months last year, imprisoned in the Tower? The darkness. The loneliness. The fear. It gave him a shudder to think of her in any kind of pain.

He offered Parry his best wishes for a happy Christmas, and then strode across the hall to Elizabeth. Bowing to her, he rattled off the expected public pleasantries—glad to see her looking so well, and all that. He was no courtier, and was eager to get her alone, so he got to the point. "The *Elizabeth* is ready to launch, my lady. If you can spare some time away from your friends, I'll bring you up-to-date."

She looked at him as though he were a common seaman who had stumbled in from the street. "Friends, sir, before business. Always," she said with icy precision.

He was taken aback by her coldness. What had changed her from the ardently grateful girl who had nursed him with such tenderness?

"You are welcome to wait," she said, flicking her fingers as though to flick him out of her sight. He got the feeling that she meant to leave him cooling his heels indefinitely.

"Pardon, my lady, but I have little time. My ship awaits."

"Then you had better return to her."

Outright dismissal. Adam thought how his stepmother wanted this girl to be queen, and for sheer imperiousness she was halfway there. The men around her were watching them with idle interest. He didn't much care what they thought, but he was not going to leave Elizabeth this way.

"Give me five minutes," he said to her. "Alone."

He hadn't meant it to sound like such a command. God knew he had no business ordering her. The looks of surprise on her friends' faces signaled his clear transgression. Something wild leapt into Elizabeth's eyes. Fury at his audacity? An itching to do battle?

"Five minutes, sir," she said, almost spitting the words. "Come." She rose like an empress and swept past her friends. He followed her out of the hall. Almost immediately she turned into an alcove, a stuffy, windowless nook for servants to hang guests' cloaks and shelve parcels. The moment they were alone she turned on him in anger.

"You take a liberty, sir!"

"I'm sailing the *Elizabeth* to Calais with a cargo. I wanted you to know your investment is going to pay off."

She fixed severe eyes on him. "How will you bear to be parted from your wife?"

He was stunned. "Wife?"

"I hear I am to wish you joy on your forthcoming nuptials."

"Good God, who told you that?"

"Lady Cavendish heard it from Margery Neville. *She* heard it from the lips of your betrothed."

He almost laughed. "And who is my betrothed?"

"The sister of Baron Grenville."

"Frances?" The thought was so absurd he'd blurted her Christian name without thinking, and now he realized the intimacy it suggested. "It is not so, believe me." His need to assure Elizabeth of the error was as strong as his surprise—his delight—that she felt so passionately about it. "Your friend is dead wrong."

"She heard the lady wax most eloquent about you," she shot back witheringly, "and your many charms."

It sounded so foolish to Adam, he had to laugh. "And from that your friend pushed me into the marriage bed?"

She stared him down, her eyebrows tugged tight in anger. But Adam sensed it was now for show. She couldn't hide the tiniest smile creeping over her lips. "Well," she sniffed, conceding with a toss of her head, "she may have misheard."

"I warrant. And you should know how to value court gossip. If the lord treasurer tells his wife there's a cut in the price of bread, his footman reports to the barmaid that the baker will lose his head."

She stifled a laugh. "True. I have sometimes heard tales about *myself* that have astonished me." She looked into his eyes, a sly smile curving her mouth. "So the baron's sister is no more to you than . . . a sister?"

He shrugged. "She's building a priory. She's asked my advice a few times." The thought of Frances talking about him at all, let alone about his "charms" and hinting at marriage, made him squirm a little. He could think of nothing he had done to give her such ideas. He should have a talk with her, he supposed, straighten it out. But at the moment she was the last thing he wanted to think about. Not with Elizabeth so near, and so . . . interested. It thrilled him. And made him reckless. "There's only one lady I hate to part from. I gave my ship her name so I would feel her always near me."

Her sly smile vanished, and she looked at him with such clear-eyed fascination it made him go still just to hold that look and drink it in.

Her voice became hushed, urgent. "Show me."

If any other woman had said it he would have had her in his arms before she took the next breath. But a princess? He felt frozen, even as her eyes kindled fire in him.

Her gaze dropped to his chest. "Show me," she whispered again. "Our bond."

Now he understood. And what a sweet command. He unfastened the top buttons of his doublet and tugged loose the lacing at the collar of his shirt. He opened the shirt to just below his breastbone. Elizabeth's eyes fixed on the puckered scar. She touched it with her fingertips.

It shot an arrow of arousal through him. He swallowed, finding it hard to keep his hands away from her. The ruby necklace caressed the cream-white skin of her breasts above her bodice. Her breath was warm and smelled of sweet cloves.

She looked up into his eyes and gently laid her palm flat over his wound. The heat of her hand, and that smile in her eyes, that skin—it unfroze him, firing him with desire. He covered her hand with his, and pressed her palm against him, hard.

Her lips parted. He bent his head and touched his lips to hers. She pulled back, blinking as though startled. Then, instantly, she raised her face to his for more. Adam took her in his arms and pulled her tightly against him, and she gave a slight gasp as she felt his hardness. He covered her mouth with his in a kiss that set him on fire.

A noise. Someone was coming.

They pulled apart. Adam was breathing hard and unwilling to let her go, even as he saw Parry from the corner of his eye. Elizabeth, too, was catching her breath, and staring back at him in a way that tempted him to make a lunatic lunge and kiss her again, damn Parry and anyone else.

"My lady, Mistress Thornleigh is come, asking to see you."

Adam's gaze snapped to him. His stepmother? It seemed almost laughable, like some stage comedy, his parent marching in to box his ears. He almost *could* have laughed, Elizabeth left him so light-headed.

But Parry's serious tone was anything but light. "An urgent matter, she says. She has come for Master Adam."

They found her waiting in the foyer. Adam took one look at her pale face and knew that something had happened.

"Pardon this intrusion, my lady," she said to Elizabeth. "There has been—" She stopped, clearly needing a moment to steady herself.

Elizabeth said, "Mistress Thornleigh, what's amiss?"

"I have just left Sir William Cecil. The bill . . . in Parliament. The Exiles Bill . . . it was defeated."

"Ah," Elizabeth said, clapping her hands in delight. "Good news, indeed."

Adam felt a surge of pride. His father had played an important part in this victory. But why was his stepmother not smiling? "That's not all, is it?" he said.

She shook her head, and he suddenly saw the vast effort she was making, as though to fend off panic. The look of a sea captain who sees disaster looming but forces a calm face for the crew.

"Your father. He and their friends went to Sir William's house on Canon Row to celebrate, and—"

"And what?" said Adam.

"When the Queen heard the vote result she dissolved Parliament. Lord Grenville marched to Sir William's door with soldiers. He arrested Richard. Adam, he has taken your father to the Tower."

❧ 17 ❧

The Plot

March 1556

"**B**less me, Father, for I have sinned. It has been six weeks since my last confession."

A busy six weeks, John Grenville thought as he said it. He leaned close to the bronze grill that separated him from Father Paxton in the confessional and tallied his gains. In those six weeks he had bought a lucrative manor in Cornwall with three very productive tin mines. Had concluded negotiations for a young niece's marriage to a duke's son, a brilliant step up for his family. And, most satisfying of all, had delivered Richard Thornleigh to the Tower. *The day that murderer becomes gallows fruit,* he thought, *Father can rest in peace.*

His confession was brief. His sins were few.

In five minutes he and the priest met outside the confessional. They were alone in the chapel, part of John's family suite at Whitehall Palace, and John said pleasantly, "Father, I have been busy on your behalf. Bishop of Wealham. Does that appeal to you?"

The priest, who owed his living to the Grenvilles, beamed. "My lord, your generosity humbles me."

"Nonsense, Father." John made a graceful, courtier's bow. "Your service to God humbles *me.*" He did not mention all the favors he had called in. He always followed his father's rule of liberally funding friends in the church, and the churchmen now had come through with this appointment for his candidate. Paxton as bishop would be a fine ally amongst the other bishops in the House of Lords, and a strong voice for God in John's community. Every ally was needed against the pernicious Protestant vermin.

"Will you sup with me in the city, my lord? A few of us have a table at Rimbaud's tonight. Their roast venison is superb."

"And Rimbaud's stock of the best burgundy is vast," John said with a knowing smile. "I thank you, Father, but I have an appointment in less than half an hour that I cannot shirk. In the meantime, I will pray."

They parted, exchanging wishes of "Godspeed."

John waited until the priest was gone. The chapel was quiet. It was a nasty night with icy rain, and most of the palace's inhabitants were snugly sitting at supper before fires in their chambers. John stepped inside the priest's side of the confessional and closed the curtain.

He didn't have to wait long. Roper was always punctual. He slipped into the other side of the confessional and settled himself, catching his breath as though he had hurried. He leaned into the bronze grill, and John could smell wood smoke on the man's clothes and brandy on his breath. His pockmarked face looked reddened from his walk. Or maybe from the brandy.

"The whole mess of them are at it tonight, my lord. A planning meeting at the printer's shop."

"Names."

Roper rhymed them off. A few new ones, John was delighted to hear. He gloried in imagining the Queen's gratitude. This could earn him an earldom. He asked for more details and Roper filled him in. Then he asked, "Has Dudley set a date?"

"Early May, that's his wish. I imagine they'll agree on it tonight. I left early, soon as he gave me my orders. I'm to sound out Sir Humphrey Grandin, and if he's game, bring him into Kingston's company."

"Let me know once you talk to Grandin."

Silence. Roper cleared his throat. "It gets more dangerous for me, my lord, the closer they get to action."

"Yes, yes. Another twenty pounds." John was already pushing aside the curtain to step out. "It will be delivered to the tavern."

A sleety rain was falling as Honor rapped cold knuckles on the printer's door. The shop stood among the crumbling buildings of the sprawling old Blackfriars monastery hard by London Wall, where the monks' former haunts had been converted into a rambling maze of shops and houses. The new pushing out the old, Honor thought. A fitting place to plot the overthrow of the Queen.

Behind her, Adam moved close to her back to conceal her from two men trudging past. The men followed a linkboy who lit their way with a torch that hissed in the frigid rain. When the light died Honor knocked again, daring to be louder, anxious now as she looked up at the dark, shuttered windows of the printer's shop. She could hear no sound within. Had something gone awry with the plan? She did not think she could bear more delay. She had never felt so tired. Every muscle was worn, and her mind was frayed from nights of thin sleep, tortured by nightmares of Richard suffering in his prison chains. But they were so close to taking action now, and the thought sent fresh determination coursing through her. She lifted her fist again, but before she could knock the door opened a crack.

The round face of Thomas Germinus appeared above the candle he held. Honor sighed her relief. No words were necessary as he opened the door to let her in. She had been buying books from the Fleming for years.

"All right then?" Adam asked her quietly the moment she was across the threshold.

She nodded. "Yes, go." Having escorted her here he would now make his way across the city to the Charterhouse to pick up an essential member of the group—the man with the money.

"Godspeed, Master Adam," Germinus whispered. Adam touched his dripping hat in a quick salute and then was gone down the narrow street, cloaked by the rain and the shadows of Blackfriars' walls.

Germinus closed the door. "A foul night," he said, keeping his voice low.

"A blessing for us," Honor said. "Safer."

She followed him through the shop, where his candle's flame flickered over trays of moveable type, casks of ink, and the two shadowy presses. They had to duck their heads under sheets of printed paper pegged to dry on strings that crisscrossed the room, a spider's web whose dangling catches would create books on everything from mathematics and medicine to philosophy and music. Not hanging were the contraband Protestant broadsheets Germinus occasionally printed in the dead of night with the shutters closed.

He led her up a narrow staircase and opened the door at the top to a slope-ceilinged room. Firelight glimmered from a peat fire smoldering in the grate. Fifteen men stood around a table. Fifteen faces turned to Honor.

She hated to interrupt, but felt some response was necessary, and in truth her heart brimmed with gratitude for the risks these men were taking. "My lords. Gentlemen," she said, "you are well met."

Sir Henry Dudley, their leader, bowed to her. "Madam, thanks to you."

His deference moved her, knowing it was his mark of respect for her part in bringing them all together. Each of them had been driven here by intensely personal reasons—religious conviction, outrage at the Queen's tyranny, a hunger for potential spoils, perhaps a mix of all three—but she sensed that each one respected what was driving her: Her husband could hang if the Queen decreed it. "Please, go on," she said.

They turned back to the table where maps were spread, and resumed their discussion, which Honor gathered was about the Queen's defenses on the Welsh border. As Germinus went back down the stairs, closing the door, she moved to the fire to warm her chilled hands. Its heat was meager, but no matter—this assembly warmed her as nothing else could. Some of them had ridden far and the cramped room smelled of wet wool. She thought it also smelled uniquely of men: leather, sweat, and horses.

"Henry," someone asked, "what French troops are promised us?"

"Ambassador de Noailles guarantees a thousand, trained and armed. And once they land we'll raise twenty thousand English."

There were murmurs of approval at Dudley's forthright pronouncement, and it thrilled Honor. A thousand mercenaries fi-
nanced by the French king would soon file onto ships and sail for
England, and with those veteran troops as the backbone of their
army, the men here would topple the Queen. She was impressed
by Dudley, a commanding figure, black haired, black bearded, and
dressed all in black. Except for the jewels gleaming on his sword
hilt, he could have passed through the dark streets as invisibly as a
black cat. It was Cecil who had recommended him as commander.
"A lifelong soldier. Used to be captain of the guard at Boulogne,"
Cecil had told her. Dudley had tried three years ago to prevent
Queen Mary from ascending the throne by joining with the forces
of the Duke of Northumberland to make Lady Jane Grey queen
instead. When that venture ended in failure and tragedy, Dudley
had removed himself to France. "He has many friends among the
French," Cecil had said, "and that will pay off now."

She scanned the rest of the company, feeling full of hope for the
venture. How could it fail in the hands of such men? Sir Anthony
Kingston, beefy but fighting fit. Tall, white-haired Sir John St. Loe,
a former sheriff of Somerset and former marshal of forces in Ireland. Nicholas Throckmorton, who had ridden as a captain with
Wyatt's doomed rebel army. Sir John Perrot, sheriff of Pembroke-
shire. Richard Uvedale, captain of the fortress at Yarmouth. They
were all experienced soldiers, battle-hardened in England's past
wars with France and Scotland.

At the far end of the table were Sir William Courtenay and Sir
Henry Peckham, who, with Perrot and Kingston, had stood with
Richard as MPs in the turbulent House of Commons that the
Queen had summarily dissolved. Honor also recognized John
Daniel, a friend of Princess Elizabeth. And Lord John Bray, Eliza-
beth's neighbor at Hatfield. Pity pinched her heart when she saw
Roger Mitford. Hardened by grief after his father had been burned
at the stake, Roger had been one of the first Honor had contacted.
His brother Timothy had fled to Antwerp, where the organizers of
the Sustainers of the Refugees were now recruiting for Dudley
among the exile community. And there were several others, men
she had never seen before.

She did not doubt the commitment of any. Almost three hundred innocents had been burned at the stake, and the men here had seen friends and neighbors perish in the flames. Most also had family and friends who had been forced to flee to the German lands because they were not safe in their own homes. All were incensed about the proposed royal bill to declare Princess Elizabeth a bastard and bar her from the succession. Murder and tyranny marked Queen Mary's rule. Now, they were going to end it.

Dudley was saying, "With the trained companies Sir Anthony will raise in the Welsh borderlands, we'll have the west covered. That is, if Anthony can keep his horse-thieving neighbors from stealing his mount this time."

There was quiet laughter.

"I'll press the blackguards into service," Kingston shot back with a grin, "and assign them to you, Henry."

More laughter and some backslapping. Honor smiled. Their camaraderie warmed her after the desolate weeks since Richard's arrest. Six hectic weeks of conferring with Cecil, enlisting Ambassador de Noailles, meeting Dudley and coordinating his messages to the rest of these men, and their messages back to him. She had beaten back the nightmare images of Richard in prison, because it was the only way she could carry on with what had to be done, but there were moments, especially late at night, when she could not fend off the torture of her imagination. She had not been allowed in to visit him. The Tower guards had turned her away, even when she had offered bribes. But she knew what it was like in those dungeons. Years ago she had visited Sir Thomas More in his cell. She would never forget the stench and the cold, and the small, terrifying sounds from far-off cells. In her mind she saw Richard sprawled in filthy, bug-infested straw, his skin red from insect bites, his wrist scraped raw from the iron manacle, his throat parched with thirst, his mind racked with fear—for himself, for her, for Adam. The Queen might keep him there indefinitely, for years even, before he could expect a trial, and even then, though he had broken no law, a judge and jury could be terrified into condemning him to hang. Honor was so desperate to free him she would have fought the Queen with her bare hands.

"Then it's settled. We aim for mid-May, six weeks from today," Dudley said. "Any questions? Tomorrow, Norton and I will sail for Le Havre. I'll hire the troops while Norton arranges for the ships to carry them. Roger Mitford and George Lowry will sail to Antwerp and raise our exiled friends. Four hundred are pledged to us, many with some fighting experience, and if need be they'll hire German soldiers to bring that complement to three companies. At home, Sir Anthony Kingston will raise men and arms along the Welsh frontier."

He tapped his finger on the map, at the south of England. "Captain Uvedale commands the key fortress of Yarmouth here on the Isle of Wight. He will open Portsmouth to my troop ships. Once I land the invasion force we'll march on London, Sir Anthony coming from the west, me from the south. The rest of you will raise the trained bands among your own retainers and tenants, and reconnoiter your local armories, and stand by for my orders."

There were nods of approval all round. It was clear that Dudley had the undisputed confidence of these men who were trusting him with their lives.

"That leaves just the reason for it all," he said, looking at Honor. "Mistress Thornleigh, will Princess Elizabeth honor us with her support?"

They all turned to her, and she felt the hope in their eyes. They all wanted Elizabeth on the throne. She was considered a Protestant sympathizer; as queen, she would not burn their neighbors and friends at the stake. "I cannot answer for her, my lords, but I will inform her of your plan," Honor said. She would not send anything in writing to Elizabeth, and they all understood that. The Queen still suspected her sister of seditious involvement with Wyatt's failed rebellion, and any complicity with Dudley set down in black-and-white would be grounds for executing her as an outright traitor. But to encourage them she added, "My lady cannot fail to be moved by your bravery."

Dudley nodded. It was the best they could hope for, for now.

Germinus slipped into the room with bottles of wine tucked under his arms and goblets on a tray, a welcome diversion that broke the group up into small knots, who set to pouring wine and discussing tactics. Dudley offered Germinus some money, but the printer held up his hands in refusal. "No, sir. When you have rid us of this wicked queen, come back and buy my books."

"A date I shall keep with pleasure, sir," Dudley said. Honor saw him beckon the printer closer. He handed him a gold coin, an angel, worth ten shillings, and asked him to split it in two on his vise. Germinus looked mildly surprised but went downstairs to comply. Lord John Bray led a couple of toasts—to the mission, to Elizabeth. When the printer returned Dudley announced, "My lords, gentlemen," and everyone quieted at his tone, like a call to arms. His face beamed a confidence that was infectious. Honor felt it, and saw it light every other face.

Dudley held up the two halves of the coin, displaying their snapped edges. "One half of this angel is for Sir Anthony Kingston." He tossed it across the table to Kingston.

"Don't spend it all at once, Anthony," Lord Bray joked, making everyone laugh.

Dudley went on, grinning, "When I land at Portsmouth with the troops, I shall send a fast rider to Sir Anthony with this matching half. It will be my signal for him to raise our pennants—and march!"

The men cheered, abandoning caution for one excited moment. They immediately settled down for prudence's sake, but quiet laughter continued with more backslapping of Kingston and Dudley, and a deep current of comradeship that Honor found very moving.

There was a sound at the door. Swords scraped an inch or two out of several knights' scabbards.

The door opened and Adam walked in. He pulled off his hat, flinging cold raindrops. His red-rimmed eyes showed how little sleep he had allowed himself recently, and his mud-spattered clothes spoke of the long miles he had covered as a go-between for Dudley. Living in his boots and spurs for days on end, he was unshaven and dirty—and Honor had never been more proud. She marveled at the change in him, remembering how they had once argued, Adam insisting that the wise thing was to go along with the Queen's policies. How he had scoffed at Richard's warnings about the Grenvilles. But the day John Grenville arrested Richard at the Queen's command, Adam had become the Queen's enemy, and Honor's right hand as they had allied themselves with Dudley. He had ridden tirelessly through the countryside from shire to shire, village to town, mansion to manor, alerting supportive men to their cause. He had become a bulldog for bringing down the Queen.

Dudley welcomed him now, and told the gathering, "For those of you who don't know him, this is the man who took an arrow meant for Princess Elizabeth. Almost died." He raised his goblet. "To Master Thornleigh."

They all toasted him. "To Master Thornleigh." They downed their wine.

Adam took a goblet offered him and knocked back some wine, but Honor thought he looked strangely uncomfortable. And the ambassador had not come into the room with him. Caution prickled her scalp. "Adam, where is Monsieur de Noailles?"

He wiped his mouth with the back of his hand, hesitating, as though preparing to deliver bad news. "Not budging from his house." He looked at Dudley. "He sends his deep regrets, sir. It seems that King Henri of France has just signed a truce with Philip of Spain."

"What does that signify?" one of the younger men asked, looking around at his comrades. "France and Spain have been warring off and on forever. Their quarrels do not concern us."

But Honor saw that the truce did. And that it spelled disaster.

Dudley saw it, too. His face darkened. "It means that, for the moment at least, King Henri does not wish to destabilize Philip's position in England. He no longer wishes to involve himself with bringing down Philip's wife. It means, my friends, there will be no money from France."

There were groans of dismay. Then silence as the full, deadening impact sank in.

Throckmorton said flatly, "No money, no troops."

Honor fought a clutch of panic. No hired troops meant no uprising. Queen Mary would stay in power. Richard would stay in prison. Or walk out to be hanged. She looked from face to face, hoping desperately to see in them a will to go on regardless.

"So," said Dudley with grim acceptance, "if there is to be no money from France, we must find it in England."

She could have hugged him. He was not giving up. "Sir Henry," she said, "how much do you need?"

If her interruption startled him, he did not show it. "Twenty thousand pounds, at least."

An enormous sum! The impossibility of it swamped her. No man here could raise a tenth of that, not without selling every acre he owned.

As if speaking her thoughts, Courtenay said, shaking his head, "I've already sunk as much as I dare into this. I cannot beggar my family."

"No one expects that, William," Dudley said.

"We need another prince to finance us," said St. Loe, though there was little conviction in his voice. If there had been such a benefactor, Dudley would have recruited him by now.

Peckham said wryly, "Perhaps a loan from Her Majesty?"

No one could even muster a smile. The situation was too bleak.

Honor was frantically trying to think. There *had* to be a way. "I know a room that holds a hundred thousand pounds, and more," she found herself saying.

They all looked at her as though her words made no sense.

Kingston said with some irritation, "Unfortunately, madam, the pope's treasury does not lie within our reach."

But, she thought, *the Queen's does.* The royal treasury was no more than the personal funds of the monarch. Much of it was kept under guard at the Tower, but not all. She knew this from her days as lady-in-waiting to Queen Catherine.

She looked at Nicholas Throckmorton. Four years ago, during the reign of the young King Edward, he had been a member of the privy chamber and under-treasurer of the mint.

"Sir," she said, "you know the room I mean. You used to pass by it every day. In Westminster."

❧ 18 ❧

Blood and Treasure

April 1556

Westminster Palace was eerily quiet as Adam led four of his crew, men he'd handpicked from the *Elizabeth*, down the corridor toward the office of the Exchequer. He had chosen Palm Sunday. Most of London would be in church.

Holy Week had begun with a freakishly hot spell and they were all sweating under the heavy, loaded leather packs slung over their shoulders. Above the sound of their boots Adam could hear the clanging of church bells all across the city, calling the faithful to come in procession to the churches with their palms and crosses—sticks of willow or boxwood that the priests would bless to ward off evil. Was Elizabeth kneeling at mass among the worshippers in some royal chapel, dissembling for her sister who kept her in such a purgatory of fear? And Father—listening to the church bells, was he sunk in despair that he would never see the sky again? Adam hoped to help free them both with this day's work.

His heart beat faster as he approached the two armed guards standing at the Exchequer door. He tightened his fingers around the shoulder strap of his load to keep himself from gripping the hilt of the dagger in his belt. Too nervous. The plan, so exhilarating when he had volunteered it and himself to Dudley, suddenly seemed impossible.

"Good morning, Captain."

"Sir."

Adam handed over his papers, hoping he wouldn't have to use the dagger if the man decided to inspect their loads and dig beneath the top layer of coins. "I warrant we'd both rather be fanning ourselves with palms than sweating here, eh, Captain?"

"Your name, sir?"

"Christopher Martin, assistant to Lord Paulet," he said as the guard looked over the paper with its official stamp. It was Treasurer Paulet's directive to deposit fifteen thousand pounds in silver transferred from the Tower treasury. An obsolete directive. Sir Nicholas Throckmorton, one of Dudley's confederates, had scrounged it from his own papers kept from his former tenure as under-treasurer. Adam had smudged the date with a drop of wine.

"My lord treasurer usually brings Her Majesty's bullion himself," the captain said, glancing at the four burly crewmen, then down the corridor to where Adam's escort of a half dozen soldiers from the Tower guard stood waiting. Except they weren't soldiers but Roger Mitford and his friends, dressed in breastplates and helmets. Adam hoped the palace guardsmen and those of the Tower didn't know each other well.

"My lord's a pious man, Captain. Especially when Her Majesty commands her whole council to accompany her to mass."

The guard handed back the papers. "Aye, sir. Easter is a blessed time."

Adam touched his cap to him. Maybe they *were* blessed. No inspection.

He opened the door. They'd made it inside the Exchequer office.

The master teller, Peter Forbes, was alone, pacing in front of the long counting table. His sallow face and soft hands proclaimed him worlds apart from Adam's sea-weathered crewmen. "You're late," Forbes said in a frightened whisper.

"No, sir," Adam said. "Perhaps you were early."

"Shhh, keep your voice down," Forbes said, fumbling for keys on a ring at his belt. It seemed to Adam that whispering was a sure way to arouse suspicion.

Forbes unlocked a door and Adam and the crew followed him

into a compact room with one small, barred window set high in the wall. There was a counting table, and behind it a wall with pigeon-holes bristling with scrolls. Another wall was lined with shelves stocked with identical wooden, iron-banded coffers with domed lids. Each was about two feet square and a foot high, small enough for one man to lift. Each had a thick iron lock.

Forbes closed the door as Adam and his men slung their heavy loads off their shoulders. Forbes hurriedly unlocked several caskets. "Now be quick, for God's sake," he whispered. Beads of sweat glistened on his forehead.

Adam's men gaped at the massed silver bullion. "How much do you reckon is twenty thousand, sir?" Jack Curry asked him.

Adam said wryly, "Whatever we can carry, Jack."

"Four coffers," Forbes answered, wiping sweat from his upper lip. "Now hurry!"

Adam and his men emptied caskets, dumping the silver coins into heaps on the table. Then they upended the heavy leather packs over the empty caskets and poured out the contents of pebbles and sand. Adam scattered a layer of coins on top, then shut the lids and relocked them, and his men hefted the caskets back onto the shelves.

Adam counted out the teller's cut of the bullion and shoveled it into a separate, smaller leather pack. Forbes greedily watched every single coin drop in, and then looked up, suspicious. "Let me count it," he said.

Adam didn't like Forbes's inconsistency. A moment ago the man had been hell-bent to get this over with as fast as possible. He held out the pack to him. "Take it right now if you want to be sure."

Forbes looked horrified. "Good God, no. They could find it on me."

"Nobody's going to be looking. Not if you sit tight."

"No, you idiot. Stick to the plan. Send it to the address I gave you, in Amsterdam."

Adam bit his tongue. He couldn't waste time trading insults. "As you wish."

He and his men set to work scooping the bullion from the table and filling the pouches hidden inside their clothes. They stuffed coins into the front pouches until they swelled like beer bellies, and into long narrow ones down their thighs, then helped each other fill the pouches at the small of their backs. When they were done and had rearranged their clothes, Adam took a few steps to test the weight. It was hard to walk like he wasn't laden down with an anchor fore and aft. He caught the dismay in his men's eyes as they, too, realized the challenge.

He gave Jack Curry's arm an encouraging slap. "It'll build muscle, Jack. Don't worry, we'll have this load halfway to France before they know it's gone. Then you can buy your wife a fine new Easter gown."

The men managed smiles.

"Come away now!" Forbes said in a fierce whisper. "It's my neck if you're caught."

But ours first, Adam thought. "Ready?" he asked the others.

"Aye, sir," they said.

Forbes escorted them out through the antechamber, where he sat down at the counting table and set to looking busy at scribbling in his ledger. The plan, once they were gone, was for him to continue at his desk, then lock up a couple of hours earlier than usual and tell the guards he was going to church. Attending mass today was the law, after all. But instead of praying he would be leaving England this evening on a ship bound for Amsterdam.

Adam opened the outer door. The two guards were talking and stepped apart. Adam couldn't let them get a good look at him and his crew. Wishing them a happy Easter, he beckoned to his counterfeit soldiers down the corridor. Roger Mitford immediately marched his men toward him, and Adam quickly ushered his crewmen out so that they were swallowed up by the soldiers. They all marched off together down the corridor.

Adam's back muscles strained to counter the ballast around his stomach, and his legs were so heavily weighted that each step made him breathe harder. From the corner of his eye he saw the others' tight-lipped efforts to manage their burdens, too. Their exertion seemed so obvious, he half expected to hear the captain yell after them, "Halt!"

But no shout came. They marched out of the palace and down the stone steps into the heat of the day. Adam led them into the shade beside the stairs, where a vine-covered trellis masked them. He turned to Roger's friends. They were a motley mix of young gentlemen—a couple of goldsmiths like Roger, an Oxford don, two lawyers—but they had acted their military parts well. "Good fellows. Off with you now. Roger, you're with us."

"Godspeed, Master Thornleigh," one said.

"And to you. When next we meet, we'll drink a toast to our fair new queen." They grinned, and as he watched them march away Adam allowed himself a stirring thought of Elizabeth, beaming as she thanked them all, and saving a special, warm smile for him.

Roger stayed, pulling off his breastplate and helmet as planned and ditching them. He, too, was no soldier, but Adam was glad of such a committed lieutenant. They shared a dedication to Dudley's rebellion. Roger had lost his father to the Queen's cruel oppression. Adam was bent on saving his own father from her.

Now, he had to get his men to the palace wharf where the skiff would be waiting. Not everyone in Westminster's sprawling precincts had gone to church yet, and he and Roger and the crewmen passed among the scattered courtiers and servants traversing the courtyard. For a moment Adam felt relieved to blend in, not be so exposed. But he realized that it was a false comfort. If an alarm were raised from the palace they would be surrounded, easy to capture.

He decided a detour would be wise. He turned down a narrow alley hemmed in by stone walls. It snaked around by the kitchens. The roundabout route would take them a little longer, but it was empty of people.

"Adam," Roger said, "he's coming after us."

Adam turned. The teller, Forbes, was running toward them. He was whey-faced and out of breath when he reached them, and Adam feared the worst. "Trouble?" he asked.

Forbes shook his head between gulping frantic breaths. "No . . . no trouble."

What nonsense was this? "Then go back. You'll draw them after us."

"I want my money. Now!" He looked wild-eyed with fear.

Adam saw that it was alarming his men. He had to satisfy the bastard. He tugged open his doublet and shirt and dug into the belly-pouch for two big handfuls of coins. "Here," he said, handing over the money. "Now get back to your desk. Act like nothing's amiss and we'll all be fine."

"That's not enough. Not nearly what we agreed!"

Damn his eyes, it was probably far more. "We'll settle accounts later, man. Now go."

"You can't cheat me!" Forbes lunged for Adam's waist and pawed out handfuls of coins. They spilled out and fell clattering on the cobbles.

A window shutter above them banged open. A woman's voice called, "Susan? Is that you?"

Adam shoved Forbes backward against the stone wall. Roger and the men shrank back beside them.

"Susan?"

Adam looked up at the window. He couldn't see anyone. The window casement jutted out, so anyone up there couldn't see him and his men, either, squeezed right up against the wall. He looked down at the bright coins scattered over the cobbles. He couldn't leave the money there. It was clear evidence—and a trail. He lowered himself, awkward under his burden, and began to pick up coins.

"Mine!" Forbes cried. "Leave them! They're mine!"

"Roger, shut him up."

Roger clamped one hand over the man's mouth. Bending his other arm against his chest he pushed him back, pinning him to the wall. They stood face-to-face, Forbes snorting breaths of fear and fury.

"Susan! You get up here with that cream or I'll skin your worthless hide."

Grabbing coins, Adam didn't see the rapier flash out in Forbes's hand. Even when he heard Roger's surprised gasp he didn't realize what had happened. Not until Roger clutched his side and Adam looked up to see blood seeping through Roger's fingers. But he still pinned Forbes against the wall with his other arm.

Forbes raised his blood-smeared blade and slashed Roger's face, slicing his cheek.

Adam jumped up, pulling his own dagger. Roger still hadn't let the man go and Forbes lifted his rapier, ready to stab it into Roger's heart.

Adam lunged. His dagger slashed Forbes's throat. Blood pulsed out, spattering Roger. Adam jerked Roger clear.

Forbes gagged, clutching his throat. Eyes bulging, he slumped against the wall and slid down it. He collapsed on the ground, dead. Adam and the others stared at the blood pooling around the coins. Roger swayed in Adam's grip. Blood trickled down his cheek.

"Hoy! What's going on down there?" the woman called from above.

Adam fumbled his dagger back into his belt. "To the wharf," he whispered to the others. He threw an arm around Roger and pulled him down the alley.

They all moved as fast as they could under the burdens strapped to them. Adam felt shaky, what with Forbes's blood on his hand and his fear that soldiers would soon be after them. He told himself that brawls were common around here, and so were palace rats—robbers who infested the precincts. Whoever found Forbes's corpse surrounded by coins would chalk it up to a fight over money. Just before they broke out of the alley he pulled off his doublet and threw it around Roger to mask the blood that soaked his side. One of the other men had a handkerchief and he cleaned the blood off Roger's face as best he could.

They slowed down, panting, as they reached the palace wharf. A few gentlemen stood haggling with oarsmen whose wherries nudged the water stairs. Servants unloaded hogsheads of beer and crates of cabbages from a dirty barge. Adam and his men halted, catching their breath, trying to appear calm, though Adam was soaked with sweat and he could see it dripping down the faces of the others. Roger's gashed face was gray. Adam held him close and scanned the boats, looking for John Daniels in the skiff from the *Elizabeth*. All he saw were wherries and lighters and barges and tilt boats. At the far end of the wharf was an alehouse where fishermen sat on benches in the sun, repairing a net. He scanned the boats again. Where in God's name was Daniels? They had to make it to the *Elizabeth* before the two o'clock tide.

His heart banged painfully in his chest. He had just killed a man. Roger was losing blood. The six of them were covered with stolen silver. And there was no skiff.

"One word of support from you, that's all they want," Honor urged Elizabeth. "It would mean everything to them." She was trying to keep up with the Princess on the sand-packed garden path that ran from Somerset House to the river. Elizabeth walked briskly and her long legs covered the ground faster.

"I don't want to hear about it. You have put me in peril by just *telling* me."

Honor held back her anger. She had expected some excitement from the girl on hearing of Dudley's venture, an eagerness for details. Some nervousness, too, of course, which they all felt. But not this wall of denial. She stuck by Elizabeth's side as they passed through the orchard where cherry and apple buds were swelling in the heat.

"You cannot let these men fight for you without giving them *some* encouragement."

"I did not ask them to fight."

"But you will accept the throne if they win it for you," Honor snapped. "Can you deny that?"

Elizabeth glared at her. "It is treason to say so." She stomped up the steps to the raised flowerbeds that offered a view across the garden's riverfront walls. The Thames swarmed with Easter boat traffic, Londoners coming and going to church.

Honor followed her. "Don't pretend you haven't *thought* about being queen."

Elizabeth turned on her. "I have thought long and hard about imprisonment and execution. About the axe that cut off the head of my sweet cousin Jane when *she* tried to be queen. My sister ordered that death, and she hates me more than she ever hated Jane."

"My lady, this venture is worlds away from that sad time. Lady

Jane had no goodwill of the people, only her madly ambitious father. He propped her up on a stolen throne. You have the people's respect as the daughter of King Henry. You have their love. You embody their hope for ending your sister's tyranny. And many powerful men are loyal to you. The whole realm would welcome you as queen."

She saw something spark in Elizabeth's eyes. Eagerness after all? A desire to hear more? To make this cause her own? Elizabeth had just returned from chapel where she had dutifully attended mass, and she still held a rough stick cross, twisting it now between her fingers in nervous contemplation of Dudley's enterprise.

There was a burst of ribald laughter. They both looked over the westward garden wall. Beyond the neighboring nobleman's estate smoke drifted up from a cooking fire in the derelict tenements of the Savoy. Built decades ago as a poorhouse cheek by jowl with the great mansions of the Strand, the Savoy had degenerated into a squatting ground for petty criminals and vagrants. Elizabeth watched the smoke rise, absently twisting the stick cross in her hand. "It's easy for you to talk so recklessly. You don't know what it's like to be in prison, to wonder every day if it will be your last."

"I think I do. My husband has been in the Tower for four long months. Every day I wonder if it will be his last."

Elizabeth looked more annoyed than sympathetic. "That's the real reason you're planning rebellion. I know you. All you think of is your family."

Honor was taken aback at the heartless insult. Elizabeth had spent time with Richard at Hatfield when they had sat by Adam's bedside.

"No. No, that's wrong," Elizabeth said quickly, contrite and flustered. "Good Master Thornleigh. He has my pity."

Honor decided she could build on that. "I have learned that family is everything, my lady," she said. "You need to think the same way. If you're going to rule, the people of all England will be your family. That's why, when brave men stand up for you, you must stand up for them."

Elizabeth threw down her cross like a petulant child. "I don't want them to! I didn't ask them to. I don't *need* them to. I have the protection of my brother-in-law. You said it yourself, he needs me next in the line of succession in case my sister dies. To keep my cousin Mary of Scotland from becoming queen of England. I'm safe—as long as I don't make trouble."

"A queen cannot run from trouble. A queen must meet trouble and transform it."

"I am not queen!"

Honor bit her tongue. "Think, please think, of the fine men who are wagering all for you. Sir Henry Dudley, a bulldog for your rights. Lord John Bray, your good neighbor at Hatfield. Faithful old Sir John St. Loe, whose son has served you so well as the captain of your guard. My son, who saved your life. Sir Nicholas Throckmorton, who—"

"Your son? What does he have to do with this?"

Honor was startled by the sudden keenness in the girl's tone. She hesitated, unwilling to leak the information that Adam had just robbed the Queen's treasury. "He is sailing for France at this very moment," she said. "To help raise an army for you."

Elizabeth looked horrified. "Why? Why *him?*"

What a question. "He believes in you," Honor said tightly. She wished she could say she felt the same. She was beginning to wonder if this selfish young creature was fit to rule.

Elizabeth's eyes narrowed in fury. "This is your doing. You *made* him."

"I? How could I? He is his own man."

"He could die! I shall never forgive you, woman. Leave me. Leave my side at once!"

Noon, and no sign of the skiff. They would miss the two o'clock tide.

Looking downriver from the palace wharf, Adam cast his mind to the *Elizabeth* moored off Billingsgate Wharf, waiting for them. Two tides daily. Five hours for the ebb to end and the next flood to begin, then seven more hours until high tide. So the next time he could weigh anchor was two o'clock in the morning. A neap tide, at least, and there would be some moonlight. Little comfort, he thought. What the devil was he to do for twelve hours, with Roger half fainting from his wound, and his crewmen anxious to be gone, and palace guards maybe already out looking for them? Should he hire a tilt boat to take them? But that would leave an oarsman who had seen their faces and seen them board the *Elizabeth*. He didn't want to add another corpse to his sins today. He would wait. If Daniel hadn't come by dusk, he would steal a boat and they would take their chances.

But they could not tarry on the wharf for hours, laden down so awkwardly and dangerously with silver. He had to get Roger out of sight. And the treasure.

"I could use a swallow of that," Roger groaned with a feeble smile.

Adam followed his gaze to the servants hoisting the last hogsheads of beer out of the barge. They were hefting the barrels as though they were weightless. "Sorry, my friend, they're empty," Adam said. The palace had its own brew house. This was a shipment of fresh barrels. Then a thought struck him. *Bless you, Roger.*

He explained the plan to his men.

They crossed the wharf to the alehouse. Adam settled Roger inside, in the cool of a heavy-beamed alcove, and left Jack to watch over him. A few shillings bought Adam five empty hogsheads from the barkeep's store. A few more shillings to the fishermen outside bought their nets. He and his crew rolled the hogsheads behind the building to a small courtyard filthy with fish refuse and littered with broken casks. A few minutes later they rolled the hogsheads, no longer empty, out to the wharf edge and onto the spread nets. The fishermen watched, idly interested, as Adam and the men used the nets to lower the heavy hogsheads into the water. They'd all seen it done by fishermen on countless wharfs during the dog days of every summer. A fine way to cool ale.

Dusk was falling. In the purple shadows Adam prowled the wharf with Jack, looking for any craft left unattended. The wharf wasn't busy, just a lord in blue satin instructing his servant, and a small knot of gentlemen who stood arguing about where to go for supper. But every watercraft was manned by at least one oarsman.

Waiting for trade, the oarsmen sat lounging, one whittling a stick, one taking pulls from a bottle of wine. Adam passed them, feeling more desperate. He would steal anything, even a sculling boat. He had left his other three crew keeping watch over Roger, who lay delirious in the dirty courtyard behind the alehouse.

"Sir," Jack said under his breath, nodding to a boat.

Adam saw it, a wherryman lying stretched out in the stern, snoring. The river rocked him like a baby in a cradle.

Adam and Jack exchanged a look, and Adam nodded. Going down the water stairs without a word, they climbed into the wherry quietly so as not to wake the man. Jack took the oars. The wherryman snuffled in his sleep. Adam went to the short single mast, not much taller than himself, and hoisted the sail, so small it took just two pulls on the halyard. He left the sheets slack as Jack, rowing, nosed the boat out past the other craft.

A snort from the wherryman, awaking. "Hoy!" He sat up. "What—"

Adam clamped his hand over the man's mouth and pulled his dagger. "Quiet. Or you'll swallow some river bottom." The man tensed, no more struggle.

Adam kept his dagger at the man's throat as Jack rowed them over to the alehouse, past the two drunken stragglers on the bench. Adam tied up the boat and whistled softly. His three crewmen came out from the back of the alehouse, helping Roger stagger over to the water's edge. They settled Roger aboard. He moaned, his face as white as the washed-out sail, and Adam wondered if his friend could survive even the river journey, let alone the crossing to France. But he would not leave him. They hustled the wherryman to the back of the alehouse and gagged him and tied his wrists and ankles with ropes.

It took all five able-bodied men to haul up the fishing nets with their cargo of dripping hogsheads. No one at the other end of the wharf heard the silvery clinking inside the hogsheads as the men loaded them into the wherry.

With all his crew aboard, Adam hardened the sheets and took the tiller, and the evening breeze carried the small boat, with its six men packed knee to knee, out into the middle of the river.

It was almost midnight when London Bridge loomed dead ahead. Lanterns and torches blazed from its three- and four-storied houses and shops, lighting the water below like quicksilver. The river roared, compressed by the twenty huge stone arches, sounding like a waterfall. The arches were thirty feet apart. Adam picked the seventh from the south shore and tacked, preparing to shoot the bridge. It would be rough—the small boat was not made for such white water.

The crew braced themselves, two of them holding Roger between them to cushion the impact. The little boat jerked and pitched as it hit the rapids. The bridge lights above them were eclipsed as Adam steered through the roiling water of the sixty-foot-high stone cavern. Then, the angry water shot them out the other side. Adam hardened the sheets and within moments they were sailing smoothly again.

He steered for Billingsgate on the north shore, navigating between the scatter of lofty galleons and caravels moored near the wharf. Flags fluttered from their masts with the colors of France, Spain, Hungary, Poland.

When he spotted the *Elizabeth* it lifted his heart like a summer breeze lifting a becalmed sail. As welcome as Elizabeth's kiss.

He steered over to her, and she rose above the little boat, as proud and shimmering as her namesake. Lanterns winked in her stern cabin window as she rocked gently in the river swells, and reflections of the painted designs on her hull—chevrons of bright green, gold, and red—danced on the lamp-lit water.

"Ahoy!" Adam called up to the stern rail.

Faces of Adam's crew appeared over the rail. Then the face of Sir Henry Dudley himself.

"Thornleigh?" he called down. "Good Lord, man, you made it!"

Adam had his men board first, carrying Roger, and he ordered his friend's wound seen to. Then he took over his ship. He set three of his crew to load the hogsheads of silver while he oversaw preparing the *Elizabeth* to sail. Dudley, marveling at the treasure, gave a low whistle of appreciation. "Well done, Thornleigh. It's enough for a king's ransom."

My father's ransom, Adam thought as he watched the sails unfurl. As he took the wheel he looked back at the Tower rising up just past the bridge, its turrets and battlements etched against the moonlit clouds. His father was there, his only company for four long months the rats of his stinking cell. *For him, and for me*, Adam thought, *this rebellion cannot come soon enough.*

They were underway with the tide. They cleared Gravesend and soon broke free of the estuary with a fresh, following wind at their back. Once out in deep water Adam felt buoyed by the clean night wind rushing past him at the wheel. It felt like Elizabeth's hand gently pushing him on, and her voice whispering in his ear, *Do this for me . . . do this for me . . .*

❧ 19 ❧

The Queen's Net

May 1556

"Five hundred pounds?" Elizabeth said in amazement. Honor had stopped her on the broad staircase of Somerset House. "You must be mad."

"You refused to send Sir Henry Dudley even a word of support," Honor said sharply. "The least you can do is send—" She paused to let two maids carrying armloads of bed linen trudge past them, going down the stairs. When the maids were out of sight, Honor took Elizabeth's hand and pulled her up the last steps and into an alcove where no one could hear them.

Elizabeth snatched her hand free. "Are you deaf? I told you days ago that I would not suffer your company more. I marvel that Master Parry let you in."

"Parry has your best interests at heart."

"I would that he would *act* so."

Insufferable girl. Honor had never felt such bitter disappointment in anyone. But she had to press on, had to try everything possible to help the rebellion succeed. To do less was to condemn Richard to prison indefinitely. "The least you can do," she insisted, "is send this token amount to feed Sir Anthony Kingston's troops. They are massing on the Welsh border. They must eat."

"Token? It is enough to beggar me. God's wounds, you may as well ask for my blood."

"I ask no more than any prince would gladly offer to brave men, ready to shed *their* blood. And all for your cause."

"Your hearing must be defective, indeed, for I have told you again and again this is *not* my cause. Treason is not my cause! And," she cried with a catch in her voice, "if blood spills, it will be on your hands!"

"*My* hands? What possible connection—" She stopped, astonished to see tears glistening in Elizabeth's eyes. It seemed that the girl *did* care, and deeply. How unaccountable! Or was it? She remembered the warm look that had passed between her and Adam when they parted at Hatfield. *It's him she cares about. And now she thinks I've roped him into doing battle.* Perhaps she could build on those soft feelings.

"My lady," she said, changing tack, "have you heard any news of my stepson's ship on her maiden voyage?"

"The *Elizabeth*? What has a cargo of wool cloth to do with—"

"At least, you will surely have heard of the recent robbery of the Queen's treasury." The reports three weeks ago had shocked London. A gang of ruffians, it was said, had gotten into the Westminster treasury in the full daylight of blessed Palm Sunday when almost everyone was in church. Such sacrilege!

Elizabeth's tone was tinged with impatience. "I do not follow the doings of common criminals."

"Oh, not so very common," Honor said with a swell of pride for Adam. She glanced around to be very sure that no one was near, then whispered, "Adam masterminded the treasury mission."

Elizabeth's mouth fell open. "Good God. Why?"

"To raise troops in France. For your cause."

"Really?" Fascination flitted across her face. "But how did he manage it?"

"He and his men marched in, pretending to deliver treasure from the Tower. Instead, they stuffed their clothes with silver coins and marched right back out."

Elizabeth looked ready to laugh in delight. Then she sobered, instantly concerned. "But is he safe away?"

Honor nodded. "He sailed the *Elizabeth* to France with the silver, and with Dudley. The French are our friends in this. Ambassador de Noailles has assured me that his king will smile on our victory." Naturally, since the overthrow of Queen Mary would hurt France's enemy, the Queen's cousin, Emperor Charles. "We are so close to success," she went on eagerly. "Dudley is hiring a thousand soldiers. Adam and his friends are raising more among the exiles in Antwerp. I imagine it's already done and they're on their way here with the troops, even as we speak. Our friend Captain Uvedale of the fortress on the Isle of Wight will open Portsmouth to Dudley's troop ships, and in the west Sir Anthony Kingston and his English musters stand ready, and together they'll march on London. But, my lady, Sir Anthony desperately needs cash for his men." She took hold of Elizabeth's hands and said with all the urgency she felt, "It is all so nearly within your grasp. The crown. An end to tyranny. Honest stewardship of the realm. Justice for your people. I beg you, embrace the courage of these men ready to fight for you. It will so gladden their hearts, they will fight ten times harder and you will be victorious. Do it, Elizabeth. Or lose the chance forever."

Elizabeth stiffened at the shocking use of her Christian name. That one word shattered the spell that Honor had cast. Elizabeth jerked her hands free. "Have a care, madam. God made me the daughter of a king."

Honor stifled a groan of frustration. "Then he may have wasted *His* chance."

"You are insolent!"

"And you are a selfish child."

Elizabeth's hand flew up to slap her. Honor caught her wrist before she struck. She dropped the girl's arm in disgust. "You are not worth fighting. Or worth fighting *for*."

"Leave! This moment! Or must I call the yeomen of my guard to seize you and throw you into the street?"

"Do not bestir yourself to such exertion. Pray, continue hiding amongst your ladies and musicians and dancing masters. I will trouble you no more with the doings of brave men. I am done with you!"

Honor was trembling with anger as she went down the staircase. She would not waste another moment on the ungrateful girl, not another thought. She wrenched her thoughts back to Dudley. She would go immediately to consult Ambassador de Noailles. Though his monarch would not fund the rebellion outright, Noailles had assured her that he would do anything else in his power to help. He might lead her to some other source of cash to feed Kingston's men.

She was almost at the door when she heard Thomas Parry's raised voice.

"Where is she?" Parry was running in from the courtyard, leaving startled servants and a yapping lapdog in his wake. He spotted Honor and rushed up the bottom stairs to meet her. He looked frightened. "Oh, we are undone. Where is my Lady Elizabeth?"

Honor pointed up the staircase. "What's happened?"

"Soldiers. They turned me back from the gate." He dashed up the steps. She followed.

They found Elizabeth in her bedchamber, settling down with three friends at a card table for a game of primero. As they burst in, Elizabeth and the ladies held their cards motionless, suddenly aware of the commotion in the courtyard. "My lady," Parry called to her, pointing at the window. "Look."

They hurried to the windows that faced north toward the Strand, Honor and Elizabeth and Parry crowding in at one window, the three ladies at the other. Down in the courtyard, soldiers wearing breastplates and helmets were marching in from the street, armed with swords and pikes. They were taking up positions every twenty feet or so along the walls. Servants scurried in fear across the courtyard. One stopped to help up an old woman knocked down in the panic. A little boy stood bawling in a doorway. An officer on horseback gestured to two sergeants as more soldiers marched around to the far sides of the house.

"The Queen's guard," Elizabeth said, a quaver of fear in her voice.

"But . . . why?" Dorothy Stafford asked, her face suddenly pale. The troops made way for two lords riding in. "Sir Henry Jerningham and John Norris," said Parry, identifying the Queen's agents. The soldiers closed the gate.

Elizabeth shrank back from the window, hugging herself in fear. "Dear God, it's happening. She has come for me."

A breathless footman ran in. "They're out back, too, Your Grace," he reported. "They've tramped straight through the garden. Taken up positions along the garden walls right to the riverside gate."

Elizabeth turned to Honor. She thrust her hands out to her, begging reassurance—a gesture of pure need, like a frightened child turning to her mother. Concern for the girl flooded Honor. She grasped Elizabeth's hands and held tight, feeling she would do anything to defend her. "Take heart, my lady. If Dudley is on the march you can be victorious yet."

"If?"

Honor hesitated. *Could* Dudley have struck so soon?

Raised voices sounded down the stairs. The clomp of boots.

They rushed down to the great hall, and there Elizabeth received Jerningham. Parry and Honor stood at her side. Ranged behind her were her gentlemen ushers and her nervous ladies. Jerningham bowed to the Princess. She stood ramrod straight, hands clasped at her waist, but her knuckles were white and Honor could see the effort she was making to keep from trembling in Jerningham's presence. "What is the meaning of this outrage?" she demanded.

Like a queen, Honor thought. *Brave girl.*

"Pardon the intrusion, my lady. Her Majesty the Queen is investigating reports of a planned insurrection."

So, Honor thought, *the fighting has not yet begun.*

Elizabeth managed to maintain her stern voice. "What has that to do with me?"

"Until Her Majesty can put down the traitors, she wishes to ensure your safety."

"My safety?" she scoffed. She gestured at Parry. "Then why have you kept my steward from going about his business in the city?"

"Madam, my orders are to strictly guard your house. That is all I can tell you." With that he bowed, apologized for any inconvenience, and left.

"Like Woodstock," Elizabeth said in a thin voice of desperation. "She has made me a prisoner. Again."

Honor was trying to think. "Dismiss these people," she said quietly to Parry. "We need to talk." He did so, asking the ladies to retire to their rooms and telling the gentlemen ushers to go and await further instruction. They left in a flurry of whispering.

Elizabeth stood still with fear. "Woodstock was a paradise compared to the Tower." She turned to Honor, her lower lip trembling. "And if the Tower again, mayhap this time she will dispatch me to the scaffold."

"My lady, do not despair," Honor said. "What we need is information." She was thinking aloud. "If we could somehow contact Ambassador de Noailles, find out what's happening. If Dudley and Kingston are on the march, there is everything to hope for."

"Think you so? But, they need aid, you said. Money. Support." She seemed to be wrestling with her own demons. "If I commit to their fight, how can I be sure of their success?"

"You cannot," Honor admitted. "There is no way to predict the outcome."

"If I do nothing, Dudley and his men may still win. If I help them, they may still lose."

Honor could not dispute it. She would not lie to this princess she had sworn to advise.

Elizabeth lifted her head high. "I will not sit meekly and wait to see if my sister will triumph over my supporters . . . and kill me. Come with me, both of you." She turned on her heel. "Master Parry, bring your keys," she called over her shoulder as she strode out of the hall. "And a candle."

Honor and Parry shared a startled glance, then quickly followed.

Downstairs they went, Parry lighting their way along a stone-walled basement passage to a locked storeroom. Elizabeth took the candle while Parry fitted his key into the lock and opened the door. Inside was a counting table and on it, as well as on the floor,

were a variety of steel-banded caskets, perhaps fifteen in all, rang-
ing in size from that of a small jewelry box to a coffer that would
take two strong men to lift. Elizabeth had Parry unlock a midsized
one, and as he lifted the lid Honor saw that it was tightly packed
with gold coins.

Elizabeth cocked her head at Honor. "Five hundred pounds,
did you say?"

Honor blinked at her in awe. What a startling girl. Humors of
quicksilver—but a gallant heart withal! "Thank you," she said,
hardly able to find her voice. "To your friends, this will make all
the difference. Just knowing you are with them."

"Friends?" Parry asked. Elizabeth explained, and he immediately looked all eagerness. "But how shall we get this money to Sir
Anthony Kingston?"

"I'll take it to Ambassador de Noailles," Honor said. "He has a
network of spies, good at evading the Queen's agents. And couri-
ers on fast horses to race the gold to Kingston."

"The question is," Elizabeth said, "how do we get you there?"

Honor hesitated. The house was tightly surrounded. The soldiers would be watching every move. She questioned Elizabeth
and Parry about the building, all its ins and outs. Was there some
secret passage? Some forgotten side door in a stable wall? Some
gardeners' tunnel in the orchard? But they knew of no such exit.

Parry raked a hand though his hair, thinking. "Mistress Thornleigh, remember the ruse we devised to get you into Woodstock?
Do you think—"

"The Princess's laundress," Honor said, pouncing on the idea.
"It got me in. It might now get me out."

"All very well," Elizabeth agreed, "but how do we hide *this*
from them?" She gripped the casket by its handles to show how
awkward it was.

Honor lifted the thing. Awkward, indeed. And heavy. She
grinned at Elizabeth. "Adam's trick?"

A smile danced in Elizabeth's eyes. "Will you grow suddenly
fat?"

"Just ugly. Call me Hunchback."

* * *

It took them less than an hour to prepare her in the privacy of Elizabeth's bedchamber. A homespun dress borrowed from a kitchen maid. Hidden straps of leather rigged by the stable's harness master, the crisscrossed affair ingeniously holding the engorged pouch of gold coins high on her back. A head shawl borrowed from another maid to cover the hunchback. As Honor was fitted with this gear she marveled yet again at the bone-deep loyalty of Elizabeth's people. None hesitated to cast their lot with her. The servants. Parry. Adam. *Me.*

"Ready?" Parry asked her.

Honor took a wide stance under the load on her back, and hoisted the laundry bundle over her shoulder. She nodded. "How do I look?"

"Like a right witch," he said.

They shared a nervous laugh.

Elizabeth looked on, and Honor saw the worry in her eyes, fear lurking there again. If Honor were caught, Elizabeth could see the inside of the Tower before nightfall. They could all pay with their lives.

Honor came to her. "Trust in me, my lady. I will not fail you."

In a sudden, impulsive move, Elizabeth threw her arms around her. Honor hugged her in return, feeling too much to speak.

Elizabeth pulled back. She laid a gentle hand on Honor's shoulder and said, "Godspeed."

"*Aspirat primo fortuna labori,*" Honor replied. Fortune smiles on our first effort. It was the quote from Virgil that Elizabeth had greeted her with the first time they had met.

Elizabeth matched Virgil with Virgil. "*Audaces fortuna iuvat.*" Fortune favors the bold.

Honor had never admired the girl more.

Crossing the courtyard alone, Honor tried to control the drumming of her heart. The heavy load on her back demanded a plodding gait, but she made use of that, trudging like a lowly working woman whose labors continued unchanged, whatever the change in her masters. She welcomed the itch of the homespun dress, coarse as bark against her skin. Welcomed the pinch of the shoes. Welcomed the reek of cooking grease in the shawl that covered her false hunchback. These clothes were her frail armor against the Queen's soldiers.

She made for the closed main gate. Soldiers were posted, a pair on each side of it. Near the right-hand pair, Jerningham sat on his horse, consulting with a lieutenant on foot. Every fiber in Honor wanted to avoid Jerningham—he had seen her inside the house, next to Elizabeth. But the guards to the left of the gate could too easily discharge their responsibility with a flat denial. Jerningham, with his more subtle commission, was her only hope. And surely he would not recognize a hunchbacked servant as one of the ladies he had seen inside, would he? She could only hope not. Bargaining that his orders, whether to "protect" the Princess or keep her under house arrest—or both—did not include depriving her of the privileges of her status, she made her way toward the two guards near him.

The taller one stopped her. Told her to go back inside.

"And leave Her Grace with filthy underclothes?" she asked. "Nay, I'd rather fight the likes of you than face the wrath of the Princess."

"Don't talk rubbish, woman. No one leaves. Go back."

"Nay, I will not. I cannot. I'm that afraid of a whipping from the master steward."

"Fool." He grabbed her arm to shove her.

She cried out, protesting.

"Here, what's this ruckus?" Jerningham said, trotting his horse over to her.

"Woman was trying to leave, sir."

Jerningham didn't even look at her. "Well, send her back."

"I will go out, good sir, if you please," Honor insisted to him, "just as I go out every Wednesday morning."

He frowned at her, then asked the guard, with a nod at Honor's bundle, "What's she got there?"

"Laundry, sir."

"Her Grace's laundry," Honor clarified. "Which I must take away."

"You'll do as you're told," Jerningham said sharply, "or it's the stocks for you."

"I have my orders, sir, and that's to take Her Grace's smalls every Wednesday and wash and bring them back sweet smelling. I warrant you have your orders, too, a fine lord like yourself, and where would we be in this muddled world if we didn't follow our orders?"

She waited, sweat prickling her back. His scowl did not bode well.

"Where were you heading?" he said, his voice dark with suspicion. "There's water enough here for washing."

"The Cheapside conduit is sweeter water, good sir," she said, frantic for an answer. "And my sister lives nearby it and keeps special lavender that's a favorite scent with Her Grace."

Jerningham's scowl deepened. "Have a look at what she's got in there," he told the guard, nodding at her bundle. Honor's stomach clenched. "You too," he told the other guard. "Look for any paper. A letter. A message."

One guard opened the bundle and both of them poked through the linen shifts and bodice linings and stockings, examining every item. Honor swallowed. How far would they search?

"No papers, sir."

"Search her clothes."

The guard reached out to pull off her head shawl. Honor flinched as his fingers brushed her shoulder. An inch of padding under her dress was all that covered the gold on her back.

"Jerningham!"

The imperious shout from the house turned all heads in the courtyard. Elizabeth emerged from the door and swept across the courtyard with all her ladies and her gentlemen ushers in tow, demanding, "What insolence is this, man? Let my servant pass."

Jerningham bowed stiffly in his saddle. "Pardon, madam, but I must search the woman." He nodded to his guards to continue.

They turned back to resume their duty, but Honor sensed their reluctance as Elizabeth came near. These soldiers, like so many other common folk, admired the Princess. But they had their orders. They searched the sleeves of Honor's dress. Searched the pockets of her apron. Even looked inside her shoes. The tall one reached again for her head shawl and this time he tugged it off.

"God's wounds, my lord," Elizabeth said indignantly to Jerningham, "are you so affrighted that you must molest this unfortunate hag? Can you raise your sights to no fitter enemy than a crippled washerwoman? Pray, when you finish do come in and search my lame scullery boy. Oh, and the blind donkey in the stable. Heaven knows what contraband we might have fed the creature."

There were smirks from the guards. Jerningham glowered a reprimand at them and the smirks vanished. But the damage to his authority had been done.

"Bah," he said to Honor in a burst of bad temper. Then, to the guards, "Open the gate."

She was out—saved by Elizabeth. What a brazen gamble on both their parts! It gladdened Honor's heart that they had triumphed together. Now she was on her way to Noailles.

Leaving Charing Cross in her wake, she walked east as fast as she could manage under the burden on her back. She ducked into a stand of beech trees at the side of a tavern and dumped the laundry bundle into the bushes, but she could not remove the gold, for there was no other way she could carry such a load. Hurrying again along the Strand, she could hardly wait to find out from Noailles what was happening. Was Dudley already marching to liberate London? Was Adam with him? Would the city welcome them, eager to be rid of a queen despised by so many, a city ready to champion the popular Princess?

As she made her way along the busy thoroughfare and headed up Ludgate Hill, she noticed troops of soldiers everywhere. She spotted some posted at Ludgate to watch the traffic of country women carrying baskets of produce to market and a farmer herding sheep. She passed more soldiers posted outside the Belle Sauvage Inn beside Ludgate in London Wall. She glimpsed some at the entrance to Goldsmiths' Hall and Haberdashers' Hall, the headquarters of two of the city's great livery companies. She lowered her head as she walked by more of them under Newgate's massive arch and, as she went north, more posted along the road to

Pie Corner. This show of the Queen's strength was unnerving, but also bracing, for it could only mean that they were preparing to fight Dudley. She yearned for victory. Elizabeth on the throne!

She hurried through Smithfield, skirting the milling throng who had come for the horse fair. Her stomach turned queasy at the very air—it seemed to hold the cinders of George Mitford and hundreds of others burned at the stake. She left the execution ground as fast as she could, passing Long Lane, and finally reached the Charterhouse where the French ambassador was lodged. It was a private estate now, but had once been the home of the Carthusian monks, and its sprawling grounds, too, held an odor of death. Over twenty years ago, in his edict to dissolve the monasteries, King Henry had met resistance from the Charterhouse monks and so had ordered their prior hanged, drawn, and quartered. Ten other monks had been held in Newgate Prison where nine starved to death. The last had been executed on Tower Hill. Now Queen Mary, having sent hundreds of men and women to die in the flames, had shown how truly she was her brutal father's child.

Honor entered the Charterhouse by the garden gate, so as not to be seen on the street, and made her way past the well-kept beds of tall yellow iris and climbing pink eglantine, then around to the front entrance. She knocked. The lanky porter opened the door. She knew him from her clandestine visits, ferrying messages between Dudley and Noailles.

"Bartholomew, I must see the ambassador. It's urgent."

The porter stood squarely in the doorway, making no move. It's this cumbersome disguise, she thought. "It's me," she said, slipping the shawl off her head. "Honor Thornleigh." She tried to look past him for his master. "Let me in. I must see Monsieur de Noailles."

"Madam, I regret that that is not possible." He looked oddly pale.

"He's not here? Good Lord, Bartholomew, then tell me where I may find him. Lives hang in the balance."

"Indeed they do, Mistress Thornleigh," a voice behind him said. The porter stepped aside, head down in shame.

Honor's heart gave a painful thud, then seemed to stop. The man who had spoken was John Grenville.

"It seems," he said, "that neither of us can speak to your French friend unless we travel to Paris. Monsieur de Noailles has fled."

He nodded to the half dozen of the Queen's guard who stood with him. Two soldiers stepped forward and seized Honor's arms.

Grenville stepped close to her, his narrow face inches from hers. She could smell the metallic bite of his sweat. "An odd costume, mistress. Going to a beggar's ball?"

With his eyes fixed on hers, he pulled a dagger from his belt. She stiffened in the soldiers' grip. Grenville raised the dagger high above her head, aiming its tip for the base of her skull. The soldiers drew in a shocked breath.

He plunged the blade into her back. Her knees buckled at the impact. Fabric ripped. Metal screeched against metal. Gold coins spilled. As Honor righted herself, the soldiers gaped at the coins clattering around her feet.

Grenville smiled.

❧ 20 ❧

The Tower

May 1556

"Whose gold is it?"

Honor forced her face to remain unchanged, though if John Grenville saw her terror it was no more than anyone brought to this place would show. Few prisoners who left the Tower went farther than the executioner's block. From the stool where she was being interrogated she looked up at him standing over her. She had to lick her lips, dry as canvas, before she could reply.

"The lady Elizabeth's."

"Did you steal it?"

A trap. It would be easy to protect Elizabeth with that lie. But he would surely have found out from Jerningham how the Princess had insisted the gate be opened for her washerwoman. Grenville wanted to catch her in a lie.

He asked again, slowly and clearly, as though to encourage a dull child, "Did you steal it?"

She could hear his two servants adjusting long screws on the apparatus in the corner. The rack. She thought of Richard's tenting yards, where cloth stretched over a frame was tightened by tenterhooks. "No, my lord," she answered. "I am no thief."

"Are you saying the lady Elizabeth *gave* it to you?"

"She did."

A smile of satisfaction tugged his thin lips, turning white the hard rib of scar above his lip. "Good. We are making progress."

How she hated him. Elizabeth was his real quarry. The prize captive to deliver in chains to the Queen.

"Now," he went on, "why were you smuggling the Princess's gold to the French ambassador?"

"For my husband."

He frowned, caught off guard. "What nonsense is this? Your husband is the Queen's prisoner."

"And I hoped to set him free."

"What? How?"

"Monsieur de Noailles has many contacts. I hoped he could extend an inducement to my husband's guards."

"A bribe?"

"A reward. The gold can be yours, my lord, if you will set him at liberty."

He scoffed. "The gold is not yours to bestow. I have delivered it to Her Majesty." He added pointedly, "Whose humble loyal servant I am. Now, do you expect me to believe that your husband matters so much to the Lady Elizabeth that she conspired with you to smuggle out five hundred pounds of her treasure?"

"She is a bountiful lady. As you know, I went to serve her at Her Majesty's express wish, and I have come to admire the Princess's generous spirit."

He stared at her, pondering this. Then suddenly laughed. "You are ingenious, mistress. A most artful fantasy." His eyes narrowed, his voice hardened. "But I am not the brain-sick fool you take me for. Now, let's have the truth. Where was the gold destined? To which of the rebel leaders?"

"Rebels?" She swallowed. How much did he know? "I know of no such men, my lord."

Grenville glanced at the rack. "Keep up these lies, mistress, and I shall trouble you with questions no more. Not until my men have stretched your memory."

Her stomach threatened to heave.

He looked back at her with unmasked enjoyment at her fear. "Your confederates, you know, have already confessed."

She could not hide her shock. Who had he captured? Her thoughts flew to Adam. Outside, a troop of the Tower guard clomped across the yard and Grenville moved to the barred window to idly look down at them. In his place the bright sun struck Honor and she had to close her eyes against it, the pure warmth so at odds with the ice water that seemed to fill her veins. Nor could the sunshine's purity cleanse the stench that rose from the stone floor, the residue of former prisoners who had lost control of their bowels.

Grenville turned back to her. "When did you last see Lord John Bray visit the Lady Elizabeth?"

So he had Bray! Had he tortured him to talk? She mustered feigned confusion. "You mean, at her home in Hatfield? They were neighbors, so Lord Bray came to dine quite often. He brought gifts. Venison. Strawberries. Once, a brace of pheasants. To give strawberries, my lord, is no crime."

"Treason is," he said evenly. "Did you see Sir Henry Dudley visit her?"

He had *Dudley?* She could scarcely breathe. Did that mean he had Adam, too? "My lord, you speak of a gentleman I do not know."

"Dudley's the ringleader."

"I see. Have you captured this man?"

He looked away in irritation. It shot a spark of hope through Honor. If he had captured Dudley he would crow about it, would he not?

"You will tell me what men visited the Princess at her London house," he went on doggedly. "Did you see Sir John St. Loe? You do know *him?*"

"I do, but as far as I know, he has not come to see my lady Elizabeth for well over a year."

"Sir Henry Peckham?"

"No."

"Sir William Courtenay? John Daniels? Sir John Perrot?"

Her throat was parched, her palms damp. Had he really arrested all of these men? "I never saw these gentlemen visit, God rest them."

"God will do no such thing, for they are the vilest of traitors."

He knows everything, she thought. He was listing names to prove it, to test her. She was ashamed that her sympathy for them did not go as deep as her burning need to know about Adam. Was he among Grenville's captives?

"One has proved himself a very *enemy* of God," Grenville went on, "for we were bringing him into London to stand trial when he took his own life with poison. That proves his guilt and damns his soul for suicide." He gave her a searching look. "Are you not keen to know who it was?"

If he said Adam she would fall down here and die. "You seem keen to tell me."

"Sir Anthony Kingston," he said, watching her reaction.

Richard's colleague in Parliament! She gripped her hands together to keep from crying out in pity for the brave old soldier. And the thought of Richard himself pushed her to the brink of despair. Was he even alive? Richard . . . Adam. *Will any of us leave here alive?*

Grenville heaved a sudden, angry sigh. "This cat and mouse game grows wearisome." He pulled a paper from his doublet pocket. "You will sign this."

"What is it?"

"Your confession. The Princess conspired with these men to overthrow God's anointed, Her Majesty Queen Mary, and you are the witness, and enabler, of her crime."

"She has done no crime."

"Ha! You claim ignorance of the rebels, yet declare her innocent of plotting with them."

"She has not plotted. I would pledge my life on it."

He snorted. "Your life is a paltry thing. I would my father had snuffed it out before your husband murdered him." Honor felt his hatred like a fire reduced to embers but no less scorching. "However, the life of the heretic Princess is worth a great deal. And I will allow you to go on enjoying yours, if you will sign this statement of her crime."

She could not speak. *Elizabeth's life for mine.*

He held the paper out for her. "There is pen and ink," he said with a nod at a small table by the window. "Stand, and sign."

Silence was her answer.

He cocked his head at her. "It disconnects the joints, you know. Shoulders. Wrists. Ankles. Hips. Tears the tissue out of the sockets." He was looking at her—no need to look at the apparatus.

She *dared* not look. It would force out the scream threatening in her throat.

"I will ask you one last time. One last chance, you understand? Will you sign this paper?"

Yes. The unspoken word squirmed behind the silent scream.

"It is not a difficult question. Yes or no?"

Yes! Give me the pen! She did not move.

He shook his head like a teacher disappointed in a pupil. "Your choice." He nodded to his servants. They pulled her to her feet. Dragged her toward the rack. She knew she could not hold back the scream.

But the rack went by her. They dragged her on, all the way to the wall. Two iron cuffs hung on chains from a high steel frame. She had not seen them before. Had seen only the rack.

They clamped the cuffs around her wrists, their iron cold as stone. The sunshine blazed on her face, making her squint, turning Grenville into a blur. She heard the pulleys squeal and felt her arms lifted. Felt her whole body lifted off the floor like a carcass. Her shoulder sockets screamed. Her panicked brain made her hands grope for the chains to take up the slack, sheer instinct, futile. The pain was so sharp it sucked out her breath and churned her bowels.

"Enough?" Grenville's face was so close, the bony scar above his lip seemed to smile.

Pain. Panic. "Stop . . . please . . . stop!"

"Agree to sign this confession, and it will stop."

Stunned by the pain, she retched.

"Will you sign?"

She made herself move her head in answer. *No.*

He nodded to the men. The pulleys screeched. The pain was so fierce, bile shot up her throat.

"Think about it," Grenville said.

Gagging, she saw his blur go out the door. Leaving her. To suffer. How long? Panic overwhelmed her. *Don't leave me!* But he was gone. Her head lolled in agony between her stretched arms. Leaving her to suffer . . . to faint . . . to die.

No. She had not come this far to abandon everything—everyone—by giving in to death. She forced her head up. Squeezed every drop of strength to fight down the bile and the terror. She blinked in the sunshine. Was it shining on her home? On her garden? On the tender blossoms struggling to live? Even as her shoulders and wrists screamed, the thought of her flowers soothed the core of her suffering. An oasis in the desert of her pain. She gave herself to it. Her roses. Climbing the trellis by the copper sundial. Damask roses, red and white. Yellow pansies with sly, winking faces. Violet nasturtiums fluttering in the breeze . . .

Her vision darkened. She slipped into the void of darkness.

"Will you sign?" Grenville was back.

Her head jerked up, a snap of pain. His narrow face loomed close to hers. The thin lips, the scar turning white as he smiled. She was disoriented by pain . . . had he been gone for hours? Minutes? The sunshine had darkened to dusk. A feeble purple light chilled the room. So, hours . . .

"Enough?" His horrible face! It shot fresh fire through her wrists and shoulders. She closed her eyes and struggled to stay in the oasis. Herb garden. Rosemary, thyme, mint, sage. Brush past them with the hem of her skirt and smell the fragrance. Tap the morning dew off the pink eglantine . . . stroll past tall, purple-red poppies . . . tissue-thin white marshmallows . . . bold oxeye daisies . . . the riot of daffodils that tumbles down to the water meadow . . .

"Sign, and this ends."

His face swam before her. She could barely focus. Barely force out a croak. "No."

He glanced at one of the men, and she gasped feebly, waiting for the screech of the pulleys and worse pain.

The screech came. But not pulling her higher into agony. Lowering her.

Her feet touched the ground. She staggered. Her legs were afire with the numb torment of pins and needles and would not support her. She pitched forward. Her arms were so stiff she could not break her fall. She twisted just in time and fell on her side.

They hauled her to her feet. Dragged her to the rack. Her mind screamed *I'll sign! Sign with my blood if you want! Just don't* . . .

They dragged her past the rack. To the door. "Let her go," Grenville said.

They let go of her arms. She swayed in place. Instinctively, her hand shot out to Grenville's arm for balance. She rocked back, sickened by the thought of touching him.

"Walk with me," he said.

To freedom? She ached for it, ached so hard it was torture.

Down a corridor they went. She shuffled as fast as she could, trying to keep up with him, his two men at her heels. Anything to get free. Yet, how could that be? What could have changed to make him release her? They went down a stone staircase that wound like a corkscrew, and the farther they went, the darker the stone vault became. They carried on down another corridor, narrower and cold as ice, passing occasional torches that flickered in wall sconces, giving just enough light for her to glimpse black slime on the walls. Feeble voices sounded from somewhere, the moans and whimpers of prisoners, sending a shudder through her. The smell was so foul she had to hold her breath.

Terror seized her again. She was not being taken to freedom but to something worse than before. Death? Shivering overtook her. Her legs refused to go on.

The two men gripped her arms and forced her along the last twenty feet to the end of the corridor. They stopped in front of a cell whose door was iron bars. The cell was no bigger than the space for a dog to turn around in. Its floor glinted with black wetness and the stench was putrid. A man sat there, his back against one wall, knees pulled up to his chest, boots touching the opposite wall. It was so dark that all she could make out at first was his hulked shape and the bushy beard that engulfed the lower half of his face. Then he saw her. He struggled to his feet, and a shock knifed through her. *Richard.*

"Honor?" He lurched to grab the bars. *"Honor?"*

Tears scalded her throat. "Oh, my love," she moaned, "my love . . ." His filthy clothes hung on his bony shoulders like rags. She wrapped her hands around his fingers on the bars, and the familiar roughness of his skin made her tears spill. She pressed her body against the bars to reach in to touch his face, but Grenville jerked her back.

"None of that."

"Why is he kept like this? He has done no crime!"

"Other than murder my father?"

She wished she could scratch out his eyes. "But it's information on the rebels you want. He knows nothing."

"You do. Sign, and he's a free man."

Free! She looked at Richard's sunken eyes blinking at her, glinting with anguish, with love, with fury. He had not lost his wits. Despite everything, his fierce spirit seemed stronger than ever. His suffering cracked her heart. She would gladly die to let him live.

"Honor . . ." His hoarse voice was parched from thirst. "Whatever he says . . . don't believe him."

"Quiet, Thornleigh, or see your wife altered. How fetching do you think she'd look with her ears cut off?"

They both lurched to the bars again, desperate to touch each other.

Grenville's men hauled her back with such brutal ferocity it brought a roar from Richard. They dragged her away, down the corridor. She twisted to look back at him, but he was a fading shadow among shadows, shouting.

She hardly knew how she stayed on her legs all the way back.

"I have been easy on you," Grenville said when they returned to the room with the rack. "Perhaps that was a mistake." He strolled around the apparatus as though appraising it. He patted its wood frame and fingered one of the screws like a master craftsman sure of his work. "Eventually, I promise you, you will sign. Nevertheless, my offer stands. Sign now, and your husband will go free."

He walked past her to the door and beckoned his men to follow. "Take the night to think about it," he said, as though making a reasonable business offer.

When they left, they took away even the stool.

The long night was more horrible than she could have imagined. She relieved herself, skirts hiked up, into a gutter whose vile effluent streaming from several other cells trickled out a hole in the wall. She lay on the stone floor as cold as a block of ice, and curled up to hold on to a flicker of body heat. Did Grenville have Adam crammed in some foul cell, too? Could Richard survive another week? His misery tore her apart, worse than any rack, as she thought of him in that filth, that cold, that darkness. A corpse in a coffin had more space.

If I leave him there he'll die, slowly, in agony.

If I sign Grenville's confession, Elizabeth will die, her head severed by an axe.

Both nightmare images sawed her mind until, exhausted in mind and body, she sank into a pain-fogged drowse. Clanging at the barred door jerked her awake. It was Grenville's men, banging to keep her from sleeping. Every half hour or so they clanged and shouted, leaving her lurching between desolate nightmares and even more desolate wakefulness.

When dawn lightened the frigid room, they came again. Grenville wore a fresh linen shirt under a sumptuous yellow velvet doublet. Honor struggled to her feet, shivering. Every bone throbbed with pain. Every muscle felt shredded.

"I hope the night's rest has cleared your mind to see the wisdom of cooperating," he said.

"I have tried—" she began, but she was so weak her words came out slurred, and this humiliation seemed harder to bear than all the rest.

Impatient, he did not wait for more. "Here are your choices. You can sign the statement, in which case I will immediately escort you to a room upstairs, where a breakfast of fresh bread and Dutch cheese awaits you along with clean clothes, and you will see your husband sent home this very day, unharmed. Or you can refuse to cooperate, in which case I will stretch your body on that rack like a hog's hide until your shoulders and ankles spring from their sockets. Your screams will not interest me. Only your signature. You have one minute to decide."

She was almost thankful. No more torture of thinking. "I do not need a minute."

"Good." A slight smile.

She struggled not to slur the next words. They might be her last. "This morning, my lord, I find I am not hungry."

His rage was all the worse for being controlled.

She willed control, too. She had decided just before dawn, remembering Richard's words. *"Don't believe him . . ."* He was right. Grenville would never release the man who had killed his father. And he could not be holding Adam. If he were, he would have used him, too, to threaten her.

They dragged her to the rack. Tied the straps. Fitted the screws. She willed her mind to wind inside the flowers of her garden. *Pale pink rose petals, warmed by the sun* . . . the leather straps cut the skin of her ankles and wrists. *Sprightly blue speedwells, jeweled by the dew* . . . the long screws creaked . . . her body was elevated, suspended . . . her legs spread, her head lolled, her panic roiled . . . *Maroon veins of iris . . . blood red gillyflower . . .*

❧ 21 ❧

Lord and Master

June 1556

The *Elizabeth* hit the bottom of the wave trough with a bone-shuddering crash. Adam and his crew staggered to keep their footing and their handholds. The next monster wave picked up the ship and hurled her into the sky. Everyone hung on, suspended in air, stomachs sickeningly lifted, waiting for the next shuddering descent. Rain lashed their faces. Wind screeched in the rigging. The ship crashed down and men reeled, some tumbling to the deck. One cried out to Jesus.

Adam, at the wheel high on the sterncastle deck, swiped rain from his eyes and looked over his shoulder at the damage that threatened to sink his ship. The mizzenmast had snapped and crashed onto the leeward rail, trailing its canvas and rigging in the churning foam. Waves pounded the tangled mess, half drowning it, dragging the *Elizabeth* onto her side. The ship wallowed and slewed as tons of water mercilessly beat the wooden hull. If Adam could not get her under control she could capsize.

"Master Curry," he yelled to his first mate standing beside him.

Jack Curry, gripping the binnacle for balance, did not hear Adam's voice above the howl of the storm. Adam shook him by the shoulder and yelled into his ear, "Master Curry, cut loose that spar!"

"Aye, sir!"

Curry staggered away to command the nearest crewmen. At his order, five of them pulled their knives and hacked at the dripping ropes. They stumbled, knocked off balance by the giant seesaw the ship had become. Adam's knuckles whitened, his grip on the wheel never slackening. The men struggled to their knees, then to their feet, and again sawed the ropes. The last taut line severed with a crack that whipped an end to slash a man's cheek. The waves snatched the freed mizzenmast with its tangle of shredded sail and rigging, and churned it. Adam and his men watched it hurtle up through the foam as if thrashing in the jaws of a monster. It tumbled away in the black water to their stern, and into oblivion.

Adam felt the ship right itself with a shudder like a dog shaking water off its back.

Another mountainous wave reared up above the rail, about to swamp them. He wrenched the wheel over, turning the ship into the waves. The *Elizabeth* pitched and fell as she cut through the writhing hills of water, but Adam knew he could control her now. Spray flew at his head, his hair shaggy with water. He felt salt sting a gash between his thumb and forefinger, turning his blood to pink water.

Jack Curry, dripping, made his way back to him and shouted, "Captain, we should turn back."

Adam looked at the men clinging to the rails and to handholds on the mainmast, some white faced, some shaking, like so many ghosts. They were afraid. And angry. They didn't like him taking them straight out into the storm. They were only hours out of Calais, and if he turned back now they could limp into the French harbor and into warm beds by nightfall. He looked ahead at the black clouds charging him from the west. From home. *The executions have begun*, Cecil had written. Adam shook his head at Curry. "No."

With that decision, he settled into the motion of the ship, and into that space of calm that surrounded him at times like this. It was like standing in the eye of the storm itself, where there was peace. It wasn't that he relaxed, for his muscles stayed tight and his mind stayed sharp to every change in pitch of the wind's keening and every shift of balance underfoot. It was simply that he felt more alive, more in tune with *all* of life, the whole tumultuous world, when he was steering his ship in harmony with it. It was part thrill, part peace, like nothing else.

Not true, he thought. It was like looking into Elizabeth's eyes.

She was a prisoner of the Queen, again. How was she bearing it? And the poor fellows who had stood with Dudley—his heart bled for them. And raged at the only explanation that made sense. *We were betrayed.* Inside his soaked leather jerkin the letter from Cecil lay next to his breast.

> *The executions have begun. Peckham and Daniel were hanged, God rest their souls. Kingston was arrested, and on the way to London he killed himself. St. Loe is under house arrest. Courtenay, Bray, Perrot are all in custody, awaiting trial. Ambassador de Noailles has fled. The lady Elizabeth, too, is penned up in her house, under close guard. I know not what fate awaits her.*
>
> *And this sad litany is but prelude to my sadder song. Your good father, a prisoner in the Tower these many months, is kept still in that forsaken place, and now, it grieves me to tell you, so is his lady wife. Lord Grenville, it is said, is using her very roughly. Indeed, her suffering, as I have learned, would make the angels weep.*
>
> *I send you these dreadful tidings not to unman you with grief, sir, but to exhort you to bear up by seeking God's grace to endure, and to assure you that I am at your service, and ever your good friend,*
> *Wm. Cecil*

Adam's grip on the wheel tightened, steering for home. *Everyone I care about. Everyone I love.*

A shout. He looked to the foredeck as a bowsprit sheet snapped. The bowsprit sail blew out with a loud, raw rip. The ship bucked. The tattered canvas whipped in the screaming wind like a creature demented.

"Secure the sail!" Adam shouted.

"Secure the sail!" Jack Curry yelled, and men clambered up the ratlines.

Curry loped, lurching, back to Adam's side. "Turn back now, sir?"

Adam was watching the wind tear at the lateen-rigged sail on the foremast. The furious force of the wind threatened to rip it, too.

"Sir," Curry yelled, his eyes on the same sail, "if we lose that one we can't go on."

"See to your business, Master Curry. Secure the bowsprit sail. Send two men to the hold for spare canvas. Stand by the foremast."

"Captain, the men—"

"Will do as I say. To your business, Curry. Now."

Adam turned his face into the teeth of the wind. It screeched in his ears, like a tortured voice wailing, *The executions have begun.*

He was sailing home.

"I will not stand in a queue with these fellows," John Grenville said impatiently to Frances. They stood in the antechamber of the Queen's apartments with ten or twelve other milling courtiers left to cool their heels.

"Don't worry," Frances said, "I'll get you in before them." Her status as Mary's closest friend ensured that privilege. But she had something to ask of John first. If only she could think of a way to broach it without letting on about her real motive. She longed for Adam. This last separation from him seemed endless, ten heavy months so far. It had been bad enough when the witch's daughter had kept him by her side at Hatfield as he'd recovered from Sturridge's arrow. It made her ill to think how near he had come to death. But then, recovered, he had launched his ship and sailed away. Gone on business across the Narrow Seas, the servants at his house had told her man Dyer. Yet what could possibly be keeping him away for so long? *This is how people in love suffer,* she told herself with a small thrill. *To lovers, being apart for even a week is hard.*

"Who is with her?" John asked.

She turned to him. The Queen, he meant. First things first, she told herself. "Cardinal Pole and Ambassador Renard. With this rebellion terror she will only talk to her most trusted friends." She added, with some pride, "That's why it's so wonderful that she sent for you."

He nodded, his own satisfaction clear. "But why, exactly? Do you know?"

"The executions, I believe." She leaned closer to keep the other courtiers from hearing, and whispered, "I think she will put you in charge."

His eyes widened. To lead the executions of the traitors was a great honor. And it portended even greater rewards to come from the Queen's hand. Frances felt sure she would elevate her brother from baron to a more exalted rank. Earl, perhaps, or even viscount. Marquis was not out of the question. He deserved it, of that Frances had no doubt. He had captured the traitors so quickly, almost two dozen, and gotten such detailed information from them about their plot. Frances was still astonished at the breadth of the group, from lords to gentlemen to yeomen. Some of the leaders were men she had once considered loyal. Lord Bray, Sir William Courtenay, Sir John Perrot. What a wicked world. And, of course, Elizabeth. Delivering Mary's heretic sister was the greatest prize of all. A thought struck Frances, making her gasp. "John, that's it."

"What is?"

"The commission she wants to give you. You shall lead her sister to the block!"

He looked at her with eyes full of hope. Only a very high-ranking lord would be given the commission of a *royal* execution. "Think you so?"

"Yes! She wrote to her husband giving all the evidence of Elizabeth's treason. She asked Philip's permission to execute her."

"You know this for certain?"

"She dictated the letter to me. I wrote it. And Philip's courier arrived back from Flanders this very morning."

He looked so happy, it gave her the courage to ask him her favor. "John, are you still holding the Thornleigh woman?"

He nodded. "I'll get her confession yet."

"But do you really need it?"

He gave her a sharp look. "Why do you care?"

"I don't. Not really. I'm just thinking of how people talk. Unfortunately, the woman has her admirers. I don't like to hear people say unkind things about you."

"I'll do what must be done, gossip be damned."

"But haven't you got confessions aplenty to damn Elizabeth without adding Honor Thornleigh's?"

"Attend to your business, Frances, and I'll to mine."

She held her tongue. John was the head of her house. She would not gainsay him. But she wished he would not be so harsh with Adam's stepmother. Adam would be angry when he heard of it. He might even reprove *her* for it. *If Honor Thornleigh dies*, she thought, *he might never forgive me*. Unbearable thought.

The door of the Queen's presence chamber opened. Cardinal Pole strode out in a flurry of red silk robes, followed by Renard, the imperial ambassador. With furrowed brows they marched past the waiting courtiers and hurried away.

Jane Dormer, Mary's lady-in-waiting, stepped out and beckoned to Frances, then led her and John into the royal presence.

"Ah, my dear," Mary said from her gilt chair. She looked haggard from lack of sleep. She held out her hand to Frances as John went down on one knee. "And you, my good lord. How we cherish old friends in these dark times."

"Your Majesty," said Frances, taking Mary's hand and curtsying, "the Grenvilles are ever your friends indeed."

"And ever loyal," said John.

The Queen beckoned him to rise. "What an office you have done me, sir, ferreting out these traitors. We are grateful, and shall show you our pleasure in due course."

John looked pleased, but before he could reply Mary covered her face with her hands and cried, "I am surrounded by enemies! I cannot move without endangering my crown!"

They both stood silent at the sudden outpouring of emotion. Frances felt pity for her friend, but she knew that such displays made John uncomfortable.

"It is true," Mary said, taking in their dismay. "I cannot trust the

loyalty even of my councilors. And I fear assassins among my attendants. My new confessor . . . Frances, I had a dream that he is a
spy. He means to poison me."

"My lady, you must not—"

"In the emperor's court they are whispering about me, I know
it. In the absence of my husband, they say, all my authority is melt-
ing away. Yet what would they have me do? Disobey my lord and
husband?"

She was looking at John, apparently expecting an answer.
Frances saw his struggle to come up with one. To save him she
replied with some warmth, "It is quite the contrary, my lady. The
fact that my brother and your other loyal servants caught the traitors before they could move against Your Majesty shows good gov-
ernance. My brother acts in your name, and for your sovereign
glory."

Mary beamed at her through teary eyes. "God's glory, my dear.
Thanks be to Him."

John cleared his throat. Frances could tell that inside he was
squirming to bring some decorum back to the interview. "Your
Majesty," he said, "you sent for me. Is there some commission you
would entrust to me? Some service I may render you?"

Mary closed her eyes as though in pain. She looked so pale,
Frances was afraid she might faint, and she stepped closer to offer
her hand if need be. But Mary rallied and looked at John.

"A service for the King," she said, a new edge in her voice. "You
shall leave here, sir, with a grave commission indeed. I have received word from my husband. It regards my sister, now guarded
in her house by Sir Henry Jerningham and his troop. My lord's
command is to dismiss that guard and escort my traitorous sister to
a different place."

Frances shot John the briefest smile. *To the block.* Here was his
chance.

"My lord's command," Mary repeated bleakly as though to herself. "My lord and master. Frances, I know that you understand
my duty. I am a sovereign queen, but a wife first."

"As God bids, Your Majesty." She knew how seriously Mary
took the Church's teaching that a wife be subservient to her hus-

band, Christ's representative. And Philip had become a great and powerful king since his father had abdicated and handed over most of his vast domains. Philip was now monarch of half the world. He had all but deserted Mary, but she wrote to him constantly, and always signed her letters *Your loving and obedient wife.*

"I am yours to command, Your Majesty," John said.

"No, my husband's," Mary said bitterly. "You are to terminate the investigation into my sister's crimes. Escort her to her house at Hatfield. She is to be set free."

❧ 22 ❧

Adam's Bargain

June 1556

The road was awash with mud from the night's rain. Adam was spattered with it to the thigh as his horse galloped to meet the group plodding toward him—two horsemen and a horse-drawn cart homeward bound from London. He had ridden nonstop from Colchester, had been overseeing his storm-battered ship made fast to the wharf at dawn when he'd heard the news and set off. Now, with the muddy road steaming in the noonday sun, his shirt was plastered to him with sweat, and his lathered horse heaved bellows breaths as he galloped to close the distance to the small group. They were his kinsmen. Plodding on with downcast eyes, they were carrying his stepmother home.

"Uncle!" he cried out to hail them.

His Uncle Geoffrey looked up in surprise. Adam thundered up to them and reined in with such ferocity his mount almost staggered under him. Geoffrey held up a solemn hand to signal the others to stop—his son-in-law Randolph riding beside him, his teenage son, James, driving the cart. Something twisted in Adam's chest as he saw the still figure lying stretched out in the cart, her eyes closed, her face pale as a corpse. "Oh God," he groaned. "He killed her."

"No," said Geoffrey, his voice raw. "But not far from it."

Adam sank back in his saddle, overcome with relief. But as he took in the grim faces of his uncle and cousins he realized what a hellish task they'd had, fetching his stepmother from the Tower.

"What are you doing back in England?" Geoffrey asked with dismay. "It's not safe for you."

"My family is here, Uncle, not in France." He walked his horse to the cart for a closer look.

"But he's right, Adam," Randolph said. "So many have been arrested."

"For plotting rebellion, not for the robbery," James said, sounding proud. He had always looked up to Adam. "The dolts investigating the theft haven't put the two together. You covered your tracks, didn't you, Adam?"

He didn't answer. Someone had betrayed Dudley, and many men had been captured, some already executed, and Geoffrey might be right, the Queen's council might have a warrant out for Adam's arrest, too. But right now that seemed the least of his worries. He was shocked at the sight of his stepmother. Clothes matted with filth. Wrists black with bruises. One of her arms, lying at her side, was bent an unnatural way. Fury boiled up in him. Grenville had tortured her.

"How bad?" he asked. "Can she walk?"

"Don't know," Geoffrey said, raking a hand wearily through his hair. "We had to carry her out. She moaned, but no words that made sense."

"That cursed place," said James. "Adam, you can't conceive how foul. Just look at her!"

"Joan will bathe her and see to her," Geoffrey said.

"Adam," said Randolph gently, "she has weathered the worst. Don't despair."

Adam choked back his rage at Grenville, and his pity for his stepmother, knowing his kinsmen felt no less. They all loved her. But it was hard to pretend composure, imagining what she had suffered. "Grenville would have tried everything to get her to talk," he said, "to incriminate Princess Elizabeth."

"Well, she must have told him nothing," Geoffrey said. "If she had, the Queen would have grounds for arresting her sister and she would be in the Tower now, too."

"So it's true what I've heard? Elizabeth is unharmed?"

"Aye. Unharmed and at liberty."

Adam had never felt so grateful. And never admired his stepmother more.

"Word is that the Queen just suddenly dropped her investigation of the lady Elizabeth," Geoffrey went on. "Some say at the command of her husband. Seems that's the reason Honor's free."

"And thanks be for it. But my father is not." His father still lay in chains in the Tower. Was it his fate to die there?

Geoffrey's face showed how much he feared it. "Richard's case is another matter."

Randolph muttered, "He dared to fight her in Parliament and now she's making him pay."

Adam shook his head. "No, she only meant to punish him for that as a warning. She's done the same to others who displeased her—kept them in prison for a few weeks, then sent them home. This persecution is something else. It's Grenville's doing." He remembered his father's warnings, and bitterly regretted how little he had believed them. His stepmother's bruises were the sickening evidence of how far Grenville had gone to hurt her.

"But maybe now the Queen will order him sent home, just like Honor," Geoffrey said. "Grenville has to obey the Queen."

A hand gripped Adam's boot in the stirrup. He froze. His stepmother's hand. Her eyes were open. Staring at him.

"Madam," he said, hardly knowing what to ask first, "is it the pain?"

Geoffrey and Randolph kicked their horses to her other side and James twisted around on the cart seat to see her. "Honor," Geoffrey asked, "how can we help you?"

She kept looking straight at Adam. Squeezing his boot toe. She moaned, "Stop . . . him . . ."

The men shot anxious looks at each other. Her voice was so faint, Adam had to lean down to hear her. "What do you—"

"I saw . . . your father . . . cannot survive—" She winced, stopped by the pain. But her eyes never left Adam's face. "Grenville will . . . kill him." She groped for him. "Save him!" Her eyelids fluttered. Her hand dropped. Her voice was scarcely more than a breath.

"Please, Adam . . . save . . . him . . ." Her eyes closed. Her head lolled. She went still.

"Madam!" Had she died? No, she was breathing, thank God. She had fainted. He turned to his uncle and his cousins. They all looked shaken.

"Can we believe this?" asked Geoffrey.

"Believe it," Adam said.

"We should fight!" James said. "Rally our friends and ride back to London. Storm the place, swords drawn. Get to my uncle and break him out!"

"Don't talk nonsense, boy," Geoffrey snapped. "It's a bloody fortress. They'd cut us to ribbons before we got past the drawbridge."

"Hire more lawyers?" Randolph asked, sounding desperate. "The fellow we have is a snail."

"What good would more do?" said Geoffrey. "Lawyers' work takes months, even years. Richard would be a corpse before the court grinds out a ruling."

"We will save him," Adam said. It was why he had come home. He hadn't come with any plan, but he had one now. He tugged the reins of his horse, but the animal was so winded it would be cruel to ask more of it. "Randolph, lend me your horse."

"Adam?" Geoffrey asked with a frown. "What are you thinking?"

"Can't explain now. Trust me, Uncle."

Geoffrey seemed to accept that. He gave a brisk nod to his son-in-law. Randolph dismounted. Adam did, too, then swung up into Randolph's saddle. With a last look at his stepmother, he turned the horse to go. "Take good care of her, Uncle." He kicked the horse's flanks and it bolted forward.

"Where are you going?" James called.

But Adam was already cantering away.

Grenville Hall lay upstream from Speedwell House and Adam had to row against the current all the way. It was late afternoon when he came alongside the Grenvilles' jetty. The long day's heat provoked distant rumbles of thunder as he shipped the oars, climbed out onto the jetty, and tied up the skiff. A few chattering maidservants were sorting fish from the weir's nets, and Adam kept his head down, aware of the dangerous course he was charting. He had taken the precaution of buying clothes from the smith at Speedwell House. The maids, used to seeing boats land, and workmen load and unload goods, barely gave him a glance in his dingy shirt and scarred leather jerkin and patched breeches, all ripe with the smell of charcoal. But in this enemy territory it wasn't maids he needed to beware of, it was fighters. No smith would carry a sword. So all he had brought was his dagger.

He made his way along the beaten-grass path that curved up from the river to the Hall's outbuildings. He passed a noisy team of carpenters hammering nails to repair the dairy house roof, and women carrying sacks of flour into the bake house, and a groom leading a gelding across the stable courtyard to the farrier's forge. None of them paid him any mind. No one here knew him. No one except the woman he had come to see. And her brother, the enemy he had to avoid.

"You there, boy," he said, stopping an urchin carrying slop pails from the kitchen scullery. "Care to earn a shilling?"

The boy's eyes went as big as the coin Adam held up. "Aye, sir."

"Do you know the lord's sister, Mistress Frances Grenville?"

"Aye, sir."

"Can you get inside the great house to take her a message?"

The boy eagerly set down his pails. "Aye, sir, I just saw her in the pantry with the cook."

Adam tossed him the coin and the boy snatched it in midair. "Tell her that her priory partner waits for her in the stable. Let no one else hear you."

The boy scampered off. Above the carpenters' hammering, Adam heard laughter. He turned to see three men swaggering across the courtyard, laughing over some private joke. Armed with swords and carrying crossbows, they wore the lord's livery of green and yellow. Grenville Archers. Adam couldn't afford to draw their notice. Head down, he walked briskly toward the stone stable. One of its double oak doors stood open. With a glance over his shoulder to make sure the archers hadn't spotted him, he slipped inside.

The shadows were cool, and welcome after the glare outside. He didn't see any grooms. Just as he had hoped, given the time of day. Most of the household would be at supper or on their way to it, and he had seen no sign that the Hall was entertaining guests, so grooms wouldn't be needed to tend visitors' horses. A central corridor divided the stalls that lined both sides of the stable and he strode straight on down it, passing horses behind their half walls, some munching hay. He noticed straw drifting down from a loft that ran across the breadth of the place, and saw a couple of stable boys up there with pitchforks. Busy at their work, they merely glanced at him as they each tossed another forkful down to the stone floor. Adam sidestepped the falling straw and strode on as if he was on business. They would take him for a visiting smith or farrier. He spotted a stall to his right, its door open, the space empty. He slipped into it, glad to be out of sight. The stall was hung with harnesses that deepened the shadows, and the wooden slats on either side like prison bars gave him a vague sense of being trapped. Tired as he was after the rough crossing from France and the hectic ride, then rowing here, he felt jumpy at the enforced stillness. To keep moving he began to pace. Now, all he could do was wait.

Would she come? If she did, could he still expect her goodwill after all that had happened? Enough to . . . his stepmother's plea echoed: *Save him.* Frances can do it, he thought. Father was right about her brother, but I've been right about Frances. Right to make a friend of her. *She* is not the Grenville obsessed with hatred. Adam knew she had feelings for him. She had even told others. Elizabeth had heard some court gossip that he meant to marry Frances, and had been angry. So silly, that she would believe it. So thrilling that she cared. Bewitching Elizabeth—the thought of her was an arousing distraction, and he could not afford any distraction, not if he was going to save his father.

He forced his mind to focus on his course, and it was this: He had a friend in Frances and he would make the most of it. He had deliberately cultivated that friendship for any advantage it might yield—*Befriend the people who wield the power*, as he had once put it to his father—and now was the time to reap what he had sown. Was it less than honorable to exploit Frances's feelings for him? No doubt. Would only a cad lead on an infatuated woman he didn't care for? Yes. But the alternative was an agonizing death for his father. Niceties be damned.

He didn't have to wait long. He saw her hurry in, catching her breath, her eyes darting everywhere, trying to spot him. She was moving so quickly she had passed him when Adam quietly said her name. She whirled around. Seeing him, she gasped and her hand flew to her heart. He reached out and took her hand and pulled her into the stall.

"Oh, sir—"

"Shhh," Adam said, laying his other hand gently over her mouth. "Stable boys. Up in the loft."

She blinked, silent under his hand, and nodded, but slowly as though unwilling to have his fingers leave her lips. He slid his hand away, but kept hold of her hand. "Thank you," he said warmly, "for coming."

"Of *course* I'd come," she whispered. "But what—"

He took hold of her arms, gently but firmly. "Forgive my boldness, but I had to see you."

"I'm so glad. You've been away so long. Are you well? Your wound . . . I heard you suffered an arrow."

"I am well now that I have a chance to talk to you." He drew her a little closer, and felt her small gasp at the closeness of their bodies. "I've come on a matter of grave distress, and you alone have the power to bring comfort."

"Oh, yes . . . if I can. But I'm afraid it is not safe for you here. If my brother finds out—" She stopped, her face tight with worry, as if she found the subject impossible to broach.

"Your brother is why I'm here." How much did she know? How much did she care? He had to tread carefully. "Acting for the Queen, he—"

"I know. Your stepmother. He oversaw her interrogation as a lady of Her Majesty's sister. And I'm so sorry. I tried to persuade him to be less . . . well, not so harsh with her."

"Did you?" He smiled, surprised. "That was kind."

It brought a smile from her, too, hopeful and eager. "I believe he has just released her. And I pray God she is well."

"She is home. Recovering." He took her hand. "Thank you for attempting such a merciful intercession." He lifted her hand to his mouth and kissed the back of her fingers. He felt her shiver of pleasure.

"I am so glad to see you," she whispered. "What kept you so—"

"Frances." Again she shivered, this time at the intimacy of his using her name. "I need your intercession once more. For mercy's sake. My father remains a prisoner in the Tower. I fear he cannot survive long. I must have your help."

"With my brother?" she asked, anxious. "I can't—"

"No, with the Queen. A word from her will set him free. I need you to ask Her Majesty to have mercy and release him."

She stiffened. "But . . . he was rebellious in Parliament."

"That is the privilege of the place. And he did no more than scores of others."

"Last year he marched with the traitor Wyatt against Her Majesty."

"So did hundreds of others, and when it was over they swore allegiance to her and she accepted them as loyal subjects."

She bit her lip, unable or unwilling to make further argument.

"Frances, he has done no crime."

"Other than murder my father?"

It stopped him short. There it was. The blood feud. Her blood. She could not forget it, just as he could not forsake his father. "Where will this stop?" he said. "If my father dies at the hands of your brother, my kinsmen will seek retribution. It will go on and on, death after death. But you and I, Frances, we could stop the mad spiral. Forgive. Start afresh."

She gazed at him as though moved by his words. She murmured, "Forgiveness. A Christian duty."

"So it is. And it must start with us. I beg you to ask this favor of the Queen. You are her dearest friend. She loves you. She will not deny you."

Her face showed her misery at feeling so torn. He pulled her closer to him and slipped his arm around her waist. Her breaths became quick and shallow. "Frances," he whispered, "do this for *me*."

She seemed to melt. "For you I would do anything . . . Adam." She had shocked herself, using his name, and she covered her mouth with her hand. Then dared to say it again, her eyes aglow. "Adam." She touched his mouth with her fingertips. She caressed his cheek. She leaned into him, her face upturned to his. She kissed him.

He pressed his advantage, enfolding her in his arms, returning the kiss, willing her to do as he wanted. Then, abruptly, he let her go. "So you'll go to the Queen? Can you leave today?"

She stood, almost swaying, catching her breath. "I *knew* you felt as I do. Oh, Adam, my dear—"

A clang at the stable entrance. The door banged open. Men strode down the aisle. Grooms, perhaps a dozen of them, going briskly about their business. Adam pulled Frances farther back into the stall with him, deep into its shadows, then stepped in front to shield her. He couldn't let them see her, or him. But they could both still see the commotion going on almost in front of them. A couple of grooms led a bay mare out of a stall to the left, while others prepared ropes and harnesses. They were acting under the direction of the stable master who pointed his white stick as he gave the orders, "Good, secure her there," and "All right, bring him in."

The grooms dropped an iron bar in front of the mare and tethered her to it. In a moment several other grooms led a big white horse that was snorting, stepping high, excited. Adam recognized it—the fine Arab stallion he and his father had brought Grenville as a peace offering when they had first arrived home. He realized what all the commotion was about. They were going to mate the stallion to the mare. He stifled a groan. He'd been so close to getting Frances to say yes.

She squeezed close to his side. She gripped his hand and held it tightly in both of hers, as though in fear.

"I'm sorry," he whispered. He had gotten her into this.

But a glance at her face told him she wasn't afraid at all. She was watching the horses with solemn fascination. The grooms were setting up more iron bars on either side of the mare to restrain her in place. The excited stallion, with a huge erection, was snorting and stomping, trying to rear up to get to the mare, and it took four grooms with ropes, scuffling and shouting, to hold him back. Frances looked at Adam. Her cheeks were flushed and her eyes looked almost fevered. Her breaths were quick and shallow as she pressed against him, looking almost in a trance, clearly intending to kiss him again.

"Stop!" a man bellowed.

Frances froze. Adam turned to look. John Grenville strode down the aisle. "Pull that horse away, Greaves," he ordered the master of the stable. "Now!"

"What's amiss, my lord?" Confused, the man had to raise his voice above the noise of the frantic stallion as the grooms struggled to hold it. "Was it not your lordship's order that I take a free hand?"

"That's a Thornleigh beast. I'll allow no taint of Thornleigh pollution here."

Adam felt a hot rush of rage. This was the man who had stretched his stepmother on the rack, and held his father in chains, slowly starving him. He felt an urge to pull his dagger, but he fought it. Kill Grenville and he'd hang. No use to his father then.

"You men, move the mare away." Grenville was glaring at the stallion. "Geld it."

Adam felt Frances shudder. "No!" she whispered.

The grooms looked horrified. "My lord," Greaves entreated, "you cannot mean it. This here is prize horseflesh. He'll sire the same for you, for years to come."

"Cut the beast. Do it now."

He grabbed the man's white stick and thrashed one of the grooms across the back. "Move!" The frightened grooms all lurched into action, pulling down the iron bars with a clatter, yanking the mare back to her stall, hauling down on the stallion's ropes to keep the struggling animal in place as it whinnied and reared and pawed the air.

Grenville glowered at his master of the stable. "Do as I say. Cut him."

"I beg you, your lordship, let the creature be."

Grenville whipped the stick, slashing the man's cheek. Greaves gasped, hands to his face, and backed away. Grenville strode toward a table of tools, coming nearer the stall where Adam and Frances stood hidden. Adam yanked her back farther, right to the wall. Grenville picked up a gelding knife. "I'll do it myself." He ordered the grooms to rope the stallion. "Hold him down. Or else lose a hand yourselves."

Adam's rage burned as he watched it all. Grenville butchering the horse's genitals. The horse's screams. Its flailing hooves. A groom, kicked in the head and sent sprawling. Grenville, raising the knife in victory, hands glistening red with the horse's blood.

When it was over, Grenville tossed the knife and walked out. The stunned grooms shook themselves into action. They dragged the suffering horse away. Others scrambled after it to see to its wounds. Adam and Frances stood alone, looking out at the empty corridor where the stone floor was slick with blood. Horses in stalls whinnied in fear at the smell of it.

He looked at her. Her face was white. He was stunned himself by Grenville's barbarity. And dismayed at what to do. All the precious intimacy he had built with her, shattered.

"Are you all right?" he asked.

She nodded stiffly.

"Frances . . . my father. I beg you to consider his plight. Won't you—"

"Do not ask me. I cannot. I wish I could. For you. But it's John."

"The Queen has the power, not him."

"He has the power over *my life*. He is the head of my house. I cannot go against his will."

"You have free will. We all do."

"Yes, free to live in penury, as his punishment. Or be forced into a nunnery. That is not the life I want."

Adam lowered his head, bowed by his failure. Exhaustion

rushed over him. The mad dash from France, beating through the storm and limping into harbor with broken spars, then riding like a demon to reach his uncle. The horror of his stepmother's suffering. Grenville's barbarity. His failure with Frances. The weight of it all collapsed the fight in him. His back was against the wall and he slid down it and sat on the stone floor. With elbows on his drawn-up knees, he lowered his head onto his arms. "You should go," he said, not unkindly. "You don't want your brother to find you gone."

He heard the rustle of her skirt as she knelt at his side. He felt her hand on his shoulder, a comforting squeeze. Her hand lingered. "Adam," she whispered with longing. She stroked his hair, caressing. He didn't want this, and he hadn't the heart to continue the charade with her a moment longer. He started to raise his head.

"No, don't," she said quickly. "Don't look at me. If you do, I won't be able to say this."

He rested his forehead again, barely listening, fighting despair.

"I love you, Adam. I loved you the moment I saw you. When I said I would do anything for you, I meant it. There is a way for me to ask Her Majesty for what you want."

He jerked up his head to look at her.

Her eyes were shining. "There is one man who would have a greater power than my brother's. One man whose authority I would have to obey, by law, and under God, even if it meant opposing John."

He stared at her. She couldn't mean it. He had never intended such a thing . . . never had a single thought of it. His struggle to hide his dismay brought an embarrassed smile to his lips, and she smiled back as though they were intimate accomplices.

"That's right," she said. "My husband."

The night was dark as death. Too dark to see the gathering storm clouds, though Adam sensed them as if they pressed down on him as he crossed the Grenville Hall garden, making for the hedge maze. In the darkness he could see the black bulk of the maze only because torches flared beyond it, lighting the way down to the riverside jetty. Ten o'clock she had said. So he had waited by the river, under a willow that trailed its branches in the water.

Had watched it flow past Grenville's lands and then rush on to his family's. He thought how it gave fish for the Grenvilles' table, then fueled his father's fulling mills. Watered Grenville grain, then his stepmother's roses. He had waited until the very last moment. Ten o'clock.

He reached the maze and turned to take a last look at the great house. Candelabra and torches glowed behind the windows. There was a faint sound of singing. He turned back and stepped inside the maze.

The hedge walls reached just over his head, severely clipped box yews with foliage so dense it blacked out even the glow of the riverside torches. Adam chose the left-hand turning and struck off down the narrow alley, the thick grass spongy underfoot. A minute later he reached a dead end. He backtracked and started again, this time on the right-hand alley. It twisted, drawing him nearer the center of the labyrinth. Another dead end. Back again he went a little way, then onto a new path, but soon felt sure it, too, was wrong. He stopped and stood still, listening for any rustle of clothing, any hint of voices. Bats swooped over the foliage walls, a cold swoosh past his ears, and were instantly swallowed by the blackness of the maze.

Then he saw pinpricks of light. He followed the trail, the pinpricks strengthening into a brassy shimmer that brought him at last to the center. Frances stood under a yew tree where a lantern hung from a branch. A black-robed priest stood murmuring with her. The lantern light glinted off the jewels she had carefully arranged in her hair. Adam had a fleeting thought of Elizabeth. Sunlight on her hair.

Frances smiled when she saw him.

"Ah," the priest said. "Shall we begin?"

Adam stood at Frances's side and the ceremony began. Betrothal. A solemn pledge to marry. Both church and state considered it a formal contract. People considered it almost as binding as marriage itself. Country folk often took it to *be* marriage, sanctioning sexual relations.

"It will have to be our secret for now," she had said in the stable. "I'll need some time to bring John around." At Adam's silence—

his grappling with this desperate bargain—she had pressed the point. "A secret, Adam, you understand? As will be my urgent request to Her Majesty."

"I understand," he had said. One word from the Queen and his father would live. It was a lifeline. He told himself that a drowning man does not quibble about the kind of rope he's thrown.

The priest concluded the ceremony, intoning, "For the servant of God, Adam, and the servant of God, Frances, who are now betrothed to one another, and for their salvation, let us pray to the Lord." They bowed their heads. Adam's eyes stayed wide open. "And may an Angel of the Lord go before them all the days of their lives. For you are the One who blesses and sanctifies all things, and to you we give glory, to the Father and to the Son and to the Holy Spirit, now and forever."

When it was over she kissed him lightly on the mouth. "I'll leave first. Go home, Adam. And take heart. Things will change, in time. Even John. Then we can marry. I will make you a good wife. I promise."

He watched her go, leading the priest out. The lantern light died.

❧ 23 ❧

Homecoming

July 1556

Ahook ripped flesh from her shoulder . . . razors sawed her ankle . . .

She awoke with a spasm of terror. "Stop!"

"Honor, my dear! What is it?" A soft voice.

Not his. She looked around for him, fear clogging her throat. "Where is he?"

"Who?"

Grenville. Wind whipped something against her cheek. *Where am I?* She tried to swipe at it but could not move her arm. Panic flooded her. "Richard! Where's Richard?"

"He's . . . it's all right, dear." A woman's face, a soothing voice. "He's fine."

But where? "Where's Adam?"

"He sailed to Amsterdam last week, remember? He's fine. Don't worry. You're home. You're safe. Everyone's fine."

The nightmare splintered. Her sister-in-law was leaning over her, gently squeezing her shoulder. Honor slumped in relief, her mouth too dry to speak. She went to touch Joan's hand in thanks, but could not lift her right arm. She'd forgotten.

"You fell asleep, dear. It's the sun."

Honor swallowed the last bitter trace of fear. They were sitting in the garden in the bright July sunshine, she in an armchair soft with cushions brought from the house, Joan on a bench beside her. "Sleep," she said, rubbing her forehead. The headache never quite went away. "That's all I do." Three weeks at home, and she had spent it almost entirely in bed.

"Just what you need," Joan said. "Sleep, and plenty of it." She settled down on the bench, taking up her embroidery hoop again with its needle and yellow thread. "You're still as weak as a kitten."

"But it puts so much on you. You're overseeing everything. Kitchen, bake house, dairy house. Everything."

"I quite like it. Your cook has quicker wits than mine, and your dairymaids are less prone to romancing the grooms. I might just stay."

Honor managed a faint smile. She couldn't begin to express her gratitude for her sister-in-law's tender nursing since Geoffrey had brought her home from the Tower. Still, she felt sure that Joan, the capable governor of her own large household at Blackheath, must be eager to get back to Geoffrey, who had already returned to their family.

Home. Joan's words echoed: *You're safe.* Yet Honor felt a twist of worry as she noticed three men walking back and forth outside the garden gate, each armed with a sword and dagger. Patrolling, obviously. Who had set them to this task? Watching the youngest one, who seemed almost too young to *have* a sword, she realized he was the gardener's apprentice. Jeremy something. And wasn't one of the others Peter, a new footman? It made her uneasy. This did not *feel* like home; more like being a prisoner inside her own grounds. She already felt like a prisoner inside her body—every muscle still felt frayed, stripped of strength. The wind, too, made her jumpy, a turbulent wind despite the heat. It tossed the boughs of the pear trees by the garden wall, setting the leaves to rustling as though whispering an urgent message. The wind was heavy with the scent of roses. It was a rose petal that had blown across Honor's cheek as she had lurched out of the nightmare. It had fallen to her lap, and with her good arm she picked it up. A petal red as blood. She looked across the sand path at the mass of red roses climbing the trellis against the far wall. Nodding near them in the wind were tall yellow lilies and crimson poppies. Grenville's face suddenly reared up, that hard white rib of the scar above his lip. She winced, closing her eyes.

"Pain?" Joan asked.

She quickly shook her head. "No, I'm fine." It was true, the worst of the pain was behind her. But there was desolation in her heart, like ice at her core, as she gazed at her garden. In the Tower, stretched on the rack, she had tried to bear the agony by imagining her beloved flowers, but Grenville had almost broken her. Would she ever see roses and irises and lilies again without seeing that face, that bony white scar? Would she ever smell the scent of flowers without reliving the terror and the pain? She hated him for befouling a love.

But that was just a surface hate. Far deeper, colder, flintier, was the hate she bore him for what he had done to Richard, chained for months in that coffin-sized cell. He had been so weak when Adam had brought him home, with gray skin and a wild, tangled beard. And so thin that his clothes hung from his shoulders as though from sticks. He had insisted on riding, refusing the humiliation of being brought in a wagon, but from her bedroom window where she'd had the bed moved, waiting for him to come home, she had seen, when the two of them rode through the gates, that he was barely able to hold himself upright in the saddle.

Again, that twist of worry in her stomach. "Where's Richard?"

Joan plied her needle, studying her expert stitches. "Oh, you know—at work."

"But where, exactly?" Since his return she had been haunted by a need to know his whereabouts at all times, to satisfy herself that he was alive, and nearby. That John Grenville had not snatched him again. She was profoundly grateful for whatever had moved the Queen to let him go. The best explanation she and Richard could gather was that their lawyer's petitions had finally convinced the Queen of the illegality of keeping him a prisoner. But she still imagined Grenville, like a wolf deprived of a kill, lying in wait for his next chance.

"Well, there's the new housing for the Flemish weavers," Joan said. "Two of those roofs are still unfinished and the carpenters are at odds with the joiners, so he may be there, sorting things out. Or he may be down at the mill with the master fuller. I hear there's a broken paddle wheel."

Honor felt sure Joan was hiding something from her. Absently, she shredded the rose petal, wondering, as always in these past weeks, where Richard went every day. And how did he find the strength? He had been sleeping in another room to let her recover, but he was barely recovered himself, his once sturdy body still weak, moving with a slight stoop, yet while she had kept to her bed all day he had pushed himself to go out, seeing to his workers, leaving early every morning, coming back late. Every day began the same. He came in to see her, bearing a single rose and a look of tense wonder, as though relieved to find her still alive. He would bend to kiss her, then tuck the rose into the already full vase by her bedside, then sit on the edge of the bed and take her good hand in his and ask how she felt, how she had slept, whether there was anything he could do for her, or have the servants fetch for her.

"A new body would be nice," she had said the other day. "Preferably one twenty years younger. And with fair hair this time."

"This one has served you well. And me," he'd said, the glint of a smile in his eye.

Gently, she ran her fingertips over the welts on his wrist gouged by the iron manacle, scabs that stretched in a band as wide as her hand. He was clean shaven, exposing how winter-pale his lower face still was from his prison beard. He wore a black doublet of thick, winter wool, needing its warmth even in the July sunshine. Tears pricked her eyes as she imagined what he had suffered, but she forced them back. She would not let him see how it wrenched her heart. He spoke to her of domestic things, and she was glad to go along—a servant's wedding, a lame horse, Joan's menu for dinner. Neither could bear to go deeper.

Every morning ended the same. He would give her a long look in silence, turning very sober, as though a cloud had passed over his face, then push himself to his feet like a veteran soldier hearing the trumpet call to horse. "Must go." If she asked where, he always muttered, "Business." He would kiss her again. And then he was gone. Each day she worried that Grenville would be watching and waiting. That Richard would not come back.

"I never see him from one morning to the next," she said now to Joan, not a complaint so much as a plea. *Tell me he's safe.*

"Well, you know how it is with Richard. Always one task after another."

Honor knew the truth of this. He had always hated being idle. But in his weakened state, how could his body take the way he was pushing himself? And why would Joan not look her in the eye?

"Why don't you try it again, dear?" Joan said, changing the subject. She gave a nod to the writing materials on the bench—a quill pen, and paper tucked under an inkpot to keep it from blowing away.

Better than tormenting myself with worry, Honor thought. She positioned the paper, then picked up the pen. She had been practicing writing with her left hand, a frustrating effort. Her right hand worked as well as ever, though stiffly, but her right shoulder was so damaged she could not move the arm, could only lift it with her other hand, as though it belonged to someone else, and awkwardly place the right hand where she wanted it. The doctor's opinion was that shoulder ligaments were ripped, the damage permanent. She dipped the pen in the inkpot and tried writing a few more words of the letter she had begun to her wine purveyor—*The shipment of burgundy arrived.* She stopped and looked at it. Awful. A scrawl worse than a child's.

"Keep at it," Joan coaxed. "It will come, in time."

Honor continued writing—*and my clerk's accounts show*—but her clumsy left hand refused to do what she wanted. Disgusted, she tossed the pen on the bench.

Joan had the wisdom to accept temporary defeat. "Oh," she said, suddenly remembering, "Ned came while you were napping. This was delivered for you." From the grass at her feet she picked up a burlap bag the size of a mop head and set it on the bench.

"Delivered from whom?"

"Ned didn't know. And he said the gentleman who delivered it didn't know either. But he arrived with an escort of three armed men. Must be worth something."

Honor opened the bag. Inside, a rope of pearls was coiled on top of a purse of crimson leather. She loosened the purse strings, revealing a mass of gold coins.

"Good heavens," said Joan, "the pearls alone are worth a small fortune! Who can it be from?"

A paper was tucked beside the purse. Honor unfolded it and silently read the short note.

> *Madam,*
> *For your loyalty, a hundred pearls. For your pain,*
> *five hundred crowns of gold. For the love I bear you, a*
> *thousand years will not suffice to honor you.*

It was unsigned, but she knew that confident handwriting so well. "Princess Elizabeth," she told Joan. It moved her. A gesture full of meaning, those crowns—one gold coin for every pound that Elizabeth had given her to take to Noailles for Dudley's venture. A tragic, failed venture. She had been heartbroken to learn that Sir Henry Peckham and several others had been executed. Sir William Courtenay and Lord John Bray had been arrested, but with friends in high places they had been released after paying heavy fines. Sir Nicholas Throckmorton had escaped to France. Honor would be forever grateful that none of them, apparently, had implicated either her or Adam. She gazed at the crowns, thinking of Elizabeth's gold confiscated by John Grenville, and again the image of him forced itself upon her, twisting the knot in her stomach.

"You did such a brave thing, protecting the Princess," Joan said warmly. "I'm sure she knows the true cost to you. This reward is a mere token."

Honor found that she could smile, knowing Elizabeth's tightness with money. "Oh, no. For her, this is most generous."

"All I can say is, thank heaven the Queen saw fit to order your release."

"Thank her husband," Honor said. They had all heard the rumor that Philip had ordered the Queen to drop her investigation of Elizabeth, and last week Honor had received confirmation of it in a letter from Sir William Cecil. "Or perhaps I should be thankful that the Queen, for all her ferocity against heretics, is such a timid wife. She jumps like a spaniel to do her husband's bidding."

"Strange, isn't it? A queen, yet so cowed. Geoffrey has never found *me* to be a spaniel."

Thinking of the lovesick Queen, Honor almost felt pity. Love, she thought. The power that commands us all. "Joan, where is he?"

"Who?"

"Richard. And don't tell me at work."

Joan gravely plied her needle and thread. "All I can tell you is he's busy."

"So you do know."

Silence.

Honor pushed herself out of the soft armchair.

"What are you doing? Sit down."

"I'm going to find him." The jolt of standing so abruptly made a hammer start pounding in her head. She felt rocky, and groped the chair for balance.

Joan jumped up and took her elbow to steady her. "Honor, stop. If you plague yourself about this you'll make yourself sick again."

"About what? Good Lord, Joan, what's happened? Tell me, or I will be sick indeed!"

Joan's face showed how torn she was. "He didn't want you upset. He's seeing . . . some men. He's at the tithe barn."

It was a huge building, half stone, half wood, one story high but long enough that a horse, if sent from one end to the other, could trot for minutes. It had been the abbey's collection depot and winnowing barn for the grain of its tenant farmers, who gave a portion of it as a tax to their church overlord. The farmers still used it as a barn, though a couple of added storerooms now held Richard's raw wool. It stood in hulking isolation in a fallow field on a slight rise above the river, the highway that carried both the grain and wool to London's markets.

Honor hurried as fast as she could along the path that ran parallel to the river. Her legs were still shaky, but stronger than a week ago. As she approached the tithe barn she saw several horses tethered to the rails. The huge double oak doors were closed. It took all her store of strength to pull one of them open.

It was as though she had walked in on a battle. Dozens of men, hacking at each other with swords, firing arrows, running, shouting war cries. Yet none seemed to be drawing blood. Before she could make sense of the mayhem, a beefy soldier in a breastplate stepped in front of her, clanking with weapons, barring her way. His face was made fierce by glowering, bloodshot eyes.

"Turn around and walk out," he said quietly. An order.

Honor gaped at the knife he held, a brutish weapon as long as his forearm, and pitted from use. He had not raised it to threaten her but held it idly, familiarly, as though it was a part of him, which somehow made it more menacing. Beyond him she spotted Richard. He sat on a stool with his back to her, hunched over a table laden with weapons where men were milling. A man at the far side of the table saw her, and his look of consternation made Richard turn.

The soldier with the knife scowled at her for not leaving and grabbed her arm to shove her out, but she dug in her heels, an almost panicked reflex at being manhandled as she had been by Grenville's guards in the Tower. She sensed it was stupid and dangerous to stand up to this rough fighter, but what kept her rooted to the spot was that she recognized some of the men. They were completely unlike this soldier. They were farmers. Tenants.

"Stand down, Captain," Richard said, coming over to them. "This is my wife."

The soldier let go her arm. "Sorry, sir."

"Richard, what is all this?" Her eyes were on the man's ugly knife as he sauntered away, lifting his arm over his shoulder to sheath the knife in a scabbard strapped to his back between his shoulder blades. He sheathed it with a single, practiced motion even as he called out to another soldier, "Lieutenant, show that man how to wield his pike or I'll have your guts for garters."

"Go back to the house, Honor," Richard said. "This is no place for you."

"But who is that soldier? Captain of what?"

"Go home," he said to her, scowling at a knot of men who had stopped their fighting and turned to look at her.

"Not until you tell me what—"

"Not here," he said tightly under his breath. He took her elbow and hustled her into a storeroom. He shut the door behind them and dropped the wooden bar into its iron bracket to lock it, then turned to her. "What are you doing out of bed? I told Joan to—"

"To keep me in the dark? Why? What's James Althorpe doing out there with a crossbow? And Arthur Heneage, thrusting a sword at his brother? What in heaven's name is going on?"

"Sit down. You're too weak to be traipsing the fields."

"I wouldn't have to if you'd told me where—"

He held up his hands to forestall her, then beckoned her. "Come." The room was crammed with canvas sacks stuffed with raw wool, plump oblongs as long as a man and wide as a bench, stacked up in rows that almost reached the ceiling. He guided her to an unfinished stack that reached just to his shoulders and pulled the top woolsack down to the floor. It landed in a thud of dust. "Sit," he ordered. "You shouldn't be up. It's—" He didn't finish. His face went suddenly pale, his eye glassy. Honor saw that the effort of pulling down the heavy woolsack had made him dizzy.

"Here, sit down," she said quickly, taking his arm and guiding him. He sank onto the sack. He leaned over, elbows on his spread knees, head down. Honor sat beside him and gently rubbed the back of his neck. She had to use her left arm, awkwardly reaching across her body. "What a pair we are, my love," she said with a sad smile. "Damaged goods."

He glanced up, and seemed to wince at the way she was reduced to using one arm because of Grenville. He did not smile. His voice was a growl. "Damn his eyes."

"Richard, you're not well. Come home. Let me take care of you."

He shook his head. "Can't."

"You can and you must." She longed to keep him indoors, by her side, away from their enemy.

He straightened up and looked at her. "Don't you see? I've got to fight him."

Terror gripped her. "Fight? You can barely stand."

"Not alone. I'm forming a home guard among the tenants. That's what you saw out there. I hired Captain Boone to train them. He's battle hard, a veteran of Scotland and France."

"A home guard? You can't be serious. Farmers with battle-axes? The most dangerous weapon most of them have ever touched is a scythe."

"They'll do. Boone handpicked them. The strong and the quick. A few are experienced fighters. And they're loyal."

"As long as they're paid."

"A necessary expense. I've extended our loan."

"I don't care about the money. I care about you."

"Honor, I'm doing what has to be done. For our family."

"No. What you should be doing is nothing. You should be resting. Getting better. Not calling Grenville's attention to us. Not giving him any reason to come against you."

"Just keep our heads down?"

"Yes!"

"Hide under the bed until the dragon goes back into his cave?"

She glared at him. "Don't mock me, Richard. He would have killed you if the Queen hadn't signed your release. He *will* kill you if he can."

"I know." He looked at her hard, as though gauging whether to go on. "I'm going to kill him first."

Silence cut between them like a sword. Beyond the door, men shouted their mock war cries.

"No," she said. Her mouth had gone dry. Her heart beat painfully. "Richard, you'll hang."

He looked away. Gave a grim shrug. "I'm already a dead man. Have been since I killed his father."

"Don't say that. Don't talk like that!"

He looked at her. "Honor, we deluded ourselves from the start. The pardon Cecil wangled for me, it means nothing to Grenville. No, that's wrong—it means everything. An injustice he can't abide. It's his license to take the law into his own hands."

"But there *are* laws."

"For law-abiding people."

"But, this is insane, this . . . fatalism. There's got to be another way."

"Peace?" He shook his head. "Not possible. He'll never stop. Not until I'm dead. Maybe not even then. He'll go after you. And Adam. I will not let that happen."

"You cannot know what he'll do. But you can be sure that if you kill him you will hang."

"We're beyond *choosing*. You said it yourself—he meant to finish me. And since he was forced to release me, he'll expect that I'm now out to finish *him*. Even if I weren't, he'll think I am. He's already expanded his own guard, added fourteen more crack fighters to the Grenville Archers. Beefed up his retinue of armed retainers, too—thirty men now ride with him wherever he goes." He took her hand in his, his voice becoming urgent. "Honor, don't you see? He expects me to attack him, so he'll know that his best strategy is to attack me first. It's come down to this. Kill or be killed."

It made her feel sick. "This is what I see. If Grenville comes for you he'll kill you. If you try to attack him, his men will kill you. If you somehow manage to kill him, they'll hang you. Every way, you die."

"Maybe not. There's a chance I can kill him and get away with it, and that's the chance I'm going to take. Because otherwise I'm dead for sure. Honor, someone has to do this. If I don't, Adam will. I won't risk him getting hanged. That's why I've sent him to Amsterdam on business. It's up to me."

She snatched her hand away from him. "You've been lying to me. Every morning. Chattering about the maid's wedding and what's for dinner. All the while planning and plotting this."

"Hardest thing I've ever done. Pretending I won't make him pay for what he did to you."

"You're still lying. You *want* to kill him."

He glared at her. "You think this makes me *happy?*"

"I think you're mad. Mad with rage. Mad to get even. And it's going to get you killed! Well, I will not stand quietly by while you commit suicide!" She stalked to the door and threw up the wooden bar and grabbed the door handle.

And froze.

She took a sharp breath. Her hand flew to her mouth.

"Honor?"

She whirled around.

"What's wrong?" he said anxiously. "Pain?"

Tears scalded her eyes. "This. You and me. So wrong . . ."

"You've got to try to understand. It's the only way—"

"No, I don't mean that." She was trembling. "I mean fighting. You and me. Like at the Crane." It was the last time they had been together before Grenville arrested him and dragged him to the Tower. They had fought over him organizing the opposition in Parliament. She'd been terrified since her interview with the Queen, with Grenville itching to interrogate her, and had threatened Richard that if he continued organizing in Parliament she would flee to Antwerp alone. He insisted he *would* continue and her last furious words had been, *If you go out that door, consider it locked.* He had stomped out, and she had not seen him again for five months. By then, Grenville had broken her on the rack and starved Richard almost to death.

"I don't know what's in Grenville's mind," she said now, "and I don't think you can know, either. I pray that he has had revenge enough, that by hurting us he has slaked his bloodlust. But if you're right, if he won't stop until you are dead—" She had to swallow before she could go on. She came to him, face-to-face. "Richard, if we're going to die, I don't want the last words we say to each other to be in anger. Fight him if you feel you must. From this day forward, let there never be anger between us again."

He gazed at her in wonder. He took her face between his hands, tenderly, lovingly. "Let's live, and I'll hold you to that."

It moved her so, she threw her good arm around his neck. Her right arm hung useless at her side, an ugly weight. *I'm a cripple*, she thought, and the tears she had held back brimmed and spilled. She could not stop them.

"What is it?" he asked, his face tight with concern.

"I can't even hold you."

His smile almost broke her heart. "But I can hold you," he said, and pulled her to him, wrapping his arms around her.

She nestled her face against his neck and closed her eyes and said, "I've missed you." She pulled back a little and looked at him, the craggy face she loved. She brushed her lips over his. "Missed you lying beside me."

He kissed her. A hungry kiss. But he quickly broke it off. "I . . . didn't want to hurt you."

His gaze on her was filled with longing, but he made no move. She sat down on the woolsack and pulled him down to sit beside her. She took his hand and slipped it under her skirt and shivered at his warm, rough palm on her thigh. She said, "There's nothing you can do that I won't like."

He grinned. It was a longstanding love jest between them. Years ago, at their first lovemaking, she so inexperienced in the ways of men, she had touched his erection and misinterpreted the look on his face as one of pain, and asked, "You don't like it?" He had laughed and said, in a voice husky with need, "I like it, believe me. I like it." Then, more ardently, "There's nothing you can do that I won't like."

Now, she pressed his hand against her thigh and said, "There's nothing you can do that will hurt me." She looked deep into his eyes. "Except leave me."

He slipped his other arm around her waist and lowered her onto the woolsack and brought his mouth to hers. "Then, my love, there is nothing at all."

❧ 24 ❧

Princess at the Threshold

January 1557

Adam rode hard from Colchester, Elizabeth's letter driving him on through gusting snow. The morning had brought sleet that made the road a treacherous slide of icy mud, and now the wind-whipped snow needled his face with such force he could hardly see the road ahead, but he did not slacken his pace. Just a note, she'd sent. Barely that. Two lines. *If you are within the realm and receive this by Twelfth Night, come in all haste, I beg you. If you fail me, I am lost.* He had barraged her road-weary messenger for information—What had happened? Was the Princess in danger? What was it she feared?—but the exhausted man had no answers.

It was dusk when Adam galloped through the gates of Hatfield House. The wind and snow had finally abated as though worn out by their assault on him, and he found the courtyard deserted and quiet. That eased one of his fears—the place had not been overrun by the Queen's soldiers come to arrest Elizabeth.

"Here he is!" a voice called out.

Adam turned in the saddle, his neck stiff from the cold, and glimpsed a maid's face at an open second-story window before she disappeared. Agnes? He'd gotten to know most of the household when he'd recuperated from his arrow wound—she had brought him his meals. A young groom dashed out from the house, calling over his shoulder, "He's here!"

Adam swung down from the saddle, shedding a flurry of snow from his cloak even before the boy reached him to take the reins. "What's going on, Tim? What's the trouble?"

"I know not, Master Thornleigh. Only, we was told to keep an eye out for you."

Burning to know why, Adam strode for the front door and was taking the steps two at a time when the door swung open and the chamberlain beckoned him in, looking anxious. "Blessed Jesu, what a storm you braved. Come in, Master Thornleigh, come in."

"Where is she, Bates? I got word—"

A rustle of skirts at the top of the staircase, and then a cry. "You came!"

He knew the voice and whirled around, and there she was, rushing down the steps toward him. Relief flooded him to see her alive, unhurt. As beautiful as ever—more beautiful, her loose hair streaming behind her like liquid flame, her black velvet dress hugging her body. He bounded up the steps, tearing off his ice-stiffened gauntlets, and they met in the middle of the staircase. She stopped one step above him and stood eye-to-eye with him, and her look of pure trust fired him with such desire, he had to hold himself back from taking her in his arms. He jerked his head in a bow. "My lady, I got your letter. What's happened?"

"There's no time to waste. Come." She grabbed his hand, then stopped in dismay, eyeing his sodden clothes. "Why, you're freezing." Her hand was so warm, he knew how icy his must feel.

"You said to come or you would be lost. What did you mean?"

She bit her lip, and he saw fear in her eyes as she murmured, "I may be lost yet." She managed a small, tense smile and said, "But I knew you would not fail me." Squeezing his hand, she turned on the step, bunched her skirts in her other hand, and pulled him up the stairs after her. She led him down the passage and into a bedchamber where two of her ladies, Bess Gordon and Mary St. Loe, stood watching with wide eyes as he came in, his spurs clanking, his boots dripping melted snow.

"Begin," Elizabeth told them. "Be quick!"

They gaped at her. "Oh, my lady, are you sure?"

"Sure that I want to live? Please, Bess!"

The two exchanged an anxious look, then nodded to her. They burst into activity, one pulling out drawers in a high chest, the other opening a trunk. Before Adam could press Elizabeth to tell him what was happening, she called out, "Agnes! Dorothy!" and then hurried to her dressing table where she pulled the lids off jewel boxes. The two maids rushed in.

"Your Grace?" one asked.

"Help them pack," she said with a nod at the ladies as she scattered her jewels on the table. "My red brocade gown, and the white silk sewn with pearls, and at least five others. And don't forget my sables. Go!" The maids ran to a closet. The ladies were already busily folding clothes and packing shoes and hats into trunks. Elizabeth beckoned to Mary St. Loe. "Mary, go fetch your father. He must assign my escort." Mary hurried out.

A voice came from the doorway. "So it's true."

Elizabeth's steward, Thomas Parry, stood glaring at Adam. He came straight to Elizabeth. "My lady, this is rash. Do reconsider, I entreat you."

"There's no time for that!" she snapped.

"At least wait until you can consult your friends."

"My friends are here." She swept her arm to indicate the busy women, and Adam. "*They* stand with me."

"You know my meaning. Sir John Thynne. Sir William Cecil. Lord Admiral Clinton. Sir William Paulet. Men of standing. Men of power."

"But no power to help me!"

He looked pained. "If you do this—"

"You have said your piece, Thomas. You may go." She was pawing through the jewelry—necklaces, rings, broaches, earrings, ropes of pearls—shoving selected items into a leather pouch.

"You, sir," he said, glowering again at Adam, "I marvel that you will abet such a desperate scheme."

Adam bristled. "Parry, I know not why I am here or what—"

"Silence!" Elizabeth cried. "Thomas, you are dismissed!"

Parry opened his mouth to protest, then closed it in frustration, turned on his heel, and walked out.

Elizabeth, fumbling with her jewels, knocked a large ring to the floor. "God's wounds!" she cursed. Adam quickly moved to pick it up, an eye-sized diamond circled by sapphires. She went to take it from him, but he closed his fist around it, keeping it from her. He'd had enough of this. "Answers, madam. I need some answers."

She went very still. Her eyes locked on his. Her face was pale. "Three weeks before Christmas I was summoned to court. I knelt before my sister and she gave me her command. I am to marry."

It knocked the breath from him.

"Why so surprised, sir? It is the lot of women. Duchess or dairy-maid, we must each of us be ruled by some man." Her tone was bitter. She took the ring from his unresisting hand. "I must marry, and they have chosen my bridegroom."

"Who?"

"My sister and her husband."

"No. Who is he?"

She seemed to shudder. "The Duke of Savoy."

Questions flooded his mind, but before he could speak Mary came back with her father, Sir William St. Loe, who marched in with his lieutenant. St. Loe, the veteran soldier, bowed to Elizabeth, asking, "Your orders, my lady?" She led him to the window where they looked down on the courtyard at the guards he commanded. There were now so many people in the room Adam could not hear all that Elizabeth and St. Loe said, but he heard them agree on the number of her escort—thirty men. Then she immediately came back to Adam and laid her palm gently on his chest, on the spot where he'd been wounded, and said warmly, for everyone to hear, "They will serve alongside my loyal champion, Master Thornleigh."

The glowing look she gave him squeezed his heart. Now he knew why she had called for him. She was preparing to travel somewhere to be married, and she intended for him to take pride of place among her bodyguard. It horrified him—how could he hand her over to another man? He grasped at a mad, faint hope that the marriage contract could not have been concluded yet, not so quickly. She was royalty, and this foreign duke must be close to

it. The two governments would have to hammer out details, nego-
tiate terms. That took time.

Elizabeth went back to hurriedly sorting her jewels beside him.
"His name," she said tightly, as though making a great effort to re-
main calm, "is Emmanuel Philibert. A name for a player in a comedy, don't you think? A mincing, perfumed dandy? But it is not so.
For this is no play, sir, it is life in earnest, and my duke is made of
sterner stuff. A military hero in Spain's conquest of the people of
Flanders. Lieutenant of the Netherlands, named so by Emperor
Charles before he abdicated. He is a cousin of my brother-in-law,
the mighty King Philip of Spain. His drinking crony, so I'm told.
All one big happy Hapsburg family. When my intended is not
bashing the heads of the stubborn Dutch who fail to appreciate the
Spanish yoke under which they groan, he entertains Philip with
nights of carousing, debauching the Dutchmen's daughters—all in
good fun, of course. This, sir, is my duke. Am I not blessed?"

Adam could find no words. He was lost in imagining her in this
man's bed.

"My sister wants me out of the way, and what better place than
under the iron fist of a Hapsburg husband?" She dropped her pretense of jesting and looked at him with undisguised fear. "In truth,
she wants me dead. But she has not yet convinced her council of
the need of that, so this marriage will serve her, for it pleases her
husband. Indeed, I understand it was Philip's idea. It will
strengthen his grip on England to have me the submissive wife of
his Spanish kinsman, his chief general." She shot a look at Bess
and the maids, who had paused in filling the trunks and were listening with such sad faces that Adam realized they knew the situation. "I do not need your pity," Elizabeth told them brusquely. "I
need you to pack."

They went back to it, and Elizabeth returned to her jewels, and
Adam was left to his own tormented thoughts. He knew how it felt
to be trapped into marriage. He had told no one about his betrothal
to Frances Grenville. He'd spent the last six months plying the sea
roads between Colchester, Antwerp, Amsterdam, and London,
turning some profit in his father's business, keeping deliberately

far from Frances and avoiding her frequent letters. But Elizabeth was staring this marriage in the face.

She gave him a wan smile. "I was as stunned by my sister's order as you seem to be, sir. So much so, I blurted to her that I must respectfully decline the duke's hand."

His heart jumped. "You refused?"

"I did." She lifted her chin, defiant.

Adam loved her for that. But he knew her boldness was a mask. No one could defy the Queen and get away with it. "But she did not accept that answer?"

"She raged at my intransigence. Ordered me home, and told me to come back with a better answer by the time her husband arrives."

Again he grasped at a lifeline. King Philip had not set foot in England for over a year and a half. "But he has made Flanders his home."

She shook her head. "My sister is getting her way in all things. She has pined for her absent lord and now he is on his way. Since France broke its truce with Spain, he needs money to wage his war against King Henri, and Mary saw her chance. 'Come home,' she told him, 'and I will command Parliament to grant you money.' " She took a sudden, sharp breath and her eyes glistened with tears. "She told me if I do not agree to the marriage by the time he arrives, she will have Parliament proclaim that I am not my father's child. Proclaim my bastardy and disinherit me. And if I continue to refuse, she threatened me with death."

Her mouth trembled. Her tears spilled. She clutched a handful of Adam's doublet at his chest. He gripped her elbows, longing to pull her to him and hold her safe from the world, from the Queen, from the brutal Duke of Savoy. She ducked her head, using his body to hide her tearstained face from the others in the room. He stood still, her shield, while she quickly dried her eyes with her sleeve.

"So now," he managed to ask, "you're returning to give her your answer?" He held his breath.

She looked up at him. "I have only two choices."

He couldn't bear to imagine either one. Marry or die.

"Marry," she said. "Or flee."

For a moment, so mired in dread, he didn't understand.

She said, with a new edge in her voice, "I will not marry with a sword to my throat. Where is your ship? Where is the *Elizabeth*?"

It crashed over him in a wave of excitement. "Colchester Harbor." He threw all decorum to the winds and grabbed both her hands. "My lady, I am yours to command. As is my ship."

She smiled her gratitude. "Thank you."

"Where shall I take you?"

"The French ambassador has offered me safe haven."

"To France, then. What harbor is safest for you?"

"I . . . had not thought. Calais?"

"No. Too many English merchants. Bruges might be best, then overland to Lille."

That brought a wry smile. "In this, sir, it seems I am *yours* to command. I place myself in your good hands."

It made him heady, like he'd drunk a mug of French brandy. "When can you leave?"

"As soon as they have me packed."

He looked around at her friends and servants bustling to prepare her for the journey. Her ladies, her maids, the commanders of her guard. He marvelled, not for the first time, how all her people stood by her, no matter the risk to themselves. And the risk was great in aiding a princess to flee the realm—the Queen could make them suffer for it. Looking back at Elizabeth as she tugged tight the strings of the pouch with her chosen jewelry, he felt a pang. If the risk was great for anyone helping her escape, it was truly terrible for Elizabeth herself. What she was planning could be considered treason. It could lead her to the execution block. He thought of Thomas Parry's brief attempt a few minutes ago to persuade her to reconsider.

"My lady," he said, laying his hand on the pouch to stop her. "Have you really thought this through? It's clear that Master Parry thinks—"

"Parry is a fretful old woman. He cares nothing for my dire need to be gone. He thwarts me."

"He is your true friend and cares only for your safety, and you know it."

She pulled the pouch away from him. "And you, sir? What are you? Are you with me, or will you thwart me, too?"

There was a desperation about her that made him uneasy. She was not making sound decisions. Someone had to make them for her.

"Dismiss these people," he said quietly.

"What?"

"Tell them you've changed your mind. That Parry is right, it's too dangerous to attempt to flee."

Elizabeth fixed hurt eyes on him. "I thought I could trust you."

He shook his head. "The baggage train of a princess, complete with your ladies and men-at-arms? How could you hope to evade the Queen's spies, whether in the village or on the road?"

She looked defiant. "All manner of noblewomen travel thus. Even wealthy merchants' wives do. If I disguise my appearance, I could pass as anyone."

"But you are not anyone. You are the woman the Queen wants dead."

She went as pale as if he'd slapped her.

"I will not take you as a princess," he said. "I will take you as common folk like me. And alone."

They met with Thomas Parry in his chamber.

"Master Thornleigh says it must be so, Thomas. You must give out to the household that I am not well and am keeping to my bed."

Parry paced beside his desk, clearly still reluctant, but listening.

Adam said, "And the routines around the Princess must carry on as usual. That's essential, Parry. The servants must bring her daily trays of meals, take out the nightly chamber pot, deliver letters."

"You do not trust her people?" Parry challenged.

"Wholeheartedly, in the main. But it takes just one to succumb to an agent of the Queen, or of the imperial ambassador. Those men can be generous paymasters."

Parry nodded grimly and conceded, "Always my fear." He cast a worried glance at Elizabeth. "But, to journey with no protection for my lady, no guard at all. I cannot see—"

"What soldiers does a merchant's daughter need?" Adam said.

"Merchant's daughter?" Elizabeth asked, looking daunted.

"Makes sense, since you're traveling with me. You're about the same age as my sister."

She looked intrigued. "Really? What's her name?"

"Isabel."

He caught the hint of a smile as she considered it. "Perhaps a half sister. Isabel Fitzroy."

He smiled at that. Fitzroy meant son of the king. Daughter, in this case. "Here's our story. We stopped here so I could pay my respects to Princess Elizabeth, and now we're continuing on our way to the wedding of our cousin at Braydon."

"Do you have a cousin at Braydon?"

"No. But it's a good cover in case anyone asks you."

"Asks me my business?" she said with royal hauteur. "Who would dare?"

"Almost anyone who's curious. People on the road like to chat."

She looked dismayed. Whether by the prospect of such forward behavior, or uncertain how to join in the habits of common folk, Adam couldn't tell, but he needed to know before they both risked their lives. "My lady, it's a two-day ride, three if the weather's foul, with only humble inns for shelter, and you'll have no attendants to fetch for you, dress you, make you comfortable. We'll have to shift for ourselves. If you feel unsure—"

"Never mind that," Parry said to her. "It's the *danger* you must consider. If a spy should suspect you, you'll have no protection from an assassin getting close enough to do the deed."

Her eyes flicked between them with growing concern. She fixed her gaze on Adam. "No protection? Not so, Master Parry. This man has proved his mettle. No, the one I fear is me. What if I betray myself?"

It was all Adam needed to hear. "Take courage," he told her. "I know how you love to watch the players. Comedy or tragedy, I've seen you marvel at their nimbleness in shedding their given selves and taking on the heart and soul of another. Now you must be as nimble. Act the part. Can you do it?"

She lifted her chin and said bravely, "I must."

The next day dawned bright and brittle cold. The Hatfield courtyard was quiet. The whole household was at morning prayers, called by Parry to ask God to return good health to the Princess, who'd been struck in the night with a fever and was keeping to her bed.

Adam helped Elizabeth mount her horse, then swung up onto his horse beside her. She wore simple clothes—a homespun brown cloak, a wool dress of a dark reddish brown like a hickory nut, and beneath it a plain white chemise—but her consternation was that of a princess as they watched the gatekeeper's men push open the gate, the iron fittings clattering as they walked the double doors apart. Adam had never seen Elizabeth so nervous. Never before had she passed through these gates as anything but a royal personage, the daughter of a king, the center of a grand entourage. Now there were no men-at-arms and liveried retainers surrounding her, no ladies keeping her company, no train of household officers, gentlemen ushers, secretaries, servants, and lackeys, no bustle of baggage carts and packhorses. Just Adam, with a couple of well-worn leather bags of belongings strapped near the rumps of their mounts.

The gates stood open. They started forward at a walk. Elizabeth suddenly jerked her reins, halting her horse. She stared out at the yawning gulf beyond the gates—the slushy road with its straggle of villagers—as wary as if it were a foreign land, treacherous and threatening.

Adam waited, hoping she could gather her nerve. She seemed to shrink back under the bright sunshine, as though afraid that it exposed her to the world as an imposter and revealed her to the court's spies.

"You'll be fine," he said. He gave her an encouraging smile. "Ready?"

She turned to him, and for a moment she seemed lost. He reached out, offering his hand. "Here. We'll do it together."

She took his hand. Then took a deep, steadying breath. "Ready."

They passed through the gates hand in hand, their horses at a walk. Adam tossed a shilling to the gatekeeper's man, thanking him for his pains and wishing him a good day. Elizabeth's horse sensed the journey ahead and quickened its step, pulling her hand free from Adam's.

❧ 25 ❧

The Royal Commoner

January 1557

Riding side by side, Adam and Elizabeth kept their horses at an unhurried walk as the gates of Hatfield closed behind them. Elizabeth tensed as they approached the scatter of villagers on the road going about their business. Though she wore commonplace clothes, Adam thought her beauty shone more brightly, no longer hidden under lavish ruffs, gold embroidery, lace trimmings, and jewels. He almost feared *too* brightly—couldn't these people see how glorious she was? Despite everything they were risking, and the suffering that her capture could bring them both, he couldn't help feeling a rush of happiness just to have her beside him, alone.

They carried on through the village, where plenty of people were out, trudging to and from the winter-dirty shops and market stalls. They passed housewives haggling with a meat vendor whose cuts of beef and pork roasted on spits over a charcoal fire, and market stalls where men and women loudly hawked winter apples, honey, turnips, dried herbs, and live rabbits. No one made way for them, as Elizabeth was used to having done for her. She had pulled her cloak's hood up over her hair, and with each person they passed she lowered her head, eyes cast down as though she feared that every farmer plodding behind his ox might be a spy for the Queen, every housewife on a donkey an agent of the imperial ambassador.

"Don't hide," Adam said quietly. "Just look them in the eye."

She tried it. Timidly at first, but then, as the next person trudged past without a second look, she gathered courage. "It works." She gave him a cautious smile of surprise. "They don't seem to notice me."

"Too busy with their own concerns. The price of bread. The baby's cough." They passed a middle-aged couple on foot, the woman nattering angrily at the bleary-eyed man, and Adam said with a wry smile, "The drunken husband who didn't chop this morning's wood."

Elizabeth laughed, then covered her mouth to bottle up the sound, but delight shone in her eyes. As they overtook a limping priest, she ventured quietly, "The mule who threw him yesterday."

Adam grinned. "And the doctor's bill." He jerked his chin to indicate a young farmer on a shaggy workhorse trotting toward them with a dreamy look. "The pretty girl he saw in church, and what's the best way to meet her."

Elizabeth smiled at him. It warmed him to his boots.

They struck out onto the main road that led out of the village and he felt Elizabeth tense up again, as though preparing herself to cross this threshold into the wider world.

"All right?" he asked.

She looked at him, pale faced but clear-eyed, and nodded.

They left the village behind and rode on past fields sleeping under quilts of snow. The road sloped down to a narrow river frozen in its bed, and their horses clomped over the wooden bridge. The earthy smell of wood smoke reached them as the road rose up on the other side. Elizabeth began to relax. Adam could see it in the way she let her hood slide back off her hair, the way she let the reins slacken a little, the way she let her body sway with the horse's gait. Most of all, the way she let herself look around, her anxiety yielding to curiosity. Her worried concentration on herself seemed to melt under the strengthening sunshine, and her gaze stretched out to roam the white expanse of the countryside. They rode on in companionable silence, Adam loving this easy camaraderie with her. They trotted through a hamlet of five or six thatched cottages that hugged the riverbank, where a work party of mud-spattered men were mucking out a ditch. A child sat in a doorway skinning a rabbit. A bell pealed from the squat church that thrust its steeple into the bright blue sky. Dogs barked. Leaving the hamlet, they rode again past snow-quieted fields that rolled out on either side like drowsy ocean waves. Sun sparkled on the sea of snow.

Elizabeth heaved a sigh, almost like a moan.

"Tired?" Adam asked. They'd been riding for several hours, and it was cold. Had he pushed her too far?

She shook her head. "It looks different," she said almost in wonder. "So different from when I'm out hunting or hawking. There's always such a noisy company of people and servants and horses and dogs. All my friends chattering and gossiping."

He remembered it. "Gentlemen wagering on the hunt."

"Ladies bickering."

"Everyone jockeying for place."

Her smile was sly. "Toadying."

He laughed.

She looked over the land and let out another sigh that sounded like contentment. "Inside that moving court I never see this. Never *hear* this."

He knew what she meant. The silence.

She suddenly looked very serious. "How fares Mistress Thornleigh?"

"Better. The months spent quietly at home have done her good."

"I am glad to hear it. But, dear Lord, to be stretched on the rack. And never, under such terrible duress, to speak of me. It humbles me." A sly smile flitted across her face. "Though I'm sure she thinks such an emotion quite foreign to me."

Adam hid his own smile.

"And what of your good father?"

"Better, too." He said nothing about how his father now kept a guard around the house. How he never left home without armed retainers. How his private war with Baron Grenville simmered, threatening to overturn all their lives. There was a temporary ceasefire, ever since Frances had written in one of her letters to Adam that the Queen had dispatched her brother to Ireland to oversee a commission for keeping the peace. But in a few months he would be back, and then, Adam thought, what lay in store for his father? But he said none of that to Elizabeth. To speak of John Grenville would be to face the fact of his betrothal to Frances, and that Adam refused to do. He had banished Frances to the backwaters of his mind.

"I owe your family much," Elizabeth said.

"You owe us nothing. Except to stay exactly as you are."

"Willful and obstinate?"

He grinned. "That, of course. Who would want to follow a timorous princess?"

They stopped beside an old churchyard where a stone bench slumbered under a stand of ancient oak trees, their bare boughs plumped with snow. Adam brushed the snow off the bench, and they sat and ate bread and cheese and hard-cooked eggs from the saddlebags, washing it down with ale that came ice-cold from the wineskins. As they bent their heads over the shared meal that lay between them, he loved the way her breath, steaming in the cold, blended with his. The horses nudged the snow-covered ground around the crooked tombstones and munched the few tufts of grass.

"Strange," she said, looking at the snowy expanse that stretched beyond them for miles. "It's as though I've disappeared."

"Into thin air?"

"Into England." He caught the sadness in her eyes. "And yet, it may be the last time I'll ever see all this."

"In France you'll have plenty of English friends. You'll make a little England of your own. You'll be its queen."

She looked cheered at that, happy to indulge the fantasy. "And will you stay at my court and join our English revels?"

"What, with all that bickering and gossiping?" Smiling, he handed her the wineskin. "No, I'll be the admiral of your navy and sail to Cathay."

"Ah, you would leave my happy little English palace?"

"Only to fetch you riches to furnish it."

Their fingers touched as she took the wineskin. Neither of them moved their hands apart.

"And what will you bring me?"

"Ships bursting with spices and silks and ivory and gold."

Her eyes sparkled. "Let me sail with you."

His heart leapt. "Is that your wish, my queen?"

"Wish? Bah! As your queen I *command* it." She held out her hand in mock majesty.

He took it. Kissed the back of her fingers like a courtier. But he did not let go. He turned her hand over and kissed her palm. He felt her shiver. With pleasure? He looked up at her. At her lips parted in suspense, red from the cold, red as if from kissing. At the tendrils of her hair that danced with the faint breeze. At the soft white skin of her throat where her blood pulsed. He hungered to kiss her. They were alone. No one to see. Nothing to stop him.

Nothing except that look of pure trust in her eyes. His mission was to protect her. Not ravish her.

"Time to move on," he said, and got to his feet.

The winter days were short, and soon the trees' shadows lengthened across the fields as if longing to lie down and rest. Adam was glad to reach the Boar's Head Inn outside Aldbrook. The holly-wreathed windows, where a few candles were already lit, invited two cold and weary travellers, and the sound of singing inside promised cheerful company. Adam gave their horses' reins to the boy out front, handing him a penny, and as they opened the door they walked into a cloud of warmth, damp with the breath of ale drinkers who seemed to fill every table, and pungent with the oniony aroma of mutton stew. Drinkers lounged at the bar as well, loudly singing a ribald ditty that Adam knew from the taverns of London—an ode to a large-breasted girl from Dover. Elizabeth, wide-eyed at the scene, kept close to him as he nudged past the singers to ask the barkeep about lodging for the night. He almost had to shout to be heard.

"*Two* rooms?" the barkeep shouted back. "Sir, I cannot give you even one. We're that full up, I've got these gentlemen sleeping three to a bed. It's the winter fair at Hertford."

A wiry man beside Elizabeth with a nose the color of a raw beet jerked his grinning face around to her, sending the ale atop his tankard foaming over his hand. "Plenty of room in my bed, lass. Just me and Peter over there, and he's dead to the world. Oh, and Jock, of course," he added, leering down at his codpiece then back up at her. "A fine, upstanding fellow is Jock. You're welcome to join us."

Adam winced. He'd promised her the real England and damned if she wasn't seeing it.

She blinked at the man and blurted stiffly, "My brother and I are going to Braydon for the wedding of our cousin."

Adam almost laughed as the drunk tried to focus on her face, mystified at her recitation. "Are you now? Well, he's welcome, too," he said good-naturedly. "Mayhap Nan from the kitchen will join the romp. She's a game wench." He flung his arm around Elizabeth's shoulders, his hand dripping ale, but before it landed on her Adam pushed between her and the lout. "Come, Isabel, we'll be on our way. Barkeep, how far to the next inn?"

"No need to travel so far, sir," the barkeep replied. "Make your way to the Bents' cottage a half mile along the Hertford Road. Three beech trees mark their lane. They take our overflow. You'll find good vittles there, and oats for your horses. Tell them Ralph sent you."

Adam was navigating Elizabeth to the door as the beet-nosed man began singing,

"A lass making her way up to Braydon,
Through snow and through ice came a-wadin'.
When she reached the Boar's Head
It was three to a bed . . ."

Adam pulled her out the door but she turned back, enthralled. "A poet."

"... So the lass lost the head of her maiden."

They found the cottage dreaming under the moonlight. Adam knocked on the door, and a woman in a neat cap and apron opened it, balancing a baby on her hip. Adam smiled and asked if he and his sister might break their journey for the night. "Ralph at the Boar's Head said you might have two rooms."

The woman glanced at the figure on horseback behind him in the dark. "A cold night to be a-journeying, sir. You're right welcome. You'll share a bed with my father, and your sister can share with my two little girls. If that suits, 'twill cost you six shillings. Comes with bread and small beer at dawn to break your fast."

He thanked her gladly and beckoned Elizabeth. She dismounted without looking too much like a princess who had always had a groom to offer a step down from her saddle. He ushered her inside under the thatched roof that smelled familiarly of musty clover, like a stable. Following her in, he bent his head to go through the low doorway. The room was dim, but warm from the glowing peat fire in the hearth. They seemed to have interrupted the family at supper, for a scatter of people sat in a ragged semicircle before the hearth, four adults on stools with wooden trenchers of bread and sausage on their laps, five children on the floor spooning up bread in milk from wooden bowls.

A ruddy-faced man stepped forward, wiping his hands on his breeches. "Where are you bound, sir?"

"Chelmsford," Adam said.

The man offered his hand. "Walter Bent." He jerked his chin toward the woman who was taking Elizabeth's cloak and showing her to the hearth. "My wife, Katherine."

The ceiling was so low Adam's fingers brushed its beam as he pulled off his cap. He shook the man's hand. "The name's Fitzroy. And we thank you for your hospitality, Master Bent."

He was finding it hard not to guide Elizabeth and pull up a stool for her like the lady she was, but he could see that she was relieved just to stand before the fire and warm her hands. A thin young man got up from his stool and genially offered it to her, saying, "Sit you down, mistress." She sat, stealing glances around at the cottage with barely hidden interest at its foreignness. The floor was beaten earth, the wattle-and-daub walls were whitewashed all over, and the room's main furniture was a battered trestle table. There seemed to be just two rooms on this level, the common one and a kitchen at the rear, bisected by a staircase of five bare steps leading to a low-ceilinged upper floor. The room was smoky from the peat fire—Adam saw it was making Elizabeth's eyes water—but every-thing was clean, the hearth well swept, the table scrubbed smooth and boasting a pair of wax candles, though unlit since wax was ex-pensive. This was no rough laborer's hut, but the home of an in-dustrious yeoman, a farmer of some means.

"Will you and your sister sup with us, sir?" asked Bent.

"Thank you. I'll see to the horses first."

"There's a byre. Only Kat's cows there, so plenty of room. Just nudge Buttercup and Old Nut aside. Help yourself to oats for your horses. Willy, go show him."

A boy of about ten sprang to his feet and Adam was about to go with him, but caught Elizabeth's anxious look at the prospect of being left alone with the family. *They won't bite*, he wanted to assure her. He said to the woman, "My sister would be glad of a little warm milk if you can spare it, mistress. The ride was cold."

"With pleasure, sir," she said as she laid her baby down in its cradle. "And a little honey in it, mistress? I warrant 'twill do you a world of good. Margaret, fetch some milk." A little girl scampered into the kitchen.

Adam went out with young Willie, who told him all about a newborn foal as they led the horses around to the byre. The boy helped him unsaddle the horses, and then, using his hand, chopped the film of ice on the water in the trough and filled a bucket while Adam scooped out oats.

"Shall I brush them for you, sir?"

"Thank you, Willy." He handed him a penny, which the boy ea-gerly pocketed, then he headed back to the cottage, not wanting to leave Elizabeth too long. When he walked in he was surprised to see her chatting happily in the midst of the family circle.

"Adam," she said cheerfully, "this is Master Horner, who is Mis-tress Bent's father." A hunched and toothless old man nodded in

Adam's direction, though his milky eyes bespoke blindness. Adam said a respectful "Hello, sir," and Elizabeth went on to introduce the others—an aunt Cecily and a son, Arthur—the young man who'd given her his stool—and his wife, Meg, who was heavily pregnant. "Arthur and Meg," she reported with the pleasure of an insider, "plan to move into a cottage of their own in the spring."

"Aye," Bent said with some pride, "in the heart of the village. They would have moved in right after the wedding at Christmas, but a storm toppled an old oak on the place and broke its back."

"We'll have it mended by Easter," said Arthur.

"Better have," Meg said with a teasing nudge in his rib.

Adam, sitting down to join the circle, caught Elizabeth's glance at Meg's swollen belly as though calculating the wedding less than a month ago. She looked at him with obvious surprise at the family's indifference to the situation. He shrugged with a smile that said *Country people get on with life.*

The lady of the house, who'd been busy at the hearth, handed Elizabeth a steaming bowl. "Here's your warm milk. Fresh today. None gives better than Old Nut."

Elizabeth looked delighted as she took it. "I thank you, mistress, with all my heart."

"You have a fine property, sir," Adam said as Bent handed him a tankard of ale. A shaggy sheepdog padded over to him and laid its head on his knee. Adam gave its ears an energetic scratch and the dog closed its eyes in bliss. "How many acres?"

"Speak that again," the old man said suddenly.

Everyone looked at him. "Speak what, Grandfa'r?" Arthur asked.

"Not you. The young mistress. The traveller. Speak that again, what you just said."

A few faces idly turned to Elizabeth, but others went back to their supper as though used to the old man's oddities. But his demand made the hair stand up on the back of Adam's neck. Before he could warn Elizabeth, she replied as though it were some parlor game she was eager to join, "I will right gladly, sir, if you will remind me what I said. Are we to make a rhyme of it?"

"It's her!" he declared. "The child of Old King Harry. The young princess."

Mistress Bent frowned at him. "Don't talk daft, Father. Here, have some ale."

But the old man was struggling to his feet. "I'll never forget that voice." He looked in Elizabeth's direction, his fingers groping blindly as though to touch a mirage. "I was on the road to St. Alban's, me and my wife, the Lord rest her, when you came to London. Eleven year ago it was, come Lent. A hundred men or more rode with you. Least, that's what the road shook like, for I heard their horses and choked on their dust. But you stopped them all to speak to a housewife who'd run out with flowers, calling for you to take her bouquet. People thronged from every door and lane, but I was near you and I heard you sweetly tell that housewife, 'I thank you, mistress, with all my heart.' And the people cheered 'God bless the lady Elizabeth,' and my good wife, Lord rest her, said you were the bonniest maid she'd ever seen. 'I thank you, mistress, with all my heart,' that's what you said. Lord bless us, I'll never forget it, not as long as I live." He bowed low to her. "Your Grace."

The room went silent. They all stared at Elizabeth. Even the children, who caught the change in their parents and gazed up, expectant, in wonder. Elizabeth looked like a frightened doe seeing hunters in the bracken. It went straight to Adam's heart. The chance to dissemble was lost.

Warily, with heart pounding, he stood. "Your memory serves you well, sir, where sight cannot. And, just as you heard true majesty in my lady's voice, I hear loyalty in yours. Please, tell me I am not deceived."

In the silence the old man said stoutly, "Need you ask, sir?" He bowed again. "I am Her Grace's faithful servant."

Elizabeth looked at him, her chin trembling. "I am heartily grateful, good sir."

Bent slowly got to his feet in awe, his eyes never leaving Elizabeth. His wife stood up as well, equally dumbstruck. They shuffled back a step or two, as though aware they must not stand so close to royalty. The aunt and the son and his wife followed. Then the children. Elizabeth was left sitting all alone. The whole family, gaping at her, seemed frozen.

It sent a chill up Adam's spine. Could he really trust these people? Elizabeth's life, and his, lay in their hands. But something struck him. Their utter lack of fear. There was no shrinking and quaking. They looked at Elizabeth as extraordinary, golden, perhaps even closer to God, but still a fellow creature who had eaten bread with them, warmed her hands at their fire, laughed with them. She was special, but she was theirs.

"Good people," he said, "you have shown us great kindness this night. I must now ask even more of you—that you keep my lady's presence here unknown. The stakes are no less than life and death. Will you take pity and gift her with your silence?"

Slowly, they all nodded. Tears of relief glistened in Elizabeth's eyes. She insisted that they all sit down again and finish their supper. Slowly, they took their stools, moving them back a little way from her, and sat.

In the silence, a horse outside whinnied.

Then little Margaret whispered to her mother, "If she's a princess where's her crown?"

That brought a tense laugh from some. Then a wave of giggles. Then peals of knee-slapping laughter. Adam grinned at Elizabeth. She beamed back at him. She was safe.

But Mistress Bent insisted on one essential alteration. The princess must be given her own, private room.

Late that night Adam bedded down in the byre. At first he'd been crammed into the common room with the old man and four small children, all of them displaced by the royal personage given an entire room in grand isolation. The dog, too, had joined the crowd, curling up at Adam's side. After an hour of the old fellow's snoring, and the grunts and sighs of the children, who squirmed endlessly in their sleep, and the dog's breath in his face, he'd decided to stake out a quieter spot, and headed outside to the byre. He had created a makeshift bed in the straw of Bent's wagon, beside the horses and cows.

It was damn cold. And stank of cow dung. And there was a jagged hole in the roof as big as a saddle, where the frigid air swept in, making him wish he had more of a blanket than his cloak. But there was plenty of room to stretch out, and as he lay back in the straw, arms folded under his head, and stared at the stars that winked at him through the hole, he felt that this had been the happiest day of his life. He and Elizabeth had made such good progress he reckoned they would reach his ship in Colchester by midday tomorrow and then, with any luck, catch the late afternoon tide. With her on his mind, it took a long time to fall asleep.

The horses' nickering woke him. A shape slid by in the dark. Adam shook his head to clear it of sleep. Moonlight silvered the rough wooden walls. A scuffling sound. Someone was in the byre. "Who's there?"

"I'm sorry. I woke you." It was Elizabeth.

He hopped off the end of the wagon. "Are you all right?"

She stood beside one of the horses. She bit her lip as though unsure. "My whole life I've had people around me. Servants. My ladies, sleeping in my chamber. I've never been . . . all alone."

The catch in her voice tugged at his heart. He came close to her. "You're not alone. You have me."

"Yes. But for how long?"

"As long as you need me."

She looked up at him and her pale face seemed to glow in the moonlight. Her hair flowed over her shoulders, the ends kissing the drawstring of the chemise that peeked above her breasts. He tried not to imagine untying the drawstring. She shivered. She had come out without her cloak.

"You're cold," he said. He grabbed his cloak from the wagon and whirled it around her shoulders, then reached for the saddlebag on a peg beside her and pulled out a flask and opened it. "Here."

"What is it?"

"Go ahead. To warm you."

She took it, her fingers brushing his, and took a swallow. She smiled. "Brandy."

Her fingers felt so cold he took her hand in both of his and rubbed it.

"You're no better," she said. "Cold as ice. Here," she said, offering the brandy.

He knocked back a swallow, though he didn't need it. He was burning up, wanting her.

"I'll tell you how we can both get warm," he said, tucking the flask back in the saddlebag, eager to have both hands free to rub hers again. "Forget France—it's just as freezing there. I'll sail you to the Indies. To the Spanish Main, where the sun shines every day and the flower petals stay forever warm. The sand of the beaches is hot and soft, like new-baked bread, and the water's as warm as melted butter."

She laughed. "You sound hungry."

He noticed something glint at her throat. A thin gold chain around her neck. "What's this?" he asked in a mock scolding. "You managed to sneak out some jewelry?" He had insisted she leave it all behind, for if anyone searched them the jewels would betray her identity.

She seemed to blush, though he couldn't be sure in the dark. She tugged up the chain from its hiding place between her breasts and Adam was surprised at what hung at the end of it. His captain's whistle of carved horn. The one she'd asked him to give her on the day she'd agreed to invest in his ship.

"When I was little," she said, fondling the whistle, "my father had a whistle such as this made for him, but of pure gold. He loved to stride up and down the decks of his flagship, the *Great Harry*, playing admiral." She looked up at him. "He kept it for sport. I keep this to remember you. I wear it always."

He felt too much to speak.

He kissed her. She didn't stop him. He kissed her again, harder. Her lips tasted sweet, of brandy. She still held the whistle, her bent arm a barrier between them, and he took the whistle, warm from her body, and let it fall on its chain inside her chemise.

He nudged the loose cloak off her shoulders and it fell to the floor. He unfastened a tie at the front of her dress. She let him. He untied two more. She helped. He tugged loose the chemise drawstring and kissed her skin beneath it, then pulled the chemise down over her shoulders, exposing her, and she took a sharp breath of surprise as his hands smoothed over her bare breasts. Her skin felt burning hot against his cold hands, her nipples as hard as holly berries. His need burned so hard he pressed her back against the horse's side, forcing her to splay her arms wide, leaving her breathless as he kissed her mouth, her throat, her shoulder, the inside of her elbow, thrilling to the feel of her, the taste of her.

Catching her breath, she fumbled to unfasten the ties of his doublet. He wrenched off the doublet, tossing it to the ground, and her hands slipped up under his shirt, her cool fingers on his chest firing his hot skin.

He pulled off his shirt, then lifted her up by the waist and set her down on the back of the wagon. He jumped up beside her and they sat shivering together, breathless together, burning together. He took her face between his hands and kissed her, and she thrust her fingers into his hair, kissing him back. He lowered her onto the wagon's bed of straw and slipped his hand up under her skirt, and heard her gasp as he ran his palm up her outer thigh, her skin so thrillingly smooth and warm. He bent his head and kissed her knee and shoved the skirt higher and glimpsed the triangle thatch between her thighs, a flash of flame in the moonlight. He undid the ties of his codpiece fast, gazing at the glory of her, and she threw her arms around his neck and pulled him to her. He ran his tongue over her navel and squeezed her thigh, his senses aflame with the melding of opposites—cold air and hot skin, his hardness and her yielding softness. His breaths were ragged, his need overpowering. But her legs were tight together. Was this her limit?

She pulled back her head to look at him. "I've never—"

"I know." The yearning in her eyes was shadowed, hesitant, unsure. But above all, yearning—and he took that as his answer. He smoothed her hair back from her forehead, his other hand still on her thigh, and whispered, "Open your mouth."

She did. And when his tongue found hers he felt her thighs loosen. She moaned and pulled him down again and held him, the whistle between her breasts caught between their bodies. Gently, he spread her legs with his knee. Slowly, he entered her, holding back, which took all of his might, until she was ready to take all of him. She gripped his back, and pulled him to her, and he thrust into her with a need more fierce than he had ever known. She arched. She cried out at her climax. He held her so tightly as he spilled his seed, the whistle dug into the wound on his chest.

They lay there, catching their breath, she still holding him tight.

Adam felt snowflakes kiss his bare back. He rolled over. Clouds had drifted in, masking the stars. In the waning moonlight he could see the shadow of blood on the inside of Elizabeth's thigh. And a small smear of blood on his chest from his abraded wound. And the look of wonder on her face.

He kissed her. A lingering, loving kiss. It was the happiest day of his life.

Clouds as gray as armor marched across the gunmetal sky, and the sea heaved up steel-colored swells as if to meet it in a counter-attack. But the wind, strong and steady from the northwest, was all Adam could ask for. It swept over the *Elizabeth*'s quarter, filling her sails and snapping her flags as if to salute her namesake, on board for the voyage to France. Standing at the wheel, Adam looked over his shoulder at her.

She stood with her back to him, gazing over the stern rail at England's coast. With this wind, he thought, they'd soon be out of sight of land. He was glad. He didn't want her to dwell on every-thing she was leaving.

He was glad of much more than that. He felt brimful of glad-ness. To have her here with him, on his ship. To be carrying her to safety. To know that she was his, and might still be his in whatever quiet life of exile awaited her in France. Her royal state might well dwindle once she was in exile. Dwindle and even expire. Why could he not hope, then, that one day she might be his forever? The thought rippled happiness through him, like the flags cheer-fully snapping overhead. If he were any happier he'd have to dance a jig.

Still, his eyes kept sweeping the sea lanes, for they were not out of danger yet. Spies were not a threat on the water, but there were plenty of rovers and corsairs who were. Pirates all. Whether Dutch, Spanish, Portuguese, or Swedes, their crews would lick their lips to capture a prize like Elizabeth and demand a princely ransom. Adam had ordered two men aloft to keep a constant lookout.

"Hoist the topgallant, Master Curry," he called.

"Aye, sir," his mate called back across the deck, and in a moment the boys were clambering up the mainmast and shimmying along the spars etched against the gray sky.

Elizabeth left the rail and came beside him at the wheel, her cloak billowing around her, her cheeks pink in the cold air. If she had been gazing at England in sadness she had rallied now, for her eyes sparkled. Whether it was from tears that she had banished, or from a quiver of excitement at the future, Adam loved her for her courage.

"Not queasy?" he asked. It delighted him to see her get her sea legs so easily. He had watched passengers go green with sickness, but she seemed in her element.

She shook her head. "I always loved it when my father took me on his ships. He was proud of his navy."

"So you'll sail with me to Cathay, and adventures beyond? Battle the natives, win some treasure?"

She grinned. "My sword will leave them quaking in their boots."

"A swordswoman! By heaven, madam, you are a changeling."

She looked deep into his eyes. "Since last night, I am changed indeed."

He would have kissed her if Curry hadn't been so near. He'd told the crew she was a kinswoman joining her family in France. Hard to explain the captain in a passionate embrace with his cousin.

"Boat off starboard quarter!" a voice yelled from aloft.

Adam looked behind him to his right. A skiff was bearing down on the *Elizabeth*. He could make out five men aboard, all of them as rigid as soldiers as they kept his ship in their sights. His heart lurched. The Queen's men, coming after Elizabeth? He was about to order Curry to lay on more sail to make the *Elizabeth* fly, when he realized that he knew the skiff. That battered prow and maroon foresail—he would recognize it even in a fog. Hugh Poulton's fishing smack, out of Colchester Harbor. A woman was aboard, he noticed, standing foremost, skirts flapping in the wind. Poulton was a long way out, he thought—was he in need of some aid? Calculating a maneuver to slow the *Elizabeth* and hail the skiff, Adam turned his eyes back to the sea ahead.

"Why, that's Mistress Thornleigh!" Elizabeth cried.

Adam shot a glance over his shoulder. Good God, it *was* her. It was so strange to see her on that skiff, his first thought was a pang for his father. Had Grenville struck? She shouted something, but her voice was too faint at this distance, drowned by the wind.

"Master Curry, shorten sail," Adam ordered. "Prepare to heave to."

The *Elizabeth* slowed, and the skiff came alongside, and Adam ordered a boarding ladder thrown over the rail. His stepmother climbed aboard with difficulty, still unable to use her right arm, and weak on her legs from the mad dash here, her face drained of color. Adam and Elizabeth hurried to her, but before he could ask her what had happened, she collapsed.

⧽ 26 ⧽

In the Presence of the King

January–February 1557

"You must go back . . ."

Honor found it hard to squeeze the words out with the dizziness in her head, the ringing in her ears, the blur of faces, the barrage of voices. Adam's. Elizabeth's. A crewman who was questioning her like a doctor. She tried again—"Listen to me—" but they kept on with their questions.

"Can you sit up?"

"Why have you come?"

"Here, sip this"

"Stop!" she cried.

They all went silent. Honor tried to get her bearings. She was lying on the berth in the captain's cabin. She must have fainted. Adam was standing over her, and Elizabeth sat beside her, holding her hand. The crewman was bent over her, trying to get her to drink from a cup. She pushed his hand away and sat up, pain thumping in her head. "Leave us, please," she told him.

The man looked to Adam for orders.

"I'm fine, Adam," Honor assured him. "I must talk to you and . . . this lady."

Adam nodded to the man, who set down the cup, picked up his satchel, and left. The moment he closed the door Honor said to them, "You must turn back."

"Is it Father? Grenville?"

"No, your father's fine."

"Then what—?"

"The Princess must return home."

The two exchanged a startled glance. "Impossible," Elizabeth said to Honor, letting go of her hand. She stood. "You do not understand the situation. I barely escaped the wrath of my sister. Your son is taking me to safety."

"I do understand. The Queen's order that you marry the Duke of Savoy. Master Parry's message explained it all."

"Parry?" Adam said in surprise. Then, darkly, "The turncoat."

"No," Honor said. "The realist." She lowered her legs over the edge of the berth and lifted her useless right arm to lay her hand on her lap. Rubbing her throbbing temple, she looked up at Elizabeth. "I wish you had listened to him."

Elizabeth turned to Adam, anxious. "We *will* carry on, won't we?"

He smiled at her. "With these winds we'll be there by tomorrow night." He reached out to her and she clasped his hand and smiled back at him.

Honor watched them in wonder. She had long thought that there was a special bond between these two and now, as they stood before her, ardent and handfast, it was heartbreakingly clear. Adam loved the girl. And she loved him.

"I know your concern is sincere," he said, "but the Princess has made her decision. You are unwell, madam. You need to rest. And I need to hoist sail. We are bound for Bruges. If there is anything you need, ask any of my crew."

She could not fight them both. "It's true," she said, sinking back against the pillow. "I am very tired." She closed her eyes. "Go, Adam, see to your ship."

"Take heart," he said quietly to Elizabeth. Honor heard him walk out.

"Your son is right. You need rest," Elizabeth said gently as though to an invalid. "I will let you sleep."

She was almost at the door when Honor pushed herself off the bed, overtook Elizabeth, and closed the door. With her back against it, she said, "You cannot leave England."

Elizabeth looked shocked. "I have no choice."

"Everyone has choices."

"Not like the ones I face. This marriage—"

"The demand that you marry some day was inevitable. You are a princess of the blood royal. Arranging your marriage will always be an option of state business."

"Princess. Hah. I am a pawn."

"Whatever you call it, you must have known that both Queen and council would one day make a marriage for you to further some policy of the moment."

"Not with a sword at my throat!" She paced in the cabin's small confines, hugging herself. "Always she holds this over me, this threat of execution. She hunts for ways to call me traitor—she *invents* them. For colluding with rebels. For heretical beliefs. For being my father's bastard. And now, for obstructing the Crown by refusing this marriage. I have lived in the shadow of her threats for too long. I will abide her terror no longer. I will be *free* of her."

"You cannot leave your people."

"My people?" Elizabeth scoffed. "What phantom flocks are these?"

"Neither phantoms, my lady, nor sheep. They are your friends. Your supporters. The loyal gentlemen and yeomen of England. There are more of them than you know, living quietly throughout the length and breadth of the realm. They keep you in their hearts because you are King Harry's daughter."

"And may God keep them all," she said acidly, "but forgive me if I leave without bidding them farewell. When Mary threatens me with the axe, such 'quiet' friends are little use."

"Nevertheless, a day may come when you will need them. And they will not be there for you if you forsake your country."

"You do not seem to understand. She threatened me with *death*."

"If you flee you *will* die. Think. In exile you will be unprotected, friendless, alone. She will take full advantage of that, may even bless you for escaping. It perfectly opens the way for her to dispatch an assassin to kill you."

Elizabeth seemed to suppress a shudder. "You are wrong," she said, looking up at the ceiling as if imagining Adam striding the deck above them. "I have a protector."

Honor sadly shook her head. "Yes, Adam stopped one assassin's arrow. And I can see that he is ready to stand with you and do so again—ready to hazard all for you." She came close to Elizabeth so they stood eye to eye. "That is why you must not ask it of him."

"I? I have asked nothing of him but passage to France. I—"

"I . . . I. Can you think of no one but yourself? What of Adam? If · you do this, you make him your accomplice. To interfere with a princess of the blood is treason. At best, he will have to remain in exile all his life, never able to come home again. At worst, the Queen's men will hunt him down. You know the penalty for treason. They hang the victim by the neck, then cut him down while still alive and disembowel him and hack his limbs off one by one."

Elizabeth looked aghast. It was hard even for Honor to go on. But she did.

"And what of faithful Master Parry? Another accomplice. Another victim bound to die in agony as an example to the people of the consequences of treason. And your loyal servants—they, too, will pay a price. Imprisonment. And afterward, shunned and masterless, destitution."

"Have you no mercy?" Elizabeth cried. She pushed past her in a rush to the door.

Honor grabbed her arm to stop her. "The misery will not stop there. Throughout the realm, those who now silently support you as a bulwark against the Queen's tyranny would see you gone— their best hope, gone—and would despair of any change coming to England. Despair breeds bitter judgment. Blaming the Queen for your flight, they might revolt in small cohorts, unprepared. Acting in such disarray, leaderless, what chance would they have to overcome her forces? She would crush them. Executions and mass hangings would bring the country to its knees."

Elizabeth covered her ears with her hands. "Stop."

"And then, having cut down all the brave men who would oppose her will, the Queen will turn with a vengeance to the task she calls her true mission. The extermination of heretics. Already she has burned hundreds. With no check on her, she will order the fires lit regularly in every market square, and as masses of her innocent victims burn she will praise God for keeping her throne and her people safe from *you*."

"Stop!"

"You alone can save your country from this fate. Do not condemn Adam and Thomas Parry to a traitor's death, and your servants to beggardom. Do not condemn countless innocents to perish in the flames."

Elizabeth lowered her hands from her ears with the agonized reluctance of someone going to her death. Her voice was as thin as a child's. "And so I am to sacrifice *myself?*"

"I know you, Elizabeth. You may have been selfish, but you are not heartless."

She said bleakly, "What you are saying is that I must submit. I must marry Savoy."

"No. That is the Queen's way of neutralizing you, sending you out of the realm. You must stay with your people. You must refuse the marriage."

Elizabeth blinked at her. "Refuse? Again? To her face?"

"Yes."

"And be sent to the scaffold," she wailed.

Honor shook her head. "She will not make good that threat. She does what her husband wants, and Philip needs you alive. If you are gone, Mary of Scotland stands to inherit the throne, and she is betrothed to the future king of France. The last thing Philip wants is France controlling England. He saved you twice before from his wife's wrath. It is in his interest to do so again."

Elizabeth looked desolate. "To you it is all politics. To me, it is my life."

They are one and the same for you, Honor wanted to say. But she held her tongue. It was hard enough for Elizabeth to bear this moment. She was not yet ready to accept that her life would be forever confined by the immutable fact of her royalty.

"But even if you are right about my sister, Philip wants this marriage as much as she does. A state policy of his own, to marry me to his Hapsburg cousin. Am I to refuse to his face, too?"

"Yes."

Elizabeth looked overwhelmed. "You expect much of me."

"Because you can win this. Philip cannot arrange the marriage without your consent."

"You say that he will stand by me again, but since he has come home to ask his wife for war funds, this time she may get her way." She lifted her chin, raising her troubled eyes to the small port window that overlooked the sea path to France. "No. You cannot ask this of me."

"Not I, Elizabeth. You must ask it of yourself."

The huge audience chamber at Whitehall Palace was splendid with sumptuous hanging tapestries and the lavish, bejewelled apparel of dozens of courtiers. The courtiers kept their distance from the royal dais where the Queen and King were receiving Princess Elizabeth, and they confined their talk to whispers, not for the sake of discretion, but in eagerness to overhear any snatch of the royal interview. The King's Spanish entourage watched in excited approval of the proposed marriage of the Lady Elizabeth to one of their princes, the Duke of Savoy. The English watched in sullen suspicion that her union with the family that ruled most of Europe could turn England into a Hapsburg client state. No one had forgotten how recently the Queen, in declaring that she would marry Prince Philip, now King of Spain, had so angered Englishmen it had triggered the Wyatt rebellion that had almost lost her her crown. But she *had* married Philip and she remained queen, and the English lords and gentlemen here kept their sights firmly on that reality. Even an event not in the best interest of England could be one that might improve their personal fortunes.

To Elizabeth, as she curtsied low before the Queen and King, the chamber had never felt so vast and the audience so threatening. The Spaniards were watching her like hyenas waiting to pounce for the kill, the English waiting to see which way to jump. Gone was Mistress Thornleigh's brave voice to give her courage. Gone were Adam Thornleigh's strong arms to protect her. And before her sat the two people who held her life in their hands. Mary, languidly fanning herself with a Spanish pearl-encrusted fan, all smiles at having her lord and master home beside her. Philip, as haughtily certain of God's plan in making him king of half the world as if it were Scripture. Elizabeth had never felt so alone.

She straightened. Standing before their thrones, she waited, for etiquette decreed that she must not speak until in answer to Their Majesties. She wished the silence would go on forever—that she would never have to say what she had come to say. It had been hard enough to find the courage to tell Adam to turn back the *Elizabeth*.

"You don't have to listen to her," he had said, his voice raw with anger. "Listen to your heart. In France you can be free."

She loved him for all that he was ready to risk for her sake. And loved him too much to ask it of him. "You would not run away thus."

"It is not my life at stake."

She looked up at the billowing sails of the *Elizabeth*. "If your ship were in peril, would you forsake your crew? If a reef in a storm threatened to tear her apart and fling your men to drown in the sea, would you jump to safety in a boat and leave them to their fate?"

He had looked at her in agonized silence. It almost broke her heart.

"Notre soeur," Philip said, eyeing her as he crossed one leg sheathed in white satin over the other. Elizabeth was not surprised that the interview would be in French, since Philip still had not learned a word of English. She was just grateful that he had called her, not unkindly, "our sister."

Mary snapped her fan closed, her gaze on Elizabeth hardening. Philip's tone hardened, too, as he modified his phrase with emphasis. *"Notre soeur têtue."* Our stubborn sister.

That sent a chill through Elizabeth. *Mistress Thornleigh is right,* she kept telling herself as she curtsied again. *He needs me alive. He cannot lose me as heir. And Mary follows him in all things.*

Philip went on in French, "We trust that you have had sufficient time to reconsider the offer of my cousin Savoy's hand in marriage."

"Indeed, Your Majesty," she replied in French, "I have thought long and hard on it."

"Excellent." He looked over her head in the direction of the aristocrat who represented the duke, and lifted a hand, about to beckon the man.

"And I must tell Your Majesty," Elizabeth interrupted, "that such a marriage is an honor for which I do not consider myself worthy."

He stared at her. "Pardon?"

Mary spat, "It is *life* you are not worthy of."

Philip held up his hand to quiet his wife. Her eyes on Elizabeth narrowed in anger, but she obeyed her husband. The rapt courtiers had fallen silent. The whole room seemed to hold its breath.

"Perhaps, sister," Philip said carefully, "I misunderstood you. To be joined in holy matrimony with my kinsman Savoy is a great honor, to be sure. As great as my own wish to see the union take place. So you may rest assured that your consent is entirely to our liking. And consent is, surely, the answer you intended."

"You did not misunderstand, your Majesty. I cannot accept this most gracious lord as my husband."

"For what possible reason?"

I must stay with the ship, Adam. "My reasons, Sire, are between me and God."

"Spoken like the heretic you are," Mary cried. "A personal relationship with God—that is the depraved cant of all the heretic vermin. I have decreed that every one of them be burned to death like rats. And those in high places," she said pointedly to Elizabeth, "will not escape the fire."

Philip jumped to his feet. "Death to heretics, yes."

Elizabeth felt the breath sucked out of her. Breath and strength and courage. She dropped to her knees and bowed her head low. *Mistress Thornleigh was wrong!* a voice inside her wailed. *And for her error, I am going to die.*

"But you will live," Philip said with a contempt that seemed to scald her, "and live to regret this answer. Amend it, madam. This instant. Or long life shall be yours, indeed—lifelong imprisonment at our pleasure."

She did not speak. Could not speak for trembling.

"Captain of the guard," Mary called out, triumphant. "Bring your men. Arrest this woman."

"I promised you to my cousin," Philip fumed, "and by God, you will not make a liar of me. He is a prince, and not to be trifled with. The negotiations are concluded. The marriage contract drawn up. Who are you to interfere in such matters of state?" Guards marched up to Elizabeth. Philip railed on. "It galls me to see you so ungrateful when I have agreed to a princely sum for your dowry and named you my wife's heir. But this hard-won contract shall not be in vain. You will do your duty, and our will."

Mary was staring at him in dismay. "My heir? My lord, our son shall be my heir."

"And where is he, madam?" Philip said testily.

She looked stung. "God will bless us, soon."

"Then at our son's birth I shall rejoice. But in his absence provisions must be made."

"My lord, forgive me, but this contract cannot stand."

"Madam, these details are my concern."

"Details? At my coronation God entrusted this realm to me."

"And, with our marriage, to *me*," he snapped. He beckoned the Spanish lord representing the Duke of Savoy. "Sir, come hither. We will conclude this matter."

The man came forward so that Elizabeth, still on her knees, was flanked by him on her right side and the guards on her left. But all of them looked unsure of which monarch to obey. Elizabeth knew no better than they did—except to realize, in despair, that Philip, far from being her savior, had become as implacable an enemy as Mary.

"My lord," Mary said. She looked agonized at contradicting her husband, but driven nonetheless. "The marriage cannot take place under these terms."

"I have promised Savoy these terms," Philip said hotly.

"Then you must renegotiate."

"I have given my word."

"And I have a duty to God. I will not allow this realm to fall into the grasp of a heretic. The bastard of a criminal who was punished as a public strumpet."

Philip glared at her. "Your duty is to me, madam. As God ordained. I marvel that you forget that."

She looked as if he had slapped her.

They both turned to Elizabeth. She felt a shift in the air so sudden, so powerful, it almost took her breath away. They were in a deadlock, and they needed her voice to break it.

"Consent, madam," Philip told her. "Do it now, and you will be named heir to the throne."

"Do not consent," Mary said to her. "I *never* shall."

Elizabeth fixed her eyes on her sister, astounded that Mary should need her on her side. Both monarchs stood waiting for her answer. The whole court was waiting.

She got to her feet. It surprised her to find that she was no longer trembling. Far from it—a new tide of strength rushed through her. Something in her quivered with pleasure at the sense of power. Her life, she saw, lay in her own hands.

❧ 27 ❧

Battle Lines

May 1558

A year had changed the kingdom. When Philip had arrived last
spring to ask his wife for money to fight the French, Mary had
gone to the council to get it for him, but they had refused, unwilling to be drawn into Spain's war. Furious, Philip told Mary that unless she persuaded them to release the money, he would leave
England and never return to her. She, in turn, threatened the
councilors with the loss of their estates and imprisonment, and
they finally capitulated. Exploiting rumors of a French invasion,
she then demanded their support for her to go a fateful step further by declaring war on France for her husband's sake. By summer, England was at war. Philip planned his military campaign,
and Mary basked in his satisfaction with her, selling thousands of
acres of Crown property to raise additional cash for him. By the
time he sailed away with ten thousand English soldiers and ten
thousand cavalry, he left Mary elated at the certainty of being
pregnant. At Christmas, joyfully, she let it be known that her heir
would be born in March.

The campaign began well. Philip's forces, commanded by the
Duke of Savoy, along with Mary's, commanded by the Earl of
Pembroke, defeated the French at St. Quentin in such a resound-
ing triumph that thousands of foot soldiers and dozens of the most
prominent nobles of France were taken prisoner. Stirring suc-

cesses in Italy followed, and victory seemed at hand. But England's involvement in the war soon turned into catastrophe. For over two hundred years, since 1347, England had held the territory of Calais in France, the last remnant of the Anglo-French empire that dated from the Norman invasion, and this bridgehead to Europe was an essential conduit for English trade. Its complex of fortresses seemed impregnable, but on New Year's Eve the French attacked, taking the English defenders by surprise, and Calais fell. The loss was a disaster for English merchants, and a national humiliation.

Even more devastating to Mary, she discovered she was mistaken about being with child—for the second time. Having believed she was pregnant right up to the ninth month, she became a laughingstock for anyone who dared to laugh. Even those who supported her shook their heads at her folly. Pamphlets of ridicule—and of sedition—multiplied. Mary cracked down, ordering that all such writings be burned and anyone found in possession hanged, and she stepped up her policy of exterminating heresy, burning religious dissenters on an average of one every five days. She avoided her council, ordering them to report to Cardinal Pole on the financial crisis, and she withdrew from public appearances. The government seemed rudderless. The country was insolvent. Philip had not returned.

Neutral ground. That's what Frances had called it in her letter. Adam didn't feel that way as he rode up to St. Botolph's Church in Colchester with its adjoining new priory buildings, which looked almost finished. The walls of Frances's grand project rose so high they eclipsed the sun and cast into shadow the squat houses of the poor people that barnacled the outer enclosure walls. By neutral she had meant neither Grenville nor Thornleigh, and he knew she intended to put him at ease by arranging this meeting in the priest's rooms, but to Adam the Church was the lethal, long arm of the Queen, making this enemy territory. He did not want to be here, and would not stay long. Before dusk he had to rendezvous with his father and Lord Powys's men to make his report and help unload the guns.

Frances opened the door, all smiles and blushes. For a moment he thought she might throw her arms around him, she looked so eager.

"Welcome home, sir."

He bowed. "Madam."

She laughed. "So serious. Don't worry, we are alone. You may kiss me . . . if you like."

She blushed so deeply, and looked so hopeful, Adam smiled in kindness. "I would not take such a liberty."

"Oh, it is no liberty—we're almost man and wife."

He made the kiss brief. "The construction is going well, I see," he said as he strode to the window that looked out at the priory works. Roofers atop the building destined to be the monks' dormitory were crouched on the rafters, hammering, while others hauled sheets of lead. Glaziers on a scaffold tapped a stained glass window into place. "At this rate the brothers will be moving in by Michaelmas."

"You have been away so long," she said, coming to his side. "Tell me all. Where have you been, and what have you been doing?"

He looked at her. *In the Low Countries, organizing the exiles to join us.* "Just the dull business of trade," he said. "Loading wool cloth, sailing in rain and fog, unloading in Antwerp. Coming back with cargos of pins and glass and leather. Nothing very exciting."

"I have missed you so."

He managed a smile. "What I want to know is what have *you* been doing? How is life at court? How fares Her Majesty?" It came out so blatant and blunt he was afraid she would turn on him in suspicion. He was not good at this business of spying. But she seemed to accept his question as one of natural concern for her royal friend.

"Melancholy, I'm afraid. She weeps a great deal. The baby, you know."

Adam could not muster a kind word about the Queen's phantom pregnancy. The woman was delusional and, given her hatred of her sister, her unbalanced state of mind threatened Elizabeth. Men throughout England were now preparing to bring down the

Queen, but Adam's worst fear was that she might strike at Elizabeth before they were ready.

"No sign of the King returning?" he asked. Again, too blatant. But he needed to get a sense of whether Philip might land Spanish forces to help the Queen fight a rebellion. If so, extra defenses would be needed.

"Come, drink, you must be hungry," Frances said as she poured him a goblet of wine. He saw that the table was set for two. "I have ordered dinner for us," she said brightly. "There is so much to discuss."

"Discuss?"

Smiling, she handed him the goblet. "Our wedding day."

He drank a quick swallow. The Queen was not the only woman who was delusional. The wedding was never going to happen, and not just because it was the last thing he wanted. Frances was too afraid of her brother. They both knew that Grenville would burn down his own house before he would let his sister marry a Thornleigh. Their secret betrothal was a dead end. Adam was not proud of leading Frances on to get the intelligence he needed. It felt craven. But lives were at stake. Elizabeth's, and all the men organizing with his father. "Shall we eat?" he said.

They sat, she settling into the seat across from him as if they were already married, and she made a great fuss about serving him herself as the priest's servants brought in dish after dish that she had obviously taken great pains to order. Oysters. Poached bream in saffron sauce. Roast venison with currants. Fresh figs. Strawberry tart. Adam ate without appetite. A memory glimmered of the humble supper of sausage and brown bread and beer that good yeoman Bent and his family had shared with him and Elizabeth when they had come in from the cold. Best meal he'd ever had. On the happiest day of his life.

"I am sorry for the Queen's troubles," he said. "And I hear that the royal council is little help to her."

"Oh, their insolence infuriates me. All they do is squabble, right to her face."

"About what?"

"Money, always money. They claim there is none. It can hardly be true."

"Perhaps it is. The war must be a terrible drain. Imagine what it takes just to keep the fleet manned and afloat. Do you have any idea?"

"I know exactly. Fifteen thousand pounds a month."

He probed deeper. "For how many men?"

"Pardon?" She was cutting slices of tart.

"How many sailors and gunners and soldiers on the ships?"

"Fourteen thousand, I've heard."

"And they must have their daily ration of biscuit and two pots of ale and two pounds of beef, or there'd be mutiny. Hard to find money for all that."

"The lord treasurer is trying to arrange loans in the Antwerp money markets."

"At exorbitant interest rates, no doubt." This was all useful information. The treasury sounded nearly bankrupt.

"Have some salad." Handing him a dish of borage and radishes, she pointed to the blossoms that decorated it. "Rosemary flowers." She asked coyly, "Do you know the message?"

Courtiers made much of the hidden meanings of flowers, he knew, but he had no idea what they were. Likely something about love.

"It means, I accept your love," she said, her eyes sparkling.

She bantered on about the flowers and he waited for a chance to steer the talk to the Queen's defenses. He said he hoped Her Majesty was ready in case of a French invasion, and asked what commanders the earl marshal had in place, and where. She mentioned some names, enough to be helpful intelligence to Adam, but her interest in the topic soon waned. "But here's news," she said cheerfully. "The Count of Feria, King Philip's envoy, is in love with one of Her Majesty's maids of honor, Jane Dormer. The Queen is openly promoting the match. Just think, Feria will marry Jane and take her back to Seville as his duchess." She added, blushing, "I wish you and I could make it a double wedding."

"Frances, I'm afraid we'll have to wait a little longer. Things are so unsettled. This war with France, and the unrest in Ireland. Unless," he added, "the Irish situation looks like it will soon be resolved. What does your brother say? Has he enough troops to keep the peace?"

"Oh, it's a quagmire there. Her Majesty had to send six thousand more soldiers, John says."

Good. Troops fighting Irishmen were unavailable to fight Englishmen.

She leaned closer and her voice became low, intimate. "Adam, I know you didn't *want* to stay away so long. You felt you *had* to, for fear of my brother. I understand why, after his . . . well, his harsh behavior. It's why we've had to keep our betrothal secret. But a promise to wed is one thing, marriage is quite another. A union under God that no man can break asunder. Not even John."

"You don't mean . . . marry now?"

"In his last letter John said he won't be back for at least two months. We don't need a lavish wedding, just a private ceremony. A priest and a witness. By the time John returns, we will be man and wife. He'll *have* to accept it."

"Or disinherit you. Frances, I do not want to be the agent of your ruin."

She said with a despairing look, "But I am so tired of waiting. I fear we'll go on like this forever, betrothed but apart."

"It's safest."

"I am ready to take a chance. Will you?" She slid her hand across the table as though to take his hand, but stopped short, her fingertips almost touching his. "I know it was not your idea to marry me, Adam, but I will make you happy. Truly. I will be the most devoted wife in Christendom."

He could not meet her eyes. He moved his hand to swirl the wine in his goblet.

She stiffened. Her voice took on a new edge. "I did what you wanted, back then when your father was in the Tower. I persuaded Her Majesty to release him."

"And for that I will be forever in your debt. But you must see that at the moment everything conspires against us."

"Even you, apparently." She looked at him severely. "Did you *ever* intend to marry me?"

He hesitated. If he was not a good spy, he was a worse liar. As captain of his ship he was used to giving orders and having them obeyed, used to aboveboard dealings, not subterfuge and deceit. "I owe you much, Frances, for saving my father's life. I will never forget that," he answered sincerely. "Even if we do not marry, I will always honor you, and will find a way to repay your kindness."

She was silent, regarding him as though hearing him for the first time. She looked out the window at the workmen finishing the religious house she had re-created. "You vowed to marry me, and God was our witness. I would have you honor *that*." She looked back at him, a new hardness in her eyes. "Honor. It is a thing your father's wife knows little of, despite her Christian name. Indeed, I shudder to say *Christian* in speaking of her. It profanes the sacred word."

The switch of subject was so sudden he was totally at a loss. "My father's wife? I beg your pardon?"

She got up from her chair and fetched an ironbound box fastened with a lock, the kind commonly used to hold important papers. Adam had one aboard the *Elizabeth* to protect his log books. She sat down and withdrew a key from her pocket and clicked it in the lock. The papers she took out looked worn at the edges but the writing seemed clear.

She smoothed her hand over the top page. "This document is twenty-three years old. It was copied from the records of the court of the bishop of London for the year of Our Lord 1535. It is a record of the heresy trial of Honor Thornleigh. The verdict was death by fire. I spoke with the priest who oversaw the case. The condemned was taken to Smithfield to burn, was chained to the stake, the fire lit under her. But depraved persons led by a villain attacked the proceedings and spirited her away. This priest, who saw the whole calamity, swore it was Satan himself who freed her." Her eyes locked on Adam's. "You probably did not know this, since you were a mere boy at the time. You have not been aware that you were raised by a criminal damned in the eyes of God."

His mouth had gone as dry as stone dust. He had been part of that rescue adventure—had been in awe of his father's brave wife. Brave, and always his friend.

"She lived among the German heretics," Frances went on, "while our poor realm saw chaos under three shifting reigns, so that even the bishop's court lost track of her. By the time she slipped back into England, everyone had forgotten. But I will not forget. Her death sentence is irrevocable."

She set the document back in its box and locked it. In the silence between them, the hammering on the priory roof sounded like nails going into a coffin.

"The archbishop visits Grenville Hall next week," she went on. "He is always a welcome guest, and takes delight in treating John's children shamelessly with sweetmeats. His kindness to my nieces and nephews is matched by his vigilance in overseeing Her Majesty's desire to cleanse the realm of heretics. If he were to see this document, I think Honor Thornleigh would see the inside of a cell beneath the archiepiscopal palace that very night. And the flames of Smithfield soon after."

Her voice became low, intimate, confiding. The voice of a wife. "It has troubled me, Adam, knowing this vileness about your family. I must confess that the decision to keep it secret was difficult, since it is my duty as a Christian to decry heresy. But I did keep it to myself, for your sake. It has troubled me more since I became sworn, by our betrothal, to join your family. But I take my vow to God as sacred, not to be broken because the time is inconvenient. I charge the same of you. As part of your family, I will do my duty to keep this secret still. But if you break faith with me, and with God, by breaking your vow, then I can no longer deny my greater duty."

She poured him more wine, refilling his goblet. "I would like our wedding to take place in three weeks, on the feast of St. John. It will be a private ceremony, known only to us until I can safely tell John. I trust that date will be convenient for you." She smiled at him. "Midsummer Day. Just think, all the flowers will be in bloom."

*　*　*

Adam hardly knew how he covered the twenty-three miles to Drayton after he left Frances. His fury at her was so violent it seemed to haze his vision, and the fields and people and houses passed him like ships in fog. More than once he was on the verge of galloping back and telling her that she could take herself, and her malicious threat with her, to the gates of hell. But each time he was about to turn his horse, he thought of his stepmother, and the hard facts pounded, over and over, like a catechism drilled into him—*can't let them seize her, I had to agree, there is no choice*—and he pressed on. One ray glimmered through the fog, and in his mind he steered for it. If they could overthrow the Queen, and if Elizabeth took the throne, Frances's menace would evaporate, because Elizabeth would never allow his stepmother to be harmed. *And if we can do it before Midsummer Day . . .*

So many ifs.

He jerked the reins to halt his horse. He had reached Drayton and the main street ahead was clogged with people. They all seemed to be thronging the market square. He cursed under his breath. It was getting near dusk and he could not afford this delay. He was to join his father and uncle and Lord Powys's men at the mine two miles past this town. They had crisscrossed the county, gathering stockpiles of weapons.

He nudged his way past people, moving into the thick of the crowd where he sensed anger in the air. There were sullen faces, and the chatter was the grumbling resentment of a mob. He asked a wiry man on foot what was going on.

"The baron's men, sir, arresting the miller. Possession of seditious pamphlets."

Adam raised himself in his stirrups to get a better look. The crowd had converged on the market cross, where armed men in Grenville's green and yellow livery sat on horseback. Near them stood several town officials in rich robes, a couple with their chains of office askew on their chests, as if thrown on in haste. They glared at the victim, whose hands were being tied behind his back. His hair and clothes were faintly dusted with flour. The miller. Sitting on horseback beside the officials was a man expensively dressed in fur-trimmed green velvet, his hand resting lightly on the hilt of his very fine sword. Some local lord, Adam reckoned, maybe kinsman to Grenville. And no weakling, if his imposing bulk and severe expression and sharp eyes were any guide. It made Adam all the more impatient to move on. His father was organizing secretly under the aegis of Lord Powys, but the preeminent authority in the county, and the district's principal lord, was Baron Grenville. This town was completely under his influence. The tyranny of this spectacle sickened Adam. The poor, wretched miller would hang. "All for a scrap of paper," he muttered.

"A potent scrap, sir," said the man. "It calls the Queen 'Bloody Mary' and worse."

Adam wished he'd kept quiet. Any insult against the Queen was considered a criminal act.

The man spat in the dirt to show his disgust. "Bloody Mary, indeed. Light words, if you ask me, for one who's burned hundreds of folk. If she fought the French with the fury she shows her own people, we wouldn't be losing this war."

Adam relaxed. The fellow was no supporter of the Queen. "I'd say we've already lost it."

"Aye, when she lost Calais, she lost all. And England's dignity with it."

Adam couldn't help admiring the man's grit. All the laws in the world wouldn't silence an irate Englishman. He was about to ask if there was another way through town, when he saw, a few house-lengths ahead, his father and uncle on horseback. They were at the head of a train of three wagons, with Powys's mounted retainers surrounding the vehicles. Adam's heart thumped in his chest. His father's party, trying to pass through, was hemmed inside the throng just as he was, and they were dangerously close to the town officials. If anyone got a glimpse of what was under the wagons' canvas tarps, they would all hang.

He pressed his horse forward. The people suddenly moved closer to the market cross like a tide rushing out, leaving his father's party marooned, alone but for some stragglers. It allowed Adam to trot his horse over to them, and as he reached them he heard his father say in a fierce whisper, "I won't stand by and let them string him up. Let me go."

Geoffrey had gripped his wrist to restrain him, and spoke in the same forced undertone, "Not here, Richard."

Adam reached them. "What's happening?"

"Thank God you're here, Adam. Your father wants to protest. Wants to barge over there and confront the mayor. It's madness."

"It's only right! Thomas the miller has been with us from the start. If we don't stand up for him, what the hell are we doing this for?"

"Sir," Adam said, "my uncle is right. This is not the place."

"I know, I know, I must content myself," he growled. "Let go, Geoffrey, I'll be still." He looked back at the miller being led away. "It's just so damn wrong."

"That's why we're going to make things right."

He nodded. "It's good to see you, Adam."

"Look." Geoffrey jerked his chin to indicate the hard-faced lord in green velvet. He was looking in their direction, scowling, and began to trot his horse toward them.

"Christ," Adam's father muttered.

"Richard," Geoffrey warned in a whisper, "hold your tongue."

"What's going on here?" the lord demanded as he reached them.

Adam said, "Good day, my lord. We're passing through with some loads of household furnishings. My father is anxious to get along before dark."

The man looked back at the wagons. At the seven grim-faced retainers. Adam held his breath.

His father said genially, "My wife will have my guts for garters if I break any of her mirrors or crockery. Sorry for the commotion, my lord. We'll be on our way." He signaled the carters driving the wagons, and Powys's men. The wagons rumbled forward. Adam, riding with his father and uncle, didn't look back, though he felt the eyes of the lord on them all.

Two miles later, the buildings of the mine came into view across the heath. When they arrived, there was still enough daylight as they dismounted in the tangled grass and the wagons clattered up. Adam and his father and uncle helped the men throw off the tarps and carry the heavy boxes inside. The rough building was caked inside with windblown grit from the cave mouth that yawned beside them, and they kicked up a lot of dust as they worked. Adam was glad of the loyalty of Lord Powys's men. Powys was not the most powerful lord in the county, but he was the richest—so wealthy he could stand a small army—and his early involvement in the cause was what gave Adam hope of success, despite the dangers. Sir William Cecil had brought his father and Powys together. Powys was committed, but did not dare stockpile the weapons at his home, so Adam's father had volunteered to take them. Years ago he had bought this piece of property for its lead mine, but because of his lack of capital had been unable to operate it. Sitting idle, it offered an ideal hiding place.

Adam finally had a chance to report to him. They had to raise their voices above the noise of the men trudging in with the boxes, coughing from the dust as they thudded down their loads and shoved them in place. Geoffrey passed out wineskins of beer as the men worked, to mitigate the dust.

"First," Adam told his father, "Grenville will not return home for at least two months."

"She told you that?"

"Yes. He wrote to her."

Geoffrey said with a wink as he passed a wineskin to him, "Handy having the lady in love with you."

Adam downed several mouthfuls of beer, his rage at the woman matched only by the desire to keep secret his unholy bargain with her. There was nothing his family could do to help him. He wiped his mouth with his sleeve and handed the wineskin on to his father. "He asked the Queen for six thousand more troops to quell the Irish, and got them."

"Good. The more there, the less here. What's the situation abroad?"

"In France, Sir Henry Dudley is with us. He has the silver, and will sail the moment we send word. And Throckmorton will raise two hundred men." After Dudley's failed rebellion, Sir Nicholas Throckmorton had fled to Paris. Adam went on to report on some of the other exiles. There were hundreds of men, many of wealth and power, like Lord Bedford, who would stand with them, too.

His father clapped a hand on his shoulder. "Good work. Can you ride to London and tell Cecil?"

"For God's sake, Richard," Geoffrey said, "let him snatch a bite of bread and a few winks. Look at him—he's a wreck. He'd fall asleep in the saddle."

His father smiled. "Aye. Rest tonight with us, Adam. We're bound for the Hart's Horn Inn."

Adam was aware of a sudden silence. The men had stopped working. He turned to see a figure standing in the doorway. The hard-faced lord in green velvet.

"Household furnishings for a mine?" the man said, looking at them with unmasked suspicion.

Adam's eyes flicked to his father, who said, "A stopover, my lord. I own this property."

"Unusual warehouse."

"You take a lively interest in my trade, sir. May I know your name?"

"You may not."

Adam's hand slipped to his dagger handle. He saw Geoffrey move slowly to the door to block the man's retreat.

The man caught both movements and brought his own hand to the hilt of his sword. "I am not alone," he warned calmly. "Come for me, and ten men who ride with me will cut you down."

Adam could feel the tension in Powys's men. They stood expectant, uncertain.

"Trade, eh?" The man looked down at a box near him whose lid had come ajar. He kicked the lid off, revealing the contents. "Are guns your stock in trade?" He added, very quietly, "You could hang for this."

Adam swallowed. Every box held the evidence. Arquebuses, pistols, swords, pikes, armor, crossbows, and hundreds of arrows.

"My respects, sir," his father said, bowing. "It's clear you are a gentleman of high standing and no doubt proud to do service to Her Majesty the Queen. Do you find yourself quite satisfied with the state of the realm?"

The man looked flummoxed. "What?"

The hair stood up on Adam's neck. His father had decided to take a gamble.

"Happy that the price of everything has doubled in the last few years? Happy with our success in the war with France?"

"Success? You're either brainsick or incompetent at your underground trade. England's beaten."

"Then perhaps it is the burnings that please you? The hundreds of so-called heretics who suffer in the flames, a number unheard of in the days of old King Henry. Or perhaps it's the sight of poor men arrested, to swing by their necks just for reading a pamphlet."

"I like none of these things. Is that the appropriate reply?"

Adam wasn't sure what to make of him.

The man gave a wolfish smile. "Is your name Thornleigh?"

Geoffrey took an audible breath of surprise. The man noted it. "I'm on my way to the Hart's Horn Inn. I've been sent by my cousin, Lord Powys. To meet you." He grinned. "The name's Palmer. Sir Arthur Palmer. I have an armory you'll want to see."

❧ 28 ❧

Midsummer Day

June 1558

Adam threw himself into the work of treason, spending every day in the saddle, and many nights, too. So many prominent men had secretly joined the cause, he was riding to all corners of the county, arranging the stockpiling of weapons and coordinating the communications between gentlemen with armories. The most recent recruit was Sir John Thynne of Longleat, the richest land-holder in Wiltshire; the most exhilarating, the officers of the north-ern garrison of Berwick-upon-Tweed who were tacitly waiting to throw their support to the rebels. Many of the foremost men were friends of Elizabeth, but for her safety they kept their preparations secret from her—if all failed, the treason would be theirs, not hers.

Adam rode from village to town, and manor to manor, constantly hoping that the call would come, the attack would begin, and the Queen would be routed—all before Midsummer Day. But as he sat in on strategy meetings, his frustration became excruciating. There was no finalized plan. Though men throughout the length and breadth of England stood ready and willing to fight, they lacked a central leader, a figure to rally them. And so, no call had come when the morning dawned of the longest day of the year, high midsummer, when the country basked in the lengthened hours of sunlight.

To Adam, it was the darkest day of his life.

"Going to church, sir?"

Having just come down from his room at the inn, Adam was startled by the landlord's question. The wedding was secret—how could the man know? Frances had arranged the thing, summoning him to this isolated village, and he had arrived after a late-night ride down from Cambridge. She would be there already, in the parish church down the street, preparing and primping.

The landlord was patiently awaiting a reply. "Most folks like to go before they break their fast, is all."

The feast of St. John, Adam realized. If only his visit to the church could be about just that—mumble a prayer or two, then go on about his business, a free man. If he could say a prayer and have Frances miraculously disappear from his life he would be on his knees, prostrate before the altar. But he had never believed in miracles. He was coldly resigned, telling himself he was hardly the first man to make a loveless marriage. Fellows did it all the time, to obey a father's command or to move up in the world. Why should he be any different?

"Later," he told the landlord. He ordered breakfast. He had no appetite for food, but even less for pacing in his room. It was nine o'clock. In an hour he would be standing with Frances before the priest. *Until death do you part . . .* He was distractedly tearing a piece of bread, forcing his mind onto practicalities, onto how he could continue the stockpiling operation away from Frances's notice, when the landlord came back.

"A visitor for you, sir."

"Visitor?"

"Your sister. She's outside."

His heart jumped. It could not be Isabel.

He found her at the back of the building on a grassy swath leading down to a stream, standing under a huge willow tree that rose higher than the inn. She hadn't seen him and her back was to him as she looked at the water. She had pulled up the hood of her cloak, but he would know her anywhere, even without the telltale strands of bright hair. He was stunned to see her. Why was she here? Had she fled again? Was she in danger? Gripped by this fear, he came up behind her and blurted, "What's happened?"

She whirled around. Her eyes blazed fury. "Treachery, that is what."

"My God, has someone betrayed you?"

"Betrayal, indeed. Falseness. Rank unfaithfulness!" Throwing back her hood, she tugged off a necklace, the whistle he had given her dangling from it, and hurled it at him. It hit his chest and fell to the ground. "How *could* you?"

It staggered him. Frances. She knew.

"Yes, your sordid secret is out." Her voice was harsh with contempt. "Your lady's maid is a cousin of my chamberlain's stepdaughter. Your lady is apparently overeager, and blabbed."

He clenched his teeth. "Do not call her my lady."

"Oh, shall I say your sweetheart? Your dearest? Your darling? How long have you loved her?"

"Love? I hate her."

"Ha! Is that why you've rushed to cobble together this furtive, backstreet wedding? You cannot wait to enjoy her!"

"Good God, if you knew the reason—"

"Oh, I dare say there's a reason. Is it money? A baron's sister must bring a handsome dowry. Are you building another ship and want her moneybags?"

"Money?" he shot back. "Her brother is like to cut her off, penniless."

"How sad. Then perhaps the reason is more of the barnyard variety. Perhaps you *must* marry her before her belly has swollen so huge her kinsmen will hunt you down."

"Enough!" Damn her. He could have borne the wretched wedding with some shred of dignity if only she had not come. "Why are you here?"

She gasped. "How can you ask that? How, after all we have been to each other? You *dallied* with me, and now you marry another woman. I am the injured party!"

"You! *You* don't have to make a marriage you loathe. They wanted you to, and I was ready to take you anywhere, brave any danger, to save you from that fate. As for injury, I will bear the scar forever of the arrow I stopped for you. If you want to talk of hurt," he said, thumping his chest, "look no farther than here."

"Ah, yes, your past great deeds for my sake. But it seems you have tired of loyalty and faithfulness and care not who sees you for a liar, for now you have chosen *another*."

"I tell you, I did not choose."

"You are a free man!"

"As free as a prisoner in chains! *Less* free, because if I escape I doom a friend to death. You call that choice? The choice of the devil. And this devil is forcing me to clamp the chains on myself."

"Death? What new lie is this?"

"No lie. I have *never* lied to you. I am marrying this woman to buy her silence!"

She gaped at him. "About what?"

He had gone too far to go back. So he told her everything. All about his stepmother's heresy trial so many years ago. The rescue. Frances's knowledge of it. And her threat to use it.

"Dear Lord," Elizabeth whispered in horror. "What a terrible thing to hold over you."

Now that she knew, Adam felt an overwhelming relief. Just to know that she understood. But at what a price. In place of his anger there was a bleak hollowness. He had told her, and it changed nothing.

"She *is* a devil," Elizabeth said with a shiver. And then, in a tone of awe, "But a devil who must love you very much."

"If that is love, then let me live in hate." He heard the rustling of the vast canopy of willow leaves above them and drooping all around them, the arched boughs bending lower than their shoulders, and for a moment it felt like a refuge, a place to hide from the world, as children would. They stood in the canopy's shadow, but the sun winked through the leaves, sprinkling them with warmth. Everything in him longed to be away from here, with her, and her alone.

"Adam," she said suddenly, hopefully, "in law, coercion to marry is grounds for annulment."

"But I cannot protest. Not as long as this queen reigns." He shook his head. "No, there is no way out."

They stood still together, lost in the misery of it. The church bell tolled. To Adam it sounded like a death knell.

He heard a quiet cough, and noticed two burly men standing at the corner of the inn, their backs to him and Elizabeth, their eyes on the road. They wore her livery, though their swords and vigilant stances were proof enough that they were guarding her. "Where is the rest of your guard?"

"Waiting at the edge of town. I had to see you. Alone."

They guarded a royal princess, he thought, the stark reality so clear. "I used to have a fantasy that I could marry you," he said. "The day we traveled through the snow together, as friends, and that night found each other, as lovers. I was so drunk on loving you I made myself believe I could have you and keep you. But it was a lovesick fool's dream. Never possible."

"Then I am a fool as well, for I had the same dream."

It fired him with such desire it was pain. "You love me," he said, gripping her arms.

Tears glistened in her eyes. Her chin trembled. "Love you, yes. For the arrow you stopped with your body. For the worlds you showed me—the one we traveled through, and the one inside of me."

This was harder to bear than her fury. "I cannot have you. You are a princess of the blood. And one day you will take the place of your sister."

"I may not," she said, sounding desperately hopeful. "Anything can happen."

"She has no heir of her body and is past bearing one, even if her husband ever returned. Her throne must pass to you."

"Others may claim it. My cousin Mary of Scotland, backed by France. Or Philip himself, backed by the might of Spain."

He said nothing. Princess or queen, she had always been too far above him, and they both knew it.

"I wish I *were* queen," she wailed. "I would have the power to stop your wedding. I would forbid it. I would make you free."

It was tearing him apart. To have her love, but know he could never have *her*.

"But I am not queen," she said with a hollow voice that matched the hollowness in his heart. "And the one who is would send Mistress Thornleigh to the stake." Tears brimmed in her eyes. "And so, you must marry. And I must wait for a crown."

It was hard to stay silent. He could not tell her that the crown might soon be hers, that half of England stood ready to fight for her. That he would fight to the death.

He bent and picked up the whistle from the grass. He lowered the necklace over her head and let it settle on her breast. He slid his fingers into her hair at her temples. "Like flame, I always think. And you, bright as the sun." He smiled, the saddest smile he had ever felt. "I flew too close to the sun. I had to fall."

She turned her head and kissed his palm. "Burned?"

"No, made alive by your fire."

Her tears spilled.

He kissed her tears. Kissed her mouth. She returned the kiss with a passion that Adam knew he would remember until his dying day. He pulled her to him and held her. "Remember me," he whispered.

"Always."

And then, he let her go.

A more pleasant Midsummer Day Richard could not recall. A sultry, drowsy morning with just a lilt of breeze. Quiet, too, since half his household was at church to observe the feast day. Half the country, for that matter, which was why he was taking the day at home, away from the organizing work with Adam. The riding, and the danger, had been constant for so many months, it was a blessed relief to take a break. He was only sorry Honor wasn't here to spend it with him. Besides, over at Blackheath, where she was visiting Joan, she was missing her roses looking their best. Big and blowsy, the way she liked them. He was cutting some for her with his dagger. A bunch of roses beside the bed—she would like that when she got back home tonight.

"No, not that way," Geoffrey said, lolling back in his garden chair, hands clasped behind his head. "God's teeth, man, you're lopping off half the branch."

Richard nicked his thumb on a thorn. "Christ, I don't know how she does this without cutting herself bloody. I'm a pincushion. Look." He sucked the drop of blood.

"She uses gloves."

"Armor would be better."

"And she uses scissors. You're not butchering a steer."

Richard cut higher, closer to the flower.

"Lord, that's worse. You're decapitating the poor thing."

"There, that's thirty," he said, flopping the last flower onto the heap of them on the grass. "Think that's enough?"

"Enough to sink the fleet."

"Maybe stick in some of those others?" He pointed to the morning glories climbing the brick wall.

"They'd just fall over. No backbone."

"Those?" Irises growing around the sundial.

"That would make it a mess of different colors. You need to stick with one."

"Why?"

"Well, they would, I don't know . . . clash."

They looked at each other. Richard laughed. "Clash?"

Geoffrey chuckled. "Joan would claim some such nonsense. Women's thinking. It's beyond me."

Past the garden Richard saw Captain Boone sauntering over to the house gates. "Like clockwork," he said, admiring the tough veteran. "No matter how much sack he's drunk the night before."

"And for breakfast."

They watched Boone take up his position outside the open gate. "He's a good man," Richard said. "Though Honor hates that brute of a knife of his." The fellow was never without the long knife, sheathed in its dirty scabbard strapped to his back.

"Fat Mary in the kitchen doesn't seem to mind his blade, especially out of its sheath."

Richard smiled. "You've got to know our little household too well. Time we sent you back to Joan."

"The Lord knows I'm willing. All this traipsing around the country is for younger men." Geoffrey turned serious. "Think we'll strike soon?"

"Powys hasn't got word yet from Lord Bedford."

"What does Adam say?"

"Haven't heard from him in two days."

"God's teeth, I would these high and mighty men could form a plan."

"Well, my plan today is to finish off that plum pie from—"

A sharp sound made him stop. It came from beyond the gate. Like a scream.

Geoffrey stood up. "What was that?"

Richard's eyes were on the open gate. He could see nothing but the dusty road and trees. But then there was another scream. And a low thunder that he felt judder the ground. Horses. Many horses.

A glance at Geoffrey, then they were both running into the house for weapons, Richard shouting over his shoulder, "Close the gate!" In the great hall he tore open the arms cupboard, yelling "Fletcher!" He snatched his sword.

"Who's out there with Boone?" Geoffrey asked, grabbing a longbow.

"Not enough." Damn the feast day. Damn his own lack of vigilance. Fletcher, his steward, rushed in, asking, "What is it?"

"Sound the alarm. We're under attack." Turning to go, he ordered, "Geoffrey, stay here. Take Fletcher and Hoby. Guard the house."

Geoffrey nodded, and Richard dashed out of the hall. Running out the front door of the house he almost collided with James Alford, his clerk, running in.

"Horsemen!" the clerk said, breathless. "Almost at the gate!"

"James, you're with me." The alarm bell was clanging behind him as Richard and James ran across the courtyard, Richard yelling again, "Close the gate!" A scatter of servants had come out of various doorways, looking shocked, uncertain. "Arm yourselves," Richard shouted to them. The men amongst them dashed toward the great hall. The women scurried back inside.

"Close the—" But it was too late. He wasn't even halfway across the courtyard when the attackers burst through the half-closed gate, horses at the gallop, men yelling war cries, swords slashing. Andrew the brewer was fumbling to buckle on a sword when a blade from horseback chopped his shoulder, slicing off the arm. He screamed and toppled, blood spurting.

Richard faced a charge of pounding horses and swirling dust and bloodthirsty yells. Cut off from James, he was surrounded by horsemen before he could even swing his sword. In the middle of the pack rode Grenville.

"I want him alive!" Grenville shouted.

Men swooped off their horses around Richard. Two grabbed his arms, a third kicked the sword from his hand, another grabbed a fistful of his hair and wrenched back his head so that he could not move it. Leather ties bit into his wrists as another man bound his arms behind his back.

A thump. A horseman of Grenville's cried out and toppled from his saddle, an arrow in his gut. Another thump, and a horse with an arrow in its belly staggered and fell, hooves flailing, crushing the rider's leg beneath it. Another horseman shouted, "Up there!"

At the second-story windows Geoffrey and Fletcher stood with longbows, quickly fitting fresh arrows.

"Stop!" Grenville shouted up to them. "Keep loosing arrows, and this man will get his throat cut. Lay down your weapons and come out peaceably, and he will go free, unharmed."

"Don't!" Richard yelled. "He's lying—"

A fist smashed his jaw. The blow knocked him to his knees.

Geoffrey and Fletcher came out the front door, hands high. Grenville nodded to his archers at one side of the pack. Two archers took aim and their arrows flew, slamming Geoffrey and Fletcher in the chest with such force they fell back as if jerked by wires.

"No!" Richard yelled, but his cracked jaw distorted the sound in a gurgle of blood. Grenville moved his horse up to him where he knelt in the dirt, and lifted one foot from the stirrup. His boot was the last thing Richard saw as Grenville kicked him in the head.

Adam found the small church empty except for Frances, who stood waiting just inside the door. He took her by the hand without breaking his stride and led her toward the altar. *Let's get it over with.*

She stopped before they reached the altar. "I saw a body of men ride through the village in the livery of the Lady Elizabeth." Her eyes narrowed. "She came to see you, didn't she?"

"Yes." He looked around. "Where's the wretched priest?"

"It is not right, Adam. She has no right to—"

"Let me make the terms of our arrangement very clear. I will proceed with this ceremony and make you my wife, and in return you will agree to keep to yourself, forever, the information you have about my family. This is the boundary of our relationship. I will brook no interference in my business affairs."

"I only wish—"

"What you wish is not my concern. How we conduct our married life together is. I will manage my affairs as I see fit, and that includes associating with whomever I see fit. Is that understood, madam?"

She seemed about to object, but shut her mouth. She nodded.

"Then," he said, "we have a bargain."

"Adam, I know you are angry now. But you will not regret this. I promise. I will make you a good wife."

"Doubtless, madam. Get the priest."

The ceremony began. They exchanged vows. They exchanged rings. The ceremony ended. Adam partook of the small feast Frances had ordered at the inn, and he drank a great deal of wine to wash it down. So much wine, that when they retired to their chamber and he bedded her, and brought her to her climax, and his, he rose afterward and left her sleeping and rode away with a head still fogged with the liquor, and with little recollection of having enjoyed his bride.

❦ 29 ❧

Midsummer Death

June 1558

"W̲ho's that fellow, I wonder, coming at such a hell-bent pace?" said Honor's groom, Ned.

Riding beside him, Honor at first saw only dust. The rider and his horse in the distance were a mere speck enveloped in the brown cloud. Gradually they took shape, and she thought he looked like a cavalryman on a charge. "Wherever he's bound," she said, "he had better slow down soon." The road around her and Ned was busy with traffic on horse and on foot, and farmers carting produce into Colchester.

"I wager it's to do with Princess Elizabeth," said a nearby man on horseback, having overheard them. He looked smugly pleased with his information. "She's not six miles down this very road."

"How did you hear that, sir?" Honor asked, astonished. The last she had heard, Elizabeth was still at Hatfield.

"I saw her," he replied proudly. "I just came from visiting my nephew in Leaside village, and I saw the Princess and her guard ride straight down the main street. A fine horsewoman, and the fellows with her all in her red livery. It's a sight I'll never forget."

Could Elizabeth be coming to visit Speedwell House? Honor wondered. "Was she riding east or west, sir?"

"West, mistress. Mayhap on her way to London town."

Away from Speedwell House, then. It was puzzling. What

would have brought Elizabeth into this vicinity? Visiting Lord Powys? Had someone finally told her about the risky preparations being made in her name?

It made Honor all the more eager to get home. She had left Joan's house at Blackheath as soon as she'd got Richard's message that he was home for a brief visit. The stockpiling of weapons had kept him away so long, and was sure to take him away again soon to rejoin Adam, and she didn't want to lose even an hour of this time with him. She wanted to hear everything. Who were the latest recruits of note? How close were they to a coordinated uprising? The cause had drawn so much clandestine support that she dared to hope success was now possible—bring down Queen Mary, raise up Elizabeth, and thus eclipse the power of John Grenville. As she idly watched the rider gallop nearer, she imagined how sweet it would be to sit with Richard in the garden on this lovely Midsummer Day, among her roses, and hear his stirring news.

That was the last thought she had before the rider thundered to a stop in front of her, and the last moment of peace she was to know. His news brought the end of her world.

"My lady, you are undone! We are all undone!" He was no soldier hardened to rough riding, he was the young apprentice of her brewer, and he juddered to a stop, gasping for breath, and almost toppled sideways from the saddle in nervous exhaustion. "They attacked us! It is all ruin! It was terrible! Terrible!" He lowered his head to gulp down air.

"Attacked? Who?"

"Villains!"

"Thieves?" Ned, her groom, asked in shock.

"Murderers!" The young man looked up, his face ashen. "Lord Grenville . . . and an army. Blessed Jesu, my master is dead!"

Honor froze. "Master Thornleigh?"

"My master!" he wailed. The brewer, she realized. "It was slaughter! So sudden . . . our men could not fight."

Slaughter. "My husband, is he—" She could not say the word.

Ned burst in. "Did they kill Master Thornleigh?"

"Yes! They must have."

"Did you *see* it?" she cried.

"What? No, it was terrible . . . they were all around him with swords and knives and—"

"Then is he dead or no?" Ned demanded.

"I . . . I know not. They . . . I think they took him."

Took him. She looked homeward. Four miles. Adam was some-where north, safe, thank God. With her good arm she whipped her startled horse into a trot, then kicked until it galloped. She pounded down the road toward home, hanging on, kicking the horse until its skin wept blood.

Speedwell House was in flames.

Honor stopped at the smashed-open gate. Orange flames writhed over the black skeleton of her house, the fire so loud it roared in her ears and blasted her with scorching gusts. All around it the outbuildings were on fire. People were running, shouting. Some were crying. A metallic smell of blood smoked the air.

Honor's terrified horse stumbled and reared. She clung to the saddle, and when the hooves thudded down again she saw three bodies sprawled in dirt and blood. Richard had posted these men at the gate. One lay on his stomach with an arrow between his shoulder blades. Beside it, a long knife was sheathed in the scab-bard on his back. Captain Boone. She thought, This veteran sol-dier had not had the chance even to draw his knife. What chance could Richard have had against such a lightning attack?

The fire, the smell of blood, the shouting—it all made her horse so frantic it was staggering in circles. She no longer had any control of the animal. She abandoned the reins and tried to slide out of the saddle, but it was impossible with only one good arm and the horse's wild motion, and she hit the ground in a painful sprawl. The horse bolted.

Honor struggled to her feet and looked at her burning house. Was Richard inside? *Taken away,* the apprentice had said, but so dazed and confused in the telling, what if he was wrong?

She hurried on unsteady legs across the courtyard, making for the house. Monstrous orange tongues of flame crested the top floor and licked at the blue sky. The lovely blue sky—it made no sense to her stunned mind. Fireballs burst from the great hall as curtains caught fire, billowing out of the smashed windows in sheets of flame. She stumbled on a sword hilt. She looked down at it, disoriented. Blood on the blade. Sparks rained down high above her, borne by a wind of heat. Cinders fell on her clothes like black snow. Men ran past her carrying buckets of water that sloshed over the rims, making mud at her feet. She walked on through the muck, and as she neared the fire its heat seared her cheeks and parched her eyes. Smoke made her cough. The front door was ablaze, and in front of it two men lay on their backs. One was too far away to see clearly, but clear enough for her to know it was not Richard. But on the other she saw the familiar round belly, the ginger beard. "Geoffrey!"

She ran toward him.

"My lady! Stop!"

A hand hooked her elbow and she lurched to a stop.

"Let me go!" She coughed in the smoke. "It's my brother-in-law!"

"You cannot go near. You'd perish." It was James Alford, the clerk. A timber pitched down from the second story and crashed near their feet, showering sparks. James wrenched Honor backward, away from the blazing timber and the fire's killing heat.

"He's dead, my lady. I'm sorry."

She looked back at Geoffrey and saw the arrow in his chest. Had he been trying to defend the house? She thought of Joan, widowed though she did not know. The horror of it almost felled Honor. And Richard? Geoffrey would have been at Richard's side. Was he lying unconscious behind the blazing door? She tried to tear free of James's grip. "My husband . . . he may be inside."

"No," he said, pulling her back. "He's not, my lady. They took him."

Again, *took him.* "You're sure? You saw it?"

He nodded. "I was beside him one minute, the next minute horsemen were bearing down on us. I jumped clear of a big charger and landed on my arm. But I saw them surround Master Thornleigh. They tied his hands. Slung him over a horse and rode out with him."

Then he could still be alive! James stifled a groan of pain, and

Honor saw that his arm was in a makeshift sling, a belt. Soot streaked his clothes. Dried blood caked the corner of his mouth, and his eyes were bloodshot and rimmed with red. He had lived through the hell of the attack. She forced her mind to work. "How many dead?"

"Eight. That we know of." He gazed around at the blazing outbuildings. His voice was raw. "It was like an army swooping down."

"Baron Grenville."

"Aye, Grenville Archers, some of them. The rest, I don't know. Not men of hereabouts. Hired brutes."

Killers. And they had taken Richard. And murdered Geoffrey.

"Mistress!" a woman cried out, running to her. "Where are we to go?"

Honor blinked at her. Susan, a housemaid, with two crying children in tow. Honor's home, being eaten by fire before her very eyes, had been their home, too. The home of almost twenty people. And many more who lived in Colchester and came here to work were now masterless. She wrenched her mind off Richard and tried to think. "James, has any place been spared the torch? The stables? The tithe barn?"

"Tithe barn's burning. Stables, too."

She gasped. "The horses!"

"Burned by now," he said grimly. "We could not get in past the flames."

She was speechless, imagining the animals' agony.

"But there's the abbey," he said. "They smashed everything inside, looms and all, but there's no fire."

She looked to the west across the stream. The abbey's tower stood free of flames against the sky. Of course, she thought in fury. Grenville had murdered and laid waste, but had spared the abbey as sacred ground. "Susan, take your children to the abbey," she said. "It shall be shelter for our folk." The maid and her little ones scurried away, and Honor turned to James. "Where's Fletcher?" She needed the help of her steward.

"Dead, my lady." He nodded toward the body beside Geoffrey. It was too much. She felt herself shaking. "Who is . . ." Who could take Fletcher's place? "Arthur Hoby," she said. Young, but capable. "Is he alive?"

"Aye. He's yonder at the dairy house, I think. Helping put out the fire."

She looked in that direction and glimpsed the men's frantic activity—their small buckets of water, the raging fires. "Hopeless," she murmured, fighting despair.

"My lady!" Two men came running, filthy with soot and sweat. Word had spread that the mistress was here. She recognized one of the men, a shepherd. He started to speak but his voice soon choked with weeping, so the other man blurted out their desperate report. Grenville's men had slaughtered all the livestock. "Thirty-four cattle beasts," he said, eyes wide at the awful tally. "Twenty-nine sheep. Fourteen pigs. Five goats."

They all stood dumb at the catastrophe. Honor could hardly take it in. More people were gathering round, some bloodied, most dirty with soot, all frightened, and they were looking at her for a glimmer of guidance. She swallowed the grit of cinders in her mouth. "James, the buildings and animals are lost. But our people are not. Tell Arthur Hoby to send the women and children to the abbey." She looked around at the desperate faces. Feeling lost, she wondered aloud, "What else?"

"Victuals, my lady," James said. "Nothing's left. Not a crust nor a bone. Come morning we'll need food."

Of course. She tried to think. Lord and Lady Powys had always been her friends. "Forget Hoby, I'll find him myself. You ride to Highlands and tell Lord Powys what's happened. Tell him we need bread and meat. And blankets."

Hesitating, he ran a hand through his sweat-stiff hair.

"Your arm," she realized. The one in the sling. Was it broken? "Can you ride?"

"I can, and would gladly, my lady, but I have no horse."

"My horse is loose . . . somewhere. Get some of these people to help you nab it. If you cannot, then set out on foot for Highlands. Off with you now!"

He ran. Honor set out to find Hoby. The courtyard was a chaos of shouting people and crying children and barking dogs, of mud and household things that people had wildly thrown out of the burning buildings—crockery, shoes, ropes. People kept running to her to report, to ask for help, to merely weep. She had no way to help them, which made her feel sick. At the house a section of the roof crashed down into the garden in an explosion of sparks, bringing screams and sending people running. Honor came upon Hoby, looking exhausted from slinging water from buckets on the blazing dairy house alongside other exhausted men. She told him that he was now her steward and instructed him to round up the women and children and send them to the shelter of the abbey. He seemed energized by the mission, and set out toward the bake house and brew house, calling names as he went.

Honor forced her shaky legs to continue on to a huddle of moaning people. The injured. Burns and cuts and broken limbs. They must be helped. She had glimpsed Mary Carter, a kitchen worker, pumping water at the well. Fat Mary the men called her. Honor knew her to be a strong woman, clever, and not squeamish. She went to the well.

"It's poisoned, mistress," Mary grunted as her hefty arm pumped water to fill the men's buckets. "They dumped a bleeding pig carcass down it, belly slashed to the entrails. Water's fit for nothing but these here buckets." Honor told her to leave the well and take charge of the injured people. She called to two men and instructed them to assist Mary, then set a sturdy apprentice to man the pump.

There were so many people to see to. For an hour or more she went from one group to the next, trying to bring order, reassurance, information about relatives. Every glance she took at the burning house left her shivery. Every thought of Richard left her struggling with a dull panic. Why had Grenville taken him? *Where* had he taken him? Was he already dead? There was a sharp pain in her foot. She had lost a shoe . . . somewhere.

A shout. A racket of horse's hooves. Honor twisted around in horror. Grenville?

A single horseman. It was Adam! He pounded past the smashed gates, his cloak flying, his horse lathered, and thundered to a stop beside her. His face was tight with shock and rage.

"Are you all right?" he asked from the saddle.

She nodded. "But some are dead. Geoffrey . . ."

"Dear God," he murmured. He cast a frantic look at the blazing house. "Where is my father?"

"Grenville took him."

"What do you mean, took him? Alive or dead?"

"Alive."

They stared at one another, and the sickening knowledge that Honor had been refusing to face bit into her. If Grenville wanted Richard alive, it was for only one reason. To make him suffer.

Adam knew it, too. He said quietly, hollowly, "As he kept you alive in the Tower?"

She could hardly stand. She gripped the harness of his horse to hold herself up.

"Madam, let go." She looked up and saw pure, cold fury in his eyes. "I will find him."

"No . . . you cannot. Grenville has a whole company of killers."

"I will not go alone. I will raise our men. And hire more. And get weapons. And strike down this murderer once and for all."

He spurred his horse forward, calling to men to come meet him at the well. Honor watched in horror. He was going to attack Grenville. Grenville would kill him. Then kill Richard.

She was about to run after Adam when he turned his horse in a wide circle and doubled back at a gallop. But not toward her. He was racing for the gate. A woman had ridden in and stopped. She wore rich clothing and behind her rode a manservant. Honor gasped. It was Frances Grenville! How did she dare to come here? In fury Honor started walking toward the woman.

Adam thundered up to Frances and halted his horse and leaped off. She sat stunned as he stalked toward her. He snatched her by her arm and hauled her down from her saddle. She screamed and staggered as her feet hit the ground, almost collapsing in fear and shock. Her manservant jumped off his horse and pulled a dagger. Adam turned and chopped the dagger from his grip, then punched his jaw, and the man sprawled backward and fell in the dirt.

Adam turned on Frances. "You knew! He was coming for my father, and you knew it!"

"No!" she cried.

"You had me at that church because you knew he was coming here! You told me he would not be back for months. I told my father, and he left just three men at the gate. You knew!" He raised his hand to strike her.

She cringed, tears streaming. "I knew nothing!" Adam stopped, the flat of his hand inches from her face. She dropped to her knees and begged him, "Please, you must believe me! I had no idea!"

He grabbed her arm and wrenched her to her feet. "Where is he? Where's my father?"

"I tried to save him," she whimpered.

Honor reached them. "You did what?"

Frances flinched at her voice. "They brought him in—"

"To Grenville Hall?"

She nodded, weeping. "I saw from upstairs. He was bound and bleeding." She looked at Adam. "I ran out to my brother and begged him to let your father go. But he shook me off."

"Where is he now?" Adam demanded.

"What?" She looked dazed.

"My father! In the hall? The lockup? The stable? Where?"

Frances shook her head. "I know not."

Honor said, "You told us you *saw*."

She blinked, snivelling. "I left."

Honor slapped her. "Get out! I will not have you here."

Frances gasped and covered her stung cheek.

Adam was mounting his horse. "Grenville will pay."

Frances wailed to him, "I have nowhere to go! Please, Adam, I told my brother everything. That your father is *my* father now. He raged at me. He cast me out. I cannot go back!"

Honor ignored the woman's babbling and tried to focus her fractured thoughts on Richard—how long could he survive? And on Adam—how to stop him from tearing off to Grenville Hall?

But Adam had heard. He glared down at Frances. "Let her stay."

Honor was dumbfounded. "Stay?"

He said with disgust, "She is my wife." He kicked his horse and bounded away.

The two women stared at each other. Adam's words made no

sense to Honor. All that did make sense was her need to get this Grenville woman out of her sight. "You can go to the abbey—join the other people your brother has made homeless. If they do not scratch your eyes out."

"Please, no! Don't put me with them. I am your son's wife!"

"You are no such thing."

Weeping, Frances whimpered her confession. Listening, Honor was too stunned to speak. Bastwick and the bishop's court . . . the death sentence upon her . . . Frances's threat to Adam to expose her . . . their wedding this very morning. Frances confessed it all and wept while Honor's mind reeled at Adam's sacrifice, and her house burned, and her terrified people struggled to salvage their lives from the ruin Grenville had wreaked on them, and Adam shouted for men to join him.

"Stop him! Please, stop him," Frances begged. She was on her knees, clinging to Honor's skirt. "If he rides to my house my brother will kill him!"

"Your house? It seems *this* is your house now." She swept her arm at the flames all around them and said with fierce bitterness, "Welcome to your new home."

She wrenched her skirt free. Frances fell back on her heels, weeping so uncontrollably her breaths were shudders and her body shook. Her misery was so profound Honor almost pitied her. She saw that the Grenville manservant felled by Adam's blow was now on his feet, looking around him in dazed fear. Someone had tethered the two jittery horses they had ridden in on. Honor stopped a groom as he ran past with a bucket and told him to leave what he was doing and escort Frances to stay with Lord and Lady Powys. "Use her horses."

Then she walked away from Frances. She did not know where she was going. She did not know how her legs were still holding her up. Despair hovered over her without mercy. Geoffrey and good men of her household lay murdered. Her home was ablaze. Richard would be tortured to death. Adam would die fighting Grenville—his brother-in-law. She stopped in the middle of the courtyard, unable to take another step, feeling the fire's gusts of heat as if she were truly in hell.

"Your shoe, mistress?"

She turned. A little boy, grimed with soot, was holding up an embroidered leather shoe.

"I told them it was yours. So fancy."

She reached out for it. It was wet with mud. The child's small hand was muddy, too. But he was smiling, proud to have done this service.

"Thank you," she said, shamed by his composure. She slipped on the shoe. This was no time for despair. Her murdered people she could do nothing for, and her house was lost. But Richard and Adam were alive. For how long, she did not dare think. But as long as they *were* alive she might *keep* them alive. Adam, at least, could not attack Grenville until he had gathered more men from outside, and found horses. That could take a day, maybe longer. But how was she to help Richard? There was no time to seek justice through the law, and even if there was, Grenville had the favor of the Queen. For that very reason no one else would interfere to help the Thornleighs. Grenville might eventually pay some official price for his barbarous acts, but by then Richard would be dead. Adam, too. Honor gazed at the insatiable flames, feeling utterly alone. She was powerless.

And then she realized that she knew someone who *did* have power.

She ran to the groom who was helping Frances toward the two horses. "She'll ride pillion with you," she told him. "Help me onto the other horse."

❧ 30 ❧

A Plea to the Princess

June 1558

Elizabeth's entourage was miles ahead, and Honor knew neither their route nor their destination. She had to ask a cobbler on a donkey, and later two travellers on foot, for signs of where they had seen the party turn. She finally learned that Elizabeth was breaking her journey for the night at Bramley Hall as a guest of Sir Harry Whitcombe.

The road was hot, even as the midsummer sun sank nearing dusk, and Honor was parched with thirst and saddle sore by the time she cantered up to the gatehouse. Through the iron bars she could see men in Elizabeth's livery strolling in the courtyard.

"Halt," the guard ordered.

"I must see the Princess," she said through dry lips. "It's a matter of life and death."

He gave a wary smirk and looked about to send her away as a tramp. She knew how she must appear—dirty, dishevelled, riding frantically, all alone. Soot streaked her face and pinprick holes pocked her clothes burned by cinders. She gritted her teeth. There was no time for this!

"Sir William!" she cried. William St. Loe, the captain of Elizabeth's guard, was walking with another soldier just inside the gates. He looked startled at hearing a woman call his name, and even more so when he saw her.

"Mistress Thornleigh? Good Lord."

"Tell your men to let me pass. I must see Elizabeth!"

"Have you been assaulted?" he asked anxiously, signaling his men to let her in. "Highwaymen?"

Honor did not stop to answer him as the gates opened. She slid out of the saddle, her useless arm making it impossible to dismount with any control, and hit the ground with a painful shock to her legs. Shakily, she hurried across the courtyard toward the front doors, leaving St. Loe ordering a groom to see to her horse. She heard him calling her name, but she kept on. The servant at the door, like the guards, looked instinctively about to shut her out as a vagabond, but St. Loe shouted across the courtyard for her to be let in.

She hurried inside and heard laughter. Waves of laughter from many throats. She reached the great hall and found the whole household assembled and watching a play. Gentlemen and ladies of Whitcombe's house, as well as a score of Elizabeth's retainers, sat enjoying the antics of the players on a makeshift stage, while pages and servants threaded among them serving wine and strawberries. Honor's eyes flashed over the faces, searching. There were many she knew, but she could not see Elizabeth.

"Mistress Thornleigh, whatever brings you here?"

She turned to see the round face of Thomas Parry. "Where is she, Thomas? I must see her."

"Perhaps refresh yourself first?" he suggested diplomatically. "And then let me introduce you to our host—"

"No time! Please, tell me where I can find her."

He hesitated. "She asked to be alone. She is somewhat indisposed."

"Not sick abed?" Honor asked in dismay. She needed Elizabeth strong.

"No, I would call it . . ." He searched for the word. "Melancholy." His eyes drifted to the window. Honor caught a glimpse of tall apple trees. A garden? She left Parry without another word and made her way through the hall, skirting the play-watching crowd, ignoring the wondering looks of the ladies and gentlemen she brushed past. She reached a passageway where the smell of roasted meat told her it was the route to the kitchens. A maid was coming in a side door with a basket of pears. Honor went out and found herself in the garden. It was huge—an orchard, raised flower beds in row after row, a trellised pavilion, a tiered fountain. But it looked deserted except for a maid on a ladder picking pears.

She looked to the west where the sun was setting over a man-made lake dug in the shape of a crescent. A small boat with one sail drifted, an old man in servant's attire slouched comfortably at the tiller. A curving walkway of sand led out to the lake and there, on the grassy shore, stood Elizabeth. She was watching the sailboat and hugging herself, not tightly as though from cold, for the evening was balmy, but as though she were deep in thought.

"My lady!"

Elizabeth turned, astonished at the sight of Honor hurrying toward her. "Mistress Thornleigh!"

Honor poured out the terrible account. The telling brought back all the horror of the deaths and Richard's abduction and the fire, and when she had finished she felt emptied of every ounce of strength. Her voice trailed in misery as she said, "Grenville will kill my husband."

"And your son?" Elizabeth asked, her face pale.

"Away when it happened. But he came back, saw the ruin . . . and heard about Richard. He is so enraged he means to attack Grenville Hall."

"Has he set out?"

"Not when I left. He is gathering men."

"Then he may cool down," Elizabeth said as though trying to convince herself as well as Honor. "He is sensible. He will not charge off on a rash attack." She looked toward the garden, and Honor distractedly followed her gaze. Parry had come out and stood watching them, concern on his face. Elizabeth motioned for him to go back in, a gesture that also told him she was all right. He turned and went inside.

Honor saw it, but was lost in her own nightmare. "Grenville's place is a fortress . . . He has a small army. Adam will die . . . Richard will die." Dizziness swamped her. Her vision dimmed.

She felt her legs buckle. She dropped to her knees and sank back on her heels.

"Mistress!" Elizabeth crouched bedside her. "You are ill. I will call for help—"

"No! Call no one. It is you I want. You alone can help us."

"Of course. Whatever I can do for you, I gladly will." Honor's teeth were chattering, and Elizabeth murmured, "Oh, dear lady, you are so ill." She called to the maid on the ladder at the pear tree and told her to fetch a cloak and some water, then said to Honor, "Baron Grenville must be brought to heel. We will take this to the judges of the Star Chamber."

Honor shook her head. "No time."

"That court exists to dispense swift justice."

"Swift? Weeks! Richard will be dead."

The maid came with a cloak and Elizabeth wrapped it around Honor, saying, "Come, can you stand?" She helped her to her feet and led her to a bench and guided her down on it. She offered the cup of water the maid had brought as well, and Honor took it with trembling hands and gulped it down. Elizabeth handed the empty cup back to the maid and told her to leave them alone but to stay near. She sat beside Honor, saying, "I owe you my life, Mistress Thornleigh, and I will do everything in my power to help you, I promise. You shall have all the people of mine that you need to set your ruined house and property in order, and all the money you require to rebuild. And do not fear for your son; he is too wise to launch a suicide attack. But as to your good husband, I know not what can be done. We can pray that Baron Grenville will not stoop to cold-blooded murder. In any case, I fear I have no way to help him."

Honor swallowed, the burned taste of ash still in her mouth. Elizabeth was wrong about Adam. He would die fighting to get Richard out. Wrong about Grenville, too. He would torture Richard unto death. "Yes," she said. "There is a way."

"How? Tell me, and it shall be done."

Honor tugged the cloak tighter around her. Laughter lilted from the house. She looked Elizabeth in the eye. "You must become queen. Now."

Elizabeth looked taken aback, then gave a sad smile as though acknowledging that her friend's terrible ordeal had understandably left her somewhat deranged. "If only that were true," she said kindly, but with a wry note. "I would decree peace for all mankind."

"It *can* be true. You can make it so. Overnight. Men throughout the length and breadth of the country have been preparing to bring down the Queen and raise you to the throne. Lords and knights. Gentlemen and yeomen. Soldiers and sailors. They stand ready, many hundreds of them, thousands. And they have the arms and the plans to do it."

Elizabeth stared at her. It was clear she'd had no idea of the preparations. And even clearer that she doubted what she was hearing.

"It's true," Honor insisted. "I know, because my husband has been involved. He has organized the stockpiling of weapons in this county. Adam, too, and many of our friends. And this is going on in *every* county, managed by men in high places. Men like Sir John Thynne of Longleat in Wiltshire. And they will have willing troops behind them—not just their own people and tenants, but battle-hardened soldiers. In the north, the officers of the garrison of Berwick-upon-Tweed stand ready to march their men under your standard. In the south, Captain Uvedale commanding the fortress of Yarmouth will also support you. And there are hundreds of exiles waiting for the word to sail home and fight. And money aplenty—the Queen's silver that Adam stole from Westminster—coming from Sir Henry Dudley in France. And many men who escaped the Queen's wrath after that failed revolt stand ready to march again. Nicholas Throckmorton. Sir John Perrot. Lord John Bray. Sir William Courtenay. Believe me, my lady, your supporters are everywhere. And they are all only waiting for a signal from you to rise up."

Elizabeth listened in rapt wonder. "But, how can this be, and I not know a glimmer of it?"

"They have not wanted to implicate you until all is ready. Especially those of your own household."

"What? *Who?*"

"Ask Master Parry. He has been sending letters to coordinate the plans. Ask Sir William St. Loe. He is pledged to protect you all the way to the throne."

Elizabeth's eyes narrowed in skepticism.

"Ask them!"

Elizabeth got up from the bench and called the maid and sent her to fetch the two men. Parry came out first, having stayed nearby. Elizabeth related what Honor had told her and asked him outright if it was true. He shot an angry look at Honor. "That was ill advised, Mistress Thornleigh."

"But is it *true?*" Elizabeth demanded.

He hesitated. To say yes was to admit to high treason. He said quietly, "Every word."

Elizabeth let out a sharp breath of astonishment. And something more. A fierce delight. Honor could see it in those sparkling black eyes. She knew Elizabeth. This news was thrilling to her. And that gave Honor such a jolt of hope she rose from the bench so quickly the cloak fell from her shoulders. "It is true. And it is *time.*"

"My lady, you called for me?" Sir William St. Loe was striding toward them.

Again, Elizabeth asked outright if he played any part in the conspiracy. St. Loe glanced at Parry with a frown, but his answer was quick—a soldier unencumbered by subtleties. "Me, my father, and my brother," he confirmed. "All at your service, my lady. We are sure to—" He didn't finish, because another man was hurrying through the garden, a gentleman finely dressed, with an air of authority. Reaching them, he bowed to Elizabeth and asked, "Have those fool actors driven you here, my lady?"

"Not at all, Sir Harry, I love a play," she assured her host. "But weightier matters require my attention."

Sir Harry Whitcombe eyed the group, including Honor and her dishevelled state. She knew him only by reputation, but knew where his sympathies lay. The other two men stood in edgy silence. None could mask their tension.

Elizabeth's eyes flicked between the three men. "All friends, good sirs?"

Parry and St. Loe looked grim. Honor entreated Whitcombe

with her eyes. He must have caught something he needed from that, for he looked back at Elizabeth and said quietly, "All friends in a righteous cause, my lady. These gentlemen are loath to name me, but I am proud to name myself." He bowed again. "Your champion."

Elizabeth's smile showed her excitement. But a careful smile. A controlled excitement.

Suddenly, everyone was talking. Not with anxiety anymore, but with determined calmness, keeping their voices low, though not a soul was near. Elizabeth led the exchange, asking about the plans, the extent of the preparations, the leading organizers. The three men answered succinctly and confidently, and with their own careful excitement now that she was one of them.

Honor waited, ignored by the others as they discussed the details of treason. She waited, feeling jumpy for action. Action, not more words! She thought of Adam charging, felled by a sword to his throat. Thought of Richard. His tongue cut out. His skin peeled off in strips.

"It's *time*, my lady!" she blurted. "The country wants you. They are only waiting. Give the signal and lead your people." She gripped Elizabeth's arm. "Be queen, Elizabeth! Stop Grenville. Save Adam. Save Richard!"

The men stared at her, startled by her outburst. Elizabeth told them, "Please excuse Mistress Thornleigh. Her family has suffered a tragedy. Sir Harry, will you escort her inside and see that she is looked after?"

"No," Honor protested, "I'm fine."

"Take the lady in, sir," Elizabeth insisted with a compassionate, sad glance at her, "and treat her as gently as you would treat me. She is my well-beloved friend."

Whitcombe's servants settled Honor in an elegant bedchamber. They brought her a silver basin of warm water, and perfumed soap and embroidered towels. They brought clean clothes, a gown of dove gray satin frothed with white lace. They brought roasted quail and wine and candied fruits. Honor carelessly splashed water on her dirty face, and crammed some food in her mouth, too keyed up to taste it, hungry only for Elizabeth to give the order to march.

She lay down on the cool, clean sheets, her muscles trembling with fatigue but bowstring tight with hope and anticipation. Everything she had done to keep Elizabeth alive and unharmed by Queen Mary, everything she had endured for Elizabeth's sake would be worth it the moment the Princess wrested power from her sister. The new queen would send her army to thunder down on Grenville Hall and release Richard before Grenville knew what had happened. Queen Elizabeth! Honor lay on her back, eyes wide, longing for morning, and action.

Darkness crept over the house, but sleep was impossible. She got up from the bed, drawn to the moonlit window. Forests surrounded Bramley Hall, and she cast her eyes to the dark, green-black horizon, looking for traces of smoke rising from her burning home, praying she would see none.

Someone was moving on the terrace below. It was Elizabeth. Pacing. All alone. Arms folded, head lowered in thought, she went slowly back and forth between huge urns that spilled over with blood red gillyflowers. The moonlight, stark and cold, made her features indistinct and her slim body look ghostly as the night breeze tugged at her long, loose sleeves. In the distance beyond her the boat on the crescent lake was tethered to the jetty. Unmanned, its single sail furled, it tugged at its rope in the breeze as though eager, like Honor, for morning.

She felt a pain at her heart. It would take time to march soldiers to London, more than a day. Two, at the least. Three, perhaps. Could Richard hold out until then? Would Adam hold off from attacking?

She climbed back into bed, too tired to stand or even to think. It was out of her hands now—and in Elizabeth's. She closed her eyes, still stinging from the fire, the ride, the fear. Her last thought before sleep dragged her under was, *It all begins with morning.*

❧ 31 ❧

The Making of a Queen

June 1558

The Queen was retching. A black-robed doctor held the porcelain pot while two other doctors hovered, anxiously inspecting the color and consistency of the vomit.

Mary spat out the last of it, exhausted from days of illness, and then pushed the doctor's hand away with surprising strength. "She is *here?*" she demanded of her lady, Jane Dormer.

"Here, Your Majesty," Jane said, still curtsying from delivering her message. "In the antechamber. The lord chamberlain thought you must have summoned her."

"Never!" Mary fell back upon her pillow, her haggard eyes wide with disbelief. "How does she dare?"

"Shall I return the message that Your Majesty is unwell?"

"No! I would not give her the satisfaction. Come, help me dress," she said, thrashing at the sheet to throw it off. Her skin was clammy and her emptied stomach ached, but she was on her feet within moments.

"Your Majesty," Jane ventured nervously, "she has come with many friends."

Honor had ridden into London in a state of almost dizzy anticipation. She rode near the middle of Elizabeth's retinue of forty retainers, grateful for the company's quick pace. Their departure had been so sudden and swift she'd had only a moment with Elizabeth, who had come to her room at dawn to say, "Mistress Thornleigh, I want you with us. It is important that you witness this." They had left Sir Harry Whitcombe's house as the sun's first rays were pinking the sky. Elizabeth rode out at the head of the company, flanked by Whitcombe and Parry, with St. Loe and his lieutenant as their vanguard.

Honor could hardly believe Elizabeth's audacious gambit. Straight to London! It was brilliant. After all, why had Wyatt's rebellion failed soon after Queen Mary took the throne? Because he and his small army had marched from Kent, and by the time they reached London the Queen had rallied her forces and the city gates were closed and Wyatt's men were slaughtered. Why had Dudley's rebels, likewise, never had a chance, even before they were betrayed from within? Because they had planned to march from the Welsh borders and join Dudley's French troops arriving in the south—all too far from London, the center of royal power. The capital was the prize, the linchpin, the key to success. Start in London, take the city, and remove the Queen before she had a chance to call out her troops. Brilliant.

But Honor's exhilaration at the strategy did not last long. As the company rode past Charing Cross outside London's wall, she realized they were not going into the city, and though the people in the street cheered the Princess as she passed, it was clear that Elizabeth was not going to join up with the organizing leaders Richard had told Honor about. No one joined them. As the entourage turned into the sprawling precincts of Whitehall Palace, Honor realized in dismay that Elizabeth had not come to London to raise a rebellion. She had come to see the Queen.

Queen Mary swept into the antechamber attended by five ladies and as many gentlemen ushers, plus several lords of her council, hastily convened. Honor dropped to her knees. Lowly in rank, she was far behind the Princess, and she watched, still stunned, afraid that Elizabeth had lost her mind. Ahead of her St. Loe, Whitcombe, and Parry were making their bows, their sheathed swords glinting. Ahead of them, Elizabeth.

The Queen stood stone-faced as Elizabeth rose from her curtsy. Someone inside the royal bedchamber quickly closed the door, but not before Honor glimpsed the rumpled bed and the three doctors in tense discussion, and caught the smell of vomit. She looked back at the Queen, at her face as white as raw pastry, at the ruff slightly askew at the throat of her orange taffeta gown as though she had dressed too quickly. *She was in bed, ill,* Honor thought. Even in her consternation at being here, she noted with surprise how gaunt and aged the Queen looked. *She's deathly sick.*

Despite the large number of people, there was utter silence. Protocol forbade even a princess speaking until addressed by the Queen, and the rustle of Elizabeth's silk skirt as she smoothed it from her curtsy was the only sound. Honor could sense her fear. Elizabeth had always been in terror of her sister's power to have her executed, and whatever bizarre gamble had given her the courage to come here today, the fear lingered. But this was a new Elizabeth Honor was seeing. Serious. Carefully confident. Her nerves controlled. Honor felt on tenterhooks, waiting to see where it would lead.

"Well?" Mary demanded.

"I thank Your Majesty for granting me an audience at such short notice," Elizabeth said, "and I beg your forbearance for so crudely disturbing your peace. Believe me, nothing less than a matter of grave urgency would make me do so."

"And what is this grave matter?" Mary asked with cool derision. "Have you lost a dancing master?" She glanced at her councilors to catch their amused response. None smiled.

"I am come to alert Your Majesty of a great danger. Forgive my blunt telling, but there is no other way. The country, Your Majesty, is about to rise up against you."

There were gasps from Mary's people. Honor saw the backs of Parry and Whitcombe stiffen. St. Loe's fighting hand at his side balled into a fist.

Mary fixed her small eyes on her sister and said quietly, "Have a care, madam. You speak of treason."

"I speak of what I see and hear, Your Majesty. And it is dire. The people live in fearful unrest. They fear that with our soldiers off in faraway wars, our country is left open to any brute invader. They fear the roaring rumors that Your Majesty's treasury is bankrupt and that this will drag down their careful businesses to ruin. They fear the burnings in every market town, which every day snuff out in dreadful agony another of their neighbors, their cousins, their kin. Most of all they fear a leaderless future, since you have no heir of your body."

Shocked courtiers stared back at Elizabeth. No one ever dared to mention the Queen's barren state in her presence. Mary herself went rigid, and livid color splotched her chalk white cheeks.

"And since you have named no one to be your heir," Elizabeth went on pointedly, "the people fear that a malicious claimant to your throne could sweep in from foreign shores and bring a ravenous army to lay waste to this peaceful realm."

The lords of the royal council exchanged bleak looks. This was their own fear.

A sheen of sweat glistened on Mary's forehead. It sprang from both fury and fever. She said with barely suppressed rage, "There is no such threat to the realm."

"But it is what the people fear. With no proclaimed heir—"

"My heir. That is the prize *you* covet. You want my crown."

"I have no such ungodly wish, Your Majesty. I am unworthy— even though it is true that you and I share the same royal blood. I love my country, and I love the people, and they know it, but I am well aware that I am not worthy to wear the crown. I am only anxious to preserve Your Majesty and the country from a bloody uprising."

"I know you, what you are. You *foment* this unrest. You lust for my crown. You lust to rule. You, who know nothing of the cares and burdens of a monarch. You, who spend your days in dancing and playacting. Spend your nights, as your strumpet mother did, in who knows what godforsaken pleasures."

The insult besmirching the Princess brought murmurs of discomfort from the courtiers. Sir William St. Loe took an indignant, protective step closer to Elizabeth.

"I am not here to speak about myself, Your Majesty," Elizabeth said calmly, "but to warn you as your loyal servant. With this instability about the succession, the country is floundering in such alarm and foreboding it could bring you to ruin."

"Who dares to plot this? Who would rise against God's anointed? I want names!"

The three men with Elizabeth did not move a muscle. Their heads could roll, but they had cast their lot with the Princess, come what may. All the courtiers and councilors knew it, and Honor read respect on the faces of several—admiration, even, for the valiant loyalty of Elizabeth's supporters. The Queen seemed anxiously aware of it. She wiped beads of sweat from her upper lip. "Names, madam," she demanded again. "Who are these traitors?"

Elizabeth bowed her head. "I cannot say."

"You *will* not say!"

"I cannot, Your Majesty, because there are too many."

There were gasps. Sir William Paulet, the lord treasurer, whispered something to Lord North, who nodded in dour agreement.

"Silence!" the Queen cried, turning on them. One of the ladies nearest her took an instinctive step away from her, as from an aggressive dog.

"I cannot," Elizabeth went on steadily, "because they throng me to tell me their fears, and how can anyone know the names of so many? If it were just one or two men driven to take action, or even ten or twenty, you might snuff them out as you would snuff out an errant spark from your grate. But there are *legions* of our fearful countrymen. The realm is a tinderbox, and one spark will ignite the whole country. Your Majesty cannot suppress an entire kingdom. To attempt it would be to kindle a blazing civil war. And that would be tragic for so wise a ruler as yourself, a ruler so careful of her people's welfare. Their memory of you would be tainted for all time. A legacy of carnage. All because Your Majesty has not proclaimed your heir."

"Again! My heir! Your lust is showing. Can you prate of nothing else?"

"I speak it because it is what the people tell *me*. They will not tolerate a foreign ruler. They would rather fight and die than see Mary of the Scots call herself their queen. She is a creature of the French court that has always been her home, and now, married to the heir to the French throne, she would sell England to the King of France. And—forgive me, Your Majesty, but I must speak the hard truth—the people fear even more that if King Philip is your heir, he would gobble us into his mighty empire and make our England a feeble, vassal state."

"Never!" a councilor blurted. He immediately looked regretful at his outburst, and jerked a deferential bow to the Queen, but there were no looks of reproach from his colleagues. He had merely spoken what they were thinking. The Queen was trembling. Her eyes looked haggard. Control of this interview was slipping away from her and she was too unnerved, too ill, and too bereft of friends to win it back.

Elizabeth kept on without mercy. "Wherever I go, Your Majesty, the people flock to me and press their petitions on me and tell me their fears. Without a named heir you leave the realm unprotected, vulnerable to any invader or to tragic civil war. Your people are loyal, but they would rather risk everything now to bring about a change than wait to see their green fields soaked with the blood of brave Englishmen who want only to protect their families, their homes, their beloved native land. Without a named heir, Your Majesty, you consign your own memory to infamy."

"Enough! You . . . you . . ." The Queen did not finish. She was swaying, fainting.

A lady cried, "Your Grace!" She and two others rushed to hold the Queen upright. The courtiers and councilors buzzed in alarm. "Make way, my lords!" one of the Queen's ladies cried. The gathering broke apart to create a ragged path to the royal bedchamber. The Queen, hanging on to her ladies, disappeared into her private chamber. The door closed behind her.

Honor heard Parry murmur to Elizabeth, "Your tale has made her deadly ill."

Elizabeth looked at the closed door and said tightly, "I hope to God it kills her."

❧ 32 ❧

From the Ashes

June 1558

Speedwell House was a smoking ruin. The roof had collapsed, and two of the outer walls and most of the second-story floor, leaving waist-high rubble, half-eaten interior walls, and a staircase that went nowhere. Wisps of dirty smoke drifted up into the blue sky as tired women and children, their faces half soot, poked with sticks through the charred debris, looking for anything of value that might be salvaged.

Honor moved slowly in the outer shadows of the house's remains. Her shoes and her skirt's hem were white with ash. White as a corpse's winding sheet, she thought. White as bone. Her mind was on death. Elizabeth had betrayed her. Betrayed them all.

The bells of Chelmsford had been ringing when she rode alone through the town on her way back from London. The town council had convened in the market square where the clerk had read out the proclamation to the people. Decreed by Queen Mary, and signed by all the lords of her royal council, it declared that in the absence of an heir of her body the Queen named Princess Elizabeth as her heir. The people cheered. Fast work, Honor thought bitterly as she kept riding. Elizabeth had so frightened the councilors with the spectre of imminent country-wide rebellion, and offered so reasonable a path to peace—herself as successor—she had backed the Queen into a corner from which Mary's only exit, no doubt clamored for by the council, was to immediately name her sister her heir.

Betrayed, Honor thought in misery. Elizabeth had gotten exactly what she wanted. While Richard and Adam still faced death.

She stopped walking when she reached the garden. Gray ash lay like a shroud over her rose bushes, the blooms as colorless as if drained of blood. Ash made ghosts of the fruit trees. She noticed a pile of cut roses lying on the parched, blackened grass. Dead now—just a heap of blanched flowers and shrivelled leaves, all dusted with ash. Dusted with death is how it felt to her. Who had cut this doomed bouquet? She saw a dagger on the stone bench. A shape only, for the dagger, too, was dusted with ash, but she recognized it instantly. Richard's. Had he cut these roses for her? A terrible pain squeezed her heart. He must have done it just before Grenville attacked. He'd had no chance even to snatch the dagger before Grenville's men snatched him and dragged him away. Two days ago. Was he alive or dead? And if alive, was he suffering such agony that he prayed God for death?

She sat down with a thud on the bench, on its shroud of ash, and struggled to hold back the scalding tears. If she let them loose, lost all control, she was afraid she would go mad.

She looked up at the blue sky. The wispy smoke of her dead house drifted up toward wispy clouds, a few long, feathery trails in the otherwise cloudless expanse. Mare's tails, Adam called such clouds. They portended rain, not soon but within twenty-four hours. A seaman's knowledge. She stared at one elongated plume that stretched itself high and lonely against the blue. Adam was about to meet his own death, she was sure of that. When she had ridden in, the anxious women told her that he had gathered together all the men of the household and almost half the tenants, and all night they had trooped the area, getting horses and arms from this neighbor and that, and now they were scouring the vicinity for more men, and Adam was offering pay to any that came armed and ready to ride with them. Untrained farmers and farriers and carpenters, about to hurl themselves with pitchforks against the Grenville Archers and the band of murderers Grenville had hired to man his fortress home.

Adam would die. Honor knew it in her bones.

Would Elizabeth weep?

"I trusted you," Honor had accused her in bleak fury as they had left the Queen. "Trusted you to save my family. But you never intended to. You will not fight. Not for anyone."

"No, I will not fight, not when fighting will lead to thousands of deaths. I will not loose barbarous civil war to get a crown. And barbarous it would be, for the Queen has many supporters, adherents of the Catholic faith, and she can call on the armies of Spain and the pope. No, Mistress Thornleigh, I will not send Englishmen to die for your family. I will not sacrifice thousands to save a few."

Honor turned from her in mute misery. She started to walk away, not knowing where to go or what to do. They were under a massive archway in the courtyard of Whitehall Palace, and beyond the arch Elizabeth's retinue were saddling up to leave.

"Stop," Elizabeth called, running after Honor. She grabbed her arm to stop her. "Please," she said in a strangled voice, "please understand. I wish to God I *could* help your family. I esteem your husband, who did such brave service in Parliament. And as for your son . . . I love him. Yes, I will say it. I love Adam Thornleigh with all my heart. Love him body and soul." Her voice wavered. "I know how deeply you love your husband. Believe me, I feel no less for Adam."

"Then how can you let—"

"Because I cannot think only of those I love! Not anymore. You once told me I need to think of all England as my family. I did not want to hear it then. I wanted no such burden. Perhaps I should have listened to you back then. If I had thrown my support behind Dudley's plan, I might at this moment be queen. I could have curbed Baron Grenville and kept your family safe. I could have stopped Adam's marriage. Well, it is too late for that." She lifted her head high. "But not too late for me to do what I must. You have tried to protect your family. I am doing the same for mine—and mine is all of England."

"You have gambled, that's all. Gambled that the Queen will name you her heir. But she may not. Then what will you do?"

Elizabeth answered in a heartbeat. "Then, I will fight. To the death."

Honor got up from the garden bench. The dead house seemed to pull her, like a ghost that haunts the living, urging them not to forget. She wandered inside, her skirt's hem sweeping ashes. She stepped over a fallen pillar of the great hall, and skirted the staircase that stood decapitated between the two floors. She looked up toward the bedroom she had shared with Richard. Half the floor had collapsed, but on the floorboards that remained stood their bed, a grotesque heap of smoking ash. Richard had always kept his strongbox of gold in the corner. Gone, now—stolen by Grenville's men. And the table where Honor kept her jewelry and combs and pins, and her cherrywood box of Isabel's precious letters from Peru—all dwindled to ash. *Isabel,* she thought with a pang. Her daughter would come home to find her father and brother slain, her mother a widow, Adam's new wife a widow.

It was too painful. She turned away.

She walked on to the roofless parlor, where the sun shone down on the rubble. Last week she had brought her jewelry box down here to show Geoffrey a bracelet she meant to give his daughter for her birthday. Poor, dear Geoffrey. His body and the bodies of Captain Boone and the six other men had been laid out by the women under the chestnut tree in the stable yard. Joan would have heard by now. Richard's kindly, sensible sister, always Honor's friend—already a lonely widow.

She turned away again. But there was nowhere to go.

Something glinted in the rubble. Green fire. Her breath caught. Her emerald necklace! She crouched and pawed at the hot ashes. The beechwood jewelry box was cinders, and the gold chain of the necklace was a distorted thing, half melted and cooled into an ugly contortion, but the gemstone shone pure. She snapped it free of the chain. It was too hot to handle, and she fumbled it into a well she made in her skirt. It was so beautiful. And so dear to her, a gift from Richard on their wedding day. Shining in the sunlight, it reflected twenty-five years of memories of him. Lovemaking. Talks about Isabel's first tooth, Adam's school, ships, business, gossip, Christmas, books. Lovemaking.

She would never see him again. Never hear his voice. Never lie in his arms. Clutching the hot gem, she ran out through the rubble and reached the parched grass and dropped to her knees, and the tears sprang. She could not stop them. She sank back on her heels, sobs tearing her chest, leaving her throat in a wail of despair.

"Aye, mistress, cry it out. We've all lost good men, and it ain't over yet."

Gulping breaths, Honor looked up. Mary Carter stood gazing down at her with sad sympathy. Fat Mary—Captain Boone's sweetheart. A sack slung over her shoulder bulged with salvaged, useful things. Tin cups, pewter plates, spoons, wire. She was wiping a soot-grimed cloth over a long knife to clean it. Boone's knife. "Can you stand, mistress? Come, I'll help you over to the tent. There's water there. And some cold vittles. And a stool to rest on."

Honor let herself be helped to her feet. She wiped the tears from her face with her sleeve, struggling to gain control, though sobs still shuddered through her. "Not over?" she managed to ask Mary, afraid to hear the answer.

"Master Adam and the men are set to ride hell-bent for Grenville Hall. Peter galloped all the way from Colchester to say they're on their way. I pray the good Lord they'll kill that bastard baron and ride back to us, every one of them. But I've found that the good Lord don't much listen to me." She looked sadly at the knife. "No more than my man ever did."

Two hours, Honor thought. Maybe three. That would bring Adam to the enemy's gates. She looked at Mary, so busy with useful work, not tears, scavenging for items to coax life back to normal. She took a deep breath to steady herself. "I'm all right, Mary. Thank you. And I am so sorry for your loss. Go on, now, see what else you can find."

Mary trudged on, and Honor watched her kick through a pile of debris. Mary was doing what had to be done. Admirable. And necessary.

She looked up at the blue sky and thought of Elizabeth, that proud and selfish girl she had come to know so well. The hoarded anger at her fell away, and in its place swelled a fierce respect. Elizabeth was a girl no longer. Selfish no longer. She might not yet have a crown, but she had transformed herself into a queen, a leader of her people, making hard choices, sacrificing her own desires. Elizabeth was doing what had to be done.

Honor lowered her gaze to the faraway horizon of forest that bordered Grenville's lands. Adam, too. He was doing what he was convinced had to be done.

And so must I. Maybe she had known it all along, known since Grenville took Richard. The answer lay with her. There was something that only she could do. It was necessary. Because Richard was necessary. Adam was necessary. Without them, there was no family. Without them, Isabel would come home to a house of widows.

Grenville Hall had been built in the dark days of unstable reigns, overmighty nobles, and the constant threat of civil war. The mossy stone walls of its main block rose five stories, topped by parapets with crenellations as shields for archers. The walls of the lower blocks were hatched with arrow slits in the form of crosses. The stone curtain wall that fronted the buildings was a parapet with more embrasures for archers. The wooden drawbridge crossed a moat of murky water where foes would wallow to their deaths. The gatehouse hulked over a massive arch manned by guards.

Honor crossed the drawbridge, her horse at a plodding walk, its hoofbeats echoing down to the dark water beneath. She looked up. Archers spiked the parapets. A flag rippled lazily, high atop the main block, lifting just enough to display the Grenville coat of arms as though to claim mastery over the feeble breeze. Guards, standing thick along the inner walls of the gatehouse arch, watched her come. They were alert but at ease, only idly interested in a lone woman on a tired mare. She obediently stopped before they stopped her. The lead guard sauntered out and asked her to state her business. She told him she had come to see Baron Grenville. "He is holding my husband."

He looked taken aback. "No good talking to his lordship."

"I believe there may be. I am here to beg him to have mercy. As a Christian."

He scowled at such a futility. "Go home, mistress. Say a prayer for your husband's soul instead."

"He's dead?"

The guard shook his head, then added grimly, "But as good as."

"Captain, if you were in an enemy's hands and your wife came to beg for your life, would you want her to give up and go away?"

His smile was wry. "Beg for me? That'll be the day." He shook his head again, though not unkindly. "Sorry, mistress. Can't let you disturb his lordship. Go home."

She looked at the other guards. Uninterested in her, they had turned and were talking amongst themselves. A few shared a quiet laugh. Honor reached into her pocket. "Let me through," she whispered to the captain. "Take this, and let me through." She handed him the emerald.

His eyes went wide. The gem was worth many times more than he earned in a year. He glanced up at her. Glanced at his companions. None were looking. He slipped the emerald into his pocket. "A chat with the baron? Why not try." He called over a young guard. Told him to run inside and tell his lordship the lady was coming. "Tell him I let her in from Christian charity."

"Thank you, Captain. And, could you help me down?" It was hard with her useless right arm.

No one took notice of her as she walked across the grounds. Servants were going about their business, men unloading firewood from a wagon, women carrying baskets of bread from the bake house, others sweeping the cobbles outside the main door. She scanned the compound for any trace of Richard. Was he down beneath the main block, chained to a dungeon wall? Or up in that squat tower, slowly dying of thirst? Or inside the stables, roped and tethered like an animal?

She walked past the women sweeping and stepped inside the door. Out of the sun, she felt the darkness of the place. Her cloak was loose, unfastened, and she pulled its edges more tightly around her for warmth. A household officer, the chamberlain, perhaps told by the young guard of her coming, eyed her as she walked past him.

She reached the great hall. It was huge, with high windows of stained glass and long stone walls unadorned except for the heads of deer with branching antlers and dead eyes. The musicians' gallery was vacant, and so was half the hall, but at the far end a small throng of people seemed about to sit down to supper. There were three tables, two abutting a head table, all set with white damask tablecloths. Men and women milled around them, chatting with the leisurely enjoyment of a family group. Honor recognized Baron Grenville's young wife. There were children. A couple of old people. A dwarf was juggling plates before some of the children, making them laugh. Servants bustled, setting down platters of meats, bowls of fruit, pitchers of wine.

Honor saw Grenville. He stood behind the head table. She had not expected that. But he was expecting her. With a hand on the back of his chair, as if he'd been about to sit down, he was watching her walk in. He said loudly, making a cold, calm announcement, "A neighbor approaches."

People turned. They had not noticed her come in.

Honor stopped. She had not yet reached the two tables ahead of her on either side. She made a deep, humble curtsy. "My lord."

Voices buzzed as a few people realized who she was and passed it on.

Grenville said, "I would invite you to join my family's modest feast, Mistress Thornleigh, but I fear you would not find the atmosphere to your liking. Now and then, disturbing sounds come from the criminals in my lockup. It is not conducive to digestion. Even my wife complains."

"My good lord—"

"Ah, I have risen to *good*. An accolade, indeed."

"I hope that all of us may rise to goodness, as our Savior taught. And I know such goodness must lie in your heart. My lord, you hold my husband's life in your hands. Without him I have nothing left, no home, no hope. I am here to beg you to take mercy on him." She knelt. "Let him go, I entreat you. I promise you we will leave England and live abroad and you will never hear from us again. Good my lord, on my knees I beg you. For the love of God, which I know fills your heart, spare my husband's life."

The people looked at her in wonder. Then all eyes turned to Grenville.

"Nothing left? Yes, so I have heard. A sad situation." He let out a small breath that sounded like reluctant surrender. "Perhaps it is enough." The edge of belligerence had gone from his voice. "Perhaps the enmity between our houses can now end." He sat down and leaned back in his chair, his eyes on her as if reassessing. "You do well to invoke the love of God, mistress. However, just as we must first confess our sins before we ask His forgiveness, the first step here, for you, is to admit your family's sins. Will you do that?"

"I will, my lord, right gladly."

"Good. Admit that your husband murdered my father."

She swallowed. Then nodded.

"Pardon?"

"Yes. He killed your father. I beg you to forgive him and have mercy."

"Admit that your son seduced my sister and defiled her."

She hesitated, trying to think. This was not working. She needed him closer. Close enough so he could see the despair in her eyes. He liked that, seeing suffering. But as a lowly petitioner she could not go to him. So she lowered her head contritely and murmured, "Yes, my family has done you much wrong. Forgive us."

He made a face of annoyance. He could not hear her. "Speak up."

Again, she mumbled her plea. Still unable to hear, he forged ahead with his inquisition. "Admit that you and your family have shown contempt for the one true faith, and blackened your hearts with blasphemy."

Again, she made her repentant response, making it too quiet.

He got to his feet with an impatient grunt and brushed past the people, coming around the tables so that he could better hear her. He stopped, still a stone's throw from Honor, still too far to really see her pain. She needed that.

"So you admit it all?" he said, frustration in his voice. He was not yet satisfied.

"Most humbly." Still kneeling, she bent and placed her good hand on the floor. She crawled toward him, her useless hand dragging. She heard a child giggle at the sight and a woman said, "Hush." Honor kept her head down, making her grovelling way to Grenville until she was just an arm's length from him. "We have sinned grievously, my lord, against you and against God."

She looked up to see him watching her with a cold glint of pleasure in his eyes.

"But I think you have overestimated my power, Mistress Thornleigh. Speaking for myself, I can forgive. But will the law? I am merely a subject of Her Majesty Queen Mary, and must obey the laws of the land like any other Englishman. Like your husband. You see, as a justice of the peace, I am merely holding him in custody. He will go to court and stand trial for the murder of my father. That is the law."

Not true. Richard had a royal pardon. Grenville must know that his fantasy of revenge would not stand up in a court of law. This was some trick. So she held her tongue.

"The problem is, he is a wildly unruly prisoner and I have had to take harsh measures to restrain him. He is so unruly, in fact, it makes me fear he may never reach the courtroom, for such reckless criminals often try to escape. Should your husband attempt that, it will be my duty to deal with him in kind."

Honor rose on her knees. She fixed her eyes on this man who had stretched her body on the rack until she had wept what felt like tears of blood. This man who now held Richard in some hellish hole and would never, ever, let him live.

He leaned down, bringing his face so close to hers that if she spit it would have landed on the white rib of scar above his lip. He finished with quiet menace, "I will cut him down like a mad dog."

She jerked off her cloak and reached over her left shoulder with her left hand. She found the scabbard between her shoulder blades and gripped the handle of the knife. The long blade flashed as she whipped it out. She stabbed it up into his groin.

There was a scream from among the women. Grenville gaped in

shock. Honor pulled the knife free. Blood oozed through Grenville's breeches. He looked down and gripped the wound, blood dripping between his fingers. He thudded to his knees before her, his eyes bulging white, locked on hers. Both were kneeling, face to face, and she raised the knife with a cry of "Richard!" and plunged it into his chest. He gave a fierce gasp as if to suck back his life.

Women screamed. Men shouted. Blood poured down Grenville's front. He clawed Honor's shoulder. She slashed his throat, crying, "Richard!" Blood spurted.

He toppled toward her. His arm clipped her useless arm, knocking him sideways as he fell, and he crashed to the floor on his back. Wildly, she stabbed his stomach. "Richard!" She hacked at his shoulder, his chest, his throat. "Richard! . . . Richard! . . . Richard!"

Guards pounded in. She was still hacking at Grenville's lifeless body when they hauled her to her feet and tore Boone's knife from her bloodied grip.

ꙮ 33 ꙮ

Colchester Jail

November 1558

A scatter of yellow-brown leaves drifted down from the oak tree. Only one ragged bough was visible through the high, barred window of Honor's cell in Colchester jail, but she had been grateful for even that small view of the world. She had liked watching the leaves through their seasonal change. At first green and resilient, glossy in the sunshine; now, brown and dry and drifting to earth, their duty done. Poets sometimes spoke of autumn's mournful mood, but Honor did not find it so. In fact, it cheered her, this eternal cycle: leaves fell to replenish the earth. True, in her garden she had always removed drifts of dead oak leaves, heaping them separately, for left in clumps oak leaves burned the soil. Eventually, they decomposed into an excellent nourishment for roses, but that took time. To grow things did take time. Like growing a hardy child. Another eternal cycle.

She turned to Richard. He stood leaning against the far wall, arms crossed, looking across the cell at the window. "Will you have more of this roast capon, my love?" she asked.

He slowly shook his head. Somewhere in the city, church bells were ringing.

"Adam?" she asked. He sat across the table from her, separated by dishes of food that both men had barely touched. Adam was crumbling a piece of bread as though lost in thought. He, too, shook his head.

"It's quite delicious," she said, and meant it. "Do thank Mildred Cecil for sending it." She savored food as never before, now that so little of life was left to her. A few days at most. Every morsel tasted fresh and rich and fascinating. Precious. Especially such fine fare sent by friends. She was fortunate, she knew. Prisoners who could not pay the jailer for their lodging and food suffered in the crowded, foul, common wards and ate what they could barter or scrounge, but Richard had paid for her to have this comfortable cell, a room of her own with a feather bed and a brazier to warm the cold nights. He had paid for it all, and for three expensive London lawyers, too, until his cash had run out, including what he'd raised from selling his mine and the last of her jewels. All that was left was the land on which their burned house stood, and Adam's ship. Honor had been deeply moved by the kindness of so many friends coming to their aid with money. Sir William and Mildred. Lord and Lady Powys. George Mitford's sons. Most touchingly, Joan. Most generously, Elizabeth. And, most surprisingly, Frances Grenville. No, Frances Thornleigh, she reminded herself. That was hard to get used to.

The lawyers had earned their gold. They had stalled the trial for weeks and weeks by submitting briefs to argue self-defense, and demanding a change of venue, and gilding the palms of officers of the court to stall some more. But, in the end, Honor's trial had been swift, all the witnesses in agreement, and the verdict inescapable. She would be hanged by the neck until she was dead.

Now, when Richard and Adam visited, it was a death watch. They were only waiting to be told by the jailer what day.

The bells of Colchester clanged on. A wedding? Honor wondered. Some young couple's life about to bloom? The eternal cycle.

"They won't do it on a Sunday," Richard said. "So that gives us another two days to see if—"

"No," Honor said, "enough." She didn't want to talk about it. She wanted to talk about Isabel. Her fingers smoothed over the letter that lay in her lap, the latest one from their daughter, in

Peru. She had almost memorized it—happy chatter about little Nicolas, and the advancement Carlos was enjoying in the service of the Viceroy, and their flower filled house in sunny Trujillo. Isabel knew nothing of the calamity that had happened here at home. It took ages for letters to go to and from the New World. Two days ago, when Richard had delivered this latest letter, Honor had told him she wanted him to invite Isabel and Carlos to come home. He had promised to do so. That thought had cheered her, a needed diversion, and she'd spent the last days envisioning her daughter's return. Now, she said to Richard, "Have you written to Isabel yet?"

He shook his head, morose.

"Richard, please. I . . . need to know that she'll come."

He looked away, as though it was too difficult to speak.

"I'll do it," Adam said.

"Good. And then, you must both go to greet them when their ship arrives."

They both gave terse nods of ascent.

Honor tried to calculate Isabel's arrival. Adam's letter alone would take months to reach Peru. "How long does the voyage take?" she asked him.

Adam shrugged. "Storms in the Atlantic this time of year. Then they'll make landfall first in Spain. So, months before they get here, certainly. Maybe by late summer."

They'll see England at harvest time, she thought. Fragrant apple orchards. Fields of green barley. "You must both be there," she said again. "There on the wharf to greet her and Carlos and little . . ." Her voice broke. Nicolas. The grandson she would never see.

Richard looked at her with pain in his face. He came to her and placed a reassuring hand on her shoulder. "We will. Don't worry, my love, we'll be there."

She laid her own hand over his and looked up at him. Grenville had kept Richard in his lockup, standing tethered to the wall by wrist chains so short he could neither lie down nor sit. For two days and two nights. Whenever Honor thought of it she wished she could stab Grenville one more time.

The bells rang on. Adam got to his feet quickly, as if the sound was too irritating. He plowed a hand through his hair. Gave Honor a look of desperation. Sat down again and poured himself another cup of wine and drank it fast. His third in half an hour. There was a scuffling sound in the corridor outside the door. Then voices, loud but indistinct. "Another fight," Adam said. "I'll go see. I don't want them brawling near here." He went out to the corridor.

Honor and Richard looked at each other.

"Books?" he asked hollowly. "Do you want any more books?"

She shook her head. "Elizabeth sent some last week." Strange, she thought, that when she had first met the Princess, Elizabeth was the prisoner and had asked *her* to bring books. Now, they had traded places. Except Elizabeth had finally been set free. *I will not.*

She shook off the thought. "Now," she said, eager to settle another matter, "has the Princess sent the money to rebuild the house? Has it arrived?"

He nodded.

"Good. When can you have the carpenters begin?"

He shrugged. Looked away.

She stood. "Richard, you need to get started. Soon there'll be snow." He and Adam were living aboard Adam's ship in Colchester Harbor, partly to save the last of their money. Joan had asked them to move in with her at Blackheath, but Richard insisted on being near Honor so that he could visit her every day. "Please, promise me you'll hire the workmen tomorrow."

"Can't do that," he said tightly.

"Why not? You have the money. Elizabeth has been generous."

"I can't because . . . I won't."

"You can't keep living in the harbor."

"There are other places."

"Where?"

He groaned, hating this. "I'll go to Antwerp."

"Antwerp?" she said in horror. "No! Speedwell House is our home. I want you to live in our home."

"I don't want to live there without you!"

They stared at each other. She groped for his hand.

"Oh, don't do this. Please, Richard. If you leave England,

what's it all been for? I did it. . . . . I killed him . . . for you. For you and Adam. And Isabel and her children."

He was shaking his head in misery.

"Please," she begged. "You once told me you would *never* leave. That day we fought at the inn. You said you wouldn't let them make us run away again. You vowed to stay and fight. And you were right. Don't let them win now. Stay, Richard. Rebuild. Give a home to Isabel and—"

He laid his hand over her mouth to stop her. She could see how hard he was fighting for control. He lowered his hand and smiled bleakly. "You've forgotten your own vow."

She was lost. "Mine?"

"When we both came home from Grenville's treatment in the Tower. Don't you remember? You made a promise. You said you would never fight me again." Tenderly, he took her face in his hands. "What a liar you are." Tears gleamed in his eye.

She struggled to hold back her own hot tears. She would not cry. Seeing her cry would kill Richard.

The door opened. Adam came in, his face ashen. "Barnes," he said. "He's coming."

Honor shivered at the name. The jailer.

The three of them looked at the door. As they waited in dry-mouthed silence, the city bells sounded all the more clamorous. Richard held Honor's hand so tightly it felt like he would crush it.

The jailer appeared at the open door and, absurdly, gave it a soft, polite knock with his knuckle. "Mistress Thornleigh?"

"Master Barnes," she managed.

He walked in looking very grave. He held a rolled paper scroll. Honor could see that its red wax seal was broken. An official confirmation of the execution? From the mayor?

"I've come to tell you—" Barnes stopped and shook his head. "God's blood, I can't hardly hear myself with those bells going at it."

It unnerved Honor despite her effort to be brave. Were they ringing bells to announce the execution? Was that common?

"They've already set bonfires in the market square," the jailer went on. "And what with all the dancing in the streets and feasting and drinking and such, I'll be lucky to keep even one of my turnkeys on the job today."

Honor could not fathom what he meant. She was trying with all her might to stay strong, to hear the time decreed for her execution and acknowledge it with some dignity.

"Bonfires? Feasting?" Richard asked, his voice raw. He glanced at Adam, who seemed just as lost.

Barnes looked at the three of them, his eyes going wide. "You didn't hear the news? God's blood, the old queen's dead. Aye, Queen Mary died in her bed just past midnight. And this morning in London the lords and gentlemen of Parliament proclaimed the new, young queen. Queen Elizabeth. Folks have gone stark mad, rejoicing. Listen to them bells!"

"Good Lord," Adam said in awe.

Honor felt a moment of deep satisfaction. The burning of heretics would stop. The country would suffer no civil war. The young woman she had counselled and cajoled had survived her sister's hate. "Queen Elizabeth," she said almost to herself, liking the sound of it. "I am right glad of it."

"Aye," Richard murmured hollowly. She looked at him, knowing his mind was still fixed on her imminent execution. This joyful news did nothing to cheer him.

"Aye," Barnes echoed. "The new, young queen is mistress of the lot of us now, and I must do her bidding. And she wastes no time in making us jump." He raised the scroll. "This here is my order, delivered straight from her hand." He put on a sober face and puffed out his chest to make a declaration. "Mistress Honor Thornleigh, in the name of Queen Elizabeth, the first of that name, I release you from my custody."

She blinked at him, not understanding.

Richard asked warily, confused, "Is my wife to be taken to another jail?"

"God's blood, man, no. No jail at all. She's to have her freedom. Her life. Your good wife is pardoned."

❧ 34 ❧

Two Ships

December 1559

Fog—a cold, wet, winter fog—lay heavy on the River Thames, making some in the small crowd on the London wharf shiver as they waited. But the gathering, the usual mix of merchants' agents, customs officials, ale sellers, chandlers, lightermen, scavenging boys, pickpockets, and whores accepted the discomfort. Every arriving ship was a floating opportunity to make money.

Honor felt the cold not at all. She was too eager to catch the first glimpse of the Spanish galleon through the river fog; her first sight of Isabel and Carlos and their little boy. Storms had delayed their landfall for weeks. Now, they were coming home. Not to Speedwell House—the rebuilding was still going on. In the meantime, Honor and Richard, befitting their rise in the world—thanks to Elizabeth, and the astonishing new wealth that came with it—had bought a London house on fashionable Bishopsgate Street. Joan, part of their household now, was there, getting everything in order for the feast to welcome Isabel and Carlos back to England. Honor and Joan had had a spirited difference of opinion this morning about whether to have the cook serve goose with preserved cherries as the first course, or pheasant. They had resolved it by ordering both.

How quickly we get used to a life of luxury, she thought now with some amusement. And yet, every day she gave silent thanks for her great good fortune. And her gratitude would be boundless at the sight of her daughter after five long years. A friend of Richard's at the customs house had alerted him about the ship en route from Seville. The ship's boat had come ahead with the passenger list, and Richard's friend confirmed that Isabel and Carlos were on board.

No sign of them yet, though. Just screeching seagulls and a few wherries either appearing out of the dirty-looking fog or disappearing into it. Beside Honor, Richard had struck up a conversation with the agent of a colleague of the Mercers' Guild. She glanced back at Frances, waiting quietly a few paces behind them, hugging herself. She already missed Adam, Honor knew. She was with child.

"Cold?" Honor asked her.

Frances shook her head with a quick, reassuring smile. Honor had come to pity her, and also, strange to say, almost to admire her. At her brother's death Frances had surprised everyone by taking Honor's part, saying she would never forgive her brother for using her to enable his attack on Richard and Speedwell House. She had made a complete break with the house of Grenville, and was trying hard to fit into the Thornleigh family, although Richard still did not trust her, and spoke to her with strained civility. But Honor could see how much Frances loved Adam. It was pitiful, really. Adam was reconciled to the fact of their marriage and treated his wife with courtesy, and even a modicum of intimacy, but it was very clear that Frances would never have his heart. Yet she made no complaint. Honor found that touching.

A manservant Honor didn't know approached their little group and bowed. "Your lordship."

Richard took no notice and kept on talking to the agent, listening with interest to the man's replies.

The servant tried again. "Pardon, your lordship."

Oblivious, Richard talked on. Honor watched with amusement. He still wasn't used to being addressed as a peer of the realm.

The servant coughed to catch his attention.

Honor laughed. "Lord Thornleigh," she said pointedly.

Richard blinked at her, then at the servant, then remembered—
he was Baron Thornleigh now. Elizabeth had ennobled him in the
flurry of her first acts as queen, and gifted him with rich lands in
Kent and Wiltshire as well as another large manor neighboring
their Essex home. Richard, grinning, had told Honor it was Elizabeth's way of thanking *her.* "Sorry," he said now to the servant.
"What is it?"

"Sir William Cecil bids you come to Whitehall for a meeting,
and to kindly come posthaste." Elizabeth's very first act had been
to name Cecil her principal secretary, the most influential man on
her newly formed royal council. "He sends you this, my lord." The
servant handed over a folded paper.

Richard scanned the note. "More talks with Gresham," he said
to Honor. "The Antwerp strategy."

"Then you must go right away." Sir Thomas Gresham was Elizabeth's expert financial agent in Antwerp. Honor knew that England's financial crisis was dire. Queen Mary had left a bankrupt
treasury, which dangerously weakened the country's security. Elizabeth was facing the first international crisis of her reign. French
troops, brought over by the Scottish queen regent, had been
threateningly posted along England's border. But Elizabeth had
no standing army, a fleet that was in urgent need of repair, little
cash, and a debased coinage. She needed to borrow immediately
from the powerful London merchants' companies in Antwerp to
consolidate her debts, buy arms, refit her ships, and rebuild confidence in the pound sterling by removing base coins from circula-
tion. She needed all the help she could get. Richard knew
Antwerp, knew the major traders there, and knew Elizabeth, who
trusted him. "The lord treasurer, too, will want to see you," Honor
said to him.

The servant bowed to Honor. "Your ladyship's presence is also
requested."

Richard smiled wryly. "And the Queen will want to see *you.*"

Honor was glad to help in whatever way she could. Elizabeth
had called her in for several private discussions to help formulate

the act that had begun her reign, an act to establish a truce in religion, a proclamation of tolerance. That had made Honor very proud. She had stood beside her as Elizabeth had prepared to make her entrance into Parliament for the proclamation, while her ladies-in-waiting fussed with last minute touches of her jewels and her robes. Honor's heart had swelled with admiration for the new queen.

Elizabeth had turned to her with a nervous look, and reached out her hand for reassurance. Honor clasped her hand and gave it a squeeze and said, *"Aspirat primo fortuna labori."* Fortune smiles upon our first effort. An echo of their very first meeting when Elizabeth had been a frightened prisoner at Woodstock.

Elizabeth had smiled, relaxing. She stood tall and said, matching Virgil with Virgil, *"Audaces fortuna iuvat."* Fortune favors the bold.

"There it is," Frances said. "The ship."

Honor and Richard turned. The Spanish galleon was sliding out of the fog. Honor strained to make it out. It looked like there were people on the decks, but the ragged shreds of fog blurred everything.

"Is that Isabel?" Richard said, excited. "There, to port of the mainmast. Look."

Honor's heart leapt. A young woman, waving, with a little boy at her side. But, no, it was not Isabel.

"That's not her. Maybe they're below deck?"

"Longboats towing them," Richard said. "No wind."

"How long till they reach us?"

"Half an hour at least. Hours more if the customs officials decide to meddle."

Honor's spirits plunged. "And we must go. You to Sir William, I to the Queen."

They shared a look of frustration. The summons to Whitehall must immediately be obeyed.

"I'll stay," Frances said. "I'll greet them. And take them back to the house."

They turned to her. She looked so anxious, so eager to please.

Pregnancy had softened her features somewhat, even her temperament. Honor was moved. "Thank you, Frances. That is kind. Get them settled, if you would. Tell them we'll be back for the feast."

"I will." Frances laid her hand on her stomach and said with a hesitant smile, "It will be lovely to have a child in the house."

Richard offered her a stiff bow of the head. But a little less stiff than usual, it seemed to Honor. "Madam," he said to Frances. It was his thanks.

Honor took a last loving, aching look at the ship that held Isabel and little Nicolas and Carlos. Then Richard took her elbow and they turned and made their way through the crowd and left the quay.

The wind was fair on the *Elizabeth*'s quarter and the sea shimmered with blue and white and gold as Adam took over from the weary helmsman at the wheel.

"Get some rest, Griffiths." The gale off Dover had kept them all on their toes. Now, they could relax.

"Aye, sir." Griffiths tugged his cap and lumbered off, glad to be relieved.

Adam watched an osprey wheeling above the sails, her head gleaming white in contrast to her rich brown body. Her heading was the same as his. He didn't know about the bird's planned landfall, but the *Elizabeth* would fetch Portsmouth tomorrow morning. He was eager to begin his mission. Meet with Sir Benjamin Gonson, treasurer of the Admiralty, and William Winter, master of naval ordnance. Elizabeth was rebuilding her navy.

"I don't know those men," she had told him when she had given him her orders. "I do know you."

What a day that had been. Her great hall at Hatfield crowded with lords and ambassadors and courtiers, and she, queen for just three days, looking radiant and confident and eager. She had knighted Thomas Parry. Then knighted him.

"Rise, Sir Adam." Her dark eyes had sparkled as she said it, and

Adam knew he was not imagining that a tear intensified the sparkle even as she smiled. She handed him a captain's whistle made of gold, and under the watch of all those people she said quietly, "The original shall stay with me, for safekeeping."

His heart was so full he'd been glad that protocol required his silence, for he would not have been able to form a single, rational sentence. It was the second best day of his life.

Now, his mission was to assist Gonson in evaluating the Queen's naval assets and liabilities. Inventory each ship's tonnage, number of men, state of readiness, condition of repair, type and quality of artillery and other munitions in the Queen's storehouses, and then calculate what would be required, at what cost, to make Her Majesty's navy into a vigorous fighting force. Adam was under no illusions. England at sea was weak. The fleet was just thirty-four ships. Of those, only eleven of the largest ships, all upward of two hundred tons, plus ten barks and pinnaces and one brigantine, were in satisfactory condition. The other twelve, including two galleys, were not worth repair. Or so he'd been told. He would see for himself. He had told Elizabeth that she could rely on private ships, too, if necessary. He estimated that forty-five merchant ships, including the *Elizabeth*, could be refitted and fashioned for war.

Because Elizabeth was vulnerable. Adam looked southeastward across his port gunwhale. There lay Spain. With its mighty forces on land and sea, its endless wealth from the New World, and a grip on the hearts of Catholic Englishmen, Spain could so easily invade England. At his stern, to the north, lay Scotland, a virtual province of France, whose troops were stationed on England's border, just waiting to march south and claim England as well.

England. When he'd left Antwerp five years ago, he had thought he was coming home. Home was where family was. He would soon have a child, and that filled him with a calm kind of joy. But Frances was not his home. And never would be.

He took a deep breath of the salt-tanged air. The *Elizabeth* felt like home. He looked ahead. Far across the ocean lay the New World. Something in him longed to see it. The *Elizabeth* could take him there, take him anywhere. But not now. Now, he had a child to raise, a country to defend, and a queen to protect and strengthen.

He steered a few degrees to starboard to keep the wind full on his quarter and fly the sea miles to Portsmouth. The osprey kept him company for another few minutes, then bore off on her own charted course.

AUTHOR'S NOTES

Readers of historical novels are often curious, when they reach the end of a book, to know how much was fact and how much was fiction. So let me fill you in.

The tense relationship between the two daughters of Henry VIII is famously true, confirmed in the writings of many contemporaries at court, including several foreign ambassadors. Mary, the child of pious Queen Catherine of Aragon, considered Elizabeth, the child of Anne Boleyn, a bastard and a heretic, and abhorred the thought of her ever ruling England. Even when the childless Mary knew she was dying, she refused to acknowledge Elizabeth as her rightful heir. Begged by her councilors to do so to prevent massive unrest over the succession, Mary added a terse codicil to her will in which she finally made provision for the passing of the throne to the sister she hated. This happened three weeks before her death—not four months before it, as my story depicts. There is no historical record of a final meeting between the two sisters during these last months of Mary's life, but for dramatic purposes I have portrayed a confrontation between them in which Elizabeth outmaneuvers Mary, leaving her little choice but to acknowledge Elizabeth as her heir.

It is part of the historical record that Mary's husband saved Elizabeth more than once from her sister's wrath. Some modern novelists have fancied a romantic interest on Philip's part for his comely sister-in-law, but this seems to me unlikely given the man's dour character. Instead, I have attributed his actions to political forward thinking, of which he was a master. His intervention was ironic, because for the next thirty years he and Elizabeth were hostile political adversaries, waging a bitter cold war that culminated in the legendary confrontation in 1588 between her navy and the "invincible" Spanish Armada, and Elizabeth's celebrated victory.

Religious zeal ruled Mary. She oversaw the burning of more

than three hundred English men and women, earning the name her subjects gave her in her lifetime: "Bloody Mary." Yet it is hard not to pity the woman when we consider what she suffered. The phantom pregnancy I depicted in the novel actually occurred—it was the talk of the court, and foreign ambassadors wrote home about it with increasing astonishment as Mary willed herself to believe she really was pregnant, right into the tenth month. Some modern scholars have attributed her malady to uterine cancer. Her trials were many: her barren state; the horrible humiliation of two phantom pregnancies; the desertion of her husband, whom she adored; the bankruptcy in which she plunged England for the sake of his wars; the resulting loss of Calais, so disastrous for English trade; and the complete overthrow of her resurrected church—the supreme mission of her life—which she could see coming with the ascension of Elizabeth. The weight of these miseries broke her in body and spirit. She died knowing that she had been an abject failure as a wife and as queen. Mary's life was tragic.

Elizabeth's life as queen was a triumph by any standard—a forty-four-year reign that saw the flowering of an unmatched age of artistry, exploration, and enterprise, an age whose glories we still refer to as "Elizabethan." Yet before her ascension this young woman spent twenty years in almost constant insecurity, in and out of her royal father's good graces depending on which wife he had at the time, endangered when rebels acted in her name, fearful of her sister. The book's opening event, in which Mary imprisoned Elizabeth in the Tower of London, is true, as is Elizabeth's purgatory afterward under house arrest for more than a year at Woodstock. She was never sure if the sister who hated her would kill her by outright execution or by other means. The assassination attempt depicted in the novel is invented, but there is historical evidence that the imperial ambassador actively considered ridding Queen Mary of her troublesome sibling. Later, during Elizabeth's long reign, there were dozens of known attempts on her life.

I have depicted Elizabeth as reluctant to support the Dudley conspiracy. She was known to have had a cautious nature. During her forty-four years as England's monarch she often frustrated her advisers with what they saw as her indecisiveness, especially during crises when the country's security was threatened. Sir William Cecil wrote that she was always loath "to have her people adventured in fights." Modern scholars, however, tend to attribute Elizabeth's caution more to cleverness and a deft management of foreign affairs. Given the astounding peacefulness of her long reign, the latter interpretation seems justified.

The following are some notes on the fate of other real personages in my book.

In the history of England, Sir William Cecil stands as a mighty oak. Elizabeth was at Hatfield House the day Parliament proclaimed her queen, and on that very day she made Cecil her principal secretary, a position we would equate to prime minister. It was the official beginning of an extraordinary professional relationship, arguably the most successful partnership in English history, and it lasted forty years, until Cecil's death, in 1598. He worked tirelessly and brilliantly in Elizabeth's interests, and she, in turn, elevated him to the peerage as Baron Burghley and enriched him with her largesse. She visited his bedside often during his final illness, even feeding him medicinal cordials with a spoon. It was said that the day he died was the only time Elizabeth was seen publicly to weep.

Elizabeth was loyal all her life to people who were loyal to her. She stood by them and rewarded them, none more so than the men who had risked so much for her sake during the failed Dudley rebellion. Upon taking the throne she made Sir William St. Loe captain of the Tower guard, made Sir Nicholas Throckmorton her ambassador to France, and knighted Thomas Parry, her wily administrator during the insecure years when she was a princess. She had been queen for just a year when Parry died. A drawing of him by Holbein survives.

The revolt in Parliament and the subsequent Dudley conspiracy, both depicted in the novel, are true, though I have invented the ways in which they happened. And I bent three facts for the dramatic purposes of my story. First, the House of Commons debated and defeated the Exiles Bill three days after passage of the ecclesiastical revenues bill; I have made it the following day. Second, the revolt in the House of Commons was led by Sir Anthony

Kingston; I demoted him to a lesser position and gave this catalyst role to Richard Thornleigh. Third, upon hearing of the planned rebellion, Mary did send her agents to post a guard around Elizabeth's house, but this happened at Hatfield House; I have changed the locale to Somerset House, Elizabeth's London home.

Regarding the robbery of the Queen's treasury—astonishingly, such a robbery did happen, and the master teller was complicit in the scheme. But my research did not uncover the mastermind. I gave that role to Adam Thornleigh.

Fictional characters in the book include the Thornleigh family—Honor, Richard, Adam, and Isabel—as well as John Grenville and his sister, Frances. The Thornleighs all appeared in my previous novels, *The Queen's Lady* and *The King's Daughter*. Honor's story as a young lady-in-waiting to Catherine of Aragon forms the heart of *The Queen's Lady*. It features Honor's conflicted relationship with her guardian, Sir Thomas More; the missions she ran to rescue the men he persecuted; and her tumultuous love affair with Richard. *The King's Daughter* features Isabel's adventures with mercenary soldier Carlos Valverde during the Wyatt Rebellion early in the reign of Queen Mary.

I have been gratified and moved by all the mail I've received from readers who've enjoyed the books. A question sent to me leads to the following note on Honor's name. Why, this reader asked, did I choose for a Tudor-era character a name that seems to come from a later century when girls were often given such names as Hope, Charity, Patience? Another reader asked why I had used the American spelling for an English character. The answer to both questions is quite simple: Honor's name comes straight out of the 1530s, and the spelling is Latin. I chose it after researching *The Lisle Letters*, compiled by Muriel St. Clare Byrne. This is a collection of correspondence from 1533 to1540, written to and from the family of Arthur Plantagenet, 1st Viscount Lisle, who was appointed by Henry VIII as governor of Calais, England's possession in France at the time. His wife's first name was Honor.

If you'd like to write to me, I'd love to hear from you. Contact me at bkyle@barbarakyle.com.

THE QUEEN'S CAPTIVE

Barbara Kyle

ABOUT THIS GUIDE

The suggested questions are included to
enhance your group's reading of Barbara Kyle's
The Queen's Captive.

DISCUSSION QUESTIONS

1. In trying to keep Elizabeth safe from Queen Mary's wrath, Honor decides to become a double agent. She pretends to be Mary's spy serving as Elizabeth's lady, but is actually keeping watch on Mary when she reports to her. Did you feel that Honor was taking on something too dangerous with this scheme? Were the stakes worth the danger?

2. Given Queen Mary's desperate need to have a child to be her heir, how did her phantom pregnancy make you feel? Did you think she was honestly mistaken, or willfully deluding herself?

3. Adam falls in love with Elizabeth almost the first moment he sees her. Later, when he is recovering from his arrow wound, he indulges in an erotic flirtation with her. Did you think this was risky behavior on Adam's part, since she is so far above him in rank?

4. Honor watches in agony as her friend George Mitford, condemned to burn at the stake, dies a horrible death. Queen Mary's policy of burning heretics was cruel, yet it was no different from the policy of other European monarchs. How do you view this aspect of the period—as necessary state orthodoxy, or religious paranoia?

5. Richard battles Queen Mary's bills in Parliament, which leads Mary to intimidate Honor. Frightened, Honor tells Richard that they must flee England, and she starts packing. But Richard stops her, insisting that they stay and fight. They argue bitterly about it, and he walks out. Who do you believe was right?

6. Honor gets deeply involved in the planned rebellion led by Sir Henry Dudley and she asks Elizabeth to give the rebels

some financial aid, or at least a word of encouragement. But Elizabeth refuses, fearing it will endanger her. Honor accuses her of being selfish, and they argue. Do you think Elizabeth was being cowardly, or wise?

7. Grenville arrests Honor and threatens her with torture on the rack unless she signs a statement implicating Elizabeth in the Dudley conspiracy. Honor knows that if she signs, the Queen will execute Elizabeth for treason. She decides to endure the torture. How did Honor's decision make you feel? Was she right to protect Elizabeth?

8. Frances Grenville is so obsessed with Adam Thornleigh that she blackmails him into agreeing to marry her. Otherwise, she says, she will turn in his stepmother as a convicted heretic. Did you feel any pity for Frances?

9. Adam finds Elizabeth preparing to flee England to avoid her sister marrying her to a foreign nobleman. Adam gladly offers to take her on his ship, and they set out together. When they stop for the night, they become lovers. In your view, was Adam being irresponsible, or can he be forgiven for hoping that "love conquers all"?

10. Grenville has tortured Honor and kept Richard in a dungeon for months. When they are back home following their ordeal, Richard tells Honor that he's had enough, so he's going after Grenville—it's kill or be killed, he says. Honor dreads that this can only lead to Richard's death, and again they argue. Did you think Richard was right?

11. After Grenville abducts Richard and burns down the Thornleighs' house, Honor decides to confront Grenville, and kill him. How did Honor's attack on her enemy make you feel? Was she justified in committing murder?